# KEY MONSTER

by Lee Dravis

*Doug,*

*Thanks for being such a good friend, and for your support. Many happy sunsets,*

*Lee Dravis*

Copyright 2000 by Charles Lee Dravis
All rights reserved. No part of this book may be reproduced in any form without written permission from the publishers, except by a reviewer who may quote brief passages in a review to be printed in a newspaper or magazine.

First printing

ISBN 1-58851-103-0
PUBLISHED BY AMERICA HOUSE BOOK PUBLISHERS
www.publishamerica.com
Baltimore

Printed in the United States of America

# Acknowledgments

The act of writing is a solitary endeavor. The art of writing is not. It would be impossible to learn and write about your subject without outside assistance. Fortunately, I have some good and well-informed friends to whom I am indebted.

For research materials on Key West, I sought out the advice of those kayaking, camping vagabonds, the Marble Man and the Marble Ma'am, Jack and Sue Hahn. Their wealth of facts and their charts of the Florida Keys kept the book from running aground.

Faith Hammond reminded me that she was the one I bounced various ideas off of, and she picked this one. So this is all her fault.

At the Voice of America, I want to thank Leonardo Bonett, for fixing my fractured Spanish; and Jean-Paul Schaub, for his endless interest and input, and for being amused rather than offended by Daiquiri Taylor.

For actually reading my first novel, and urging me to write a second one anyway, I extend my gratitude to Michelle McMarlin, Kim Wood, and my family in Florida and Jersey. Thanks for your support last time around, and again.

I must thank Carl Hiaasen and David L. Robbins for their kind words and encouragement. Thank you AmErica House for the chance. Thanks also to the city of Key West, just for being there.

And finally, I have to admit that this whole project would have foundered without the love and support of Sally. She listened to my musings, dug me out of narrative corners and took care of life while I wrote. To her, I am truly grateful.

Lee Dravis<br>
March, 2000<br>
Gunston, Virginia

# Dedication

To Victoria Lee Dravis, the cutest three-year-old on the planet, who may not read this book until her daddy tells her she's old enough.

# CHAPTER 1

*A*wakening slowly, rising above the soft brown ooze of the bottom of the great bay's tributary. The water swirling past gasping gills, colder than the day before and the day before again. Long body, turning about as it drifts upward but still well below the surface. Almost cozy here in the deep plunge within the mouth of the little river, sheltered from the rushing currents.

A small sense of hunger urges him into lazy forward motion, tail end snaking side to side, four flippers seeking purchase in the stream. No word for this in his rudimentary brain, just a hunger and the surety that today the water is indeed colder and the instinctive knowledge that it is already time to leave this place.

His flukes propel his perfectly hydrodynamic body out of the wide, slow river and into the great vast gray bay itself. Rockfish scatter, their instinct to escape, his to eat them. Scores of minute, razorsharp teeth slash the unfortunate fish. He feeds until the water grows brighter above. He is nearly sated, and then down to the mud again for dessert, a dozen or so bluecrabs whose shells are no defense against his crushing jaws.

But the water, so cold today! He allows himself to float toward the shimmery light, up from the dim depths, up to the warmth.

He feels his back break the surface of the bay, dry air and heat rippling along his hide. Cautiously, he lifts his head above the chop, unaware that some physiological switch has been thrown as his gills seal tightly and a rush of salted air fills his vestigial lungs. Large black eyes squint against the relative bright of the surface, the sky above a sheet of dark clouds and wheeling gulls.

The air warms him a little as he paddles in a meandering line, gently pushing against the soft tide. It is his nature to press against the flow of water when he can, like a salmon fighting his way upstream, though he knows nothing of salmon. He knows only rockfish and crabs, tuna and grouper, bonita and rays, and the only name he has for these is "food."

To one side, not very far off, a bobbing movement catches his nearsighted eye. After all these years, he knows of man and their mancraft, and is wary. He has heard the rumble and seen the spinning steel of their passage above him, and he has felt the sting of their needle-sharp hooks raking his body as he swum under them.

## KEY MONSTER

The bobbing movement, his undersized brain whispers, is one of the mancraft, moving alongside his flank. Upon the mancraft, doubled over and hurling chunks of its breakfast into the bay, hunches a man itself, the most dangerous animal to inhabit the surface of the water and its shoreline. It is only two or three body lengths off and parallel to his own course, more than matching his leisurely paddle through the whitecaps.

The man straightens suddenly, rising unsteadily on its two hind flippers and raises a pair of black barrels to its hideous face. Piles of golden fur adorn its head, swirling in the breeze. It snatches the black barrels away with its odd foreflippers and twists its features into a remarkable shape, mouth spreading wide into a perfect circle, eyes as wide and white as a squid's. And then back over the side of the mancraft to resume its return of its meal to the sea.

Alarmed, but not greatly so, he plunges his head beneath the waves, again unaware as his tiny nostrils snap shut and his gills once more began to flutter. Downward he swims, through the appetizing aroma of the man's breakfast, careful to avoid the churning blades of the mancraft, seeking solitude and the dark safety of the deep. And then it is over and he thinks no more about it. There is only the moment and the instincts that drive him.

He finds himself moving southward through the cold waters of the bay, dines on a stray rockfish, and feels the old urge to continue in this direction. A soft flush spreads along his underbelly, just beyond his stomach, and ancient stirrings compel him to increase his speed.

The change of season is coming, that delightful tingle tells him, and he bites deeply with his powerful flukes, remaining just beneath the wind-whipped spray of the bay that men call the Chesapeake, though he himself has no name for this sheltered body of water. The open sea calls to him, and the need to find a mate.

He rarely bothers to feed now, consumed by the intuitive drive to migrate. He just swims on. Nearby, he senses mancraft, larger by far than the ones near his northern lair, their deadly blades ripping at the water. When he chances to lift his head above the foam he spies the towering mancraft structures along the shore, a place men call Norfolk, but for which he again has no name.

The water grows even colder but the increased salinity tells him that this is right. Faster, harder currents buffet him as he forces himself against the tide, out the mouth of the bay and into the green water of the limitless ocean. Soon he feels the water change, a charge of warmth rushing along the coastline up from the south. A sweep of his tail brings him around to meet the stream head-on, undulating body progressing as a salmon swims upstream to spawn.

Yes, to spawn. To mate in the shallow, warm blue waters at the head of this mighty current. To seek another of his own kind, as few as they might be.

He crashes through a thick school of panicked yellowfin tuna and gobbles a pair unthinkingly, barely tasting, never slowing, swimming on toward his ancestral winter retreat.

\* \* \* \* \* \* \*

Winch was going to be sick again. He felt his stomach boil and his throat constrict. He snapped the hooked end of the bungee cord on one of the spokes of the boat's wheel and barely made it to the gunwale in time to heave up the ill-conceived breakfast of bourbon and LSD which seemed to disagree with his system and now wanted out. Head down, body shaking, he bent double over the side and fed the fishes.

When the aching spasms had passed, Winch tossed a bleary glance toward the bow. The boat was making slow headway against the outgoing tide, still neatly aligned with the next channel marker offshore of Cove Point. It was nearly ten o'clock on a depressingly bleak October Saturday, and he knew he'd never make it to Annapolis by eleven. The party of twelve well-heeled tourists who had paid good money for his *Festive Autumn Tour* of the Chesapeake would be demanding their deposits back, money Winch had already spent on recreational activities. That is, unless he got lucky and none of them showed up in the face of the dreadful weather over the bay. In that case, he would have to refund nothing, which was exactly how much he had left.

Except for the boat, there was damn little he possessed. The boat, a 57-foot Bay-Built, powered by twin turbocharged Detroit Diesels and outfitted for luxury cruises at outlandish prices, had been bought at auction in Baltimore almost a year ago. It had sold for around a million dollars new, and had been seized by the Internal Revenue Service in lieu of back-taxes.

The name on the transom had read *LauraLee*, which Winch had immediately painted over knowing that a sudden blast of inspiration would come to him, delivering to him a suitable appellation for his new boat. Winch had purchased the cruiser for $10,000 down and a note for $190,000, investing the money from the modest inheritance his old man had left him after he'd died on these same waters.

Captain Jack Winchell had been a lifelong waterman. Never sick a day in his life, Winch's father had passed away of an unexpected heart-attack while tonging for oysters off of Kent Island. He had been sixty-two years old, tough as a Maryland crab, and had planned to retire two years before but couldn't seem to leave the bay behind. His crew had brought his body back into port and had seen that the oysters had been offloaded and sold before they'd bothered to notify the authorities. Until then, they had kept Dad's stiffening corpse on ice along with the day's catch.

Winch's mother, rest her soul, had never been a well woman, and the shock of her husband's death broke her heart and, finally, her health. She lingered three more months before the cancer in her breast took her from Winch also. Winch mourned them both over a case of bourbon and the contents of his mother's medicine cabinet. When he came to, weeks later, he met with the attorney and collected his meager legacy.

At a U.S. Government tax auction, Winch had successfully bid on the big cabin cruiser, which had been seized by the IRS from a once-wealthy Anne Arundel County investment banker. Rootless and orphaned, Winch had planned to sail his new boat around the world, hitting all the hot spots and flesh-pots he could find along the way.

Once home with her, the huge boat bobbing alongside the shaky wooden dock behind his inherited house, Winch had scoured the freezer for any forgotten leftovers from his mother's kitchen. He'd extracted a large piece of ham, stuffed with kale, spices and chunks of oyster, a traditional Southern Maryland dish prepared and preserved by his dear departed mother. Over this emotional meal, washed down by copious amounts of whiskey, beer, marijuana and grief, Winch pledged to honor the memory of his mother by christening his new boat after her prize-winning specialty.

In an alcohol-infused stupor, and armed with a can of black marine enamel and a brush, Winch had painstakingly painted the new name for his craft in jittery lettering six inches high across the transom. Not wanting to waste good liquor, Winch had christened his boat with a bottle of warm

Gatorade, which glanced harmlessly off the bow and sank unbroken into the harbor. And thus he dubbed his vessel, the *Stuffed Ham*.

Twin disasters precluded his 'round the world cruise, however, each the result of a screaming mid-season storm that had blown up out of the Gulf of Mexico. The hurricane took square aim at his home and boat as it raged up the Chesapeake. The rickety dock gave way in the lashing waves, collapsing into driftwood and turning the *Stuffed Ham* loose upon the bay. Winch could only watch helplessly from the poor shelter of his house.

When the skies finally cleared, he'd found her aground, stern-first, on a mud-flat a mile away. Both propellers, both shafts and both rudders had taken a beating, and it cost nearly all the rest of his paltry inheritance to have her towed in and put right at the boatyard. And, with his backyard dock in splinters, he'd had to rent a slip.

Between the expenses of dockage at the Harbor Lights Marina and his drug bills, Winch faced the ugly truth of his life. He would have to postpone his odyssey and work, at least for a while.

For a few dollars, he placed an ad in the *Calvert Daily Bugle*, offering luxurious cruises-to-nowhere aboard the *Stuffed Ham*. Business was slow, according to D.J., the dockmaster at the marina, due to the fact that no one wanted to take a luxury cruise aboard a boat called the *Stuffed Ham*. Stubbornly, Winch refused to change the name. Nevertheless, he still managed to take in a couple hundred dollars a week and hardly ever had to offer refunds or make restitution. He was treading water, but still afloat.

But today was not one of those days. Getting a late start after a hard night of partying, Winch felt bad, real bad. He knew he'd have to cut it down to half a tab of acid at a time, at least if he was drinking too. Lately, the two just didn't mix. Could it be that he'd been divorced twice, busted twice, a stoner for more than twenty years and could see the big four-O just over the horizon? He tried not to think about it. It hurt his head.

Another sudden wave of nausea rocked him along with the pitching boat, his knuckles white as he clutched the rail. "Stare at the horizon, boy," came the wisdom of his father, and he gazed through the saltspray at the hazy line where bay met sky.

Something broke the surface with a splash, directly off the port beam. Winch looked, rubbed his bloodshot eyes and looked again. A long black ribbon broke the surface, less than a hundred yards off. It arched, then slipped below the swells, only to reappear seconds later. Dolphin? Whale?

Not in the bay, or this far north. He knew that a Florida manatee had been making regular visits to the Chesapeake for a couple of years now. Each time, scientists from the National Aquarium in Baltimore had captured the mammal and returned it to its home waters, and yet the manatee always returned each spring. No one knew why.

Winch spotted another loop of black, and another, in a line. A school of manatees? Not fucking likely. Fighting the rising tide in his guts, he groped for the binoculars stashed under the gunwale. He pulled them to his eyes and saw . . . nothing.

Puzzled for a moment, Winch examined the lenses and flicked off the caps with a disgusted grunt. Again he gazed through them.

Ahead of the bending backs of the supposed marine mammals, the water boiled. Something big, dark and ugly was rising from the foam of the whitecaps, rearing up, twisting.

Diamond-shaped flippers slapped at the water below and behind the . . . thing. It was a head, seal-like in shape, but vastly larger, climbing above the surface, water streaming off of it. Ponderously, the *Stuffed Ham* was gaining on whatever it was, passing it to starboard.

The horrible thing swiveled its serpentine neck and gazed placidly back at him, lidless black eyes filling the circular field of Winch's binoculars. The head rose up, almost even with the boat's flying bridge and Winch was forced to bend backwards to keep Chessie's face in sight.

The shock, the motion of the boat, the bourbon, and the reverse angle were too much for Winch's fragile system. The binoculars clattered to the deck as he pitched forward once more to offer chum to the fish. He was gagging up the last contents of his ruined stomach as the head disappeared beneath the gray water. Some thirty feet behind, a long snakelike, flukeless tail whiplashed through the air and slipped gracefully beneath the waves.

The dry heaves passed, and Winch stumbled back to the helm. Fuck the tourists. He unhooked the bungee cord from the wheel and gave it a mighty spin. His hands shook as the *Stuffed Ham* came about and he slammed the twin diesels to full-revs, beating his way back to port. He could tell no one he'd seen the legendary monster of the Chesapeake, not if he wanted to hang onto his last tattered shreds of dignity on the island. His credibility among the other watermen was already approaching zero. Babbling about seeing a sea monster was the last thing he needed. Winch swore to keep this hallucination to himself. Well, perhaps he could tell Brant about it. Or maybe he should just do his best to forget it all.

Unlatching the locker below the wheel, Winch reached in and tossed aside orange lifevests until he had uncovered the emergency pint of bourbon he'd hidden. Running south with the ebb tide, he tilted the bottle until it was dry, and home was in sight off the port bow.

\* \* \* \* \* \* \*

Felix Munoz toed the pitching rubber and tucked the ball behind his back. He took a cautious glance toward first where the baserunner dared a lead, dancing nervously, looking for the steal. Felix decided that the lead wasn't quite big enough and went into his windup. At that moment, the runner broke for second base.

The breaking ball Felix had planned instead became a fastball as the batter stepped out of the box and the wiry catcher rose to intercept the pitch. Felix ducked down on the mound to avoid the ball as the catcher rocketed it over the pitcher's head in an attempt to cut off the steal. Too late, the runner was safe, grinning at him from second. Felix hung his head in disgust and cast a wary eye toward the dugout. The manager wasn't looking at the field at all though. He was embroiled in a heated discussion with a fat stranger in a suit and tie. Felix breathed a sigh of relief.

The batter for the Cordenas Duques stepped back into the box and waited for the next pitch. The catcher squatted and gave Felix the sign, no fingers, a change-up. Felix peeked at the runner over his shoulder, but the player wasn't leading by more than a couple of steps. He took a big breath and wound up.

"*Tiempo!*" screamed the manager from the dugout in the midst of Felix's delivery. The effort to arrest the pitch nearly spilled the pitcher from the mound. Felix glared angrily at the manager of los Diablos Rojos de Pinar del Rio, who sprinted onto the field under a blazing Cuban sun.

"*Que carajo!*" Felix bitched when his boss made it to the mound.

"*Lo siento*, Felix," he apologized and signaled to the bullpen beyond the rickety fence in right field. "There's a man who wants to talk to you."

"*Ahora?*" Felix screamed. "In the middle of a pitch, with a one-hitter? Are you *loco?*"

The manager stared at the dirt and spat. He spoke so quietly that Felix almost didn't hear him. "He's with the Ministry of Sports."

Felix Munoz's face fell. Oh, Madre, he'd prayed it wouldn't come to this. Grudgingly, he turned the baseball over to the manager and trudged toward the dugout where the fat man from the government waited.

"*Señor* Munoz," the man said without bothering to introduce himself. "I have a letter for you."

Felix's hands shook as he accepted the paper, unfolding it so rapidly that it tore. He read the devastating words.

"Because of the recent traitorous activities and defection of your cousin, Arturo San Cristobal Munoz-Torres, it is the decision of the Minister of Sports that you, Felix Munoz, are hereby immediately and perpetually banned from any activities connected with the game of *beisbol* as played within the Republic of Cuba. You are hereby ordered to forfeit all payments owed to you by the State and return to your home at Los Palacios to await your work assignment."

There was more, but the tears in his eyes blurred the message. Twenty-two years old, in his prime, and they were taking it all away from him, thanks to his no-good cousin Arturo, who wasn't fit to be a batboy. Arturo had built a *balza* last spring, setting out across the Florida Straits, and today he was the darling of pro baseball in Miami. Damn him! And what was to become of Felix, the best prospect in Cuba in ten years? Why, he'd be harvesting sugarcane by the end of the week! He balled the paper in his hand and nodded at the fat man from the Sports Ministry.

"*Lo siento,*" the bureaucrat mumbled at his shiny plastic shoes. "You were a great *lanzador*. I was an aficionado."

Felix took a last look around the Pinar del Rio stadium. Five thousand voices roared at the final strikeout of the inning, leaving the runner stranded on second. A salty tear fell from his cheek.

He pulled off his glove and shambled into the clubhouse, but his mind was already churning. He'd need provisions, water, a sheet of canvas for a sail, and on and on. So many details. Damned if he would grow old, poor, unappreciated, slaving in the canefields. Damned if he would abandon the game that meant as much to him as breathing.

Felix Munoz decided right then that he was going to America.

# CHAPTER 2

James P. "Big Jim" Quinn took the call himself. Being a Saturday, he'd allowed his secretary to go home at three. He himself had lingered, awaiting this important information with growing impatience. The caller was an intimate contact in the Maryland state office for tax records in Annapolis. It had been over a month since he'd ordered the woman to dig through the files and he forced himself not to bark at her for taking so long. After all, she was pretty good in the sack, and talented and discreet boinks were hard to come by.

A wreath of smoke curled just beneath the ceiling from the hand-rolled double corona between his fingers. It was a genuine Havana, smuggled in from Cuba via Miami. He allowed himself only one per week. Genuine Havana cigars were harder to come by than good boinks.

"So, whaddaya got for me, Liza?" Liza with a Z, like the singer. God, so pretentious.

"I'm sorry it took so long, Big Jim. It wasn't easy to find."

He grunted, an indication to continue.

"I had to cross-reference the Department of Natural Resource records with the IRS. I know a girl at the office in DC, Millie? I think you met her once at that reception at the Inner Harbor?"

Big Jim's patience was just about shot.

"Who has . . . my boat?"

Over the receiver he could hear paper shuffling. That's what she was, a friggin' paper-pusher, thirty years until her state pension and a lonely retirement in a furnished condo in Florida. But today, she was *his* paper pusher.

"It's registered to a Eugene Winchell, 76 Charles Street, Solomons Island, Maryland, 20688. The serial numbers match."

Big Jim allowed himself a smile. Like his corona, it was his first one this week. Anticipation mixed with relief.

"Good job, baby, good fuckin' job."

"What're you gonna do? I mean, it's all legal, paid in full. I have a copy of the title right here."

"Don't you worry about that, honey." Big Jim slid open the drawer of his walnut desk. The Smith & Wesson .38 was still there, just within reach.

"I'm just going to talk with the new owner," he soothed. "Look her over, make sure he's takin' good care'a her. Maybe even see if he wants to sell her back."

They chatted for a few more minutes. He pointed out to Liza that his wife was up in New York this weekend and that he had tickets to the boat show tonight. How about dinner after and a little slap and tickle? Liza giggled, then agreed.

"Oh, I almost forgot," she added. "The boat has a new name. Mr. Winchell included it on the registration." She read it off to him.

Big Jim took the news hard. He mumbled an abrupt goodbye and hung up.

Swiveling in his padded leather chair, Big Jim Quinn gazed out his tenth floor office window at the panorama of downtown Baltimore. He would go tomorrow. With the .38, of course. And the spare set of keys he'd failed to surrender when the IRS had seized the *LauraLee* in that bogus tax lien case.

He bent his head and rubbed the bridge of his nose in agony.

His beautiful boat, his refuge, his true love.

What kind of fuckin' moron would name a boat the *Stuffed Ham*?

\* \* \* \* \* \* \*

Winch was crouched on the edge of the pier, tying off the bowline, when he noticed the pair of white Keds next to him. One of the Keds was tapping angrily. He stood up unsteadily and faced their owner. Oh, God, the day was getting worse and it was hardly yet noon.

Donna Jean glared at him from beneath the brim of a faded fishing hat. Hair the color and texture of old straw poked out from under it and framed her shopworn face. Between her thin, mirthless lips she chewed on an unlit cigarette. She was a big, tough old bitch, and she could've broken Winch in two if she ever wanted to. Today she looked like she wanted to.

"Don't tie 'er up too tight, Winch, 'cause 'less I see some money she ain't stayin' here."

Winch finished snugging the line anyway and dropped the excess rope in a clumsy tangle on the dock. The sea monster had been a scary sight, but DJ could be scarier.

"Donna Jean," he pleaded, "I'll pay up, I promise. But right now, I really, really need a drink."

She flicked away the cigarette and spat into the harbor.

"Look, Winch," she sighed. "You're an okay fella. We had some good times. I felt bad 'bout you losin' your dock an' all, but I gotta pay my bills too." She fished out a piece of pink paper from her shirt pocket and unfolded it: an invoice. She scanned the bill as it fluttered in the breeze.

"Seven hundred fifty-six dollars for repairs . . ."

Winch grimaced.

"Six hundred even for three months slip fees . . ."

Winch winced.

"Three hundred seventy-five for fuel . . ."

Winch shuddered.

". . . and forty-two dollars for sandwiches and stuff at the snack bar."

"Really? I didn't think I ate that much."

"For a grand total of one-thousand seven hundred an' seventy-three dollars, plus tax."

Winch groaned. Donna Jean handed him the invoice.

"Hey, bud," she said. "I know it's the weekend and you prob'ly don't carry seventeen-hunnert in your wallet, so I'll give you 'til Monday when the bank opens. I gotta close out the quarterly books this week. If I don't have the money in my office by noon day after tomorrow, you and the *Ham* are history." Her flat gray eyes drilled into his, and her nostrils flared as the wind shifted, carrying Winch's aroma.

"Jesus, you stink!" She took a step back, almost falling over the tangle of rope he'd dropped on the pier.

"An' coil that line proper," she shouted at him as she turned away and strode up the dock.

Winch watched her go. Hard to believe that they'd shared bottles and beds until recently. He glanced down at the pink paper through red eyes and pondered the impossible tally. Now he really, really, really needed a drink.

Just beyond the marina, hugging the shoreline, hunched a weather-beaten clapboard structure. The deck, which extended from the rear and hung precariously over the tide, was closed, made unsafe by the hurricane. But the bar inside remained open for business. Winch pushed open the side door and entered the gloom of the Oarhouse.

With the deck closed and the season over, only the sparse group of regulars haunted the bar at noon. One of the latest regulars was Brant, a student at St. Mary's College, who posed as a tortured artist but actually came from a wealthy family in Chevy Chase. Quite talented, he had become a fixture in the Oarhouse over the summer, spending his free time drinking light beers and drawing whatever caught his fancy on an oversized sketch pad. A shade shorter than Winch and almost half the captain's age, Brant wore his streaky blond hair in a rebelliously punk fashion, long on the top and shaved close above the ears. A diamond stud pierced his left lobe. Small round glasses kept sliding down his elfin nose. He was thinner than Winch, if that was possible, and possessed a sunny, naive and harmless disposition. Winch enjoyed the kid's company. On this particular Saturday midday, Brant was propped in a corner, tilted back in a chair, fingers working the black charcoal across the art paper.

Todays subject was Buster, one of the most ancient mariners Solomons Island had ever seen. He was entirely gray and nearly toothless and had spent the last two decades warming the same barstool. To believe in the tales he told was to accept the truth of Santa Claus.

Buster claimed he was born on May 7, 1915 on board the *Lusitania* only minutes before she'd been torpedoed off the coast of Ireland. Oddly, and incredibly, he'd somehow managed to grow up and enlist in the navy in time to participate in the sinking of a German battleship only three years later. He had also been present, he claimed, at the signing of the Japanese surrender aboard the *USS Missouri* in 1945, and had been first officer on the *USS Pueblo* when it was seized by the North Koreans in 1968. Buster's colorful sea-stories grew more colorful in direct proportion to the amount of rum he consumed.

Clustered at the far end of the otherwise empty bar perched Cap'n Mattson and his three scruffy crewmen, back from a morning oystering. They were big, tough men, hardened by a lifetime of labor upon the bay. They'd all known and respected Winch's father, but had little use for the son. Sullenly, they munched on sandwiches from the kitchen and knocked back Budweisers, pointedly ignoring the droning monologue from Buster.

Winch let his bloodshot eyes adjust to the murky lighting of the Oarhouse and shuffled listlessly to the bar. Gil, the proprietor, bartender and dishwasher, watched the captain's approach warily. Gil was an old bachelor, an ex-Marine, and hard as nails. His weatherbeaten face sagged beneath three days of beard and his hooded brown eyes narrowed, a veteran of twenty-five years of bar fights, drunks and lousy tippers. Winch nodded distractedly at Cap'n Mattson and pulled himself up onto a stool.

"Double vodka," he mumbled at Gil. "Straight."

The bartender folded his thick tattooed arms across his beer-stained apron and glared.

"You got my money?"

Winch lowered his head to the sticky bartop, letting the cool wet wood soothe the pounding in his temples. One of the watermen nudged Cap'n Mattson and grinned. Over in the corner, Brant paused in his sketch, mid-stroke. Buster raved on softly.

"C'mon, Gil," Winch muttered into the wood. "I need a drink. You have no idea how bad."

Gil turned to the cash register and rang open the drawer. He grabbed a slip of paper and slapped it on the bar next to Winch's throbbing head, where it immediately began soaking up spilled beer, blurring the numbers.

"The deal was, I stock your boat for your little charters, you collect the money, then you pay me. Right? So that'll be $326." He rapped on the countertop with a hairy knuckle, next to the deadbeat's head. Winch didn't move a muscle.

"I saw . . . I saw . . ." But his throat was closing, parched, and nothing more would come out. Damn it! He didn't want anything to come out! They already thought he was out of his mind and anything he said would only confirm that. Shut up, Winch, shut . . .

"What did you see, Winch?" called Brant much too cheerily. He liked Winch, wished he could be as self-destructive. That would enhance his image as a suffering artist and piss his parents off, too.

"I want the money," Gil threatened. Beneath the bar, his fingers found the knob of the softball bat he kept handy.

"Monday," Winch croaked dryly and glanced up at the towering barkeep. "When the bank opens," he promised, though he doubted there was enough in his account to pay this month's service charges. Gil continued to glare at him, considering it.

The bartender poured two fingers of house vodka in a greasy glass and set it in front of Winch. Winch cautiously reached for the liquor, but Gil deftly snatched it back.

"I don't see no cash on the bar," he growled.

"Aw, c'mon, Gil," Brant spoke up from the corner. "Put it on my tab."

"Stay out of this, you little pissant, or I'll kick your ass outta here, too."

Brant set down his sketchpad and got to his feet. He was as tall, but not as meaty as Gil. Cap'n Mattson and his men avidly anticipated the unexpected entertainment. Even Buster shut up, blinking blearily at Winch.

The gangly, blond art student crossed the few steps to the bar. He whipped out his wallet and slapped down a twenty, looking at Gil evenly, foolishly challenging the bartender. He had no idea that Gil had his hand on the softball bat, or that it had been used before. There were three good dents in the wood to prove it. They recorded a welshing biker, a failed bandit, and an unruly tourist from Gaithersburg.

"Double vodka, straight," Brant ordered. "Make it Smirnoff."

Face frozen, Gil slowly slid the drink back onto the bar.

"Ain't got no Smirnoff," he hissed, but commerce won out over honor. The bartender scooped up the twenty and dropped a ten and four singles down. It included his tip. Brant pushed the glass back over by Winch's elbow and slid onto the stool beside him. His eyes took in the touseled hair and vomit-stained clothes of the man next to him, his Pan.

"Geez, Winch. You look like hell." He wrinkled his nose distastefully. "And you smell even worse." Brant discretely slid his stool to the left a few inches.

Winch nodded in gratitude and sucked noisily at his vodka. Perversely, Brant admired Winch's style. If only he could be so fucked-up.

Gently, Brant prodded his friend, "So, you were saying. . . ?"

Winch knitted his eyebrows together in puzzlement, trying to remember. Then they shot upward alarmingly, eyes solid white in shock as it rushed back at him. His hand trembled as he drained the last of the vodka and he pushed the ten across the bar toward Gil.

"More," he gasped. Gil shot Brant a pained look. Brant nodded sternly, and a second double appeared.

"You said you saw something," the kid whispered. Winch was a shaman, Brant knew. Perhaps his mentor had had a vision. He inspired

Brant's art, and he always had the best women, if you didn't count Donna Jean.

Winch shook his aching head slowly and took another deep sip of liquor. How could he put this? It wasn't something you just blurted out. It was like claiming you'd seen a UFO, or had God Himself speak to you from a burning bush. But he had to tell someone or he'd go crazy.

A small thought occurred to him. What if he was already crazy? Well, if that were the case, there'd be no damage done and maybe they'd lock him up in a nice warm padded cell somewhere. He rubbed his stubbled face with his palms and peered about the barroom. It was a crazy story, but what the hell, maybe he was crazy already and this would put his doubts to rest. Everyone was silent, staring at him. He took a deep breath and let it out slowly.

"I saw Chessie today," Winch sighed. "In the bay."

No one laughed right out loud. Instead, it started as a chuckle, turned into a chortle, evolved into a guffaw and climaxed in a final belly-wrenching chorus of hoots and roars, tears running down their faces. Gil was leaning across the bar, pounding it with his fist. Cap'n Mattson tilted his gray head back and howled at the ceiling. His crewmen gasped for breath between wracking snorts and were nearly falling off their barstools. Even Brant was failing to hold back a snicker. Winch tried to tuck his head between his shoulders, while only Buster sat stone-faced in the corner. His faded features twitched. A faint smile of recognition twisted his toothless mouth. He knew he must speak the truth, fueled by five (six? seven?) navy grogs.

"It's true!" shouted the old man, lifting unsteadily to his feet, and a new wave of mirth swept the bar. He spread his hands in the air for attention in the center of the room. "I seen her wit' my own eyes!"

"Oh, this I gotta hear," gasped Gil, wiping the streaming tears from his cheek.

"Tell us, old man," cried the youngest waterman, rubbing the stitch in his side, and the others joined in. Winch felt like crawling under the bar.

"True! I seen her," Buster insisted more quietly, and the laughter gradually subsided to a level of great amusement. Winch turned on his barstool and gazed hopefully at the old man.

"T'was back in WWII," he began. "I was a seaman on a PT boat in the Pacific, the PT 109. Was early in the war, afore that Kennedy fella got there. General Doug MacArthur had to be evacuated from the Philippines and we was given the job. Well, we nearly went aground tryin' to maneuver into the beach where the General was waitin', so I volunteered to take one of the liferafts in to pick 'im up meself." Subtle chuckles swept the bar once again, but Buster forged on.

"I gets to the beach finally, dodgin' machine gun fire all the way in, an' there he is, big as life, General Douglas MacArthur. But afore he gets in the raft he turns to his men on the beach and says, real loud-like, 'I'll be back.'"

Winch closed his eyes and shook his head at the renewed burst of laughter.

"The General--he says to call him Doug--climbs in my raft an' I begins to row back out to the PT boat. Just then, a real thick fog rolls in an' neither of us can see a thing. An' all of a suddenlike, Doug yells, 'What the fuck is that?'

"I turns 'round and there she is, so close she's nearly scrapin' the sides, forty-feet if she's an inch, all black an' smooth wit' a tiny little head stickin' up outta the water. An' just like that," he snapped his fingers, "she's gone."

Cap'n Mattson snorted beer right out of his nose. One of the watermen had a coughing fit and the other two commenced to pound him on the back.

"So then what'd you do?" tittered Gil behind the bar.

"Why I said, 'Doug, sit the hell down! Yer rockin' the boat!'"

Fresh peals of laughter rolled through the Oarhouse. Brant had returned to his sketchpad and was scribbling furiously. Gil was in such a good mood by now that he poured everyone, even Winch, a round on the house. Buster accepted his drink with a good-natured, toothless smile and toasted his audience. Winch chugged the remainder of his second vodka and groaned.

For a minute there, he'd thought Buster might actually come through for him, back up his story. The legendary monster of the Chesapeake, known to the locals as "Chessie", had loomed before him large as life. No, Winch told himself. Chessie was only a story for the tourists. So maybe he was as nuts as the old man. What gnawed at Winch, though, was the nearly perfect description of the beast he'd seen--thought he'd seen--not two hours ago out on the bay.

The noise in the Oarhouse died to a level just above its usual murmur and Winch concentrated on draining his third drink. Behind him, he heard Buster's excited voice and twisted around to glimpse the rummy examining Brant's sketchpad.

"Yeah! That's her for sure! You got her 'zactly right!"

Brant grinned and got up. He walked over to Winch, shoved the pad under the captain's nose, and asked, "How's that? Am I close?"

The entire bar tilted to one side as Winch's head spun, and not from the booze or the aftershocks of the LSD.

The sketch was crude, smudged with charcoal and black fingerprints. And it was, as Buster had proclaimed, 'zactly right. Long serpentine body breaking waves, small dark head bobbing high in the air, and those unforgettable eyes staring blackly back at him from the rough paper.

"I took Buster's description," Brant said proudly, "added a little plesiosaur, with a dash of Loch Ness Monster."

With uncharacteristic force, Winch slapped the sketchpad from Brant's hand and onto the floor. The artist mewled a startled cry of surprise and protest.

"Leave me the fuck alone!" Winch drained his last glass and snarled, "I owe you twenty bucks." He leapt from the stool and staggered toward the door. Brant was stunned. He hadn't meant to be mocking, he was just trying to help. Hell, he liked Winch, sickly admired the man.

As Winch made for the exit, Gil looked up from the sink behind the bar and hollered after him, "Monday, Winch! Three hundred and twenty-six bucks!" The door slammed shut and Winch was gone.

Gil looked down at the sketchpad scattered on the floor. He shifted his beady eyes towards Brant.

"Hey, kid. Y'mind if I keep that? Might look good over the bar."

\* \* \* \* \* \* \*

He never saw it coming. With astounding force, the blow landed squarely in his gut. Winch went down like a sack of shit. He fought for breath, sure he was about to die. His acid-soaked brain projected scenes from old Jimmy Cagney movies. Marco knealt down beside the captain and grasped a handful of Winch's ruined shirt. With a disgusted start, he released his victim and Winch felt his head smack down against the gravel parking lot.

"Fuck, man! What you been rollin' in?" Marco took a step back and stared at the bedraggled sailor. Winch coughed a little as air tentatively crept back into his lungs. The day was hardly underway and the deeper he got into it, the worse it got.

"Get up, man, and talk to me," his assailant said warmly. Winch tried to rise and sank back down. Marco overcame his revulsion and helped his client to his knees, which was as far as he got before the three double vodkas topped with a sucker-punch burbled from Winch's throat.

"Aw, man! That's disgusting!"

Winch had to agree. He wiped his mouth with his crusty sleeve and used the wall of the Oarhouse to steady himself as he rose to a stooping position.

"We gotta have a talk, man. You got some serious debt, and I have obligations, too."

Winch nodded, and it seemed as though the whole world was nodding back at him. Marco was his supplier of illicit drugs and Winch couldn't seem to recall paying for them any time lately. Oh, the day just got better and better. What came next, nuclear war with his butt at ground-zero?

Marco had never resorted to violence before, though he had on occasion threatened it. But then again, Winch had never been so far behind in his payments. Marco was saying something. His lips were moving and Winch had to struggle to make out the words.

"Wha?"

"I said, nine hundred, man. I mean, I got a family to support, and my supplier don't like it when I put him off." He turned his head to display the puckerish scar along his cheek. Marco had really gotten the wound when he'd crashed his Suzuki into a ditch but he frequently used the scar to frighten people who owed him money. It worked this time, but then Winch wasn't much of a challenge. They'd known each other for too many years.

"I don't have it, Marco," he huffed, fighting for breath.

"Aw, man, don't tell me that. You got a boat. You got a house. You got friends, no?"

"Monday," Winch heard himself promising a third time.

"When the bank opens." Marco considered it a moment. He eased up on Winch's soiled shirt.

"Okay. I'll be back Monday."

"Noon. I'll meet you at the boat."

"The boat, sure, fine, noon, Monday. Okay, man."

Winch coughed deeply and spat a gob of bile on the gravel. Marco looked as though he was about to say something else and then changed his mind. There was nothing to add. His point had been made.

He shook his head almost sadly and turned to go. Halfway across the parking lot, Marco paused and called back to Winch.

"Hey, man!" he urged. "Go home and take a shower. You look like hell."

Winch had to agree.

\* \* \* \* \* \* \*

The water barely drizzled out of the showerhead and it took the better part of an hour to scrub himself clean, by which time the water had gone cold. He stood before the bathroom mirror and brushed his teeth, twice, the taste in his mouth refusing to be vanquished. Glancing in the broken mirror, Winch was alarmed to discover that the movements his body made were definitely out of sync with his reflection. That couldn't be good. It had to be a sure sign of the creeping insanity that was undoubtedly overtaking him. Too much booze, too many drugs. Or maybe he was just getting old and he had the world's earliest case of Alzheimer's disease. That would be reassuring. Maybe everything that had happened today had been an illusion, a slipping cog in his head.

He gingerly touched the red and purple bruise just below his ribcage. No, that was no figment of his addled mind. Marco meant business this time. So did Donna Jean and Gil. Winch padded into the kitchen in his underwear. No need to worry about propriety anymore. The house was empty now, and he missed his parents. He hadn't begun this treacherous slide into madness and debauchery until they'd left him. His old man had been tough, and he'd seen that his only son trod the straight and narrow path. He'd taught Winch to be a competent sailor, and had used his respect and influence to get his boy honest work at the boatyard while the other kids were cutting school and sponging off their parents. Mom had doted on him, fed him wonderful homecooked meals and made sure that he'd kept up with his schoolwork. Even after striking out on his own and failing, even after two unsuccessful marriages and a couple of brushes with the law, they'd taken him back in.

They had been the single stable landfall in his stormy sea of life. But now, without their guiding love, Winch had turned into a royal fucking mess.

Totaling today's disasters up in his head, he reviewed the damages. $1,773 owed to Donna Jean for boat stuff; $900 to Marco for his pharmacological supplies; $326 to Gil at the Oarhouse. Oh, and the $240 deposit he'd have to refund for this morning's charter he'd skipped out on. No money owed to the sea monster at least. He'd paid for that with a little piece of his sanity.

Winch reached into the fridge and automatically snagged a beer. Then, with his deceased mother still on his mind, he put it back and shut the door. Instead, he ambled over to the sofa, where the family had passed many evenings watching TV together. In misery, he cradled his head in his hands and fought the urge to just pass out.

The mail he'd collected from the box brimmed with the mundane bills of everyday life: gas, phone, electric, boat payment, insurance premium on the house. At least the house itself wasn't a worry. Dad had paid that off three years before his death, a two-bedroom Cape Cod on half a waterfront acre, with a detached garage and a shingled boat-shed out back near where the dock had once been, before the hurricane. If his dad was still here, he'd have had the dock rebuilt within a week.

Beside the sofa, so vacant now, Winch kept a battered cardboard box filled with memories. It was his last connection to his folks. Whenever he felt especially down, he'd leaf through the photo albums and scraps of paper that constituted the life he'd once known. Now, in the depths of despair, he plunged deeply into it.

Winch dumped the contents on the coffee table and sorted through the bundles of papers. There, the passports which he and his dad had gotten when it looked like they were going to Ireland for the International Oyster Shucking Championships. Mom had gotten sick and they'd stayed home to be with her, missing the trip. And here, his birth certificate, tiny inksmudged footprint gracing the bottom beneath his name, Eugene John Winchell. This one, too, his captain's papers. Important, wondering where they'd gotten to, and he put those aside. Right beneath those he found the pink slip for the *Stuffed Ham*, which he placed with his license. And the deed to the house and half acre, paid-in-full.

Hmmm. A notion stirred in his rusted brainpan. It grew into a thought and then became a possible plan.

Inspired suddenly, seeing a light at the end of the tunnel perhaps, Winch grabbed pencil and paper and toyed with the idea. After twenty-minutes of doodling, he picked up the phone and dialed. It was answered on the fifth ring.

"Hello, Skip? It's Winch. Sorry it's so late, but do you think you can meet me in your office tomorrow? . . . Yeah, I know you don't usually go in on Sunday, but it's important . . . Huh? . . . After church? When's that? . . . Uh, yeah, that'd be great . . . No, no, I'm fine, I guess, but this is really important . . . Great, yeah, I'll see you tomorrow. Thanks, Skip."

He hung up, feeling better than he had all day. This could work! He could get out of all this by tomorrow afternoon, if Skip agreed to his muddled plan. Now, for that beer.

But Winch, being Winch, didn't stop at one beer. He finished the six-pack of Bud and celebrated with a couple of strange pills he found on the floor of his bedroom, leftovers from some other night of hard partying. They might have been from the night he'd mistakenly, but happily, brought home that slightly underaged psych major from the college. It was so cool, he'd thought, that here in his late thirties he was still scoring with the babes. He grinned stupidly.

Winch churned his plan through his already churning brain and, sometime after three AM, passed out on the sofa into a fitful sleep.

# CHAPTER 3

He jerked his head up, snapping awake. The momentary fuzz of displacement burned away and was extinguished by the insistent *thump-thump-thump* of a bass drum powering the repetitive disco beat. Strobe lights stuttered across his eyes, making it hard to adjust to consciousness. The movements of the bartender flickered like an old D.W. Griffith movie with a soundtrack by the Bee Gees. Over the vintage music and manic, shouted conversations, someone tittered in a falsetto voice.

Steve Stevens realized he'd nodded off again. That he could slumber in this impossible environment was proof that this town was gradually killing him, brain cell by brain cell. Reflexively, his hands ran a quick inventory over his body. His wallet was still bulging uncomfortably in the back pocket of his khakis. The heavy Colt MK IV was safely nestled in the holster beneath his left armpit and concealed by his sportscoat. And his imitation Rolex was still snug around his wrist. In the intermittent flashes of white light he managed to read the watch's face: ten till one. He knew he couldn't have been out for more than a couple of minutes.

It was embarrassing, falling asleep on a barstool like some common drunk at the end of a bender. In any other city in the country he would have worried about being recognized and scandalized, but not in Key West. Nearly everybody here behaved like an adolescent whose parents had gone out of town without locking up the liquor. He rubbed the crinkly itch on his forehead where he'd been resting his scalp atop the bar, and his fingers came away sticky.

Fourteen dollars in change, weighed down against the eternal tropical breeze by a dirty ashtray, lay on the dewy countertop, the soft wind swirling through the open doorway fronting Duval Street. Outside, the usual Saturday night carnival was slowly winding down, the tourists, sleepy and smashed, returning to their guesthouses and motels for sex or slumber before the next morning, when they would bake in the sun and nurse inevitable hangovers. Next to the money, Steve noticed his half-finished frou-frou drink. A second nestled untouched behind it, a gayly pink umbrella shading the froth from the glittery sparkles of light thrown by the spinning disco-ball above the bar. It was two-for-one night at the Riding Crop Bar, he remembered, which explained the unordered follow-up drink. He glanced at his watch again. Only three minutes had gone by.

These late nights were going to be his death, Steve knew. He wasn't twenty-one anymore--he was twice that. And he wasn't some carefree tourist. He had a job now--not much of one, it was true--and that fucking punk Davies would jump at the chance to can him, like they'd done in Miami. He set the alarm on his faux Rolex for 5:15, which would give him enough time to rip off some wire-copy and bluff his way through the first newscast at six. It wasn't like the old days, back in Dade, where he could party all night, sleep until noon, and have the station limo chauffeur him to the studio by three. That had been the life! Big city TV newsroom, fat salary, a wardrobe allowance and all the perks of a celebrity. If only he could dig up that one huge exclusive story, he'd be back in his old anchor chair, or--dare he even think it?--wielding the power of a network job in New York!

But what were the chances of that happening in this insular tropical backwater? His newsgathering skills were rusting in the humidity of this far-flung island at the end of the road. Covering the Key West city council, though its politics were Byzantine, was hardly providing the dirt that would catapult him to national prominence. Once he had talent and flair, access to the most powerful people in South Florida and the biggest TV news ratings in Miami. And in one fucked-up evening it had all come crashing down.

Steve Stevens sipped his too-sweet concoction and grimaced. He checked his watch again, impatient for time to fly. Still almost an hour before Brenda was done dancing at The Deep down at the end of Simonton Street. The management there had a firm policy about not letting the girls' boyfriends in, claiming it inhibited the dancers and caused too many fights. So he sat, rather bored, at the corner of the bar at the Riding Crop and let time creep by.

The place was a dive, even by Key West standards, but it was his dive and he felt oddly comfortable here. He wasn't sure what made the place attractive to him; God knew he despised disco. But there was always a more than interesting mix of people, and the entertainment was exotic, to say the least. He could have gone back to his trailer after covering the zoning commission ruckus this evening. It would have been far more convenient, being just two and a half blocks north of The Deep. But he'd heard whispers of the new girl dancing here tonight, so he thought he'd stop in to check out her act. The ten p.m. show was already over by the time he'd arrived, so he'd resolved to hang around for the final set. It wasn't like he had anything better to do, and while he waited he scribbled out the zoning story he'd incorporate into tomorrow's newscast.

Enthusiastic, drunken applause ushered the satin-gowned dancer off the stage and the emcee bounded up the steps in her place. He wore skin-tight leather pants, a matching vest and a black cowboy hat. The audience whooped in delight and Steve craned his head for a better view of the coming show.

"Ladies, gentlemen, and otherwise," the host sang into the microphone. "Thank you for coming tonight, or however you reacted!" Liquored-up laughter answered him. "The Riding Crop is pleased to present our newest discovery! She's dark, she's dangerous, she's a dancing queen! Please, whip up a welcome for Miss Daiquiri Taylor!"

The lights in the barroom flicked off and a single baby spot drilled a hot white beam over center stage. The place was rocking, stomps, shouts and whistles competing with the opening bars of Donna Summer's 70s anthem, "Bad Girls".

Daiquiri Taylor swirled into the spotlight in a diaphanous gown of white lace. Her long skirt was slit suggestively up the side, high enough to showcase the strap of a daring garter which supported the silky sheer stockings embracing her fabulous ebony legs. Spangles of diamond jewelry graced her throat and earlobes. Waves of soft auburn hair tumbled to her shoulders and swung in counterpoint to her rhythmic movements. Doe-brown eyes peered through the smoky haze at the admiring throng as her delicate tongue brushed tantalizingly across her full, blood-red lips.

Steve found himself tapping his foot to the music and sipping his drink. Though he knew that Daiquiri Taylor wasn't his type at all, he couldn't help but be captivated by her sinuous shape and her sensual, animal, stage presence. He decided that the wait had been worth it and relaxed finally, allowing himself to be swept away.

\* \* \* \* \* \* \*

This wasn't right. The set was supposed to have opened with Alicia Bridges' "I Love the Nightlife." Through the irritating cigar and cigarette smoke she spied two of the other girls, Angel and Samantha, at the back of the room, laughing at her. So they were playing little games, an initiation to the Riding Crop. Fine. She could improvise, but it pissed her off. She didn't want people to get the wrong idea about her. She wasn't a "bad girl"! But, if she had to, she could play the part.

    Daiquiri stroked her hands across her torso, her long red nails delicately tickling her small breasts through the thin fabric. The crowd was going wild. Beyond the foot of the stage swayed bikers and tourists, fags and straights, lesbos and locals, all staring up at her, starstruck by her beauty. One guy at the bar stood out, conspicuous in his rumpled suit, white shirt and--my God-- a tie! Nobody in Key West wore a tie! He was having one of those disgusting rum and sugar drinks and, like everybody else in the bar, was staring at her in rapture. So she danced just for him. She always picked one handsome customer to focus on, allowing the rest of the room to recede and giving her the illusion of intimacy. It made getting up in front of a roomful of rowdy drunks easier to handle, not that the two pranksters in the back of the bar were making it less difficult for her. "Bad Girls" indeed.

    Well! She wouldn't be baited. There'd be no ugly catfight afterwards. She'd just make the best of it and show them what she had.

    Only time for two numbers in the last set, minutes before the lights came up and the bouncers started chasing everyone out the doors. She shifted gears and segued into her chosen closing, "Last Dance," still by Donna Summer. At least they hadn't messed with her finale. The music swelled and reached a climax as she twirled across the stage and, on the last note of the song, slid into a breathtaking leg split, arms thrust high into the air in farewell. The lights winked out and the subsequent torrent of appreciation washed over her.

    Daiquiri managed to find the stairs off the platform in the dark without falling over in her six-inch, size 11½ spiked heels. The bar's full lighting flared on, causing the bleary-eyed patrons to wince and whine, and reinforcing the emcee's amplified announcement that it was closing time at the Crop. She strode briskly across the front of the room, aiming for the makeshift dressing room behind the bar.

    The man in the tie gently reached out and touched her on the arm as she passed. He was a hunk, in a middle-aged, suit-and-tie sort of way, and didn't seem to be nearly as drunk as the average customer. He had TV star looks. His salt and pepper hair was clipped short and neatly parted. He lacked the pot-belly and droopy jowls of a habitual bar-fly, and his lightly tanned face told her that this man worked in an office. His sportscoat and tie indicated that he wasn't a tourist, probably a local, but not a true Conch. He leaned toward her slightly as she paused and spoke in a rich, smooth voice.

"Nice set."

Daiquiri smiled back at the gentleman and answered in her own deep, molasses-toned voice.

"Thank you, sugar. Nice tie."

He smiled too, tinged with a little embarrassment, and removed his hand from her arm. Daiquiri walked away and the customer glanced at his expensive-looking wristwatch, sighed, and picked up the frou-frou drink. He tossed away the pink umbrella and resumed drinking.

In the cramped dressing room, Daiquiri saw no sign of the two coquets who had messed with her music. They were probably out on the sidewalk, still in those outrageous costumes, hustling the passersby. They seemed the type.

Daquiri unzipped the hanging garment bag and sat down in front of the mirror. She pulled off her fake diamond earrings and unsnapped the catch on the necklace and dropped the jewelry into one of the open pockets of the bag. The high-heels came off next and she massaged her aching feet, promising she'd shop for a better fitting pair in the morning. She had just started to slip out of her gown when the curtains to the main room parted and the manager of the Riding Crop Bar poked his head in.

"You decent?"

"Come on in, honey," she rumbled. "It's not like you're going to see anything you haven't seen before."

"Great show, Daiquiri. Really. I mean it. You had 'em right in your hand."

She smiled and batted her long lashes at him, and he nearly blushed. She decided not to make an issue of the incident with the music. She could handle those girls herself.

"I've got your check right here. And I wanted to ask you if you could come back next weekend?"

"All three nights?"

"If you want 'em," he assured her. Daiquiri nodded agreeably and resumed changing into her street clothes.

"I think I'm available," she purred and tugged off her wig, revealing naturally wiry, close-cropped black hair. The manager shuffled his feet, watching her transformation in the mirror.

"I gotta admit, I wasn't sure how you, being black, were gonna go over with this crowd. Key West is a pretty white city."

"We're all just people underneath," Daiquiri said, wiping off the last of the make-up and reaching for a pair of jeans. The fake nails were pried off and tossed in the trash and a baggy gray sweatshirt went over the head.

Daiquiri no longer. Taylor now.

He zipped up the garment bag and slung it over his shoulder. Even in a pair of ratty old sneakers, he towered over the manager by a good ten inches. He kissed the boss on the forehead.

"Gotta run. I'll see you next Friday," Taylor said in his melodious voice.

"See ya later, Daiquiri."

Taylor paused at the curtain and looked back over his shoulder, raising a forefinger to remind him.

"It's Daiquiri in the dress, Taylor in the real world, remember?" And Lamont Taylor Jackson blew a kiss at the manager and sashayed out into the bar.

\* \* \* \* \* \* \*

For the tenth time, Steve checked his wristwatch. Finally. Brenda would be done just about the time he drove over to The Deep. He pushed the remnants of his drink away and slipped off the barstool, smoothing out the wrinkles in his khakis. He turned toward the door without looking where he was going and collided with a tall black man hoisting a gray garment bag over one arm.

"Excuse me," Steve apologized.

"Pardon me," Taylor answered. It was the guy in the suit. Seemed nice, but not Daiquiri's type at all.

Steve squinted at the black man. He looked somehow familiar. He couldn't recall noticing a man of such size and shade in the bar tonight. And carrying a garment bag.

Out on the sidewalk, Steve paused as the other man turned left. He thought about it for a second. Daiquiri? He shrugged as the black man disappeared into the late night crowd of Duval Street. This was Key West, after all, and he'd seen stranger things than this.

Steve swerved to the right and walked around the corner onto Petronia Street to search for his car. He was beat. He figured he'd drive Brenda home, climb into bed with her and, eventually, get some sleep.

\* \* \* \* \* \* \*

Brant hadn't been able to sleep at all. That whole scene in the bar had upset him, and he wanted to put things right. Most of the twelve-pack he'd consumed served as his fuel, and his need to atone was his inspiration.

Stocked with paints, brushes, rags, and a couple of loose cans of warm Miller Lite, Brant splashed the little rowboat into the black water. In a few minutes, he drifted with a thump against the *Stuffed Ham* and hurriedly tied the skiff along the port side.

Brant was a believer in all things romantic, and the notion of a sea monster lurking somewhere in the Chesapeake was irresistible. Though he had joined their laughter, he'd meant no offense toward Winch. And he was pretty sure he'd done a respectable job depicting the creature in charcoal. Of that he was certain, given the shock of recognition on Winch's face when the captain had gazed upon the sketch.

So here he was, bobbing upon Solomons Harbor, nearly three o'clock on a bitter October morning, painting by moonlight.

He sipped warm beer as he worked, blending the colors and fighting to keep a steady hand against the waves, the cold and the alcohol. He sweated in the pre-dawn chill. And despite the challenges of this floating canvas, Brant was sure that this was to be his best work ever.

Sunrise was only seconds away and it was done. Proudly, Brant scrawled his signature in tiny script just below his masterpiece and put away his brushes. Daylight was coming fast now as he wearily pulled on the oars and away from the huge cabin cruiser. About ten yards off he paused and admired his work, the stunning sweep of the monstrous body breaking the foaming waves and the perfectly shaped head, which had given him so much trouble, climbing up the hull just below the registration numbers along the port bow.

Fully satisfied, and sure of Winch's surprise and delight, Brant dug the oars into the water and headed home to bed, to dream of Matisse and Monet and monsters.

# CHAPTER 4

In his nightmare, the sea monster rises from the black waters alongside the *Stuffed Ham*. Gobs of seaweed drape its mottled body, flapping limply in the foul-smelling breeze. The green tendrils of weed are made up of damp hundred dollar bills. Upon two of its coils, breaking the waves, ride Donna Jean and Gil. From their perches astride the beast, they leer evilly at Winch. And that terrible undersized head slowly twists around, boring cruelly into his eyes as the creature's features dissolve into the scarred face of the drug-dealing Marco.

The dream startled Winch awake. As usual in the morning, his head hurt. Seeing Chessie in real life was bad enough, but now it was invading his dreams.

The clock in his room nagged that he was already late. Winch threw on some badly wrinkled clothes and grabbed the necessary papers from the coffee table in the livingroom, locking the front door as he slipped out into Sunday morning sunshine. He squinted against the new day and grimmaced, an ice pick of pain in his temples.

He hobbled up the main street along the riverfront, to the north end of Solomons Island. At a white Victorian, renovated into shops and offices overlooking the harbor, Winch mounted the front steps and entered the offices of Skip Miller Realty.

Now, in the off-season, weekend business was slow and only two forlorn agents sat at desks which were cluttered by the paperwork of houses they couldn't move. Both started to rise as a prospect came through the door, and then sat back down dejectedly. One of them recognized Winch and knew he wasn't a buyer, and the other simply recognized what Winch was: a penniless nobody who couldn't buy the rudest shack. They returned to their coffees and Sunday *Posts*.

Winch likewise ignored them for reasons of single-mindednesss and strode to Skip's office. The door was open and he went in.

The office was relaxed corporate, decorated in a nautical theme. A seascape graced the north wall. A deep bay window behind the desk offered a soothing view of sailboats rocking at their moorings on Solomons Harbor. On the south wall hung a framed print of a picturesque waterfront village shaded by waving coconut palms. Winch admired the scene for a second or two before looking down at the realtor and clearing his throat to announce his presence. The man behind the desk put down his crossword puzzle and glanced up.

Skip Miller was Winch's age, both of them in the same class at Calvert High. Balding now, a little on the beefy side from too many hours spent in an office, Skip smiled broadly and rose to offer Winch his hand. They exchanged pleasantries, but Winch was anxious, rocking from one foot to the other and folding and re-folding the papers in his hand.

"So, what's so important, Winch?"

Winch unfolded the papers and laid them on Skip's desk.

"I want you to buy my house."

Skip looked at his unkempt friend levelly and shrugged.

"You mean you want me to sell your house?" he asked, confused.

"No, no," corrected Winch, finally taking a seat. "I don't have time for that."

"I don't understand."

Winch pointed at the deed on Skip's desktop and said, "I need to raise some cash right away. I've got . . . people I owe money to, and I'm gonna be up shit creek by noon tomorrow if I don't take care of these bills."

"Well," the realtor offered, "I can spot you a few bucks. What're we talking about, five, six hundred?"

Winch shook his head. "More than that, lots more. That's why I gotta sell the house, but I don't have time to wait." He picked up the deed and showed it to Skip. "It's all paid for, and all I want is, like, five grand."

The businessman looked aghast. "Winch, you've got a Cape Cod on a half-acre waterfront lot. The land alone is probably worth twenty times that."

"I know, but I can't wait for you to find a buyer, do the settlement and all that shit. So here's my deal: I'll sign the title over to you, you give me five thousand, and the house is yours to sell, rent, live in, whatever."

Skip Miller paused, his fingers making a steeple beneath his chins, thinking this over. He sighed loudly.

"What's the rush? Why do you want to cheat yourself?"

"I'm leaving Solomons. Winter's coming, business sucks, and I just need to get away from here."

"Leaving, huh? Can I ask where you're going?"

Winch was taken aback for a moment. He hadn't really figured that out yet, exactly. He glanced about the room, seeking an answer, and his eyes fell upon the print of the semi-tropical village.

"Where's that?" he asked, inclining his shaggy head toward the picture. Skip's gaze followed Winch's.

"Key West," he replied. "Beautiful town," he added, smiling at the memory of his last vacation there.

"That's where I'm going," Winch impulsively decided. He savored the feel of the name in his mouth. "Key West. Warm there this time of year, isn't it?"

"Yes, it is. Year round, in fact."

"Lotsa tourists?"

"Boatloads," Skip answered perfectly. Then his tone changed, became serious. "But I can't let you sell me your property for five thousand. Your old man, rest his soul, would turn over in his grave. Not that I wouldn't want it. It would be a great listing, a snap to sell, at considerably more than you're asking." He paused and a gleam came to his eye.

"How about this?" the realtor mused. "List the house with us and I'll advance you five thousand toward the sale price."

Winch thought about that and decided he liked the idea.

"Deal. What do I gotta do?"

Skip Miller turned back into a real estate professional. He quickly drew up a sales contract. "What should I put down for the asking price?" he questioned.

"Whatever you think is good," Winch said. "I trust you." Skip smiled at that. Few people trusted real estate agents, ranking them with lawyers, politicians and journalists.

"Okay, we'll leave that blank for now. When I find a buyer, I'll contact you and you can accept or reject the offer. Then, if you want to go ahead, you'll have to come to the settlement to sign . . ."

Winch was shaking his head. "Uh-uh. I'm not coming back."

Skip looked frustrated for a moment before he had an idea.

"Power of attorney," he said, snapping his fingers. He got up from his chair and rummaged through a file cabinet, extracting another pre-printed form. Sitting again, he crossed out a couple of lines, made some additions and offered it to Winch to sign and initial. He called one of the other agents away from her newspaper and had her witness the document. She never gave either of them a glance and left without speaking a word.

"Now everything is shipshape and legal," Skip told him as he examined the papers. Winch cleared his throat again.

"Uh, and the five thousand?"

"Oh, right! Can't forget that." He pulled a corporate check register from his desk drawer.

"Uh," Winch began. "Could I have that in cash? Bank doesn't open until tomorrow."

Skip stopped writing and glanced at his friend sharply. "You really are in some kind of tight spot, aren't you? It's okay, it's me. Skip. Tell me about it." He gave Winch a practiced look.

Winch took a deep breath. "There's slip fees and other stuff at the marina. I owe the Oarhouse for stocking the boat, a couple of customers might want their money back, and there's a guy I know who's gonna break my face if I don't pay up."

"Drugs?" Skip whispered in horror, and Winch nodded in sham shame.

"I gotta get off this bay, man. Same old scenery, same old people for thirty-nine years. There'll be no business for the boat pretty soon, so I figure I'll clear up my debts and set up shop where the tourists are." He didn't add that he was scared that if he hung around the Cheaspeake any longer he'd see the sea monster again, or that he was afraid he'd start seeing worse things in his fevered brain.

Skip sucked on his lower lip, thinking again. Finally, he rolled his chair over to the office safe squatting in the corner and spun the lock. From it, he withdrew a cash box and examined its contents. Counting, he peeled off twenty-two hundred dollars. Then he used a machine to stamp out a cashiers check for another twenty-eight hundred, stuffing the package into a manilla envelope, along with his business card and copies of the agreements. He handed Winch the envelope.

"Best I can do, Gene." Skip called him by his old school name, which Winch hated. "Call me when you get settled. After it sells I'll send you the money, less costs and the five grand advance." He smiled gently, sorry to see his friend in trouble, drifting aimlessly through life. But business was business. Skip held out his hand to seal the deal. Instead, Winch hugged him.

"You saved me, man," he said earnestly. He released the realtor and turned to leave. Skip watched Winch walk away and then gathered his Polaroid and a *For Sale* sign. Might as well get this place on the market, he reasoned.

\* \* \* \* \* \* \*

Winch clutched his enveloped salvation tightly in his left hand as he pushed the battered shopping cart with his right up Solomons Island Road. Piled inside the rusting Food King cart were most of his clothes and belongings. This was his third and final trip with the cart, the detritus of earlier runs already stowed aboard the *Stuffed Ham*. The house was locked, he had said his goodbyes to his parents' ghosts, leaving the only stable life he had known behind. Tonight he'd sleep on board the *Stuffed Ham*, cash Skip's check in the morning, and pay off his bills. Then he'd be underway no later than one o'clock Monday. If all went well, he hoped to be sipping a frozen margarita in Key West by Thursday night.

Coming up on the Oarhouse, Winch and his cart were rudely driven onto the gravel shoulder by a silver Mercedes that was grossly flouting the 25mph speed limit. The driver shot him a disgusted look and left Winch choking on a cloud of dust. He wiped some grime from his tearing eyes and pushed on.

"Tourist," he cursed.

As he angled across the road, aiming the cart for the driveway into the marina, he heard someone call his name.

"Hey, Winch!"

Coasting to a stop, Brant dismounted his twelve-speed Trek beside the cart. "Moving?" he asked, looking over the mound of clothes, books and debris. From the top of a cardboard box, a bong poked out.

"As a matter of fact," answered Winch, "I am. Hoisting anchor tomorrow for *terre incognito*, soon as I get everyone paid off." He held up the envelope. "Got money for Donna Jean and Gil. Also, I gotta take care of Marco before he rearranges my face." Brant nodded. He knew all about Winch's stormy relationship with the drug dealer.

"Oh, yeah," Winch remembered and dug a twenty out of the envelope, handing it to Brant. "I owe you for the drinks yesterday."

Brant accepted the money gracefully. He might aspire to be a tortured artist, but he did not intend to be a starving artist. "No sweat," he said. "Need some help with that stuff?"

"Nah, this is the last of it. Sorry I blew up at you yesterday."

"No harm," Brant shrugged. "I shouldn't have laughed at you." He resisted the urge to confess to Winch about the painting he'd done last night. Let it be a surprise. But now that he'd thought about the seamonster again, Brant ventured, "Did you really see it?"

The question hung in the air. Winch made an uncomfortable face. His father had been a waterman on the Chesapeake for forty years and he'd never seen Chessie. Maybe his son hadn't either. If only it hadn't seemed so real. Winch could recall every detail vividly, much too vividly to pass it off as some psychotic episode, though lately he seemed to be having plenty of experience with those. Brant looked at the ground and kicked at a pebble with the tip of his loafer. After a long moment, Winch answered.

"Nah. Too much partying, that's all." But his tone caused Brant to disbelieve him.

Brant nodded. "I was just going to the Oarhouse for a beer. Care to join me?" he offered.

"No, gonna finish loading, check a few charts, get the *Ham* ready to go. Maybe I'll stop in later, say goodbye." And pay off Gil while he was there, he thought. He had enough cash for that now, and it would be one down and two to go.

They parted company. Brant climbed back on his bike and wheeled away while Winch trundled off in the direction of the *Stuffed Ham*.

\* \* \* \* \* \* \*

*Stuffed Ham,* my ass, Big Jim Quinn seethed as the Mercedes 500SL ignored the speed limit southbound on Rt. 2. First, Liza had kept him up half the night with her sexual acrobatics. And then, once he'd managed a few hours of sleep, he'd remembered that he had a nine o'clock tee-time with the president of the firm. Now he was hours late getting started. So distracted had he been by the nearness of his prize that he'd come close to beating the old man before self-preservation had kicked in and he'd purposely sliced into the woods on the eighteenth hole, thus ensuring he'd lose to the boss by at least two strokes.

Finally, just before the high bridge into St. Mary's County, Quinn took the turnoff for Solomons Island, tearing down the main street. On the seat beside him lay a yellow legal pad with the address of one Eugene Winchell. It wasn't a big town and he figured finding the house would be a breeze. But the village was a maze and he grew angrier by the minute, driving up and down narrow lanes in his frustrating search for Charles Street.

Back on Solomons Island Road again, cruising past quaint antique shops and waterfront restaurants, he was disgusted at the sight of a filthy street-person pushing one of their ubiquitous shopping carts. Bad enough in Baltimore, but, Christ, even here, in this quaint village, the homeless had established a beachhead, driving down real estate values and fouling the scenery. Purposely, Big Jim edged the Mercedes to the right, kicking up gravel and sending the bum a message. He chuckled at the rear-view mirror as the homeless man wiped grit from his eyes.

In his left pocket he had the spare keys to his yacht. Tucked snuggly into the holster on his belt, hidden by his trenchcoat, was his .38. The checkbook was in the inside pocket of his coat. Once he found Winchell, he thought, he'd slip aboard the *LauraLee* and use the spare keys to steal her back. If he had to negotiate, he would. He was prepared to offer up to ten grand to get his boat back. But if he couldn't steal her, or if Winchell wouldn't sell, Big Jim was ready to take her by force. He already had a man ready to alter her registration numbers and appearance, and a slip at a remote marina on Kent Island where he could hide her.

But first, damn it, he had to find her! It was past one o'clock, and he was pissed. Getting hungry and thirsty, too. He pulled the silver sports car into the next restaurant he came to, a grubby looking dump that fronted the harbor. The side door was propped open and he went in.

There was a bar and a dozen or so tables, nearly all vacant. A spiky-haired kid in a college sweatshirt and loafers sat at one of them, scribbling on a huge pad of paper. A toothless old man sat drunkenly against the far end of the bar, staring into space over a glass. He was quietly mumbling to no one in particular. A couple of locals hunched over tables, drinking beer and eating fried oyster sandwiches and crabcakes. Big Jim tugged his trenchcoat closed to better conceal his weapon, and took a seat at the bar.

The bartender ambled over. "What'll it be?"

"Beer, anything on tap. And a menu."

Gil nodded and grabbed a mug. "Bud okay?" he asked, already filling it. He set it on the counter along with a one page menu. Big Jim considered.

"Oysters fresh?"

"On the bottom of the bay this morning," Gil lied.

"Sandwich, then," Quinn ordered, returning the menu. Gil nodded amiably and went back to the kitchen to cook up the order.

Big Jim downed half his beer in one gulp. He glanced around the room. The old man was still staring at nothing, but now his glass was empty. The kid was working feverishly at his paper and Big Jim thought he caught the boy staring back at him repeatedly. Normally, Quinn abhored being stared at, but he let it slide. Kid was probably just looking in his direction and not *at* him. The boy seemed lost in thought. Probably harmless. Everyone else in the bar was paying him no mind.

He drained his beer just as the bartender set down a plate. Big Jim ordered another round and started on the sandwich. It was dry and crumbly. Between bites, he called to Gil.

"Bartender, do you know a guy, name of Eugene Winchell?"

Gil flicked his dishrag over one shoulder and stepped forward. Behind his sketchpad, Brant overheard and flicked his eyes up.

"Winch? Sure," answered Gil.

"Can you tell me where I can find his house? I think it's 76 Charles Street."

Gil proceeded to give him the simple directions to a street Big Jim had driven past but must have missed the sign for. When the bartender pointed, Big Jim turned on his stool as if he could actually see Winchell's house through the wall of the bar. As he revolved, the trenchcoat gaped open and Brant suddenly had a clear view of the gunbutt protruding from the holster on the man's waist.

"What do you want with that scumbucket?" Gil sneered.

"He's got something of mine," Big Jim bragged, then realized the beer was making him talk too much.

"Yep," commiserated Gil. "He owes me a pretty good piece of change too, along with half the people in town."

Brant softly closed his sketchpad, abandoned his Lite beer and discretely slipped out the side door.

Big Jim grunted in acknowledgment to the barkeep and washed down his last bite with the rest of his beer. "Thanks for your help," he said, rising and dropping some money on the bar.

Outside, he started his Mercedes and drove towards Charles Street.

\* \* \* \* \* \* \*

In the parking lot beside the Oarhouse, Brant recognized all of the cars but one, a silver Mercedes. Straddling his bike, he watched the man leave, driving off toward the foot of the island.

Brant pedaled as fast as he could toward the marina. He skidded to a stop and dropped the bike in the dust alongside the dock where the *Stuffed Ham* was moored. Still clutching the sketchpad, he pounded down the pier.

"Winch!" he barked into the empty cockpit. "Winch!"

The hatch to the cabin rocked open and the captain emerged into the sunlight, clutching a glass of rum in one hand and a nautical chart in the other. The aroma of marijuana escaped from below deck.

"Winch, there's some big guy in a Mercedes over the Oarhouse looking for you, he's got a gun, Gil told him where you live . . ." Brant burbled on.

"Shit," Winch muttered. Either there was someone else he'd pissed off recently and forgotten about, or Marco's supplier had decided he couldn't wait until Monday. Or could it be the father of that cute co-ed he'd been banging last weekend? It was only later that he'd found out she wasn't quite eighteen yet. "Shit."

If it was Marco's boss, he could pay the guy off with his available cash. But if it was another problem, like some missing virginity, and the guy had a gun, Winch didn't want to deal with that.

"Help me cast off," he yelped at Brant. Winch ran to the console and kicked over both diesels. The engines rumbled to life, protesting the cold start. "C'mon, baby," Winch urged, and they finally settled into a nice purr.

\* \* \* \* \* \* \*

Big Jim Quinn tooled slowly down Charles Street, annoyed he'd missed it the first time. It should have been so obvious, but how was he to know that when Solomons Island Road curved left at the foot of town the name of the street changed? He looked for house numbers, getting closer.

In front of a little Cape Cod, he pulled to the verge. The mailbox said 76. In the weedy yard, a chunky bald man in a sports shirt was positioning a large yellow sign with the logo, *Skip Miller Realty*.

Big Jim eased himself from behind the wheel and made sure his coat was pulled closed. He wandered over to the man on the lawn.

"Excuse me," Big Jim said. The realtor looked up and beamed. "Is this the home of Eugene Winchell?" Skip Miller's smile wavered only a little.

"Not for long, I hope," he replied cheerily and handed the prospect a card. Big Jim didn't offer his own name, but that didn't bother Skip. Prospective buyers often didn't think to introduce themselves right off.

"Do you know where I can find Mr. Winchell?"

Damn, this wasn't a buyer after all, thought Skip. He answered, "I believe he's over at his boat." At that, the stranger's eyebrows rose. Something about him made Skip nervous.

"And where would that be?" he asked coolly.

Before Skip could stop his tongue, he'd blurted out, "Harbor Lights Marina, just down the street on the right."

The man dashed back to the idling Mercedes. Oh, my God, Skip realized in horror. What had he done? The memory of Winch in his office that morning, telling him of the sudden need to get out of town, the drugs! This guy had the look of a big-time pusher if he'd ever seen one, which he hadn't. Skip stared as the Mercedes burned rubber up the road.

\* \* \* \* \* \* \*

From the bow of the *Stuffed Ham*, Brant could see the speeding silver car, sunlight reflecting off three coats of polish. He leaned around the side and yelled astern, "Winch, we got company!"

Winch dashed to the starboard gunwale and saw the Mercedes Benz diving into the parking lot. He recognized the car that had nearly run him over earlier. "Are we untied?" he called to Brant, and was rewarded with a thumbs up.

He grabbed the spring line and looped it off the cleat, dropping it into the water. The car ground to a lurching stop at the top of the pier and a big guy in a white golf shirt under a trenchcoat spilled out even before the expensive car had come to a complete halt. In fact, the Mercedes never did completely stop, inching barely forward.

From beneath the coat, the crazed-looking man--has to be the angry father, Winch decided--pulled a pistol. Winch ran for the console and shoved both throttles to their stops. The *Stuffed Ham* dug her stern into the water and jumped forward, propellers seeking purchase, hull struggling to rise up, hardly clear of the pilings.

The gunman made it to the end of the pier as the big boat churned white foam in it's wake, putting slow distance between them. Winch caught himself thinking rationally in an irrational situation: Okay, so I leave a day early. I'll send the money to Marco, Donna Jean and Gil later, when I get to Key West. No problem.

A shot split the air, then a second, and another. Winch ducked down in the cockpit, but the firing stopped. Cautiously, he stuck his head up over the transom.

On shore, Big Jim cursed himself. How could he be so stupid, taking potshots at that asshole? He could have hit the boat! Jesus, and now they were getting away!

Behind him, he heard the soft sound of tires crunching on gravel.

\* \* \* \* \* \* \*

From his crouch behind the safety of the transom, Winch watched in utter fascination as the silver sports car slowly rolled past the edge of the parking lot, bumped over the low curb, crashed to the wooden planking of the pier and traversed the dock before gracefully plunging grill-first into the harbor. The man on the pier lowered the gun and cradled his head in his hands. Winch thought he might be weeping.

With a whoop of victory, the captain stood up and ran to the wheel, angling the *Stuffed Ham* out into the river. She was planed off nicely now, running fast with the wind. He nudged the throttles back down to half-speed and stuck his head out the cockpit window.

"Hey, Brant!" he called merrily. "Where do you want me to drop you off?"

There was no answer. Winch crossed to the port side and looked towards the bow. His stomach did a flip.

Splayed across the foredeck was Brant's limp body. With shaking hands, Winch snapped the bungee cord in place on the wheel and scrambled forward. Scared, he hovered over his friend. A bloody wound scarred Brant's smooth forehead, dark blood everywhere on his face and spilling onto the deck. In anguish, Winch hoisted the artist up and dragged him back to the cockpit, setting him gently on the vibrating deck. Brant never moved, nor did Winch think he ever would again.

For a long moment, he gazed down at the corpse. Then he noticed Brant's sketchpad on one of the deckchairs, the pages flapping in the wind. Winch reverently picked it up and stared at Brant's last drawing, one he had made only minutes ago at the Oarhouse. It depicted the face of a killer.

He took the pad below and stowed it. When he reemerged, he was grasping the neck of the bottle of rum. Winch tilted it back, overfilling his mouth and splashing the warm liquor down his chin, onto his denim shirt where it mixed with the tears he didn't even know he was spilling.

# CHAPTER 5

Nearby, off the starboard bow, rose the scenic lighthouse at Point Lookout. Winch never saw it. He was busy rifling the galley for another bottle of anything. He found a pint of brandy behind some ketchup and stumbled back on deck. Something was different. Land close to starboard, that was right. Bungee still in place, that's not it. Brant's body was sitting on the transom bench holding its bloody head. Hmmm. That's what it was.

The corpse groaned and looked up at him. Winch had a fleeting memory of himself in the mirror, out of synch, and wondered about his sense of reality. He stared stupidly at the re-animated Brant.

"Can I have some of that?" the body said. "And a couple of aspirins."

"Jeez, Brant, I thought you were dead!" Winch cautiously handed the brandy over with a shaking hand and then retreated to the helm. He unsnapped the makeshift auto-pilot and aimed back into the channel. With a bleeding, throbbing head, Brant joined him and slid into the shotgun seat. He pulled a clean handkerchief from his back pocket and wiped at his nose.

"Damn," he whined. "I hope I didn't break it." He tested his beak gingerly.

"Man, I thought you were history!" huffed Winch, taking back the pint. "I thought that sonofabitch had nailed you!"

"What are you talking about? You damn near killed me when you hit the throttle!" Brant, satisfied his nose wasn't broken and that it had stopped bleeding, dabbed at the cut on his forehead.

"The guy was *shooting* at us. I had to get us out of there!"

"Well, you coulda warned me first." Brant held the handkerchief to the wound on his head and retrieved the bottle. "Who was that dork anyway?"

"Search me," Winch shrugged. "Some chick's dad, I think." He laughed under his breath and added, "Guess I'd do the same thing if my daughter was dating me." He chuckled again and this time Brant smiled too.

Winch glanced over at Brant, glad his friend was still alive, and said, "But if he was pissed off before, he's really going apeshit now."

"Why's that? 'Cause we got away?"

"That, and the fact that his fancy little ol' Mercedes rolled off the pier and took a swan dive!" He sighed, remembering. "Beautiful sight." They both laughed and passed around the bottle one more time until it was dry.

"So now what?" Brant said after awhile. He checked the handkerchief for bleeding again. It had tapered off.

"Next stop, Key West," Winch enthused. "Hey, you should come along! We'll have a good ol' time, and I could use a crew!"

Brant shook his head. "I'd like to, really. But I got mid-terms next week, and the folks . . ." He trailed off.

"I thought you were the party dude? Suffering artist on a road of self destruction, all that shit?" Winch was wounded. The kid had held such promise.

"Wish I was, and I wish I could go." He looked up at Winch. "You're like, like a god to me, man! All you do is party, and the shit never sticks to you. I could never be like that. For God's sake, I drink light beer! I've never done anything harder than pot and I've never . . . never . . ." He trailed off again. Winch almost blushed, but his cheeks were already rosy from the brandy.

"No problem, man," Winch said stoically and spun the wheel to angle up the Potomac. "You're probably right. Gets to be a time we all got to grow up." But he wasn't sure he meant it.

The *Stuffed Ham* chugged up the river. Just ahead was the pier which belonged to St. Mary's College, an exclusive enclave of money and power, an environment where Brant could feel truly at home. They rode in silence as the sun set upon the Potomac. Finally, with the pier in sight, Winch throttled down and maneuvered in.

"Do me a favor?" he called to Brant, readying the stern lines this time. "Could you stop by the Oarhouse and the marina tomorrow and tell Gil and Donna Jean that I had to leave town, and I promise I'll send them the money as soon as I can?"

"No problem. I gotta pick up my bike anyway."

"Thanks, man. I know I've got enough cash right now to pay them, but I'm going to need it to refuel the boat and eat. And if you see Marco hanging around, could you tell him the same?"

Brant hesitantated a moment. He didn't especially want to have to speak to the drug dealer. But he promised Winch he would if he happened to see him.

The *Ham* bumped against the pilings. It hung there placidly, held in place by the rising tide. Brant shook Winch's hand and wished him luck. Winch said he'd send a postcard. Brant climbed over the gunwale and stepped onto the dock. He turned to wave, spotted his mural, and couldn't help but smile.

"Oh, Winch, before you go, I have a surprise for you." It would be his last chance to see the look on Winch's face.

The captain looked uncertain and stepped over the gunwale and onto the dock. Brant pointed at the hull.

Winch turned around and stared at the mural, and all the nutty nightmares rushed into the void that was his brain. He looked at Brant. He looked at the painting. Damn, it was just about right. He considered the picture for a long minute, and he almost liked it. It was a true masterpiece. He turned his eyes to Brant again and said only, "You made the snout too long."

And without another word exchanged, Winch reboarded the *Stuffed Ham* and took her out. From the pier, Brant watched her recede until she was but a speck on the dusky horizon, and then he turned and limped off toward his dorm.

*  *  *  *  *  *  *

Maxx Rock used his flannel sleeve to mop up the spilled coffee next to the console and slipped on his Koss headphones. The last strains of Bob Marley's "Stir It Up" faded from the monitors. He hit the mike key on the board and dropped his voice an octave into "radio mode." "Mmmm, you can stir me up anytime, little darlin' . . . That's Marley and you're with the Maxx Rock Morning Mess on Key Rock 102 FM! Let's find out what's happenin' in the Lower Keys this morning with the Key Rock newshound . . . How's it hangin', Steve?"

In the adjoining booth, separated from the air-studio by double panes of glass, the newsman heard his cue in his phones and saw the red "on-air" light blink on. Steve held his copy and determined he would play it as straight and smooth as Maxx would allow. It was the last newscast of the morning and his earlier headache had finally receded into a soft throb, the result of too many late hours, too much booze and the blathering idiocy of Maxx Rock himself.

"It's 76 degrees at 8:52, I'm Steve Stevens with a Key Rock News Update." He knew that the shock-jock would interrupt him, but was never sure when it was coming or how inane it would be. "The Key West zoning commission is after houseboat row."

"Ah, man, here we go again!" Maxx shouted over his headphones.

Well, Steve thought, that didn't take long. The boss insisted upon this sort of banter between jock and newsman, and Steve just hated it.

"At an unusual weekend session, the commission heard from attorneys representing several businesses and homeowners near houseboat row..."

"How the *caca* do you row a houseboat?" *Caca* was Maxx's idea of high humor.

"They say that the houseboats, many of which are handbuilt and very colorful, are an eyesore. One of the houseboat owners at the meeting responded to the charge." Steve punched the green button on the cart deck and the actuality he'd recorded at last night's meeting bled out of the speakers.

"Eyesore? They're friggin' adorable! And the tourists love 'em! We're a friggin' landmark!"

This was too tempting for Maxx, who jumped in. "Hey! Can you say 'friggin' on the air? Friggin', friggin', friggin'!" Steve pressed on.

"The meeting ended without a decision . . ."

"All that, and they couldn't friggin' make up their minds? Well, that figures, typical friggin' government, your friggin' tax dollars at work!"

Steve finished limply, "More fireworks Wednesday afternoon."

"Oh, we'll be looking forward to that," growled Maxx sarcastically. "That friggin' story sucked. What else ya got?"

"How about this?" Steve shot back, bristling. The next story was the kind Steve hated and Maxx loved, pure fluff. "Celebrity alert! The Conch City Hotel and Marina will be hosting Mister Baseball Network himself, and his charming Hollywood bride; yes, Mr. and Mrs. Armand Pringle . . ."

"Oooo," wailed Maxx in mock excitement. "That's big! He's got a baseball team, a TV network, newspapers and my favorite magazine, *Knockers*! Hey, Steve, ya know his wife was Miss Knockers in the very first edition?"

Steve steadied himself. If not for the barrier of double glass between the booths, he'd strangle Maxx.

"No, I didn't realize that, Maxx. In any case, the fabulous couple will be yachting-in this week to vacation on our fair island . . ."

"That Mrs. Pringle, she's a babe! I'd do her!"

"The word on the street says they're in love with Blue Heaven on Petronia and Thomas and stargazers can catch them there for dinner."

"Don't ya just hate that place," Maxx gurgled. "It's just so precious! Yechhh! The food there makes me sick! Hey, haven't ya got any good news?"

"Okay Maxx," Steve seethed, trying to keep the anger out of his voice. "How about a look at the weather? Mostly sunny and pleasant this afternoon, 80 degrees our high. Hurricane Margo is still well to the northeast of us, moving up the Gold Coast and giving Daytona Beach a good beating. We'll be clear and cool tonight, low of 68, then more of the same tomorrow, high of 85. A 40% chance of thundershowers both afternoons, and we'll keep an eye on Margo for you."

"Steve! Ya got Margo's phone number for me? She sounds like a bitchin' babe!"

"Currently, under bright sunshine, it's 76 degrees at 8:54. I'm Steve Stevens, Key Rock News!"

The opening bars of Warren Zevon's "Werewolves of London" crept under his outro as Maxx howled and jumped back in.

"Thanks a friggin' lot for that friggin' news report, Steve! I'm friggin' Maxx Rock on the friggin' Maxx Rock Morning Mess, with those friggin' Werewolves of London at friggin' Key Rock 102, Key West's monster of rock, WRKW! Ah-ooooo!"

The newscaster pulled off his cans and rubbed the pain in his temples. Watching Maxx through the window, Steve remembered their first meeting two months ago. The general manager, Grant Davies, had hired one Gregory Bitzer, aka Maxx Rock, to punch up the sagging morning ratings. The first time Steve had heard Maxx on the air, he'd been impressed by the deejay's rich baritone delivery and had gone into the booth to welcome the new guy to Key Rock 102. Maxx had been regaling his listeners with a genuinely funny story about his frightening trip in a Beechcraft to Key West. Steve had been slightly offended by the shock-jock's rough reference to soiling his pants during the landing, but he understood the need for ratings, however distasteful. When the on-air light had clicked off, he'd tapped Maxx Rock on the shoulder and offered his hand, introducing himself.

"Welcome to WRKW, I'm Steve Stevens, the news director. Hey, you sound pretty good!"

Maxx had looked blandly over his shoulder at Steve and said dryly, "I know I do."

And it had all gone downhill from there. Steve knew that radio was full of overblown egos, and a little bit of self-confidence was required. But this was too much. After all, this wasn't New York or LA, it was the end of the road, literally. Steve had stalked out of the studio, hating Maxx instantly.

Now, Steve poked his head into the booth. "Hey, Maxx," he said mildly. "Do you think you can go a little easier? The news is important, and while I don't mind a little back-and-forth, you're cutting in way too much."

"News is shit," Maxx replied, wiping his nose with his sleeve. "It bores people and cuts into my time."

Steve shook with barely controlled rage. He was trying to be reasonable and professional about this.

"People want to know what's going on," he defended.

"Who gives a flying fuck about a bunch of leaky houseboats? Man, if you had half my talent, you'd still be back in Miami!"

*So, why are you in Key West?* Steve wanted to ask, but he kept his mouth shut. Maxx spent most of his free time brown-nosing the boss.

Before he said or did something rash, Steve retreated, slamming the studio door. The red on-air light winked on and over the hallway monitor Maxx started bleating, "Friggin', friggin', friggin'!"

Sitting at his immaculate desk in the newsroom, Steve put off making the first of his morning calls and mused over a cup of coffee. He'd been at WRKW nearly a year and his prospects for getting back to Miami weren't any brighter. Maxx was wrong. It wasn't a lack of talent that had dislodged him from the glitz of Dade County. It was all because of one wild night and a story that had gone horribly wrong.

Steve Stevens, crack investigative reporter for Action News, had scooped them all. Not only had his relentless digging uncovered a graft scandal involving one of the Dade County commissioners, but he had video of the pay-off! As usual, Steve had called the target of his investigative report for comment before airing the story. Instead of the expected routine denial, however, the commissioner had blasted Steve with an expletive-laced diatribe filled with warnings and threats. Steve had hung up on him and jotted on his note-pad, "no comment."

That night, four minutes into the six o'clock news, Steve had been opening his report when there came a loud crash from off the set. Steve paused mid-sentence. Squinting through the glare of the klieg lights, Steve saw the floor manager inexplicably tumbling across the concrete. A snarl of angry voices interrupted the newscast from offstage. One of the cameramen spun around in the direction of the disturbance, whipping his camera. Over his earpiece, Steve could hear the director in the control room screaming frantically for order.

A figure loomed out of the unlit part of the studio, directly before him. It was the commissioner he'd caught on tape, raising a pistol. Steve had lived in the insanity of Miami long enough to know the score, and for that reason he never went anywhere without his own concealed weapon, a US government issue Colt MK IV.

Steve dove for cover behind the plywood anchor desk just as a slug drilled through the back of his chair. He unholsterd his .45 and returned fire in syncopation to the shrill screams of Heather the Weathergirl. Cameramen and reporters hit the floor, seeking cover as Steve and the commissioner exchanged badly aimed shots.

After firing half-a-dozen rounds, his assailant fled. Steve rose up and, still live on the air, squeezed off one more bullet at the retreating shape. The weatherbunny shrieked in anguish and collapsed, a bloody red hole blossoming in her shoulder. In the pandemonium of the control room, the director finally managed to cut to a commercial, but not before all of South Florida had seen the shoot-out and its aftermath live in their living rooms.

By the next day, the commissioner was somewhere in the Bahamas and Steve was putting together his resume. The owner of the TV station had fired him personally. Heather, the weatherbunny with whom he'd been recently sleeping, refused to take his calls from her hospital bed. The video of the gunfight made the network news and Steve found that no other station would touch him. It looked like his career was finished.

A month later, still unable to find a job, Steve had been graced by a call from his old roommate at the University of Florida, Bob Davies. Bob had been the successful one. He had assembled a chain of radio stations in the southeast and was calling to offer his old friend a gig doing news at his Key West property. Gratefully, and with his American Express due, Steve accepted. Three days later he was installed as news director at WRKW-FM. It wasn't TV, but at least he was back on the air. It would only be a matter of time, he hoped, before he would get that one big story that would return him to the glories of major-market television. But the pace of life in the Keys was slow and a story of major significance remained elusive.

Key Rock 102 was run by Bob's son, Grant Davies, a reward from his father for managing to graduate from Sarasota Community College with a solid C average. Grant was all of 22, almost half Steve's age, and made no secret of his dislike of Steve and his newscasts. That the fallen newsman was still employed at WRKW was due only to the fact that Bob had ordered his son not to fire Steve. So Grant had instead tried to make life as difficult for Steve as possible, cutting his air-time, assigning ridiculous stories, and finally pairing him with that Neanderthal morning man, Maxx Rock. Steve sipped his coffee and brooded, his memories of the old days shattered by the arrival of the general manager himself.

Grant Davies strode into the newsroom like a pint-sized thunderstorm. "Steve," he began, "I don't hear the kind of chatter on the air with Maxx I'm expecting from you. He's holding up his end. Let's hear you punch up the news a little more! No one cares about houseboats and zoning meetings." Like Steve, Grant was a fairly new arrival to the Keys. Neither of them would ever be a Conch.

Steve set down his coffee. He hated Grant, he hated working with Maxx, hated shock-jocks in general, hated rock and roll, and most of all hated the weirdness of Key West. Miami was crazy, but Key West was totally nuts.

"I've got a story for you," Grant plowed on. "I want you to do a multi-part feature on the Save the Reef Foundation over on Stock Island. Bunch of coral-huggers want to keep a new marina from being built on Cow Key Channel. Damn environmentalists are gonna ruin the keys," he added without a trace of irony.

"Grant, that's a stupid idea. It's not a radio story." It also wasn't the kind of story that would give the newsman a shot at the big-time again. It was boring, a waste of time and he knew that Grant was only sending him to Stock Island to make him miserable.

"I don't care. I want you to cover it, and I want it on the air by Thursday." Grant looked smug. Steve sighed wearily, and his headache roared back to life.

"Fine," he huffed, rising to his feet. He picked up his notebook and cassette-recorder, patted his chest for the feel of his Colt, decided not to use it on the little twerp, and headed for the door. "I'll call them later," he said tightly. "But first I gotta cover the fucking Aqueduct Authority meeting." He stormed out into the relentlessly sunny morning.

\* \* \* \* \* \*

"Friggin', friggin', friggin'," babbled the incredibly annoying DJ, and Laura shut off the radio. She'd heard the weather report and that was all she'd wanted. God, this guy is worse than Greasegun back home, she thought. It was almost nine now and she would be late for her first day of work.

Her head ached, despite three Advils. The past two nights had been spent at the resort bar where she'd been trying to balance her nervousness with her determination to succeed. Each night, to her drunken embarrassment, one of the gay bartenders had had to walk her back to her room. She knew she had to ease up, but the heady taste of freedom was corrupting her better judgement. She ought to resist temptation and concentrate on the task at hand, rebuilding her life.

Laura looked through the window. Where was that damn cab, anyway? She stood alone in her spartan motel room and gazed out at the dazzling tropical sunshine. Back home, the leaves were turning red and gold, but here in Key West there was only the endless green and yellow of bending palms. A happy couple, two men, passed by her vista of Simonton Street, hand in hand. Laura hadn't known when she'd booked two weeks at the Rainforest Resort that she'd committed herself to fourteen days of living in the midst of Key West's number one gay and lesbian beach resort.

Laura watched the gaily plumed pair stroll by and she fought back a tear, thinking of the ruins of her marriage.

Did he even miss her yet? She'd been gone almost three days now. Twice over the weekend she'd fought the urge to phone him just to say that she was alright. But that would have led to an argument and eventually to one of his famous ultimatums. No, it would be better to wait, get settled and then call him to say she wasn't coming back home. The brief letter she'd left for him would explain it all. She didn't tell him where she was going; only that she was finally happy, doing something she'd always wanted to do, being the person she'd always wanted to be. She noticed her gold wedding band.

Without a second thought, she pried it off and dropped it in the bottom of her purse, something she should have done years ago. Outside, a pink taxi pulled up and honked cheerfully.

Laura checked herself in the mirror. She hoped the powder blue sundress wasn't too short, her heels not too high. She wanted to make a good first impression. She grabbed her room key and purse and locked the door behind her.

She gave the driver an address and settled back into the rear seat, watching the vibrant island town slip past her window. Laura Chadwick remembered sadly how Jim had first laughed at her when she'd told him she wanted to go back to school and finish her degree. And how he hadn't even shown up for her graduation ceremony when she'd taken her hard-won B.A. in public relations. He'd dashed her dreams by staunchly refusing to consider the idea of her working. She was a trophy wife, a good fifteen years Jim's junior, and as far as he was concerned her job was to look good and play the pretty little hostess.

They'd met in Negril, on the beach at sunset. How romantic. Married over six years now, but there had been no children. Jim hadn't wanted any, though she was in love with the idea of having a family. He was prone to jealous rages whenever he feared she was spending too much time chatting with other men at one of their fabulous parties, though she'd always been faithful to him. In fact, it was Laura who had endured *his* indiscreet playing around. She knew all about Liza and that drunken reception at the Inner Harbor last month. Had he really thought, carrying on in public, that she wouldn't hear about it? One of the other wives from the office had phoned her and told all. That was the last straw.

Without his knowledge, Laura had begun sending out resumes. She embezzled money from the household accounts and made follow-up calls to prospective employers using a calling card so the calls wouldn't show up on their home bill. And in an amazingly short span of time, she'd landed a real job, far away from home.

The pink taxi sped past Smathers Beach and the airport. There to the right was houseboat row, which she'd heard about on the news this morning. It really was very picturesque, she reflected. It would be a shame to see it disappear just as she discovered it. The cab turned onto US 1 and crossed the short bridge to Stock Island.

She had told Jim Friday night that she was going to New York for the weekend with one of her girlfriends to do a little shopping. She knew he'd offer no resistance to her absence, figuring he'd use the time to screw around with Liza or one of his other harpies. She didn't care anymore. It was over. In a couple of minutes, she'd walk through the doors of the Save the Reef Foundation and begin her new career as Director of Public Information, answering phones, writing news releases and dealing with the media. She shifted in her seat in excited anticipation as the cab crunched to a stop in the gravel parking lot of SRF, or "SuRF" as they called it.

Laura paid the driver and stood before the squat cinderblock building on the harbor and smoothed her long blonde hair. There was a gleam of happiness in her green eyes. She took a deep breath and strode inside.

\* \* \* \* \* \* \*

Big Jim Quinn watched the mechanic take another coffee break. It was mid-morning and the car was not yet ready. He'd managed to find someone to haul his Mercedes out of the harbor just before dark last night, but had been told that no one was available to dry it out and repair the damage until Monday morning. He'd spent a restless night at the Tiki Motel, which was unfortunately adjacent to a waterfront bar populated by sailors and college students who didn't know the meaning of last-call. Around eleven o'clock he'd tried to phone Laura, but there'd been no answer at home. Well, that was fine; he hadn't wanted to have to explain his whereabouts to her anyway. But if she was off messing around on him . . .

Big Jim's smooth hands curled into fists. He barked at the coffee-drinking mechanic to get back to work on his car and thought about his wife. Beautiful woman, but what an airhead! Had to finish college. That had cost him plenty! And now she wanted to get a job. Christ! She already had a job, the job of making him happy and running the house. And now the trouble with this Winchell asshole. Big Jim wasn't leaving Solomons Island until he'd taken care of that little shit and retrieved his beautiful boat. Winchell was going to pay for the damage to his Mercedes, too!

"Good news and bad news," said the mechanic, wiping his hands on a greasy rag.

"What's the bad news?" muttered Big Jim.

"Well, whole electrical system needs work, including the microprocessor, gotta get a replacement from up the road. Also, I gotta change your oil and filter, make sure all the saltwater is outta the crankcase and gas tank. Plus, new plugs, fuel line . . ."

"What's the good news?"

The grease-monkey grinned. "Won't hafta fill up your radiator." He chuckled at his half-wit and ambled back to the still-dripping car. Big Jim glowered at the mechanic's back and checked his watch.

Impatient with just standing around, he walked down the street and strolled through the marina again. The slip was still vacant. Where was that bastard? He had to come home sometime. Quinn's stomach growled and he growled back at it. It was a little past noon and he hadn't eaten yet. He trudged back up to the road and aimed himself toward the Oarhouse.

He was reaching for the door when it swung open and he nearly collided with the unkempt young man who was leaving in a hurry. Big Jim's dark eyes widened in recognition and he grabbed Brant by the shirtfront.

Brant had just finished explaining to Gil and Donna Jean that Winch had high-tailed it out of Solomons and would send them their money very soon. The bartender and the marina manager had been pissed, but there was little they could do. Brant had even revealed where Winch had gone in an effort to mollify the pair. But now Brant found himself in the solid grip of the man with the silver Mercedes, the man Winch claimed had shot at them last night. He twisted around in an attempt at liberty, but the big man's grasp only tightened on his tearing shirt.

"Where's that fuckin' friend of yours with my boat?" he glowered in Brant's face. Brant cringed, unable to avoid flying spittle. Big Jim shook him roughly. Suddenly, and incredibly, Brant's predicament grew even worse.

From around the corner of the Oarhouse appeared a skinny, short man with black hair. He had a swarthy complexion, pockmarked with a ferocious scar running along one cheek.

"Hey, man!" shouted Marco. He, too, had just visited the empty slip and figured that Winch had welshed. He wanted his money as promised. The drug dealer recognized Brant and grabbed the artist's arm, ignoring Big Jim's tugs in the opposite direction. "Where the hell is your *amigo* with my money?"

"Watch it, pal," warned Quinn. "I was here first."

Marco looked up as if noticing Big Jim for the first time. "Fuck you, man. I'm doing business here!"

"Oh, yeah, Jose?" He released Brant and turned to face the drug dealer. "Why don't you take the next boat back to Puerto Rico and get out of my business?"

Marco dropped Brant's arm and smiled. He took a half-step back and whipped something from his jeans pocket. He flicked his wrist and a gleaming blade sprung from the handle. Brant started to slide away, his back rubbing against the rough wall of the Oarhouse.

Big Jim smiled back at Marco. He pushed aside his jacket and wrapped his fingers around the stock of the .38. Marco stared at the gun for a second and then slowly folded the switchblade.

"Might makes right," he conceded, and grabbed Brant by the back of his shirt just before the kid slipped away. Big Jim closed his jacket and looked around the parking lot.

"I think we should conduct our business inside," he suggested, and Marco nodded.

With each thug supporting Brant by an arm, they marched into the dim restaurant and took a table deep in the corner. Big Jim signaled Gil at the bar. Quinn ordered another oyster sandwich and a beer. Marco took a beer, too, and Brant just shook his head. Gil left to fill the order but kept glancing back suspiciously. He didn't like trouble in his place and these two looked like trouble.

By now, in front of potential witnesses, Brant had calmed himself a bit. He looked across the table at Marco and stuttered, "I know why you want Winch. I was just going to come looking for you. I have a message."

"When's he coming back?" Big Jim cut in. "I got a message for him, too." He patted the bulge under his jacket.

"Hey, mister, I don't know what you want with him. Honest, Winch says he had no idea your daughter was only seventeen."

Big Jim Quinn looked puzzled for a moment. What was this guy, some retard? "I don't know nothing about no seventeen year old girl," he snarled. "All I know is that asshole's got my boat, and he owes me for my car, too!"

"And he owes me $900," added Marco, "and I'm gonna take it outta his ass when I find him!" He displayed his knife again, waggling it in Brant's face.

"Put that away, you idiot," admonished Big Jim as he saw Gil approaching with a tray of food and beer.

Gil sensed trouble. "Problem here, Brant?" he asked as he served the group. Brant sat frozen, like a deer caught in headlights.

"Our friend here was just telling us where we might find Mr. Winchell," soothed Big Jim in his best banker manner.

"Winch? He's gone down to Key West for the winter," Gil rasped. "Ain't that right, Brant?"

Brant nodded weakly, the secret out.

"You all need anything else?" Marco, Big Jim and Brant shook their heads in unison and Gil left them to return to his place behind the bar. He made sure his softball bat was handy. He still didn't like the looks of these two.

"Where in Key West?" Big Jim hissed at Brant.

"Don't know," Brant croaked miserably.

"That goddam little prick," Marco fumed quietly. "When I get down there and find him, I'm gonna rip out his lungs."

"You?" scoffed Big Jim. "He only owes you a measly nine-hundred! He's taken the thing closest to my heart! And I'll find him first. And when I do, there won't be any lungs left for you to tear out!"

"You don't know who you're foolin' with, man," Marco sneered back, displaying his intimidating scar. "I don't make my collections on time, I ain't gonna be the one who pays!"

Big Jim ran some computations through his bankers mind. He'd sweated long hours at the firm in order to afford the *LauraLee*. He'd passed many pleasurable and profitable weekends aboard her. He'd bragged of his business successes at the office and of his social conquests in the locker room of the country club, all thanks to the impression he was able to make as skipper of the massive boat. The yacht had been the envy of his circle of friends and clients. Then the feds had seized her.

Such dire news could not be kept a secret. Big Jim's standing among his peers dropped perceptibly. His dating life withered. After all, which impressed a boss, client or girlfriend more, a typical dinner in a fine restaurant, or an intimate catered cruise aboard a million dollar boat? His boat, his secret love nest, the key to his success had been wrested from him and sold to the highest bidder, a nobody.

He looked across the table at the other man and considered opening negotiations.

"Maybe we can work this out together," Big Jim said thoughtfully, sitting back and sipping his beer.

"You mean, like partners?" growled Marco. Brant's head swiveled, following the discussion.

"Maybe," Quinn said. "Lots of ground to cover, easier job if there was two of us." He paused and both he and Marco suddenly glared at the silent Brant.

"What the hell're you doing here?" Big Jim glowered.

"Yeah, man, get the fuck out of here!" Marco ordered, and Brant wasted not a second scooting off his chair and out the door. The two men turned to each other and talked.

The negotiations went on for another three beers, but in the end Big Jim and Marco couldn't agree on the logistics of a plan. Around two o'clock they parted company, but not before making a small bet on which of them would nail Winch first.

\* \* \* \* \* \* \*

The current is very strong here, but it feels good swimming hard against it. Days have passed and soon he will be in his spawning grounds.

Just below the surface, the water is turbulent. He pokes his head above the wind-whipped waves and gazes about. Hard rain lashes him, a sheet of gray water against the horizon, but water is water and it doesn't bother him at all.

He looks about and sees a mancraft not far away. It is somehow familiar, pitching violently in the storm. Some odd-sounding squealing, porpoise-like, but rhythmic, emanates from the mancraft. It is pleasant to him, appealing like whalesong.

There, along the side, hangs a man, heaving its dinner into the raging sea. That, too, is somehow familiar. Overcoming his instinctive shyness, he swims a little nearer, and he sees the man straighten up on those mis-shapen hind flippers and stare back at him. It makes a high-pitched wailing sound that is torn away by the screaming wind.

It retches once more into the water and then disappears as the intensity of the rain increases and the mancraft is lost from his nearsighted view. He dips his head back below into the relative calm beneath the surface and begins a shallow dive.

Above, he senses the rising pitch of the mancraft as it suddenly builds speed and outpaces him. And then he swims through a floating spew of aromatic waste-matter and he remembers almost clearly the day he began this migration, and the familiar smell that the man spilled into the water. It smells like food, his tiny brain whispers to his stomach.

He digs his four powerful flukes into the current and follows. Maybe the man has more food.

# CHAPTER 6

The *Stuffed Ham* climbed the wall of water rushing toward her, teetered on the crest of the wave and slid precariously down the windwardside. Winch goosed the throttles a bit and spun the wheel to keep the big boat from broaching. The gale-driven rain slashed at his face in the cockpit. Breakers smashed over the bow. Winch had done a couple of mushrooms about an hour earlier and was humming the theme to *Gilligan's Island*.

Hell of a squall, he thought. Wonder where it came from?

Winch had passed the coast of Georgia some time ago, narrowly avoiding a collision with a freighter outbound from Savannah. He'd been jamming to tunes on the tape deck most of the time and so had missed the broadcast hurricane warnings as Margo thrashed her way up the Atlantic seaboard.

In spite of the storm, the *Ham* was doing well, her bilge pumps easily keeping up with the water which spilled over the gunwales. He reckoned he was somewhere offshore of Jacksonville running more or less due south. Another burst of mushroom-induced euphoria kicked in and Winch had a sudden inspiration.

Locking down the wheel for a moment, he dashed below to rummage through his tapes. He found the appropriate cassette and popped it into the expensive Studer deck. He flipped on the remote all-weather party speakers up on the bridge, cranked up the volume and stumbled back to the helm.

Screeching electric guitars screamed from the 200-watt speakers and competed with the wind. Neil Young did battle with the storm and Winch threw back his head and joined the chorus, in off-key harmony: "You are like a hurricane, there's calm in your eye, and I'm gettin' blown away . . ."

The rain slacked off and the sea grew flatter, the swells only running seven or eight feet and the waves no longer breaking over the bow. But now, the lack of food, the mushrooms and the pitching of the *Stuffed Ham* conspired against him. Winch wasn't usually prone to seasickness, but a voice in his inner ear whispered that it had had enough. He hooked the bungee back in place and scrambled for the rail.

His meal of bologna, banana and beer burbled up and over the side. He immediately felt better. Wearily, he glanced at the rain-swept horizon. Out upon the roiling sea, something broke the surface and Winch blinked back in horror.

A tiny black head ascended from the water, lifted by a long coil of slender neck. Coal-black eyes returned his incredulous gaze. Winch let out a piercing scream that mixed with the falsetto wailing of Neil Young. He gave one more good barf over the side and retreated to the helm. As the eye passed and the storm renewed itself, Winch slammed the throttles forward and the *Ham* responded. In seconds the apparition was gone, lost in the vastness of the Atlantic. Winch didn't back off the engines until he had sighted the St. Augustine lighthouse.

\* \* \* \* \* \* \*

Quinn clenched the wheel so tightly his knuckles were turning white. Occasionally the engine coughed and sputtered, stray seawater still lurking somewhere in its workings. Belted into the passenger seat alongside him, Liza sat languidly in a red mini-dress, watching the Virginia countryside flash by on I-95. She hadn't said a word since Fredericksburg, which was fine with Big Jim. It was going to be a long drive and her constant chatter set his teeth on edge. He turned up the business news on the radio but found it hard to concentrate on market reports. His mind wandered back a day.

Big Jim had limped back to Baltimore in the Mercedes late Monday night, arriving at a dark house. He let himself in the back door and flipped on the kitchen lights. There was no sign of his wife, and the anger that had been boiling in him for the last two days steamed over.

He could have been worried about her, but instead he was only furious that she wasn't home waiting for him. Stomping down into his den, Big Jim poured himself three fingers of Canadian Club and grumped down into his recliner. He hit the remote and the 45-inch television switched on to Bloomberg for the closing stocks. His fingers searched the table beside the La-Z-Boy for a cigar, and they brushed against an envelope. He picked it up and stared at it, addressed to him in his wife's hand. He muted the audio, lit a cigar, and opened the letter. With seething anger and disbelief, he read:

*Dear Jim,*

*This is the hardest letter I've ever written. I wanted to tell you in person, but I couldn't bring myself to face you. For over six years I did all you asked of me, and more. But I have to finally face the truth. Our marriage isn't working.*

*When you refused to go with me, denying that there was even a problem, I went to counseling alone. It was Dr. Judy who listened when all I really wanted to do was talk to you. But you were never there for me. You spent all your time at the office, the golf course, or on your boat. When I finally graduated with my degree, I searched the crowd, hoping you'd come to share my joy. But you weren't there. And when Dad died last summer in Michigan, you said you were too busy to go to the funeral, so I went alone. And when I got home, I found a bra--not mine!--under the couch. But I didn't confront you about it. Maybe I should have. Maybe then I wouldn't be writing this letter. But Dr. Judy says I must be strong, so I shall be.*

*I'm so very sorry. But I have a job now, somewhere far away. I promise I'll call you when I get settled, but for now, where I've gone is my secret, the only secret I've ever kept from you. You'll find my attorney's card in the envelope, and you can expect to hear from him this week. I hope we can have an amicable settlement. I hope that you are not too angry with me and that, in time, you'll understand. Please wish me well as I wish you well also, and know that I never ever wanted to hurt you.*

*Laura*

Big Jim balled the letter in his meaty hand and knocked back the rest of his whiskey. He poured another and pounded upstairs to the master bedroom, sloshing his drink on the new deep-pile carpeting. Laura's closet door was open. Most of her clothes were gone. He sat on the edge of the bed and stared at the empty space, thinking. That bitch! She certainly hadn't gone off alone! The little mouse didn't have the courage. There had to be another man involved. And that goddam therapist, this was her fault, too! He found the doctor's number in Laura's address book on the night table and dialed. He hit Dr. Judy's voice mail.

"This is Jim Quinn," he snarled into the phone. "Fuck you, you quack bitch!" He slammed the receiver down. But it hadn't made him feel any better. He had to think. He sipped his whiskey and brooded.

Big Jim flipped through the address book and called Laura's friends, demanding that they put her on. All professed no knowledge of her whereabouts. He was sure every one of them was lying.

Okay, he decided. First things first. Laura was gone for the moment and he didn't know where. He'd track her down eventually. She wasn't smart enough to hide from him. But he *did* have a lead on his boat, and that was a priority. He'd tackle *that* problem first. He pushed Laura out of his mind, as he'd do with any business deal or affair, and began to pack. He dialed US Airways at BWI to make a reservation for the next flight to Florida. He cradled the phone against his shoulder while he booked a flight to MIA and on to EYW, and threw some clothes into a flight bag. He pulled his Smith & Wesson .38 from its holster and started to toss it into the open bag when he realized that he wouldn't be able to get past airport security with the weapon. The metal detectors and X-ray machines would rat him out. Damn! He slammed down the phone on the ticketing agent, mid-sentence.

Fine. He'd drive the Mercedes. It would only take a couple of days, he'd find the boat and sail her home. Damn it! Then what about the car? He couldn't abandon it in Florida. Why did this have to be so fucking complicated?

He placed a call to his office and left a message for the managing partner saying he had a family emergency and would be taking the rest of the week off. Carl could handle his accounts. Then he dialed Liza's number at home. She could drive down to Florida with him, he plotted, and while he sailed home, she could drive his Mercedes back north. He'd even get laid a couple of times during the trip. Sounded like a good plan. Liza had answered on the third ring in a sleepy voice.

"'Lo?"

"Liza, honey, it's Jim."

"It's late, baby," she purred.

"How'd ya like to go to the Florida Keys tomorrow?"

"I have to work, Jim."

"Call in sick," he ordered. "We're leaving in the morning."

Liza started to make excuses, but Big Jim wouldn't hear of it. He could be charming and persuasive when he wanted something and he used his arsenal of bribery and cajolery to win her over before he dropped his nuke.

"Laura's left me," he stated flatly. There was a long empty pause from her end.

"Oh, my. No, you shouldn't be alone. Poor baby. Of course I'll go with you." All said in flat tones.

Big Jim grunted. "Pick you up at ten, alright?"

Liza said okay and offered him smooches over the phone. Big Jim hung up.

Suddenly he was exhausted. With disgust, he realized he'd been wearing the same clothes for two days. Big Jim peeled them off, tossing the sticky garments into a pile for the dry-cleaners. He showered, put on a fresh bathrobe and returned to his den for a nightcap. He read his wife's letter over and over, seeking clues from her words. Finally, he had fallen asleep in his recliner while watching *Wall Street Week*.

Now it was mid-afternoon, Tuesday, and Quinn and Liza were in the two-seat Mercedes 500SL somewhere south of Richmond. The car was running rough, and Big Jim silently cursed the hick mechanic. Liza sat quietly, filing her nails. He glanced over at her, admiring the deep cleavage between her breasts, visible beneath the plunging vee of her dress. He reached over and gently squeezed her left boob. She turned and smiled at him.

"Feeling better?" she asked.

And suddenly he was.

\* \* \* \* \* \* \*

Leaning against the whipping wind which buffetted the Harry Nice Bridge as it spanned the Potomac, Marco struggled to keep his Suzuki 250 upright. He coasted down the long slope out of Maryland on Route 301 and entered Virginia. Only five more states to go! He grinned through his bug-smeared face shield.

Marco had never been very good with maps, and when he'd finally consulted a road atlas, it hadn't looked very far to Key West. He figured it would only take him a day or two at most. He hunched over the handlebars and felt the wind tug at his day-glo orange backpack. The Suzuki, which he'd crashed into a ditch a couple of weeks ago, had been repaired and seemed to be running smoothly now, although the right handlebar was still bent a bit out of shape.

Two generations ago, Marco's grandparents had come north to Maryland from Puerto Rico. His parents had been born in Baltimore and he had been born in Calvert County, where his folks owned a florist shop. During his middle school years, Marco had learned to cultivate his Hispanic heritage, finding that it gave him a mystique that set him apart from his classmates, who were mostly SMIBs, or Southern Maryland in-breds, as they referred to themselves only half-jokingly. Because he spoke no more Spanish than he had learned at Calvert High, he worked on his fake accent, finding that it intimidated his customers, who wrongly assumed that he was a tough guy from the *barrio*. He was actually a second-generation, all-American kid from suburban Baltimore. Even his wife of ten years, whom he called Maria, was really named Mary and had been born and bred in West Virginia. Like the scar on his cheek, his entire background was a fraud. One day, though, he dreamed he would return to the island from whence his grandparents came. While he had never been farther south in his life than Virginia Beach, he imagined an isle of sandy beaches, waving palms and flashing waterfalls. Maybe, he hoped, after he'd taken care of Winch, he'd sail over the Caribbean and visit his true homeland. The map showed it was only a few inches away.

Marco swerved to avoid the roadkill possum in his lane. Another bug splattered against his visor. He downshifted for a long gentle hill and continued south at fifty miles per hour.

\* \* \* \* \* \* \*

A soft breeze out of the southwest wafted over Taylor's body, the late-afternoon sun caressing him. Shapely men with pierced dicks sat in couples, rubbing sunscreen on each other. Robust women with breast tattoos and short hair read novels and chatted, seated on white loungechairs. Lamont Taylor Jackson rolled over on his flat stomach and gazed across the pool, past the sundeck and railing, at the blue-green waters of the Straits of Florida. Life was good. He felt truly at home here.

Just a few blocks from his Duval Street apartment, the Rainforest Resort offered Key West's best public, clothing-optional pool. Scattered lightly among the predominantly gay and lesbian crowd were a few heteros, identifiable by their pale northern skin. The uptight women read Danielle Steele novels and the damn-right-I'm-straight men nursed three-dollar Budweisers and stared at the topless lesbians.

Alongside the pool stood an open-air bar, tended by two gay men in leather thong bikinis, much like the one Taylor wore, except his was spandex. A spacious wooden deck was filled with lounges and baking bodies. Overlaying it all was the constant beat of pre-recorded, high-energy dance music, heavy on George Michael, the Pet Shop Boys and En Vogue.

Taylor was the only black at the pool, but no one cared. He was just another American minority, like the rest of them. He protected his dark skin with plenty of sunscreen, keeping it soft and smooth, his hairless body glistening in the sun. Though his natural pigment offered some resistance to the rays, contrary to the belief of most Caucasians, blacks too could burn. But today he had come to the pool late, avoiding the midday sun and most of the crowds. Best of all, he was enjoying the pool and deck gratis, one of the perks of working at the Rainforest.

Two mornings ago, he'd gotten word that the pool manager wanted to hire Daiquiri Taylor as the hostess for their weekly Sunday afternoon deck party. They'd been unhappy with the pushy, surly attitude of their regular hostess and had wanted to make a change. The pool manager had caught her act at the Riding Crop and had thought that Daiquiri would be perfect. The deck party had been a smash and Daiquiri had been offered the gig for the following Sunday too.

Things were going well. He had this new job here, his three nights at the Riding Crop and an offer to help out at the gallery below his apartment a couple of afternoons a week, but as Taylor, not as Daiquiri. In truth, he hardly needed the money. The estate left to him after his parent's deaths had been held in trust until he was eighteen. He'd been no fool, investing the money wisely since then, and now he had a fairly respectable stream of interest income. Mostly now, he worked because he loved to dress in women's clothing, and there were probably only a very few places in the world where he could get paid for doing just that. So, after finishing his undergrad degree at Rutgers, he'd left New Jersey and traveled for awhile.

New York had frightened him. Las Vegas had repelled him. Provincetown was too snobbish, and Bangkok was too far. Key West was just right, except for the fact that, outside of Bahama Village, there were hardly any blacks on the island. But such a remarkably tolerant community had made room for a gay black transvestite, and he'd so far experienced remarkably little open hostility in the months he'd been here.

The sun cruised behind a cloud and Taylor craned his head. People were leaving the sun-deck in a sudden rush. The reason was in the sky. Battleship-sized thunderheads were rolling toward the Keys from the west. A faint lightning bolt sizzled on the horizon, touching the sea, and moments later the first clap of thunder rolled across the pool. Taylor had become used to the almost daily afternoon thunderstorms, a fact of life in Key West. He sat up on his lounge and opened the flap of his tote-bag, placing his sunscreen next to his wallet. He stretched in the still-warm air, but was reluctant to go just yet. It would be at least half an hour before the storm swept in, and most likely it would be gone half an hour after that. In the meantime, teasingly, the sun popped out again but the sudden exodus continued. It was getting to be time to go home anyway; time to shower, catch the sunset, eat, drink, and find true love, at least for the night.

Taylor leaned back against the lounge and closed his eyes, loving the late-day warmth. But as soon as he was settled, the sun was again eclipsed. Taylor opened his eyes.

The sun was still out for the moment, but he was being shaded by two intruders towering over his chair. It was Angel and Sam, the two "girls" from the Riding Crop who'd tried to mess up his set the other night. They were out of costume now, males again. Angel wore a blue Speedo. Sam (Samantha, on stage) wore nothing but a towel draped over his shoulders. Angel sat down in an empty lounge beside Taylor. Sam grinned down malevolently.

"Well, if it isn't Ms. Daiquiri Hot-shit Taylor," Sam sneered. "I hear you got me fired and took over my spot at the deck parties."

Taylor sighed. "I had nothing to do with that. I didn't even know it was your gig, just that they called and asked me to fill in."

"Yeah, right. So you're coming back to the Crop next weekend? Gonna wow the crowd some more? Maybe we can find some white-girl music you can dance to."

Beside him, Angel snickered. He knocked over Taylor's cup of orange juice with his foot. "Oops!" The juice dribbled through the cracks of the deck and into the ocean below.

Taylor gave Angel a blank look and then returned his gaze to Sam who stood before him, hands on hips, nipple rings gleaming in the fading sunlight.

Sam glared back at Taylor. "You know," he said, "you really ought to get out of the sun. I think you're about as tan as you're going to get."

Taylor uncoiled from his chair, facing down the other dancer, Sam a little taller, a little meatier. Behind him, unnoticed, Angel rifled Taylor's tote-bag.

"You talk pretty big for a man with his jewels on display," Taylor said softly, but his heart was in his throat. "Maybe you'd like me to tie that teeny little thing in a nice bow."

Sam took half a step back, feeling vulnerable. Then he resorted to the bully's ultimate weapon, name-calling. "You watch your mouth, Sambo! Or you'll be sucking dicks with no teeth!"

Taylor drew back his arm, flushed with uncharacteristic anger, but Angel shot up to restrain him from behind. The black man shook him off. The pool boy, stacking chairs, noticed the commotion and started over towards them. Half the crowd on the deck were watching the confrontation. Angel and Sam saw the pool boy heading their way, all two hundred pounds of him, and stepped away from Taylor.

"Stay the fuck away from us and the Crop," Sam hissed. "If you know what's good for you."

They spun and left. The pool boy, the confrontation over, resumed stacking lounges. He was relieved that it hadn't been necessary to intervene. That kind of stuff made for bad tips.

Taylor watched the two dancers slip on shorts, join the exiting throng and flip him the bird before the storm hit. His palms were sweaty and his heart was beating fast. He glanced down at the spilled juice pooling on the deck beside his chair.

Lightning crackled just offshore, thunder clapped in synchronization, and the clouds opened, unleashing a deluge. Taylor grabbed his towel and tote and retreated to the adjacent bar to wait out the storm.

The two leather-clad bartenders were leisurely unrolling the plastic rain curtains which hung from the eaves, tying them down against the wind-driven rain. Just about everyone else had scattered, calling it a day before night descended and the serious partying began. Normally, Taylor hardly drank, rarely had more than one, but the scene with Angel and Sam made him want at least one stiff one. Maybe even two. One of the half-naked bartenders returned and Taylor ordered a vodka and tonic, strong stuff for him.

While he waited for his drink, Taylor noticed the only other customer left in the bar, an attractive woman--pale white, naturally--about three stools away. She wasn't dressed for the pool, wearing a khaki pantsuit and matching blazer, blonde hair combed back behind one ear. She cradled a stack of papers in front of her, which she sorted through, trying to make sense of them. She noticed Taylor staring, returned his gaze with a small non-committal smile, and returned to her work.

The bartender placed the vodka and tonic on the bar and asked Taylor for five dollars. Taylor opened his tote-bag and rummaged for his wallet. It was gone. Taylor looked up through the foggy plastic sheeting in the direction of the parking lot. Those bastards had ripped him off! Sam had distracted him and Angel had stolen his wallet! The bartender waited.

"Uh, I think someone stole my wallet," was all he could say. The bartender rolled his eyes. Taylor continued to search his bag, hoping it was just lost in the jumble.

"Dave, put it on my tab," the blonde woman spoke. The bartender looked at Taylor and then at her and nodded.

"Okay, Laura."

Taylor took his drink and raised it in a toast. "Thank you, ma'am. It's good to see there are still a few nice people around."

Laura twisted on her stool to face him and brushed a lock of stray hair out of her wide, green eyes. "Did you really get robbed?"

"'Fraid so, but I think I know who did it."

"Was it those two guys you were arguing with?" she asked innocently. Taylor's eyebrows lifted, Spock-like. Laura said, "We all saw you cussing each other out."

He nodded ruefully. "Yeah. Co-workers of mine."

"Just a little joke?" she suggested hopefully.

Taylor took a drink. The vodka burned his tongue. "No, ma'am, no joke. Seems they don't like my suntan."

Laura burst out laughing. She didn't mean to, but it struck her funny. "I'm sorry," she said, shaking her head. She extended her hand. "My name's Laura, and please don't call me 'ma'am' anymore."

He reached for her fingers. "Taylor Jackson. Pleased to meet you, Laura, and thanks again. You down for vacation?"

"No." She pointed at the papers. "I'm a working girl, now. Just finished my second day at a new job, but I think I may be in over my head."

"Well, welcome to Key West."

Laura smiled and lapsed into silence. She asked the bartender for another drink and offered to buy another for Taylor, but he politely declined. There was something about this guy that said he was safe to talk to, that he wouldn't end up hitting on her. God, that was one complication she didn't need in her life right now. Laura tried to think of something to ask him to make neutral conversation. She cocked her head and the words spilled out before she could stop them.

"Are you gay?" Oh, god, how embarrassing! Dave the bartender overheard and discretely looked in their direction. Taylor smiled.

"Yes, I'm afraid so."

Laura laughed again, pleasantly. "That's good."

Taylor and the bartender exchanged puzzled glances.

"How about you?" Taylor asked her, though he knew by her clothes, make-up and manner that she was straight.

"I'm definitely gay," answered Dave the bartender instead, and walked away, flicking a sly glance back at Taylor.

"I meant you," Taylor smiled at Laura.

"No," she replied, "but I *am* thinking of giving up men."

"Me too."

They laughed together inside the sheltered bar while rain lashed at the curtains, obscuring the view of the pool deck. Suddenly Laura cast her eyes down at the bar. She sighed deeply, sadly.

"You know, that's the first time I've laughed . . . well, I can't remember the last time."

"You have a nice laugh. You should use it more."

"I haven't had much to laugh about lately." She looked at her drink. She was past her limit and it made her talkative. "I'm getting a divorce, and I guess I've sort of run away from home." The words started pouring out.

It had been so long since she'd had someone to open up to, besides Dr. Judy. Taylor didn't seem to mind listening.

"Key West is beautiful, but I'm staying here at the Rainforest and it's just so expensive. So I've got to find a new place, something in my price range."

"That can be tough around here," agreed Taylor.

"And the job, well, it doesn't pay much and things there are total chaos."

"Where are you working?"

"Over on Stock Island at the Save the Reef Foundation. They hired me sight unseen and now I know why. They were desperate. I mean, it all sounds so fancy and well-funded, but the place is a cinderblock shack. It's entirely funded by some rich old lady up in Boca Raton. Everybody is either a volunteer or minimum wager. I'm supposed to be the PR Director, but there's no budget, no staff, and after today we don't even have a boat! How are we supposed to save the reef if we can't even get out to it?"

Taylor smiled softly. "What did you do, sink the boat on your first day?"

"*I* didn't sink the boat," she emphasized. "But one of our moron, teenage volunteers ran it aground on the very reef we're trying to save! The boat sank and the Coast Guard had to rescue half the staff. They fined us, too!" She shook her head in disbelief and pointed at the jumble of papers on the bar. "And, on top of everything else, I'm supposed to set up a media tour of the reef next week. I've already contacted half the TV and radio stations and newspapers between here and Miami, inviting them along. Oh, and let's not forget, tomorrow I'm scheduled to do my first interview and I can't even begin to make sense of the last PR director's goddam filing system. I don't have a clue about what the hell I'm supposed to say to these people!" She was beginning to rave, realized it, and stopped herself. She gripped the edge of the bar in frustration and sucked her drink dry.

Another bombshell today, unmentioned: There *was* no SuRF director or board she reported to. Only Mrs. Winters, who'd told Laura on the phone today that the PR job *was* the top job at the foundation headquarters. It was all her baby. She was the boss, the head honcho, the big cheese, and she didn't have the slightest idea what she was doing. No! Definitely not ready for this much responsibility!

Dave took pity on Laura and poured her a free drink. Last one, though, he warned her. Laura looked at him through slitted eyes. Again she offered to buy one for Taylor, and again he refused. "I hardly ever drink," he explained. "If I have anymore, I'm liable to start acting foolish." He grinned.

She took her latest drink and said, "Well, I guess I have a good reason to drink today." She was starting to slur her words and screwed up her face as though she might cry. She thumped her hand on the bartop. "I can't, I won't go back home! It's too late for that. But if I don't get things together at work, then what?" She signaled Dave, futilely. "One more, please." She'd barely tasted her last one.

"I don't think so, Laura," the bartender said kindly. "You've been in here every night, and every night Robbie or I have had to walk you back to your room."

"I'll see her back," Taylor offered. He slipped on a pair of shorts and a shirt from his tote-bag. Laura slid drunkenly off her stool. She dropped her papers on the floor and Taylor helped gather them up.

He nodded goodnight to Robbie and Dave and helped Laura outside. The rain had ended and a beautiful red sunset hung over the ocean. Haltingly, they made their way around the resort and back to her room, one of the less expensive ones fronting the street. Taylor then saw why the bartenders had been walking her home every night. At the end of the block, next to the motel, sat The Deep, one of Key West's most notorious strip clubs. Outside, a half-dozen bikers stood around their hogs drinking beer and ogling any nearby women. Hardly the best of neighborhoods, he realized.

Laura tried to get her key in the lock twice before she surrendered the task to Taylor. He let her in and turned to leave, his obligation fulfilled. She grabbed his sleeve.

"Don't go, please," she started weeping. "I'm so scared, so alone." Her drunken sobbing was punctuated by hiccups.

Taylor sighed and led her over to the bed, carefully laying her down on the spread where she curled up in a tight little ball. He found a blanket in one of the drawers and covered her.

"I'm sorry, I'm so sorry," she wept in a lost little girl voice. "I'm so stupid . . ."

"Hush," Taylor whispered. "You're not stupid, just a little drunk. Things'll look a lot better tomorrow. Promise."

He sat on the edge of her bed and stroked her long blonde hair until her sobs had tapered off and she finally fell asleep. He felt bad for her; she was obviously having a rough time. Leaving people behind was never easy.

Taylor rose softly and started to go. Then he thought of how he had arrived in Key West, alone and friendless. There were times when he was still lonely. He located the pad of standard-issue motel paper and a pen on the night table and jotted down his address and phone number. Beneath this he added, *"I'll be your friend. Taylor."*

He let himself out into the cool night breeze and walked home.

\* \* \* \* \* \* \*

The sun had just disappeared below the horizon. Finally, it was time. Felix Munoz, former star pitcher for the Rojos Diablos de Pinar del Rio, dragged his raft from the cover of the brush and down to the surf. There would be little moonlight tonight and he had an outgoing tide. It was a well-constructed *balza*, with oars, a small sail and plenty of bottled water and dried fish. As a baseball player for the State, Felix had been relatively wealthy, and he had used his wealth to commission the best boatbuilder in Bahia Honda to construct his raft.

It had to be a very good raft, he knew, for although it was only about one hundred miles to the Florida Keys, America was not--could not be-- his destination yet. He would be aiming for the Bahamas, off the northeast shore of Cuba.

His extended and perilous trip was necessary due to an oddity in Major League Baseball's free-agency rules. Felix had heard of other Cuban ballplayers arriving directly in the United States. These players were either deported or forced to suffer the indignity of the amateur baseball draft. They had no power over where they played or how much they were paid, regardless of their talent and experience.

However, those players who managed to make it to the US via a third country, such as the Bahamas, Dominican Republic or Jamaica, were declared to be free-agents. They could secure a representative, negotiate with any team and take the best deal. The difference between the two landfalls could be measured in millions of dollars.

Growing up poor in Cuba, like everyone else he knew, had given Felix an appreciation for what money really meant. His years in Cuba's big leagues had teased him with a taste of the good life, and he knew to survive in America one had better be well-paid-filthy rich if possible. Felix intended to be filthy stinking rich.

He got the raft into the water and past the surfline. He pulled himself aboard and drifted out on the tide, watching the Cuban shore recede into a black silhouette. Smugly, Felix Munoz waved *adios* to Fidel's utopia.

# CHAPTER 7

Leaving behind the choked streets of Old Town, Steve cruised North Roosevelt Boulevard east to Stock Island. Despite three cups of coffee, two of them laced with Irish whiskey, he remained in a very bad morning mood. As of two-thirty A.M., it was over with Brenda, the exotic dancer.

He had cruised by The Deep to pick her up at two, as was his usual routine these past three weeks, but she'd already left. Steve had angled up into Solares Hill, where Brenda shared a tiny cottage with two other girls. Standing on the concrete stoop outside her door, Steve was about to knock on the screen when he'd seen his girlfriend emerge from her bedroom and cross to the kitchen. His knuckles paused inches from the doorframe. She wore the flimsiest nightie imaginable, leaving nothing to the imagination in the well-lit kitchen. He grinned lasciviously and was about to wolf-whistle when he heard someone else call her name in a deep voice. From the shadows, he watched Brenda through the screen as she stood nearly naked under the bright kitchen lights. A fat guy, covered in tattoos and little else clomped across the linoleum in leather motorcycle boots, chugging a can of Bud. The biker put a hairy arm around her waist, bent over, beer gut bulging, and nibbled Brenda's breasts through the lingerie. Repulsed, Steve stumbled off the stoop and retreated to his car. It had been then that he noticed the hulking black Harley propped on its kickstand across the street. For a moment he considered knocking the bike over as he drove away, but prudently discarded the idea. Who could blame the guy? Brenda was a mighty fine piece of tail, who apparently wasn't especially particular about what went in it. As he slowly pulled away, Steve shuddered and promised himself to get tested for who-knew-what at the earliest opportunity.

Now, in the full light of day as he crossed the bridge over Cow Key Channel, Steve tried to shake it off. Brenda had been too young, too wild for him, and the conflict in their schedules had been killing him. This was Key West, after all, and there were plenty of other women out there, maybe even the right one, maybe even one who worked the same hours. His tires crunched gravel as he pulled into the parking lot of the Save the Reef Foundation.

The building that housed SuRF was a concrete block and steel bunker hunkered along the channel. A splintered dock jutted into the water from the foot of the parking lot. There were no other cars in sight and the place had an air of destitution. Steve picked up his cassette recorder and notebook and got out. He tried the front door. It was unlocked.

The interior was smaller than he'd imagined, or perhaps it was because every available space was a clutter of papers, books and brochures. Salvation Army office furniture was laid out in a haphazard maze. Steve was reluctant to enter beyond the vestibule, afraid he might trip over something. There was no one in sight.

"Hello?" he called.

"Just a minute," replied a reverberating voice from beyond an open doorway at the rear of the office. Steve waited, taking in the room.

The same concrete blocks evident outside had been painted a sickening yellow in here. Tattered posters of whales, dolphins and grunge rockers sagged on the mildewed walls, their edges curling in the muggy air. Steve noticed a ceiling fan and located the rheostat next to the front door. A threatening spark flashed from the fan housing, but the blades turned, reluctantly. A pile of papers rustled in the breeze and a mouse skittered past his feet, disappearing under a cracked wooden desk. A second later, he heard a *snap* as the unfortunate rodent found the bait. Steve winced. These were the people who were going to save the reef. Sure.

A woman walked through the door at the rear of the office. She was everything the decor was not. Long shiny blonde hair cascaded down to her shoulders. Shapely, untanned legs peered from beneath a pink pleated skirt. An off-white short-sleeved blouse did little to disguise her tempting breasts which strained at the material. Her lips were freshly lipsticked in a soft peach, and her green eyes glanced up at him and flashed as she approached, picking her way through the debris. She extended her hand.

"Good morning," she offered pleasantly. "Can I help you?"

"Yes, good morning," Steve replied, his eyes running helplessly over her body. "I'm Steve Stevens, WRKW News. I have an appointment with Laura Chadwick." Was this Laura? Oh, please, please, please!

"I'm Laura." Yes! "Please, have a seat."

Steve looked around. Finally, he emptied a chair of a pile of papers and stacked them on a desk where they balanced precariously.

"Welcome to SuRF. Can I get you some coffee?"

Steve declined. He checked his watch. Laura checked him.

He wore an immaculate gray suit, starched white shirt and black Oxfords. His hair was salt and pepper, leaning more toward pepper, not too short and combed neatly with a part on the left. About six-feet tall, she guessed, middle-aged yet with an athletic build; probably played squash. He had deep brown eyes which matched his tanned face and had just the trace of a few age lines across his brow. He opened his notebook and placed his tape recorder on the messy desk.

"So this is the Save the Reef Foundation?" he began.

"I'm afraid so," Laura replied, snapping back to reality. She glanced about the jumbled room and sighed.

"Is there something wrong?" he asked.

"To tell the truth, Mr. Stevens . . ."

He held up one hand. "Steve."

"Steve. Actually, I'm not sure today is the best day to do this. As you can see, we're a bit disorganized here. I just started Monday and I really haven't had a chance to prepare anything for you. Also, our computer went down this morning and I'm the only one here to answer the phones."

Steve glanced at the three-line telephone on the desk. It hadn't rung since he'd come in. "I see," he said, obviously disappointed. All the way out to Stock Island for nothing. Grant had his revenge. "I do need to have something on the air by tomorrow morning," he persisted. "Even a little background would help."

Laura thought for a moment. The computer support service had promised to send someone over this morning, she was trying to make sense of the files and she had three or four donation checks that had come in the mail she needed to record, deposit and write thank you letters for. And then there was still the problem of finding and renting a suitable boat to replace the one that had been sunk. The entire Foundation itself was sinking and the volunteer rats had abandoned ship. She shook her head apologetically.

"I'm sorry. I tried to call your station but they said you'd already left. Couldn't we do this later this afternoon?"

Now Steve shook his head. "I have a zoning meeting to cover at one; don't know how long that could take."

"The houseboats?" she ventured, recalling the news report from the other day.

Steve smiled. He had a nice smile, she thought.

"That's right, houseboat row. So you actually listen to my newscasts?"

Laura blushed. He seemed like a pretty nice guy, and she realized that she was attracted to him. But there was no way she was ready to hop into another relationship. She'd yet to untangle herself from her marriage and she believed in doing things in their proper order. "Yes. I pass by the houseboats on my way to work. I hope they keep them. They're cute." And so are you, she found herself thinking, much to her dismay.

Steve rose and gathered up his notebook and recorder. "I'll have to put off my boss somehow, I guess. But I still want to do this story." More than ever now, he added to himself. "Can I get in touch with you and we'll reschedule?"

Laura thought about it for a moment. "Wait. Could we do the interview tonight? Are you busy?"

"I suppose that would work," he agreed readily.

"But not here," she added. "I go home at four and it's kind of inconvenient to come all the way back." She thought about the expensive cab rides back and forth. "Is there somewhere we could meet in town? I promise I'll be prepared."

Steve considered the possibilites. Perhaps he could do the interview and get to know this lovely lady a little better. He glanced at her hands. No wedding ring, he noticed with satisfaction.

"Good idea. How about over dinner?"

Now Laura paused. Was this an appointment for an interview about SuRF or a come-on? Either way, she had a job to do, and if she couldn't do it here and now, then she'd make sure it got done later. Strictly business. She said okay and asked where they should meet.

Steve suggested a restaurant two blocks off Duval and offered to pick her up. Laura told him she could walk. They shook hands politely, business-like, and she watched him pick his way across the trashy room and out the door. Jeez, he was handsome, she thought and pushed the idea out of her mind.

Out in the parking lot, Steve got back into his car and mused, goodbye Brenda, hello Laura. He smiled the whole drive back into town.

\* \* \* \* \* \* \*

Laura skipped her usual after-work drinks at the pool. Instead, she closeted herself in her motel room and sorted through the papers she'd brought back from SuRF. The computer repairman had finally showed up at three-thirty. She'd had no luck finding a new boat that they could afford, and she'd only managed to file about a quarter of the stray papers which cluttered the office. But it was a start.

And now she crammed for her first interview with "the media." Well, two minutes on a local radio station anyway, but it too was a start. She reviewed the points she wanted to make, trying not to refer to her notes as she rummaged through the tiny closet looking for a suitable outfit.

Laura didn't want to be so flashy that she sent Steve the wrong signals, but on the other hand she wanted to look her best for the meeting. Balancing those objectives in a tropical setting was difficult. She tried on five different combinations, finally settling on a teal sundress with a dash of lace to cover her cleavage. She slipped on a pair of low heels, good for a short walk but still high enough to be fashionable, and she fussed with her hair, trying a pony-tail, swept-back, and piled up before she decided to just let it hang straight, held behind one ear with a plastic comb.

This is ridiculous, she mused as she applied her make-up. He's going to get the wrong idea. Steve's a looker, but any involvement is out of the question. Jim was fifteen years her senior and she guessed that Steve was at least ten years older than she. But that was the problem-she'd always been attracted to mature men. How could she balance her need to entice Steve enough to be really interested in SuRF with her desire to keep things on a professional level? She wasn't blind. She'd noticed him noticing her and she was flattered. She looked in the bathroom mirror and considered changing back into the tan pantsuit and flats. No time, it was getting late.

Laura had a thought. It was devious, a quality she had learned from her soon-to-be ex-husband, but a contingency plan might be necessary. She found the note Taylor had left by her bedside. Sweet man. She dialed his number.

On the third ring, the answering machine kicked in. She left a hopeful message and hung up. She lifted her purse and briefcase and closed the door behind her, walking up to Petronia before turning west, into the sunset. Her first professional interview. She was nervous and excited.

\* \* \* \* \* \* \*

Laura found Steve waiting for her at the bar in Blue Heaven. He took her hands and leaned forward to kiss her on the cheek and she ducked automatically, his lips finding only air. Uh-oh. Not a good sign, and he moves fast. She suspected that he did indeed want more than just an interview. She faked a sneeze.

"Sorry. I think I'm getting a cold. Change of climate, I guess."

Steve pretended not to be put out. He ordered drinks for them at the bar, a Beck's for him and a glass of white wine for her, over her mild objections. The hostess found them and led them through a doorway. Laura was surprised and enchanted.

The seating area was entirely outdoors under tropical acacias and palms. There were gaily painted picnic tables in shades of blue and yellow. Chickens ran to and fro through the grounds, shadowed by a dozen aloof cats, all waiting for diners to drop them morsels. Soft laughter and conversation threaded through the warm night air.

Steve and Laura were shown to a pastel green table off to one side, not far from the raised platform where a dreadlocked Rastafarian in a floral-print shirt coaxed calypso music from a steel drum. A waitress ran through the specials, took their drink orders and departed. Laura looked around. Everyone seemed to be having much too good of a time. She turned her eyes to the reporter sitting across from her and suggested that they begin the interview.

"Let's have some dinner first," he danced around her suggestion, smiling. "I'm famished."

Steve ordered the twin rock lobster-tails. Budget-conscious, Laura asked for the shrimp-salad appetizer. "Nothing else?" Steve asked.

"I need to watch my figure, and my budget," she told him truthfully.

He shrugged. "Dinner's on the station," he lied. Normally he couldn't get Grant to reimburse him for a ham sandwich. "As for your figure, I don't see that you have anything to worry about."

Here we go, she thought. Nervously, she drank some of her wine.

Their dinners came and they ate in silence. Steve was decidedly savoring his lobster and insisted that Laura try a bite from his outstretched fork. Delicately, she moved her mouth toward the utensil that had only recently been caressing Steve's lips, tongue and palate. Like a kiss, she tasted. It was delicious, and she really needed to get on with the interview before she drank too much and fell into those gorgeous brown eyes. Was this another glass of wine by her elbow? When had that come? She tried to lead the conversation in the direction of the Foundation, but he didn't seem particularly interested, preferring to divert her attention to the antics of the poultry and felines prancing beneath their feet.

Laura took another sip of wine and looked over the rim of her glass. Steve was staring across the table at her with those bedroom eyes. Oh, God. This had to stop, the hell with the interview and her job. She was considering excusing herself and leaving before it was too late when he slid his hand across the table and touched her fingers. She jumped.

"Laura!" called a dark voice, and she withdrew her hand quickly, glancing up, feeling faintly guilty for some reason.

Smiling down at them from the foot of the picnic table stood Taylor. He wore tan chinos and a black collarless shirt. The cavalry had arrived!

He bent down and kissed Laura on the cheek. This time, she didn't pull away, Steve noted.

"Here you are," Taylor enthused. "I was waiting in the bar for you."

Steve's eyes shifted back and forth between them. This tall black man was somehow familiar. Where did he know him from?

"I'm so glad you got my message," Laura beamed. "Here, have a seat." She slid over a bit and Taylor sat down next to her, close. Too close for Steve. She returned Taylor's kiss on the cheek and then looked at Steve across the table.

"Steve, I'd like you to meet my boyfriend," she said. "Taylor, this is Steve Stevens." A lightbulb went on in the reporter's head. He let Laura's alleged boyfriend speak first.

"From the radio?" Taylor grinned, shaking Steve's hand. Steve smiled back, on to the game.

"We've met before," he said smoothly. Taylor looked puzzled. "Daiquiri Taylor, I presume?" finished Steve.

Recognition slowly crept across Taylor's features. "Oh! The guy in the suit and tie!"

"At the Riding Crop last week," Steve confirmed. Taylor looked abashed. Laura looked confused. What kind of name was "Daiquiri"? Gamely, she tried to keep up the charade.

"I hope you don't mind that I asked Taylor to join us. I thought we'd be done with the interview by now."

Steve sat back and smirked. He'd been on the receiving end of a lot of brush-offs before, but he had to give this attempt extra points for cleverness. A fake boyfriend. Except she'd definitely picked the wrong guy. He let her pretend.

Taylor, for his part, looked discomfitted. He knew the jig was up. Steadfastly, Laura clutched his hand.

"No, not at all," Steve said, watching them hold hands before he dropped his bomb. "Taylor, I didn't get a chance to tell you. That was a *stunning* dress you were wearing the other night." He leaned forward and tried not to smile. Impossible.

Laura's eyes went wide and her head swung toward her date. "Dress?"

Taylor sighed deeply and released her hand. "It was a nice try, Laura. If it had been anyone but Steve here," he looked at the newsman, "it would have worked." Briefly, he confessed to her that, not only was he very gay, he was a drag queen and he and Steve had met briefly after one of Daiquiri's performances. Laura groped for her wine, finished it and signaled the waitress for a refill. Steve laughed gently.

"I'm sorry, Laura. I guess I was coming on too strong." He gazed at her a little sadly. "I'm sort of on the rebound, and when I walked into your office this morning and met you, well, I started fantasizing a bit. I apologize. It wasn't very professional of me. Or very nice."

Laura held his gaze for a moment before she burst out laughing. "I'm sorry, too. I didn't want you to get the wrong idea." Quickly she explained that she was still married, though not for long, and that while she thought Steve handsome and charming, it wasn't the right time to embark on a new romance.

"Of course," soothed Steve, "and again I apologize. But if you decide to start dating again, I hope I'll be first in line."

Laura smiled and nodded, flattered. "Promise." Steve beamed and Laura added, "Now, can we do that interview?"

Taylor rose to leave. "Well, I guess you won't be needing me here anymore." Laura grabbed his sleeve and pulled him back down.

"Stay awhile; this won't take long. I'll return the favor and walk *you* home tonight."

Steve pushed his empty plate out of the way and dug in his pocket for his notebook and tape recorder. He was about to ask his first question when the noise of the crowd escalated to an excited burble. Heads craned toward the entrance.

The hostess came first, passing right by their table. Trailing behind her followed a strikingly beautiful redhead in a beige linen suit. Immediately after strode a tall, thin man, well-tanned, with white hair and matching mustache. He carried a cane, but it was clear that it was merely an affectation. Everyone in the outdoor restaurant followed them with their eyes as the couple took their seats at an elegantly set table in one corner of the yard. The hostess removed the *Reserved* card. Steve sensed an opportunity.

"Excuse me, I'll be right back," he said absently. Laura and Taylor watched him approach the new guests. Waiters scurried like chickens.

"Who are they?" Laura asked.

"That," Taylor replied softly, "is Mr. and Mrs. Armand Pringle."

"Janet Sullivan?" hushed Laura, referring to the famous Mrs. Pringle by her stage name.

"The one and only." Taylor watched Steve schmooze the couple and saw Mrs. Pringle tilt back her head in a delicate laugh. Steve shook Mr. Pringle's hand and accepted an invitation to pull up a chair.

"Well," Laura mused, "I guess that's it for my interview. There's bigger fish out there now." She turned to Taylor. "I never got a chance to thank you for the other night. That's twice now you've come to my rescue."

Taylor waved it off. "My pleasure. Sorry I was so late getting here, and I'm sorry your plan didn't work."

"Oh, it worked out fine. You came at just the right time. I mean, he didn't buy the story about you being my boyfriend, but . . ." She shrugged. "Why didn't you tell me what you do for a living?"

Taylor hunched his shoulders. "It never came up. I'm not ashamed of it or anything. I dig wearing womens clothes and I'm good at what I do."

Laura grinned. "So, can I see your show sometime?"

Taylor smiled back. "'Course! Daiquiri's dancing at the Crop tomorrow night through Saturday. And on Sunday she's the hostess at the deck party at the Rainforest Resort."

Laura looked at him hard, trying to imagine his long, lanky frame in a sequined gown and couldn't do it. He was far too handsome to be a woman. She sighed.

"Key West," she said in amazed exasperation.

"Key West," he agreed.

A couple of minutes later, Steve rose and bade the Pringles good night. He rejoined Laura and Taylor at their green picnic table.

"I thought you'd abandoned us," Laura teased him lightly.

"I've interviewed Armand Pringle before, in Miami. Lucky for me, he remembered. I've got an invitation to call on him later this week to set up an interview before they sail for San Juan."

"Speaking of interviews," suggested Taylor, and Laura shot him a grateful look. Steve flipped open his notebook and punched *Record* on the cassette machine.

"Okay," he said, "the first thing I need to know . . ."

Chickens ran in crazy figure-eights, warily avoiding the cats. Diners finished their meals and drinks and browsed the adjacent gallery. The warm tropical wind stirred the trees, and Laura and Steve, in the company of Taylor, finally completed their interview.

\* \* \* \* \* \* \*

In a standard-issue Holiday Inn room, with a view of the interstate just north of Jacksonville, Big Jim Quinn lay sprawled across the queen-size bed on his back. His clothes were rumpled and sweat-stained, and he was battling a road-induced headache. It was 3 A.M. and he couldn't have driven another inch. The bathroom door swung open and Liza danced out. She wore a red g-string and matching silk robe and nothing else except perfume. She sidled up next to the bed. Big Jim groaned.

"Not tonight, babe, I'm beat."

She ignored his comment and traced her red-painted nails across his crotch. Something stirred. Damn his dick! Just when the rest of his body was ready for bed, his little buddy--and his girlfriend--wanted to play. Liza crawled onto the bed, straddling him, and began undoing his belt. He opened his weary eyes and took in the mounds of boob spilling from her robe, brown nipples hardening inches from his chapped lips.

She managed to maneuver his pants down around his ankles. She really wanted it. The vibration of the misfiring Mercedes had teased her all day long. She touched him with her tongue and he sprang to attention. A new kind of groan issued from his throat.

"C'mon, baby," she whispered, teasing him. "You've got exactly what I need right now. You know you have the key to my heart."

Big Jim sat up with a start, rolling Liza off his lap and thumping her onto the floor.

"Hey!" she protested indignantly.

His eyes had a wild cast to them. "Oh, shit," he muttered, launching himself off the bed. Big Jim grabbed his pants and rummaged through the pockets. Then he searched his jacket, growing more agitated by the moment. Liza watched him stomp around the motel room, cursing under his breath as he hunted for something in his suitcase. She sat hunched on the floor while he paced the room, trying to remember. And then it came to him.

The keys to the boat had been in his coat pocket. And he'd taken that coat off and--oh God--tossed it in with the dry cleaning! The boat keys were a thousand miles away, back in Maryland!

"Sheee-it!" He kicked over a wastebasket.

He'd originally planned to locate the *LauraLee* and just sail her off. So, back to plan B. He'd have to get the keys off of Winchell's lifeless body. Fine, Big Jim thought, breathing hard. He'd make that skinny little bastard pay for all this trouble!

Behind him, he heard more hard breathing, not his. He looked over his shoulder. Liza was on the floor, fingers frantically stroking between her legs, bottom arching up. He watched her climax, and then kicked off his underwear and dived on top.

\* \* \* \* \* \* \*

Bleary-eyed, he stared at the boundless sea, watching for signs of life. There was nothing. Winch lowered the binoculars. Off the starboard beam lay the first islets of the Florida Keys. The sunrise to the east painted them in glowing red and emerald.

He'd been searching the waters since first light, torn between hope and fear that he'd see the sea monster that haunted him. It had to be a hallucination. There was no such thing as Chessie. Of course not. No Loch Ness Monster. No Sasquatch. No yetis. Then what had he seen? Twice?

Was his brain just totally fried? On his way down that long slippery slope? He gave it some sleep-deprived thought, trying to remember what had happened each time the monster had materialized. Gradually, it came to him. Both times he'd been rip-roaring stoned. He never saw Chessie while he was straight! So perhaps a little experiment was in order?

Winch searched the cabin for his stash of acid. Yes, here, he still had a couple of tabs left under the sofa cushion. He did two and resumed his place at the helm, hunting the horizon. Time lost its meaning. The whitecaps became orangecaps. Seagulls flew backwards. Other boats cruised by, their hulls never touching the water, props spinning in the peppermint dawn. He saw no sea monster, acid-provoked or otherwise. Was the experiment a success or a failure? He couldn't remember, and he didn't care.

Winch cranked up the speakers on deck, some raucous Elvis Costello, and simply floated along, thoroughly enjoying his trip.

# CHAPTER 8

They'd been in Key West for three hours and, except for a breakfast bisquit and a bathroom break at a fast-food place on Roosevelt Boulevard, Liza hadn't yet been out of the dust-streaked Mercedes. Her butt was numb, her hair was a tangle and her make-up was runny. She'd pleaded with Big Jim to find a motel, but he'd ignored her, meticulously prowling the north shore of the island for any sign of the *LauraLee*. So far they'd been to eight different marinas. At each, Big Jim would leave her in the car while he checked at the office and personally inspected the docks. It was past noon now and her stomach rumbled. She wanted to change clothes. She wanted to sip a margarita by a pool. She wanted to lie in the warm tropical sunshine. What she didn't want anymore was to be trapped in this car with Big Jim.

Liza cast a sidelong glance at her lover as the Mercedes sputtered up Caroline Street along Key West Bight. His golf shirt was stained with sweat at the armpits and he was beginning to smell. In addition, the car's interior reeked faintly of the worst parts of the Chesapeake Bay. The odors were being recirculated in the cramped cockpit by the wheezing air conditioner. Jim's thinning hair stood up at crazy angles, even his eyebrows were snarled. He'd been curt and surly for the last six hours, his mood growing worse as the mile markers on the Overseas Highway clicked down to zero. Their last stop had been at a budget motel in Key Largo, where they'd grabbed five hours of fitful sleep before hitting the road again before dawn. She'd been looking forward to the portion of their trip over the long chain of bridges connecting the keys, but the Mercedes was so low to the ground that all she'd been able to see had been guard-rails and seedy strip developments. Her wild tropical fling had turned into an ordeal of cheap motels, fast food and business news on the radio. She wanted out.

On their initial circuit of the island, Liza had taken note of Key West International Airport. Big Jim was mistaken if he thought she'd drive his misfiring car home alone while he sailed back. Screw that. When she was ready to go home, she was flying! The boat and car were his problems.

The affair with Big Jim had been a disaster. He had been, in turn, bossy, petulant, manic, angry and silent. Somewhere around Ft. Lauderdale she'd realized that the only reason he'd asked her along was so she could drive his car back to Baltimore. Now, more than a thousand weary miles later, she knew she never wanted to be in a car again. And if she didn't get out of the Mercedes soon, she'd scream.

Her sweaty suitor found another marina at the foot of Margaret Street and pulled to a stop in a no-parking zone, blocking a bicycle rack. Big Jim got out without a word to her and trudged toward the office.

Liza rolled down her window and sniffed the salty air. From somewhere nearby, the music of Jimmy Buffet floated on the gulf breeze. Women in halter-tops and bare-chested men strolled past, each tanner than the last. She could stand no more.

From her purse, Liza extracted her brush and a tube of cherry lip-gloss. She twisted the rear-view mirror and swept the snags from her dark hair and applied fresh lipstick. Through the open window of the idling car came the tempting aroma of frying seafood. From her overnight bag behind the seat, she pulled a fresh blouse and a pair of shorts, and by scrunching low she was able to liberate her breasts from her Wonderbra and slip into the clean shirt. As she wriggled into the shorts, a young man passed by on a bicycle and glanced through the window at her, smiling. Half-naked, she smiled back in embarrassment and managed to pull the tight shorts past her knees and over her hips. She leaned across the driver's seat and switched off the ignition, dumping the keys in her purse. She got out and stretched luxuriantly in the sun.

Liza glanced around. There was no sign of Big Jim. If he followed the habit he'd developed this morning, it would be at least another twenty minutes before he reappeared. Plenty of time to stroll over to the place called Turtle Kraals across the street for a drink and a bite. Maybe she should leave a note, but she couldn't find a pen. Dipping into her purse, Liza took her lipstick and scrawled a red arrow on the windshield indicating the direction in which she was headed.

Inside the ancient waterfront bar, she took a seat overlooking the harbor and ordered a shrimp-basket and a Corona and lime. She sipped her cold beer in satisfaction, allowing the sights and sounds of Key West to wash over her and sweep away the hardships of the last three days. This, she sighed to herself in satisfaction, is where I belong.

* * * * * * *

In the marina office, Big Jim Quinn waited impatiently for the pimply youngster in the tank-top to get off the phone. Finally, the teen hung up and glanced at the pasty-white tourist.

"Help ya?" he offered.

"I'm looking for a friend of mine," Big Jim stated for the ninth time today. "I forget which marina he's docked at, but I think this is the one. His name is Winchell."

He waited while the kid skimmed the records on the computer. Big Jim worried that Winchell might not even be in Key West yet. Worse, he might have changed his destination altogether, and all this would be for naught. But Big Jim resolved to give it at least a week, returning to the same marinas over and over until he got his hands on that scumbag. If he had to, he'd drive back up the Keys and check every boatyard and yacht club on the way north. And, eventually, he'd get the *LauraLee* back and wring Winchell's scrawny neck.

"What's the name of the boat?" asked the dockmaster. Big Jim nearly choked trying to spit out the vile words.

"The *Stuffed Ham*."

If the kid behind the counter was surprised by the name, he didn't show it. There were lots of odd and tasteless names painted across transoms, and he'd heard them all. He tapped the keys on his terminal and squinted at the monitor.

"Sorry. No Winchell, no *Stuffed Ham*. Not even a reservation."

Quinn nodded and muttered an empty thanks. He left the office and stepped out onto the dock. There was always the chance, he guessed, that Winchell was using an alias or had changed the name of the boat. So Big Jim methodically walked up and down the docks, inspecting each vessel, searching for his. For the ninth time today, he found nothing.

Aggravated, he paused at the end of the last pier, hands on hips, staring out into the Gulf of Mexico. Boats of every description skittered across the flat water beyond the harbor. Somewhere out there, he knew, floated his boat. His eyes strained the horizon, examining every watercraft he could discern. Music crept into his ears, annoying guitar and drum-driven beats pounding from beyond the breakwater. He shaded his eyes and released an involuntary yelp.

There! Steering west out of the harbor under the white-hot sun. He could just make out her familiar lines and the large *S* and *H* painted on the transom, the rest of the smaller lettering a distant blur. A skinny guy with a mop of dirty blond hair stood at the helm, befouling the deck.

Rage seeped up from within Big Jim's black heart and he found himself fumbling for his pistol before he regained control. Winchell was too far away, there were too many witnesses, and once again he was afraid he'd miss his target and hit his precious boat.

But he was here, Quinn exalted! He'd found the little fuck! Winchell was in Key West and sooner or later he'd discover his lair. That asshole had to tie up somewhere and Big Jim would find out where if it took all winter.

He watched as the *LauraLee* disappeared behind a high-rise hotel and hurried back to the street where he'd left Liza in the car. Big Jim was so excited he could hardly breathe. He rounded the corner of the marina office and pulled up short.

The first thing he noticed was the bright red arrow pointing right that stained the windshield of his Mercedes. Beneath that, tucked under a wiper blade, fluttered a slip of pink paper. And at the rear of the car, yellow strobe lights flashing, a tow truck was easing the 500SL away from the bike rack. Big Jim broke into a wheezy trot, but the truck, with his car in tow, outpaced him. He arrived back at the bicycle rack in time to see his silver Mercedes vanish around the corner.

First he'd watched his boat disappear, then his car. Now, where the hell was Liza? He glowered to the right, in the direction the red arrow had pointed, and spotted Turtle Kraals. Through the open side of the bar, drowsing in the warm sun with a bottle of beer, he spotted her. Big Jim ground his teeth and stomped across the street. He marched to her table and towered over her, casting a black shadow across her reposed face. Liza opened one eye and smiled up at him.

"Any luck?"

\* \* \* \* \* \* \*

He hadn't had any luck at all. God, it was expensive here! Slip fees were at least double what Donna Jean charged in Maryland. Winch had spent the last day circling Key West in search of a reasonably priced marina and had come up empty. He'd spent Thursday night anchored off of Christmas Tree Island, but he needed to find a place where he could tie up and refill his fresh water tank and pump out the waste from the head. The marine toilet had clogged up two days ago and the cabin was getting decidedly rank.

At the last marina, finding that winter rates were in effect there too, he'd topped off on fuel and motored out of Key West Bight in search of a port, Lynyrd Skynyrd's "Gimme Three Steps" bleeding high decibels into the foaming wake. Winch began to fear that he'd never find a slip he could afford, and without a slip he'd be unable to establish his charter business, leaving him totally destitute. He steered a course around the west end of the key and turned east past Southernmost Point. Nothing on this side of the island except rocky beaches and the occasional fishing pier.

Rounding the other end of Key West, he encountered a narrow passage his chart labeled *Cow Key Channel*. He throttled back and angled in to explore, passing a row of shabby houseboats moored to port. At the causeway, he reversed course and cruised the shoreline of Stock Island.

He almost missed it. A decrepit, vacant, splintered and sagging dock stretched out into the channel from behind an equally decrepit and sagging building. It wore the look of abandonment. Desperate for a landfall, Winch edged the *Stuffed Ham* alongside the pier. There was no one in sight. He noticed a water line and electrical hookup and prayed they worked. The *Ham* bumped gently against the recycled tires along the pilings and he shut down the engines. There were some lines attached to cleats and he made his boat fast. The raw cinder-block building looked unused and the gravel parking lot around it showed nary a car. He tried the tap and it spewed frothing white water. Perfect. He was home.

Squatting on the dock, Winch was screwing on the water hose to run to his bone-dry tank when he heard the scrape of tennis shoes on the rotting wood. Winch looked over his scrawny shoulder, a dreadful feeling in his gut.

Slender, slightly tanned legs ran north from blue tennies to a pair of white shorts. An innie bellybutton upon a smooth, bare midriff winked at him beneath a tied-off butterscotch blouse worn over a matching bathing suit top. Long blonde hair brushed the shoulders of the shirt. Dark sunglasses shielded her eyes as she stared down at him. Winch stared back. He was in lust.

"Hey! You can't tie up here! This slip is reserved for the *Reef Explorer*."

Winch rose to his full height and looked around. "Where's the boat?"

Laura looked flustered for a moment and finally coughed out, "Sank."

"Sorry," the intruder answered, meaning it. The woman before him was beautiful, but he couldn't think about that right now. He had to take care of business, and number one on his list was finding a working bathroom. He tried to be tactful.

"I coulda swore this place was abandoned," he said. Laura slumped. "I've been looking for a place to tie up for two days. I don't mean to trespass, but could I impose long enough to fill my water tank, pump out the head and buy some supplies on shore? And I could really, really use a bathroom." Winch was beginning to hop from leg to leg.

Laura removed her sunglasses, revealing her suspicious green eyes. She bit her lip and looked Winch over carefully. He was dirty and dressed in rags, but the boat itself was glistening, obviously expensive and well-maintained. The natural wariness of strangers which had come to her so naturally up north melted away in the relaxed warmth of the Keys and she relented. "Come on in."

"Thank you, ma'am, thank you," he gushed and headed for the tumbledown building at a businesslike pace. Laura had to trot to stay up with him, keeping a thoughtful eye on his back.

Inside SuRF headquarters she pointed out the bathroom, into which her visitor disappeared gratefully. Laura gazed around the wreckage of the office. After four days, she'd managed to file about two-thirds of the mounds of documents which had cluttered every available space. None of the volunteers had returned since the Reef Explorer went down, and she'd as yet been unable to find a boat that the foundation could afford.

Mrs. Winters, the ninety-two year old president and founder of SuRF, whom Laura had never met personally, had called again this morning from her home in Boca Raton. She'd told Laura to get things in order by the end of next week or the Foundation would be shut down. And Laura would be out of a job, adrift in Key West, unable to return home unless it was on her knees, begging Big Jim's forgiveness. And that was absolutely out of the question. To save her job, she needed to drum up public interest, fresh donors, a boat and new volunteers. And she needed to do it in less than eight days. Laura collapsed in a broken chair in despair.

After an eternity, the bathroom door opened and her visitor emerged waving a magazine. "I wouldn't go in there for awhile," he warned.

Laura barely heard him.

"Is there a grocery around somewhere? And a bank? I've got a big check to cash, then I'll be on my way."

Check? Laura started out of her depression. Of course! No one owned a huge boat like that unless he was wealthy! Despite the grungy appearance of her visitor, he obviously had access to big bucks. The shadings of an idea sprang into her head and she pulled herself up from the chair. Be nice, she cautioned herself. This wraith could be my salvation. She crossed the room to him so rapidly, smiling so warmly, that the captain took an involuntary step back from her.

"Of course," she purred. "There's a grocery store at the end of the street, by the highway. And a bank right across from the store."

Winch shuffled his feet in puzzlement. What had happened to the woman who had barely tolerated his presence? Why was she suddenly being so nice? "Uh, I have to get some things from the boat first," he said. "If that's all right."

"Please, take your time. I'm sorry if I was brusque, I've just been very busy today. Here, let me walk you back to your boat." She escorted the confused mariner out the front door. "My name is Laura Chadwick." She remembered to use her maiden name. She had better get used to it. She was glad she'd registered at the Rainforest under Chadwick, just in case Big Jim came looking for her, not that that was likely. And besides, it was a sign of her new independence.

He walked beside her along the pier and checked her out from the corner of his eye. "Eugene Winchell, but everybody calls me Winch." She shook his hand again.

"She's a beautiful boat," Laura remarked as they approached the *Stuffed Ham*. "Are you down to do some fishing?"

"Nah. Hate fishing. Actually, I'm trying to start up a charter business, take tourists out on tours of the Keys." He bent over and turned on the water tap to refill the tank. "She's tricked out pretty nice, all the comforts of home.

Can I show you around?" Winch offered, inviting her aboard. She was no coed, he figured, but it might be fun.

In your dreams, Laura thought, recognizing that look in his eyes and that tone of voice.

Laura noticed the name on the transom. *Stuffed Ham*. He'll never do any business with a name like that, she mused. She allowed him to take her hand and assist her aboard.

Proudly, Winch showed her his vessel. In spite of the condition of its captain, the boat was neat as a pin, as though someone's mother had been cleaning. He led her below. It was breathtaking.

A roomy galley filled the aft port-quarter, equipped with a refrigerator, mini-microwave, a four burner range and double sink. Opposite, a spacious dining table was attached to a bulkhead, benches covered in real leather wrapped around it. Through a narrow doorway they entered the salon. A big-screen television with attendant stereo VCR and laserdisk player occupied the far wall. A plush sofa and several matching chairs were arranged nearby. There was a liquor cabinet, which was empty, and wet bar on the starboard side next to a powerful and complicated looking stereo system. Thick pile carpeting graced the deck and supported a real Italian-marble table in the center of the room. A recessed wall unit contained a library of fine maritime books, from *Moby Dick* to leather-bound copies of the latest nautical charts.

Through yet another door forward, they passed into a space the size of a walk-in closet. The port side consisted of a cubicle for the captain, with at least three kinds of radios, radar gear, sonar and a pull-out table for charts. On the starboard side was a closed door from behind which emanated a rather nasty odor. Winch apologized and reminded her that the head was in need of attention.

Finally, as the hull narrowed, they entered the final section of the boat. Three small doors led to staterooms, the two larger cabins in immaculate condition. Winch made a vain point of mentioning how comfy the bunks were. Laura returned a weak smile. The forwardmost, and smallest, space contained a windowless vee-berth and looked as though a hand grenade had gone off. Dirty laundry obscured the deck, the bunk was rumpled and unmade and empty liquor bottles were tilted on their sides. Winch made a choking noise and hurriedly closed the door to his cabin.

As he guided her back through the salon, Laura had a sense of deja vu. This was all very familiar. Although she had been on her husband's boat only once, the similarities were striking. She wasn't much of a boat person, so makes and models meant nothing to her, but her eye for interior decorating took in details which were discomforting. As she examined the layout of the main cabin, she remarked that her husband--ex-husband, soon--had owned a boat just like this one.

"And I thought she was one of a kind," smiled Winch fondly. "I've had her about a year. Got a great deal, bought her at a tax auction."

Laura spun, her eyes wide. Her voice quavered. "Jim's boat was sold for back taxes. Last year." She gazed around the salon. No, it couldn't be. Jim had been devastated when the IRS had seized the *LauraLee*. There had been no consoling him. For months it was all he'd talked about. She'd always suspected that it had been used as his little love nest, the three-day weekends when he'd disappear to the marina, claiming that he was off fishing with clients. He had never once brought home a catch. Or maybe he had.

She remembered the time she'd returned home to find an unfamiliar bra peeking from beneath her livingroom couch. Impulsively now, she dropped to her knees and peered under the sofa, Winch watching her with alarm. Laura snaked an arm under the couch and snagged some material. Aha! She pulled out a pair of black panties. "Oh, my god," she moaned, holding them at arms-length. "This *was* Jim's boat!"

"Uh, sorry," mumbled Winch, taking the panties from her shaking hand. He smiled sheepishly. "These were from last week." The memory of his underaged date warmed his cockles.

Laura fell onto the couch, suddenly emotionally exhausted. This was all a mistake, brought on by her guilt over running out on her marriage. She had to go, get back to work, straighten out her tangled life. Dizzily, she rose, thanking Winch for the interesting tour. Winch pressed her.

"You know," he ventured, "if you aren't using the dock for awhile, do you think maybe I could tie up here for a few days? I mean, I've got some repairs to make and it would only be until I can find a reasonably priced slip somewhere."

Laura found her way back on deck. It was better here, out in the fresh sea-air. She could think again, force away all those evil thoughts of Big Jim Quinn. She had to focus on saving the Foundation and her job. Her earlier idea teased at her. Why not?

She plunged in. "Look, Mr. Winchell. I'll make a deal with you. You can dock here as long as you like."

Winch gazed at her with a mixture of thankfulness and suspicion. "What's the catch?"

"Simple. The Save the Reef Foundation needs a boat. You have a boat. If you let us use it a couple of times a week, you can stay as long as you like."

Winch rubbed his stubbled chin in hesitation. "I don't know," he said doubtfully. Laura tried to sweeten the deal.

"It's a win-win situation for both of us. You need to establish your charter business, we need to attract attention to the reef and our Foundation. If you stay here and set up business, we can book tours of the reef, on your boat, and split the take 50-50."

"I don't know anything about reefs," Winch protested. "Except to avoid hitting them." Laura ignored the crack.

"No problem. We'll get someone from the Foundation to be the guide. All you have to do is steer the boat and collect the money. And you can dock here free of charge."

Winch thought it over as he helped her over the gunwale and onto the rickety pier. A free slip and some help in getting the business up and running? He was trying to find a downside and couldn't. Especially when the offer came from this stunning blonde goddess. He shook her hand with some trepidation.

"Deal."

Laura grinned back at him. "Just one thing," she said.

Uh-oh, thought Winch. Dad was right, there was always a catch.

"What's that?"

Laura pointed at the stern. "You have *got* to change the name. We won't attract a single tourist to a boat called the *Stuffed Ham*. Where in the world did you come up with that?"

Winch was wounded. His mother's honor was at stake. He shook his head forcefully.

"Can't do that," he refused. "Named for my mother."

Laura couldn't fathom that explanation. She started to speak and choked it off. Be flexible, she counseled herself. Don't offend him. It was a sweet arrangement, especially if she could clean the captain up and make him presentable. Maybe a haircut would help. Or at least a bath. She nodded.

"Please think about changing it." She turned to go back to the office. She was already planning. She could use the office copier to print up fliers advertising the reef tours, maybe even buy some ads on Steve's radio station. This could save her!

Laura was halfway up the dock when Winch called to her.

"Hey!" He was bent over the electric outlet, plugging in an orange extension cord. "Could you turn on the power out here? Flip the breaker?"

She waved in acknowledgment and continued walking.

"And, hey," he shouted again. "You don't happen to have a cable TV hook-up, do you?"

\* \* \* \* \* \* \*

He'd had all the comforts of home until yesterday afternoon. In a sudden, fierce squall which had blown up out of the Gulf, Felix had lost most of his supplies as well as his transistor radio, compass and his favorite baseball cap. Safely lashed to the base of the mast was canvas bag, filled with baseballs, an extra mitt and his lucky Louisville Slugger. In a plastic bread bag hanging from his belt swayed his most prized possession, a genuine leather Spaulding pitcher's glove. Everything else was gone, washed into the sea. Six foot waves had swept across the raft, washing his hopes of survival overboard. The sail was in tatters and his hands suffered from the blisters he'd raised rowing endlessly.

Friday evening's sunset had given him an indication of direction, but during the night he'd become hopelessly turned around. With dawn yet to arrive, Felix bobbed sickeningly somewhere north of Cuba. His prayers to *la Virgen Maria* were interrupted by a new sound, different from the ceaseless splash of water against the raft. He lifted his head and stared into the darkness, listening.

It was waves he heard, crashing against rock. "*Gracias, Madre,*" he muttered and quickly crossed himself. The roar of surf grew louder and the *balza* was suddenly pitched into the air. Felix grabbed for the splintered mast and hung on for his life as the flimsy craft stayed together just long enough to toss him onto a stony beach. He felt rocks pummel his body, and then nothing.

He must have passed out. When he opened his eyes the glaring sun was well above the horizon. Blinking against the morning light and the sand in his eyes, Felix raised his head and took a cautious look around.

The remains of his raft lay about fifteen meters away, beached above the high tide line. It was irreparable, a twisted wreckage of wood and rope. Higher up the bank, scraggy palm trees lined a low ridge of sand and guarded a thicket of brush pushing up a shallow hill. Upon a fallen tree trunk in the speckled shade of a white mangrove tree, lazed a toothless old man, his skin the color of charcoal, staring at the new arrival. Felix rolled over tentatively and checked himself for injuries. He seemed to be in one piece, despite the knot on his temple. He hoisted himself to his feet as the old man did the same and they approached each other on the hot sand.

"*Buenos dios, Marielito,*" the old one croaked.

He spoke Spanish! marveled Felix. Called him a refugee from Mariel! So he hadn't landed in the Bahamas, but on one of the Spanish-speaking isles. He was free! Ecstatic, Felix stumbled to the old man and embraced him.

"I've been at sea for three days and nights," he said in his native tongue. "Tell me! Is this Puerto Rico? The Dominican Republic?"

The old man grinned with his empty mouth and said, "Cuba."

Weeping, Felix fell to his knees. The old man, the *viejo*, circled the refugee curiously a few times before he stopped and stared at the baseball glove hanging from Felix's belt. He nodded and snapped his fingers.

"El Gato Munoz, de Diablos Rojos. 26-12 last year, 1.09 ERA, batted .286." Felix heard his statistics recited but couldn't raise his head. An aficianado. A Cuban fan. Oh, the agony, the irony. He was alive but worse off than when he'd started. He collapsed into the sand and waited for the tide to come in and take him out to sea, to his death.

He stayed that way, prone on the beach, for a long time. When Felix refused to speak anymore, lost in his grief, the old man had left, probably to summon the *policia. Carcel* awaited him, maybe even execution. Fidel had won this game.

Eventually, a chorus of excited voices rose from the brush. Felix sat up dolefully and waited for the authorities to come to arrest him. A great crowd of people emerged from the treeline and gathered around him. Felix gaped at them. There were farmers, merchants, women and children and a couple of goats. And not a single uniform. Except for the baseball uniforms worn by nine or ten of the younger men. The *viejo* pushed through the crowd and stooped down to look Felix in the eye.

"Senor Munoz," he spoke reverently. "We wish to welcome you to our humble *pueblo*, Santa Clarita. You are the answer to our prayers."

Santa Clarita! reeled Felix. He hadn't traveled more than twenty miles up the coast! He could almost walk home from here! A pretty woman in a floral skirt offered him a plate of plantain and fried goat. Felix accepted it, ravenous, and heard the *viejo* speak to him between bites.

"It is the great misfortune of our beloved baseball team, Los Angeles de Santa Clarita, that our star *lanzador* is too ill to pitch today against our greatest rivals, San Domingo." At the mention of the neighboring village, the assembled crowd hissed. Felix devoured chevron. The old man continued. "It would be a great honor if you would accept the hospitality of our village and pitch for our team today."

Felix paused in mid-mouthful. He couldn't believe what he was hearing. A man washes up on the beach, parched and half-starved, and they want him to play baseball! On the other hand, he mused, this would probably be his last opportunity in this life to take the mound and throw a perfect strike before the police took him to jail. So, *que diablos importa?* He might as well go down swinging, as they said. He shrugged, took another bite of goat, and the villagers cheered.

Many strong hands helped him to his feet. The local ballplayers clustered around him and half-led, half-carried Felix to the *pueblo*. He was taken to the home of the mayor, a fine white castle by rural-Cuban standards, where he bathed, took a long nap and ate once again.

Around four o'clock, the team manager gave him a much-mended uniform that almost fit him. The mayor shook his hand at the front door. Felix emerged onto a mud street where he found nearly the entire town waiting for him. The parish priest offered a short prayer, which included some rather uncharitable words for today's opponent, and the whole carnival escorted him to the field.

A field it was, pieces of old cane stalks poking up in the outfield (a bad place for a diving catch) and a dirt and rock infield studded with precarious potholes. Old fishing nets provided a semi-workable backstop and the grounds crew, two boys and a *burro*, were shoveling up the last of the cow, goat and donkey shit.

## KEY MONSTER

The spectators took their seats upon blankets, boxes and the occasional folding chair. About fifty people crammed onto the three short rows of rickety bleacher seats along the first base line. Felix stretched and tossed some warm-up pitches, each practice throw eliciting oohs and ahhs from the fans. He glanced at the bleachers and was panicked to see two policemen watching from the bottom row. They grinned and waved. The priest pulled on a mask, belted a sofa cushion over his chest and strode to the plate.

"*Pley bol!*"

Felix nudged the manager, standing next to him, and pointed to the cassock-garbed umpire. "Won't he be a little biased?"

The manager shrugged. "When we visit San Domingo, they use *their* padre."

Felix shook his head and took the mound. Neither of these teams, he knew, were anywhere near the caliber of the clubs in the Cuban National League. He decided to take it easy on the amateurs.

By the top of the sixth inning, Felix was in a groove, bearing down. He had a no-hitter going, and Santa Clarita was winning 7-0, largely due to his two home-runs in this miniscule park. His most ardent rooters were the two *policia*, who exchanged high-fives at every strike-out and even tried to start a wave, which more resembled a ripple in the undersized bleachers.

The game ended 12-0. Felix had blown the no-hitter after becoming over-confident and allowing a blooper single to short-right field. But he'd gotten seventeen strike-outs and had gone six-for-seven at the plate. After throwing the final strike, the crowd mobbed him while his teammates carried him off the field.

Felix was signing autographs for the adoring fans when the two bleacher cops shoved their way through the throng. One of them pushed aside a boy and they loomed before him. Felix knew it was over: This had truly been his last game. He waited stoically for the handcuffs. One of the policemen pulled a paper from his pocket. The other produced a pen.

"Senor Munoz, may we have your *autografo*?"

Felix signed, chuckling.

Before retiring that night in the mayor's very own bed, Felix enjoyed the fiesta. He was the *invitado de honor* for defeating San Domingo for the first time in six years. Felix ate and drank his fill, and danced with the prettiest *chicas* in the village. He fell into bed entirely spent, yet sleeplessly worried about what tomorrow would hold. Eventually he would go to prison, he knew. But, until then, should he stay in Santa Clarita, or go back home to Los Palacios? He hadn't the money for another raft, and he tossed and turned until exhaustion finally claimed him.

Felix slept until past ten o'clock Sunday morning. The mayor's *esposa* prepared him a bountiful breakfast, then he stepped outside the front door. Once again, before the mayor's porch, stood the entire town. Is there another game today, Felix wondered? The same toothless old *viejo* who had found him on the sand stepped forward and insisted that Felix follow.

Felix and the old man, trailed by over a hundred people, retraced yesterday morning's route back to the *playa*. As they emerged from the brush, Felix's eyes widened.

His despoiled raft had been resurrected. A new mast and fresh canvas. A dozen plastic jugs of water and a waterproof bag filled with food. A toolkit with fishing line, knife, bandages and a compass. Even a bottle of rum! Felix turned to the silent crowd with tears in his eyes.

"The tide is going out now," urged the old man. "We wish you to be on it and, when you reach America, we hope you will dedicate your first pitch in the American leagues to your amigos in Santa Clarita."

Gratefully, Felix shook hands and embraced everyone on the beach. Fresh tears washed his eyes as he climbed onto the raft and his new teammates pushed him past the breakers. The people of Santa Clarita faded from his sight, but not his memory, and Felix Munoz was once again alone, adrift on the sea.

# CHAPTER 9

Bobbing gently upon the calm, protected waters of Cow Key Channel, the *Stuffed Ham* was again beginning to sparkle after her long voyage down the coast. Winch looked up from his work on deck when he heard tires crunching gravel in the SuRF parking lot. He shaded his eyes to watch a tall, salt-and-pepper-haired man emerge from a non-descript car and stroll to the front door of the office.

After returning to his cleaning and polishing, Winch glanced up the dock once again at the tap of approaching footsteps. The man was heading toward him, led by Laura. Her face was bathed in a beatific smile and his heart went *pit-a-pat*. Winch put down his long-handled mop and tilted back his fishing cap.

"Ahoy," Laura called to him. She wore a long white sundress that showed off her smooth shoulders and slender arms. Her hair was pulled back in a golden ponytail. Her companion was dressed in a pair of pressed summer slacks and a bright yellow sportshirt beneath a tan blazer. He looked like a vacationing insurance agent, and Winch tasted jealousy as the man neared, walking so close to Laura. He waved limply back at the couple.

"Winch," Laura hailed, "I'd like you to meet a friend of mine, Steve Stevens. Steve, this is Winch." The two men eyed each other warily. Winch pulled on the bill of his cap and Steve gave a half-hearted nod of his head.

"It's quitting time, Winch," Laura grinned, oblivious of the tension between the two men. "Time to enjoy some of that legendary Key West nightlife. Steve and I are going out to dinner and then over to a club to catch a show. You game?"

Winch wrestled his glare away from the interloper and gazed at Laura. Her emerald eyes flashed at him in the late-day sun.

"I've got some more work to do before I lose the light," Winch said flatly. "Maybe another time." He stole another look at Laura's date. Trim, athletic, mature. The kind of guy a babe like Laura would go for. Winch hated him. Laura looked disappointed.

"C'mon, Winch, it's Saturday night. You've been working on the boat non-stop for two days. Take a break!"

Winch shook his head and returned to his mopping. Steve perked up. Laura had obviously wanted another chaperone tonight, but it wasn't going to happen. She might be unobtainable to Steve right now, but with a little patience he'd win her heart, and her body. He didn't need complications in the form of an aging hippie tagging along.

Laura watched Winch scrub the foredeck for a minute. She noticed the coppery red stain on the deck where he swabbed, wringing pale pink water from the mop. Steve was admiring the boat, and his eyes lingered on the elaborate mural on the forward hull. He nudged Laura and pointed it out.

"What's with the dragon?" Steve spoke for the first time. Winch leaned over the bow rail and looked at the painting upside down.

"Going away present from a friend," he answered. "Keep wanting to get rid of it, but that marine paint is a bitch to get off."

"I like it," Laura mused. "What is it, a sea-serpent?"

Winch nodded morosely. The damn thing had plagued his dreams again last night.

"What's the story?" questioned Steve, ever the reporter.

Winch shook his head. "Don't wanna discuss it." They waited silently, genuinely curious, looking up at the captain from the pier. He let out a deep breath, put down the mop and sat on the deck, his legs hanging over the side.

"It's a painting of the sea monster I saw." He waited, reluctant to go on, anticipating their derisive laughter. Instead, they only gazed up at him, straight-faced. So far.

Winch surrendered and confessed the tale of his first encounter with Chessie, back north, and of his subsequent sighting of the creature off the coast of Florida. He didn't mention that he'd been royally stoned each time he'd seen it, but he described the monster in detail.

"So, it seems to be following you," Steve noted with a small smirk.

Winch whitened at the observation.

Laura pursed her lips thoughtfully and said, "It's almost mythic. I mean, don't we all have some sort of monster trailing us, something we're all desperate to leave behind?" She had a dreamy look in her eyes and the two men stared at her. "A monster waiting for us, somewhere out there, ready to take over our lives and imprison us, complicate our happiness. A dragon we must slay." She trailed off, suddenly aware of the odd looks she was getting in the wake of her high-blown words. She had been thinking of Big Jim, *her* sea monster.

"I suppose that's true," Steve agreed slowly. He was thinking of his own monster, his shattered professional career back in Miami. He couldn't slay his past, but he could perhaps obliterate it by uncovering the ultimate scoop.

Winch was considering his own sea monster. His, however, was real. Maybe.

The three of them fell silent, only the sound of the blue-green water lapping at the boat. Winch stared down into the channel beneath his bare feet. Steve examined the mural of the sea monster. Laura's eyes beheld the splintering wood of the dock, each of them lost in thought.

Finally, Laura shook her head and glanced out to the soft tropical horizon. She was living in paradise, she reminded herself. Big Jim didn't have a clue to her whereabouts and she was safe here, among new friends and out on her own at last. Somehow she would slay her monster. Steve touched her arm, interrupting her thoughts, and spoke quietly.

"We should get going if we're going to meet Taylor for dinner." Laura nodded and the two of them said farewell and turned to go. Winch continued to hang his head, lost in his nightmare of dockmasters, bartenders, drug dealers, angry fathers and sea monsters. He roused himself to watch them depart, leaving him alone again.

"Laura," he called, and she and Steve paused. "The *Ham* is just about ready. Any plan to start this tour business yet?" Asking any question, just to keep her from leaving.

The woman in the sundress slapped her head with the heel of her hand. "Oh, right, I nearly forgot. Yeah, I printed up two-hundred fliers. I thought I could distribute them around town tomorrow. With luck, we could have our first trip put together by midweek."

"What about a guide?"

"Nothing yet, but I'll find someone. Promise." She gave him one of her dazzling smiles and Winch returned it, though somewhat sadly as he watched his dream float back up the pier with the insurance salesman. They reached the car, and the guy opened the door for her. Jerk.

Steve slid behind the wheel with Winch's dream-girl beside him, and drove sedately out of the SuRF parking lot. Winch glanced one more time at the mural of Chessie and cursed it before he stood, picked up the damp mop, and resumed trying to wash out Brant's bloodstains.

\* \* \* \* \* \* \*

The final notes of a tune by the Thompson Twins faded under the raucous applause as Daiquiri Taylor took her bows. She trotted down the steps offstage, blowing kisses to the crowd, and took a seat at a rear table, joining Steve and Laura, who were clapping enthusiastically. Laura wore a gleaming grin. She'd never seen anything like this back in Maryland. Steve automatically rose as Daiquiri sat down with them, and was abashed to realize that he had just stood politely for a man who was wearing a dress. Embarrassed, and a little tipsy, he sat back down and sipped his Beck's.

"Oh my God," giggled Laura. "You look better in a dress than I do!"

Daiquiri smiled shyly at the compliment. "All an illusion," she confessed. "But thank you." A waitress delivered the dancer a club soda with lime, and Daquiri used a napkin to dab the perspiration from her brow.

Back here, far from the stage and the P.A. speakers, the three of them could talk without shouting. Two other dancers took the stage and twirled in synchopation. Daiquiri indicated them.

"Angel and Samantha," she scowled.

"The two, er, guys who stole your wallet?" Laura asked tentatively. Daiquiri nodded and her long red curls bounced in the dim lighting. Laura looked across the table at Daiquiri in awe.

"If you don't mind my asking," she began, "how did you get started in this?"

Daiquiri flashed her white teeth. "In high school, back in New Jersey a million years ago, I knew I was, uh, different. I played a little basketball, but that whole locker-room scene always felt a little odd. I came out to my parents when I turned seventeen, and they were very understanding and supportive, rest their souls." The smile faded and Daiquiri stared into space over Steve and Laura's shoulders, remembering.

"I went to the senior prom with a date, a boy from another high school. I mean, I wasn't wearing dresses then, and neither was he. When we danced together it was a scandal! We were asked to leave. We weren't really surprised by the reaction. So, I called my folks for a ride home." Daiquiri paused a beat and sniffled, "It was my phone call that killed my mom and dad.

Steve shifted uneasily in his seat. Laura reached out across the table and touched Daiquiri's smooth hand with her own, comforting her.

"It's funny," the dancer said without a trace of humor. "My parents always made a big deal about having a safe prom night, no drinking and driving. So Carey and I hadn't taken his car. His aunt had dropped us off. So what happens? My parents get killed by a drunk driver on their way to the party to pick us up." Daiquiri's voice caught. Steve and Laura had to lean forward to hear her difficult words.

"Ma was a professor at Drew and Dad was a pediatric surgeon at Overlook Hospital in Summit. After the funeral, I moved in with my grandparents, Dad's parents, in Plainfield. My folks had left me everything in their wills, and Dad had set up a trust fund which I couldn't touch until I turned eighteen. After high school, I used some of the money to go to college, Rutgers. I had a couple of boyfriends, but I never did anything sex-wise. I was too afraid of AIDS, and I got almost as much a kick just cross-dressing as I did from sex. At nights, I got jobs dancing at a couple of clubs along the Jersey shore and studied marine biology during the day. I got my B.S. and then my masters in oceanograpy. I'd like to go for my Ph.D. one day, but I haven't ever found an interesting enough subject for a paper." She stopped and shrugged.

"So how did you end up in Key West?" prodded Steve.

"Traveled around for awhile after college, did some dancing, looked for true love, the usual. Heard about Key West from a friend and came down to check it out. Been here ever since. I like it here pretty much, though sometimes I miss the change of seasons."

"So you're a marine biologist?" queried Laura.

Daiquiri laughed deep in her throat. "Guess I could be, but I never saw myself working in some stuffy lab dissecting sharks and squid all day, wearing a long white lab coat and writing papers no one will ever read. So I dance."

More applause escorted Angel and Samantha offstage and the conversation hit a lull. Daiquiri gazed at the two rival dancers with open hostility as they flounced past the bar and into the dressing room. Laura bit her lip thoughtfully.

"Would you be interested in working with me at SuRF? Only part-time."

"You need a drag queen?"

Laura smiled. "No. I need a marine biologist, or at least someone who knows about reefs and sponges and coral and stuff."

"Well," Daiquiri murmured, "I don't really need the money...."

"It would just be two or three days a week, and only until I can find someone else." Quickly she explained her predicament at the Foundation and outlined her plan to give tourist trips on the *Stuffed Ham*.

"*Stuffed Ham*?" Daiquiri giggled. "Let me sleep on it. If it doesn't conflict with my gigs, I guess I could help out for awhile. I'll have Taylor call you, okay?"

It was a little disconcerting to hear Daiquiri refer to her male alter-ego in the third person, but, excited, Laura agreed. "I'll give you all the details when it's a little easier to talk." The volume of the music had increased and she found herself shouting over David Bowie. Daiquiri saw the manager signaling her and rose.

"I'm back on stage next. It was good to see you both. Dinner was delicious. Let's do it again soon." She patted Laura on the head and gave Steve a quick peck on the cheek. Steve covered up his embarrassment by checking his fake Rolex. He commented that it was getting late and offered to drive Laura back to her motel. They bid Daiquiri goodnight and strolled out onto Duval Street.

Daiquiri did two more sets at the Riding Crop. At last call, she retreated to the dressing room to change so she could go home. She hated walking the streets in drag, so she was outraged and hurt to find that someone had stolen Taylor's clothes, leaving only the empty garment bag.

Samantha and Angel, she knew at once. This was their work.

Daiquiri hadn't yet confronted them about the stolen wallet, reluctant to accuse them without having actually witnessed the transgression. There was still the possibility that the wallet had only been lost through Taylor's own carelessness. She had been willing to give them the benefit of the doubt. But this was too much. The music, the theft, and now Taylor's clothes.

Angrily, she folded the empty garment bag and exited the Riding Crop Bar. It was only a few blocks back to her apartment, so she guessed she could walk it in heels. And this was, after all, Key West. No one would look twice.

Daiquiri hurried up Duval, letting her mind wander and feeling her momentary anger dissipate in the warm night breeze. Past two o'clock now, the main drag was emptying out. She was flattered when a group of college boys whistled at her from across the street. Wouldn't they be surprised? she chuckled to herself. Daiquiri enjoyed the attention and unexpected thrill of walking through this tropical paradise in a beautiful dress of silk and lace, feeling entirely feminine. A pedicab driver passed her slowly, ogling her and indicating the empty seat. Daiquiri smiled at the muscular young man and whispered a *no, thank you*. She was enjoying her short walk too much, the silk brushing against her sheer nylon stockings, the sound of her high heels clicking on the sidewalk.

She paused at the corner of Truman Avenue, a block from home, and waited for the light to change. Four strong arms came out of the shadows and lifted her off the ground. Daiquiri tried to scream but a slender, beringed hand clamped across her mouth before she could make a sound. Forcefully, she was propelled backwards into a narrow alleyway between two buildings and thrown to the ground roughly, where the real assault began.

\* \* \* \* \* \* \*

Sipping a cold beer on the afterdeck, Winch watched the sun disappear behind Key West. The bloodstain had finally been washed out, the *Stuffed Ham* was shipshape once again, it was Saturday night and he was suddenly bored and lonely. Maybe, he pondered, I should have gone into town with Laura and whatsisname. Darkness settled upon the boat.

His stash was expired and he drained the suds of his last beer. He tried the TV, but, with only the antenna, all he could get was a Spanish station on UHF. It was too early to go to bed and he was restless.

Winch went below and cleaned himself up, changing into fresher clothes. Back on deck, he locked up and pocketed the keys. He ambled up the dock, past the SuRF building, and turned north, walking towards the highway.

At the intersection of US 1, he found a pay phone and called for a cab, knowing otherwise it would take him half the night to hike into Old Town. While he waited, Winch decided that it would feel good to talk to someone from back home. He dug through his wallet for the business card, wondering what was up with the old house, and dialed Skip Miller's home number in Solomons Island. He called collect and Skip accepted the charges.

"Winch!" crackled the long-distance voice. "Where the hell are you?"

"Key West," he answered, grinning. Man, it was good to hear that old Southern Maryland accent. "How're things up there?"

"Nothing yet on the house. I've shown it to a few people, but no contract so far. You sure you don't want to set an asking price on it?"

"Nah, just sell it and send me the rest of the money. Got a pencil?" Winch recited the address for SuRF, telling Skip to write him in care of the Foundation.

"Geez, Winch," the realtor breathed over the line. "I heard you beat it out of town pretty fast. It's all over town. What happened?"

"A pissed-off father took some shots at me and the boat."

"Damn!"

"No problemo, though. Brant and I got away okay."

"Oh, Winch, I'm sorry. That was all my doing. The guy stopped by your house while I was there and I told him where to find you. I didn't know there'd be trouble."

"All in the past, man. I got a new life. Hey! You were right! It's beautiful down here. You should come on down and visit sometime. I got extra bunk space on the boat."

"Maybe someday I'll get a chance," Skip replied to the invitation, though sharing a vacation with his old burnt-out high-school buddy wasn't exactly Skip's idea of a good time. Too many differences in their lives would keep them forever friendly yet distant.

They chatted for a few more minutes until Winch saw the headlights of his cab sweeping a U-turn across the highway.

"Skip, I gotta go."

"You got a phone number where I can call you?"

"Not yet, but I'm gonna try to get a phone hooked up at the dock. For now, you can leave me a message. I'm pretty tight with the girl in the office." He recited the phone number for SuRF. "Take it easy, Skip, and give my best to Brant and the guys at the Oarhouse."

"So long, Winch," Skip answered and broke the connection. Winch hung up the phone and crawled into the waiting taxi.

Based upon the driver's recommendation, Winch had a few drinks at Sloppy Joe's, which was crammed with tourists and loud music. He drifted through Old Town, sampling brews at Captain Tony's, where he danced with a cute vacationer from Ohio. Down the street at the Hog's Breath Saloon, he had a couple more drinks and then scored some righteous acid from a biker in an alley.

Feeling light as a cloud, Winch bought a fat cigar at the Conch Republic Cigar Factory on Greene Street and strolled through town leaving smoke-rings in his wake. He found a strip bar in an arcade off Duval and spent an hour stuffing dollar bills in g-strings and garters. Stoned and drunk, he bought a Jimmy Buffet tee-shirt at Margaritaville and then accidentally left it behind on the bar after a couple more beers at Barefoot Bob's. He sat on the patio at Mangoes on the corner of Angela Street until last call, watching the tourist women pass by in their mini-skirts and short-shorts. Someone at the bar told him about a party over on South Street and, when all the watering holes had finally closed for the night, he set out in the direction of the Atlantic Ocean, weaving unsteadily up Duval.

Winch managed to get across Truman without being hit by a car and had taken a couple more steps when he thought he heard a muffled moan just off to his right. Winch stopped and stared into the narrow space between two buildings and let his eyes adjust to the dark.

Another cry came, louder, and the sounds of slaps and kicks issued from the alley. As Winch's bloodshot eyes adjusted to the shadows, he saw two tough-looking guys in denim and work-boots. They were beating savagely at something on the ground between them. Swaying on the sidewalk, telling himself that this was none of his business, Winch was about to move on when a prone figure looked up at him with wide white eyes, filled with pain and fear. Her long red curls were a tangled mess and in the dim light Winch could see a streak of blood dripping from her nose.

"Help . . . me." Her mouth formed the words silently.

To Winch, there was nothing lower than a man who beat his woman. Even a space-case like himself knew that a real man never lifted his hand against a lady. Maybe it was the booze, maybe it was the LSD, maybe it was just stupidity. Winch had done a lot of stupid things in his life: taking drugs, marrying once for love and once for money, both stupid choices. And now he was about to do something supremely stupid.

Winch launched himself into the alley. He howled like an enraged rabbit, frightening himself more than anyone else. Nevertheless, startled and caught in the act, the two men paused in their assault and glanced up at the blond steamroller heading their way. They split, like the true cowards they were, pounding out the rear of the alley toward Julia Street. Winch stopped short, breathing hard, his pulse racing. He squatted in the dirt and helped the woman sit up. Despite the beating, she was a striking woman.

"Are you okay?" he puffed. "Do you need an ambulance?"

She shook her head no and her red hair started to slide off her scalp. She grabbed a handful of curls and slid them back into place.

"No. I'm okay," she groaned in a curiously deep voice. "Thanks for your help." She tried to rise and Winch assisted her. Her silk dress was torn and bloodstained. One false eyelash hung by a thread of glue, guarding a puffing eyelid. She massaged bruised ribs beneath her clothing and tried to stand. Her left ankle refused to bear any weight and she nearly crumpled. Winch threw an arm around her waist to keep her from falling. She was a substantial woman. Winch liked that. "I think it's sprained," she gasped in pain.

"You sure you're alright?" Winch didn't think she looked alright.

"I just want to get home," the woman choked. She looked across to him, almost the same height. "I don't think I can walk. Could you help me? It's only a block from here."

Winch helped gather her belongings, a purse and an empty garment bag, while she leaned against the wall for support. He guided her slowly back to the sidewalk and allowed her to cling to him as she limped along Duval. It was late now and the street was deserted. A police car cruised by and showed no interest, just two frazzled tourists making their way home after a Saturday night on the town. Carrying a pocket full of sunshine, Winch was glad they didn't stop.

Winch half-carried her up a long flight of wooden stairs to an apartment above an art gallery, shuttered now for the night. He helped her unlock the door and eased her down on a couch. It was dark in the apartment and Winch fumbled for a light switch.

"Leave it off, please," she said in the darkness. "You can turn on the kitchen light if you want, but I don't want anyone to see me like this."

Nervously, looking to make an exit, Winch banged into the dinette and groped for the kichen wall switch. He found it and flicked it on.

The kitchen was immaculate, pots and pans scrubbed and in the drainer. The warped tile floor sparkled and a full range of cast-iron cookware hung from a rack above the stove. Mrs. Winchell had always put as much effort into her housekeeping, and woe to anyone who left her kitchen a mess. Winch stood in the doorway, peering into the darkened livingroom, the woman he'd rescued but a ghostly shadow on the couch.

"If you're sure you're alright, I should get going," he told her, and started for the door. He had a party on South Street to crash.

"Do you think you could pour me a glass of wine first? I could really use a drink," she requested in a frighteningly masculine voice. Winch nodded silently and found a bottle of Chardonnay in the fridge and a clean wineglass in the drainer. "Have yourself a beer if you like," she called from the other room, and Winch located a cold bottle of Moosehead.

He carried her wine into the livingroom, but she was gone. Light spilled through the crack of the partially open bathroom door down the hall giving him enough illumination to set her glass upon the coffee table in front of the sofa. Fashion magazines were neatly stacked in a pile next to copies of *Scientific American* and *Smithsonian*. A silver-framed photograph depicted a handsome black couple, arms entwined, on their wedding day. A pair of similarly framed portraits graced the wall over the couch. One photo showed an elegant young man in a tuxedo. Its companion portrait captured the lovliness of this same woman in better times. The two faces were so similar they were obviously brother and sister, perhaps fraternal twins.

The rest of the livingroom, as far as Winch could make out in the half-light, was tastefully decorated, a jungle of potted plants lining the front window and a collection of fine African art covering the Dade pine-paneled walls. From the bathroom, he heard water running. His eyes wandered to the couch and fell upon the torn silk dress, discarded on the cushions. He glanced back to the bathroom door and took a sip of Canadian beer.

"Hey," he called. "Thanks for the brew. I took one of the Mooseheads, okay?" No reply. He glanced at the dress again, wondering what she was wearing, and something stirred down low, involuntarily. This was ridiculous. The woman had just been assaulted! How horny and desperate could he be? But still . . .

He spoke out again, trying to keep his voice light. "Hey, you know how you can tell a man who likes Moosehead? Antler burn!"

## KEY MONSTER

A deep chuckle emanated from the bathroom, scaring Winch. The light in the bath clicked off and he heard the door open followed by soft footsteps receding down the lightless hallway. He craned his head to peek around the corner, but could discern only a vague silhouette. Very shapely. Winch heard another door sigh open and then the click of a light switch. The bedroom light flashed on to reveal the sculpted back of the tall black goddess, lithe and lovely and wearing only a pair of tiny bikini underpants, who then disappeared behind the closing door.

"Please make yourself at home," she called through the door. "Put on the stereo if you like."

My, my, thought Winch. Beautiful and grateful, a perfect combination. Maybe she wasn't as injured as he thought. He found a pair of candles atop a cabinet and lit them. It was an expensive stereo, a Marantz, and he slipped in a CD, filling the room with the strings of Jean-Luc Ponty.

"One of my favorite albums," came that disturbingly low voice from the back room. Winch sipped his beer, anticipating. He heard the bedroom door open and licked his lips.

A tall, handsome ebony man in track shorts and muscle shirt limped down the hallway. "By the way," came that now familiar, honeyed voice, "I'm Taylor Jackson." He extended his hand. "Thanks again so much for helping me out."

Circuit breakers in Winch's brain tripped and his nervous system shut down. He couldn't speak. He couldn't move. He could barely breathe. The monster in his pants shriveled and died. The black man stared at him.

"Oh, my," Taylor said at last. "I thought you knew. When my wig came off in the alley. Oh, dear." He sat down on the sofa. Winch found his locomotion circuit and took a step backwards, his green beer bottle hanging limply at his side.

"Gak . . ." was all he could say. People shooting at him, sea monsters, acid of dubious properties, women who weren't. "Gak," he repeated.

Taylor rolled his one undamaged white eye at Winch, shining against his ebony face, a beacon. He sighed and admitted, "Pretty strange, huh?"

Winch finally found his voice. "Seen stranger lately," he managed softly. He glanced at the photos above the couch. Not siblings. Same animal. He swallowed more beer.

Taylor chuckled again. "Stranger than me?" Winch stared back at him.

"Much." He finished the rest of his Moosehead in one gulp.

"Please," his host offered, "have another. Help yourself. You've earned it. And I apologize for your confusion. My fault."

Winch stumbled into the kitchen and snaked another beer from the refrigerator. *Never turn down free food*, had been a saying of his father's, and by extension Winch did not believe in turning down free beer. No matter what the circumstances. He popped the bottlecap and sipped thoughtfully.

He should go, get out of here, take the beer and run. Winch poked his head cautiously around the corner and peeked into the candle-lit livingroom. Taylor was lying back on the sofa, a wet washcloth from the bathroom draped over his battered eye. The wineglass was half empty beside him. Beer-induced fog was drifting over Winch's mind. Home, back to the boat, get out now!

He spun around, unsteady on his feet, and promptly smacked his head into the open door of the fridge. Winch wheeled about and crashed into the dinette again, tumbling over the kitchen chair and landing in a blissfully dazed heap on the shiny linoleum.

Taylor heard the breaking of glassware and hobbled as quickly as his ankle allowed into the kitchen. On the floor, his guest was curled up in a fetal position, already snoring noisily.

"White boys can't drink, either," he mumbled to himself.

From his bedroom closet, Taylor retrieved a light blanket and spread it over his passed-out rescuer. He cleaned up the spilled beer and broken glass, finished his wine and put his hand on the light switch. The man on the floor snored contentedly.

"Goodnight, John-Boy."

Taylor doused the light and went to bed.

\* \* \* \* \* \* \*

He woke up groggy and stiff. Too much to drink last night, was his first muddy thought. He opened one eye warily. Where the hell am I? Unfamiliar room; too many of those lately, too. He closed his eye against the brutal morning light and sheepishly savored the memory of the woman from last night. He rolled over to cuddle against her, but her side of the bed was vacant.

Marco bolted upright in his queen-size bed at the Marineland Motor Inn. The woman he'd brought back to his room last night was gone. He breathed a breath of guilty relief and thought of Maria. Marco winced when he thought how close he had come to betraying his wife. Then he noticed his wallet, lying open upon the bureau. A wave of panic washed over him. He scrambled out of bed and checked the billfold. Empty! His last $165, gone!

Robbed! And the woman he'd met in the bar next door had seemed so nice. He couldn't remember much of anything after they'd stumbled back to his room at the motel, but apparently he'd passed out before they'd gotten to the fun stuff. Marco seethed against the restraints of his raging headache. Wearing only boxers, he flung open the door of his room and squinted against the glare of the parking lot, where his road-battered Suzuki 250 squatted in the long shade of a packed-to-the-gills minivan. He slammed shut the door and threw on some clothes.

So far, after five body-jarring days on the road, he'd suffered two flats, been blown off I-95 once by a passing semi, gotten one ticket for impeding traffic, and had been made fun of by a herd of bikers riding Harleys. He'd finally abandoned the interstate for the more civilized network of US highways, though it had cost him valuable time. His ass was sore from days in the saddle and his pride hurt at being taken for a ride, but only figuratively, by last evening's lady.

A tiny piece of Marco was deeply relieved he'd only been rolled. After seventeen years with Maria, he'd yet to break his vows. But last night, after a half-dozen tequillas in the motel bar, he'd nearly blown it after the woman with the flaming red hair had come on to him. She'd probably planned it all along. He felt stupid and used.

It was just past six on a sun-shiny Sunday morning in North Florida. A hundred yards to the east rolled the vast gray Atlantic. A hundred yards to the west uncoiled the black macadam of A1A. If he went east, he could drown himself now and get it over with. Going west would commit him to another five hundred miles on the underpowered Suzuki. But at the end of that particular fork in the road lay his target: Winch's $900. This whole nightmare journey was the deadbeat's fault. Winch shouldn't have skipped town. Now he would pay.

Marco grabbed his knapsack and pulled the door shut behind him. In the parking lot, next to his bike, he snuck a look through the tinted windows of the unsuspecting minivan. He glanced around. It was early, no one was stirring yet. There, on the floor of the passenger seat, a foolishly forgotten bag. He grabbed a handy rock and smashed out the glass. Mercifully, the car alarm didn't go off--those things only worked when you looked at a car funny. Back home they were so ubiquitous that no one paid any attention to their false alarms. He liked to call them "urban crickets."

Marco popped the door and grabbed the carryall off the floormat. Why didn't these people just paint a sign on their car that said *rob me*? A quick inspection of the bag revealed fifty-two dollars in cash and a couple hundred in travelers cheques. He stashed the loot in his knapsack and kicked the starter on the Suzuki. Blue smoke and a chain-saw noise filled the parking lot. He peeled out onto the narrow highway, cursing at Winch in broken Spanish as the sun rose to his right over the slate-gray ocean.

Marco really sucked when it came to reading maps, understanding geography and following directions in general.

# CHAPTER 10

The flat, white sun kissed the sea goodbye and they released from their nightly embrace. Long narrow pathways of orange light skittered across the calm sea as the firey star lifted higher above the cloud-speckled horizon, growing hotter by the second, burning off the morning haze. Felix Munoz was finally able to discard his rough, damp blanket, folding and stowing it carefully where it would dry after the sodden chill of the night. The drifting raft's nose was pointed dead-center at the rising sun and, in the morning light, he checked the compass and made a small correction with the oars to angle his *balza* a little more to the east-north-east. A fresh current bucked and caught the raft, sweeping it up and around the humped back of Cuba.

Felix baited a hook with a morsel of smoked pork and dropped it overboard, a breakfast of fresh fish on his mind. He kindled a few lumps of charcoal in the bottom of the coffee can and blew on the embers. The *balza* the people of Santa Clarita had constructed for him held all the comforts of home. It was a fine craft, and he was grateful to them. A nimble, deft pull of the line, a flash of the knife and Felix skewered the hapless *mojarra* to roast over the small fire.

He chewed thoughtfully and gazed to the east, the sea around him empty. This most pleasant time of the morning was also the most dangerous for him. Dawn was the favored time for *el Fuerza Aerea de Cuba*, such as it was, to fly their daily training runs offshore of the northern coast. Yesterday morning had brought a small squadron of MiGs screaming directly overhead, though fortune had placed them at too high an altitude to spot his tiny, defenseless raft. At their first appearance, three dark specks in the west, Felix had leapt overboard to bob alongside and hopefully give the impression that the *balza*, if sighted, was vacant and adrift, the *refugiados* washed into the unforgiving ocean. No patrol boats had come to investigate and by the time the sun had been at its peak, he'd finally felt safe again.

Far out into the origins of the Gulf Stream, not a hint of land could be discerned. He had no means of gauging the distance he had covered, but it mattered little as long as a generally easterly course was maintained, and the current assured him of that. Felix prayed for a landfall at Andros, Bimini or Grand Bahama. In his shirt pocket was the phone number of an agent, a Cuban-American in Miami who would arrange his passage to the United States and negotiate a fat contract with the Marlins, Cubs or Yankees. When no warplanes interrupted this placid morning, he cleaned up after breakfast and passed the time reading aloud from a tattered English primer, practicing his new language.

A flying fish broke the surface, silver scales reflecting the morning sunlight, and he glanced up from his book. A little while later, a pod of bottlenose dolphins raked the green water with their swept dorsal fins, rising and falling in undulating ribbons. Felix put the book down again and watched, smiling at their carefree antics until they grew weary of entertaining him and vanished into the distance. He dozed awhile in the pleasant sun until he heard the nearby splashing of the dolphins again. He opened one eye.

The curving backs of the mammals disturbed the surface, a half-dozen of them spread out in a long line, rising and falling in the low swells. At once, they all dove and Felix lost them, wondering where they would reappear. He recited the alphabet aloud in English, practicing. He'd made it as far as *Q,R,S* when his concentration was ripped away by an unworldly sound from beyond the stern of the raft. Felix spun and blinked.

White froth roiled the sea behind him, evidence of something that had been there a moment ago. A thud on the keel pitched the raft to one side, tilting it precariously, supplies breaking free and sliding into the sea. Felix grabbed the mast and clung for his life. The *balza* settled flatly again and all was suddenly calm. A whale? A rock? Felix dove into the warm water without hesitation to salvage the few items that remained floating nearby. He was pulling himself back onto the raft, soaked and angry, when the ocean again bubbled.

Black and sea-cow-like, the head popped out of the sea; but unlike a manatee, it rose up and up and up, carried aloft upon an impossibly long, slender neck. Thirty feet from the astonished *refugiado*, it thrashed the air as if in pain. Charcoal eyes swept over Felix and passed on. The head of the thing tilted back, aimed at the tropical sun, and its gaping maw opened around gleaming white teeth. It bellowed at the sky, a sound of wounded pride and rage and Felix's own screams melded with the sound. It glanced at the Cuban once again and dipped its monstrous head back beneath the waves, a long whipping tail following it under. Felix screamed for another full minute before he fell to his knees and prayed to *la Virgen Maria*.

At last, exhausted and drained, he collapsed on the bamboo deck and wept in fear. As a *niño* near Bahia Honda, he'd heard the fairy tales of a *monstruo marino* lurking off the coast, swallowing up unfortunate fishermen and wrecking their boats. The stories were meant to frighten and entertain the smallest children of the village and he'd stopped believing in them when he was seven years old. But now-*Madre Maria*-he believed again.

Felix ran the sail up the mast and caught the freshening breeze. He grabbed the tiller and heeled the *balza* to port, intending to give the sea monster a wide berth. The raft gained speed and Felix held the tiller in white hands, shaking and rocking back and forth, whispering Hail Marys in both English and Spanish. With his second compass lost and the sun high overhead, bearings became meaningless, except for the direction he had last seen the monster. He took pains to steer any course but that one.

*  *  *  *  *  *  *

Her heat scent is strong here in the deep water. Ahead, coiling around a coral outcrop on the bottom, he sees her, flicking her tail, teasing him. He dives toward her and she springs away, flukes roiling the sand into a brown screen, obscuring her escape. He plummets through the swirling ooze and reemerges into clear water but she is gone. Frustrated, horny, he shoots upward at full power, pierces the border between sea and sky and howls in outrage. Tricked! He sinks again and tries to catch her enticing fragrance, but he only smells the lingering, sour odor of dolphin, his ancient and distant relative.

He rises again to the surface, bumps his back against some firm object and clears it to poke his head again above the flashing waves. He peers around, blinking against the strong light, searching for her. Only a tiny, harmless mancraft nearby, a man itself standing on those queer hind flippers, and no sign of his prospective paramour.

Riven by thwarted sexual desire, he tilts his head up and bellows in grief. His hardened organ shrivels with the ebbing of her memory and the thought of food ricochets around his miniscule brain. He abandons the chase, plunges below the surface and gobbles a tarpon, though his only word for his meal is *food*. A sea turtle strokes by and he follows, swimming across the current, feeding and waiting for her delightful scent to tickle him once again.

*******

Adrift in sleep, dreaming of that long, slender black female, a piercing mechanical sound ran a sudden, serrated knife through his brain. Opening his heavy lids, the midday sun assaulted his retinas, blinding him. Cold, hard tile offered only resistance to his stiffened muscles as his arms flailed at the scratchy covering over his aching body.

Winch blinked against the light and wished someone would answer the phone. Someone did.

"Hello?"

Pulling himself up into a sitting position, Winch squinted around the sun-dappled kitchen. In the doorway, his black faux-goddess held the phone to one ear and tossed a cheery wave in his direction. Winch struggled to put his brain in drive, stripping gears along the way. The overpowering aroma of frying food was underlaid by the gentle scent of perking coffee and freshly sliced citrus. He hung his head, closed his bleary eyes, and tried to focus.

"Oh, no, it's not too early. I was already up," the tall black man with one puffy eye was speaking to the reciever. He cradled the phone, listening, poured a tall glass of tomato juice and handed it to Winch on the floor. Winch sniffed it suspiciously, tossed away the celery stalk and drank half the bloody mary. Vodka poured into his bloodstream and the world steadied.

"Of course I will," Taylor was saying. Yeah, that was his name, Winch remembered foggily. Small, incomplete details swam around his head. He discreetly dipped into his shirt pocket and pulled out a tab of acid, washing it down with the dregs of his juice and alcohol.

"A dry-run tomorrow? That would be fine. Could we get together later today at the boat? I'd like to meet the captain. Uh-huh. No, I have to work at the deck party this afternoon. How about I pick you up in an hour? That'd give us enough time to take inventory, meet the captain and plan what we need to take with us." Taylor scraped a pair of fried eggs from the skillet and added a dollop of hash browns to a pink plastic plate. He set it on the kitchen table, poured a cup of steaming coffee and indicated to his guest to get up off the floor and eat some breakfast. Winch gripped the back of the chair and hauled himself to his numb feet. He collapsed into the chair and smelled the food. Taylor gave him a warm, scary smile and Winch tried to recall what had happened here last night.

"Oh, my god," Taylor laughed into the phone. "He what? Well, he certainly sounds interesting. Are you sure he'll be sober enough to steer? Well, okay, but I'll only be a guide on this tourboat if the captain is competent and we don't all drown. What did you say his name was?" There was a longish pause and Winch pantomimed to his host that he needed ketchup for the potatoes. Taylor snagged the bottle from the refrigerator and rocked the door shut with his hip. He wore short blue cut-offs and a white silk shirt, tied in a bow at the midriff.

"Here you go, honey," he said to Winch as he handed him the Heinz. He listened to a question over the phone.

"Yes, I do have a guest for breakfast. He spent the night here. No, no, it was nothing like that! I had a little trouble with the girls from the club and this nice man was kind enough to help me out last night. His name? Well, I don't even know. He fell asleep on my kitchen floor before he introduced himself. I'm feeding him right now." He pulled the phone away from his lips and whispered to Winch, "She wants to know your name."

Winch pried himself away from his runny eggs and glanced up at the Amazon on the other side of the kitchen. "Winch," he mouthed.

Taylor stared across the room at the guy drinking coffee at his dinette. Thoughts of synchronicity crept through his mind. Into the phone, he said, "Before I tell you what he just told me, could you tell me again the name of this boat we're using? Uh-huh." There was another long pause before Taylor sighed into the phone, still gazing at the wreck of the man in his kitchen. "Yeah, I can believe it. In fact, I think he's eating breakfast in my kitchen right now. Yep, honest to God. Okay, Laura, I'll bring him along. Right, okay, see you in an hour," and he hung up.

Taylor crossed his arms and turned to face Winch across the room. From the pieces of conversation, Winch had already figured out what was going on, but he elected to stow this revelation somewhere within an acid-soaked synapse and think about it later.

"So," Taylor said to him at last. "*You* are the captain of the *Stuffed Ham*." A statement. Winch shoveled another forkful of hash browns into his mouth and nodded.

"That was Laura?" he chewed. Taylor bobbed his head.

"We're to pick her up at the Rainforest and go out to your boat in an hour. I'm supposed to be your tourguide." Winch put down his fork and wiped his mouth with his sleeve. He looked up at Taylor, the semi-effeminate clothing he wore, the memory of last night's costume of dress, wig and high-heels returning.

"So, are you going to be wearing a dress while we're working?"

No," Taylor growled.

Winch sipped his coffee and stared back, his LSD and vodka addled brain working it over. "Good," he said at last. He held out his empty plate. "Any more hash browns?"

\* \* \* \* \* \* \*

Belgian waffles, whipped cream, fresh fruit and mimosas were on the Sunday brunch menu, served by a steward in crisp whites. Steve Stevens gazed across the linen-draped table, over the blue-blazered shoulder of Armand Pringle, to where Janet Sullivan Pringle slipped out of her beach robe to reveal a stunning, microscopic floral bikini. She flicked Steve a probing glance and turned away, exposing perfectly tanned cheeks squeezed around a thong which disappeared into parts unknown, yet desired. Behind mirrored sunglasses, Steve's optic nerves sent emergency signals to his crotch.

"Steve?" Armand spoke in his untraceable European accent. "Another waffle, perhaps?" He signaled the steward with a snap of his delicate, manicured fingers. The steward removed the lid of the silver serving dish and offered another steaming pastry to Mr. Pringle's guest. To the rear, Janet slowly pasted Ban de Soleil down her long legs. The reporter wrenched his attention back to her husband with an effort bordering on Herculean.

"I'm pleased you remembered me, Mr. Pringle," he managed to say.

"Please, call me Armand," the mogul chuckled. "How could I not remember you after that wonderful feature you did when we were in Miami?

It is most fortunate we bumped into one another this week at dinner." He snapped his fingers again and the steward produced a box of cigars. Pringle selected one and the servant lit it for him.

Steve declined the proffered cigar and sat back to watch Pringle smoke. Armand Pringle was a millionaire many times over. He was sole owner, through his corporation, of a major league baseball club. Four big-city newspapers across the continent imitated the worst excesses of the yellowest London tabloids and Armand's skinmagazine, *Knockers*, was challenging *Playboy* and *Penthouse* for a share of the soft-porn market. PBC, the Pringle Broadcasting Company, was making inroads with the American viewing public, particularly in the inner cities with shows like *Big As You Want 'Em*, and *America's Wildest Fantasies*. His movie studio in California, Pringle Productions, pumped out kung-fu films and teenage sex comedies. From his stable of rising starlets he had bedded and wedded Janet Sullivan two years ago, the confounding woman who decorated this one-hundred-fifty foot yacht and was making it impossible for Steve to concentrate. As Mr. Pringle savored his panatela, Mrs. Pringle slipped out of her bikini top and massaged oil into her gleaming breasts. Armand smiled at Steve, oblivious to the havoc his wife was creating in the reporter's mind and body. He mistook Steve's loopy grin for excitement over capturing an exclusive interview with the world's most fascinating man, himself.

"I asked you here today, Steve, so we could set the terms for our interview. Now, of course I want you to do an in-depth, well-researched story, and that can't be done in the space of a single morning. I have so many facets, interests, that it will take many hours to uncover them all."

"You have a proposal, then?" Steve asked, forcing himself to look at Armand's eyes instead of Janet's nipples.

"We will be spending a day bonefishing in the Gulf. I would like you to join us, observe a typical day of our lives, get to know the real Armand Pringle. I will guarantee at least three hours of face-to-face time together and the rest of the time you may observe, question and enjoy the day."

The mid-morning sun beat down on the polished teak deck, the first hot blast of the Key West day penetrating Steve's best blue suit. Pringle removed his tailored blazer and handed it to the steward. Steve sipped his mimosa and the steward topped off the flute again. This could be the story that would propel him back to the big-time, the reporter realized. He was thinking syndication, an executive he knew at Mutual Broadcasting. Over Armand's shoulder, Janet Sullivan cast Steve a come-hither look and pursed her rosy lips.

"When do you want to do this?"

"Tuesday morning. Be aboard by noon. The following day we'll be sailing for San Juan and the French West Indies." Armand raised a warning finger. "No cameras, no assistants. Come alone. You may employ a tape recorder and notebook. You may not interview the crew and you are to respect the privacy of Mrs. Pringle." From Steve's angle, there wasn't very much that was private about Armand's wife.

"Understood," he said.

Pringle nodded and rose from the table, the preliminary discussions at an end. He offered his hand.

Steve remained seated, unable to move. Behind her husband, Janet Sullivan slipped into the on-deck hot-tub and slowly peeled a banana. Through hazy gray eyes, she smiled enticingly and teased the fruit deftly past her wet parted lips, sliding it along the yellow curve to the base of its peel. She flipped the empty skin overboard, the banana gone in one smooth stroke. Steve wavered in his chair, unable to rise, the evidence of his guilty lust straining against the fabric of his slacks.

Armand Pringle dropped his unshaken hand to his side and looked down at his guest worriedly.

"Steve," he soothed. "You should dress more appropriately for the climate, and wear a hat. I do believe you look as though you have had already too much of this beautiful sun."

Steve nodded morosely, sipped some more of his mimosa, and waited for his aching erection to subside. He stared at the blinding white tablecloth and tried to think of anything other than hot tubs, breasts, or the amazing Mrs. Pringle.

# CHAPTER 11

At the toot of the horn outside her motel room, Laura glanced up from her extensive notes. Through the salt-encrusted window, she spied a light-blue Caddy convertible, top down, idling at the curb. Behind the wheel sat a tall, well-defined and beautiful black man wearing a billowy silk shirt. Next to him, in the passenger seat, sprawled a bedraggled white man, in need of a shave and a comb. She folded her papers, slid them into her purse and trotted out to the car.

Taylor flashed her a dazzling smile. Winch opened one red eye and attempted to sit up a little straighter. They exchanged good-mornings and Laura climbed into the back seat. Taylor steered the massive car into a neat U-turn and made a right at the traffic signal onto South Street. A block later, he made a couple of turns to get them down to Flagler for the ride to the east end of Key West. Laura hunched forward on the edge of her seat to lean between the two men.

They traveled through a mostly residential area at a sedate 25 miles-per-hour, the pleasant noon-day sun warming her bare shoulders. Taylor turned down the mellow Motown on the tape deck so he could hear Laura better.

"I did some checking around with the other tour boats on the island, and I think it would be safe to charge each passenger $25 for an afternoon trip to the reef, including snacks and soft-drinks. If it's okay with you guys, we'll split the money three ways."

"Uh-uh," muttered Winch. "The *Ham* is a big boat, expensive to run. Gotta fuel her, lay in food and drinks. I'm not paying for all that outta my share."

Laura had anticipated this. "I was talking net," she countered. "After we cover all the boat expenses, then we'll make the split. I'm donating my share to SuRF anyway."

"The money's not all that important to me," Taylor said pleasantly from behind the wheel. "I'm just doing this to help out and it sounds like it'll be fun."

Winch cast a suspicious eye at the drag queen. He believed that no one wasn't interested in money. Laura pressed on.

"Each of us has a specific job. Winch will of course be the captain, responsible for the safety and maintenance of the tour boat. You'll figure the best routes to the reefs and make sure we have enough supplies on board to keep the tourists happy." Winch nodded in silent agreement.

"Taylor, since you're our marine biologist, you'll narrate the tours, give them the whole nature thing, history, fish, birds and such."

"You planned to put these people in the water, didn't you?" asked Taylor, looking at Laura in the rear-view mirror.

Laura slumped. She hadn't thought of that. In her mind, she'd imagined just motoring out to the reef and staring overboard into the water. Taylor heard her silence and filled in a solution.

"Because I'm Red Cross and PADI certified. It wouldn't be a problem at all to scrape up some snorkels, masks and fins. Then we could actually dive to the reefs, at least the shallow ones." Laura was nodding, excited. Winch looked bored.

"That's a great idea! Of course! Why should the customers hang over the side when they can actually get in the water?" She patted Taylor on the shoulder. "As for me, I'll stay in the office and schedule the tours and keep the books. Also, I'll take care of all the legal stuff, licensing, insurance."

"Where is this reef?" asked Winch, staring straight ahead through the windshield.

"I've got some charts at the office. You and Taylor can look over them and decide which reefs would be best."

At the end of the road they made a left and then a right, merging with the traffic on US 1. The Caddy crossed the bridge to Stock Island and Taylor made another right, following Laura's directions.

"So," Winch spoke up, "when do we get underway?" He sounded grouchy and Laura, wanting to keep the captain happy, reached over the back of his seat and patted his snarled blonde hair. It was like an electric shock to his system. She'd touched him! His mood shifted as the lab-bred chemicals in his bloodstream raced to the pleasure-center of his fried brain.

"If you think we'll be ready," she said gently, "I'd like us to go out tomorrow to do a dry run, just the three of us. Tuesday, we can make any adjustments we need and make sure the boat is stocked and we know what we're doing. Then on Wednesday, we've got the SuRF media tour."

"Media tour?" asked Taylor as the car rolled to a stop in the parking lot. They all climbed out and strolled onto the pier.

"Uh-huh," Laura explained. "I've been calling every radio and TV station and newspaper between here and Miami. I've got to drum up some publicity for the Foundation."

"And for the *Stuffed Ham*," Winch reminded her.

"Of course," she replied. "They go hand-in-hand. Without you and your boat, SuRF is as good as dead, and so's my job." Winch nodded. They stopped in front of his vessel.

"Any TV stations coming on this media-thing yet?" Taylor asked as he ran his eyes over the long white cruiser.

Laura looked abashed. "So far, only Steve is a definite. I've also gotten half-a-dozen 'we'll get back to you's, so I guess we'll just see who turns up. I'm going to ask Steve to make some more calls for me, try to get a few camera crews on board. After we're done here, I'm going downtown to put up the rest of the advertising fliers and then meet Steve for dinner to talk to him about it."

It didn't make Winch happy to hear the name *Steve* sprinkled so liberally through Laura's speech. He tried to be cool.

"So tomorrow we go out," Winch bitched, "and Wednesday we haul a bunch of non-paying customers. So when do we make money?"

Laura wagged a finger at him, just like his mother used to do when he'd been whining. "Tomorrow we make sure we know what we're doing. The media tour is for free publicity. Both are important. Thursday or Friday at the latest we'll take our first paying customers out to the reef. Oh," she paused, reluctant to bring up the last necessary detail she had to cover with Winch. "About the name . . ."

Winch spun on her, glaring.

"Yeah," spoke Taylor in all innocence, "I've been meaning to ask where you came up with *Stuffed Ham*?"

"It's got to be changed," Laura persisted. "Nobody is going to book a tour on a boat called the *Stuffed Ham*."

Winch breathed quickly, shallowly. This was a blatant insult to his mother's memory! He was wounded and grew sullen. Taylor sensed his tension and drifted away, pretending to study the lines of the boat. Laura stared hard at Winch for a moment, refusing to yield, and then saw how hurt the captain was. She looked down at her deck shoes. Maybe she shouldn't push it, she thought. The unfortunate appellation would be a barrier to their success, true, but maybe they could work around it, not mention the name in the fliers, keep the stern of the boat turned away from the tourists as they boarded so they wouldn't know they were going to sea in a yacht named after a hunk of pork. *Stuffed Ham* was not a name that inspired confidence.

"How about *Queen Conch?*" ventured Taylor softly. Winch shot him an evil glance. "Or *Lady Gay?* We could shoot for the pink triangle market." Laura scrunched her face in doubt. She looked carefully at the captain and prepared to offer her own suggestions.

"I know the name is important to you, Winch, but it's more important that we do everything we can to ensure our success. And, frankly, I can't see a Jewish family from Chicago taking a cruise on a boat called the *Stuffed Ham*." Laura saw the resolve on Winch's face soften and she plunged ahead with her ideas.

"How do you feel about the *SuRF Rider?*" she prodded. It had been her first choice, but Winch grimaced. She tried another. "Does *Reef Explorer* work for you?" He turned his back on her.

But Winch was wavering. He knew Laura had a point. And though he personally loved the name *Stuffed Ham,* he remembered the derision he had endured back at the Oarhouse when he'd announced the christening of his boat. Gil, Cap'n Mattson, Brant, and the others had been as amused by the name almost as much as they'd been the day Winch had revealed he'd seen a sea monster in the bay.

Taylor was sitting on the edge of the pier, his brown legs dangling above the water, gazing at Brant's intricate mural on the bow. He was fascinated. It looked a great deal like a plesiosaur. The artist had done a beautiful job, colors blending perfectly, the graceful sweep of the sea monster seemingly rising from the surrounding water. It was inspiring. In the long, tense silence, Taylor pursed his lips and let out a slow breath.

"How about . . ." he began. Winch didn't move, gazing at Houseboat Row across the channel. Laura lifted her head hopefully. Taylor pointed at the mural.

"How about, the *Key Monster?*"

Laura loved it instantly, but was afraid to speak. It would be the captain's call. Winch turned slowly and stared at the painting on the bow, but saw instead the living creature that pursued him. Taylor shrugged apologetically.

"Just a thought," he mumbled. "We're in the Keys, and it's a monster of a boat. The mural is perfect, too." He trailed off, his idea apparently rejected. Wavelets lapped against the pilings. Gulls wheeled overhead, screeching at each other. The palm trees on shore rustled their fronds with papery scraping sounds. Moments passed.

Only Winch saw the true irony of Taylor's suggestion. That goddam critter had chased him all the way to the Keys, had invaded his dreams and inspired some goofy teenager in Maryland to desecrate his boat. He might as well accept it.

"*Key Monster*," he sighed. His two partners were watching him, waiting. He sighed again. "Fuck, why not?"

Laura shocked him with an embrace and a kiss to his stubbly cheek. Taylor sat with his feet swinging over the water and applauded softly, smiling. Even Winch managed a small grin.

"*Key Monster*," he repeated again, letting the sound roll out of his mouth. Yeah, Winch had to agree. He kinda liked it. And, he was sure, Mom would understand.

\* \* \* \* \* \* \*

Sighting down the short barrel, Big Jim Quinn applied careful, even pressure to the trigger. Fifty feet away, the silhouette of Eugene Winchell presented him with an irresistible, unmoving target. Legs spread wide in a shooter's stance, one hand holding the Smith & Wesson revolver, the other steadying his wrist, Big Jim eased out a slow, well-controlled breath as he squeezed off a round at his quarry. The .38 caliber slug drilled a tunnel through the thick air and found its target, punching a small neat hole into the space just above Winchell's left eyebrow. An almost perfect head shot.

Big Jim smiled to himself in satisfaction and finished emptying the gun: two more rounds to the head, one to the throat and a pair of clean misses. Not bad. He slipped the heavy, headphone-shaped sound baffle from his ears and stepped back from the firing line to reload. The target bobbed and swayed as it raced toward him, dangling from a steel cable which ran between Quinn and the back of the room. He snapped the paper target from the clip and examined the silhouette that represented the soon-to-be-late Eugene

Winchell. Big Jim fastened a fresh target into place and pressed the button to return it to the far end of the range.

Finding a target range had been easier than he had expected. Florida was a big handgun state. The clerk at the sporting goods store on Roosevelt Boulevard, where Big Jim had purchased ammunition, had cheerfully given directions to this indoor range on Stock Island. He'd wasted six rounds, missing the target completely, until the range-master had offered a little coaching, after which Big Jim's aim had rapidly improved. He reloaded his pistol and checked his watch. He had to get back to the Pier House soon.

Big Jim hurridly paid the cashier and heaved himself into the silver Mercedes. It had taken three hours of paperwork and $250 to retrieve the car from the impound lot Saturday morning, and it still sputtered and misfired as he peeled rubber onto Route 1 south. Ten minutes later and almost an hour late, he collected a fuming Liza at the Pier House and wheeled off into traffic for their romantic dinner.

Liza spoke not a single word to him on the short ride. She remained aloof and silent as he parked the car and led her into the big white restaurant on the corner of Whitehead and Caroline Streets, a place she'd picked from one of her tourist brochures. As the hostess guided them to a table for two in the garden, he glanced at Liza's stony countenance and sighed deeply. It was going to take some serious bottles of wine to get her into the sack tonight, he figured.

* * * * * * *

Rolf Schenk eyed the ridiculous uniform. Gray shorts, blue tee-shirt with *Key West PD* stenciled on the back in yellow block letters. Black running shoes over blue athletic socks. A heavy leather belt, the only cool part of the cop's outfit, hung with nightstick, handcuffs and, tucked into a holster, what Rolf identified as a Glock 9mm. The cop confronted him from astride a silly, fat-wheeled bicycle. It was all Rolf could do not to laugh out loud.

"You've got to break up the group," the cop told him, blocking Rolf's path with the modified mountain bike. Rolf crossed his arms defiantly and stared back at the cop's strawberry hair which poked from under the white bicycle helmet. Probably a faggot, he decided. Well, no fag cop was going to order around the First General of the Aryan-American Freedom Forces.

"We have a right to be here," Rolf sneered. "Haven't you ever read the Constitution? Freedom of assembly, freedom of association!"

"Uh-huh," replied the bike cop. "I've read it, but you don't have the right to intimidate people, or to block the sidewalk."

Rolf laughed. Freedom to block the sidewalk! That's something the founding fathers forgot to put in their sacred document. When the AAFF controlled the country that would be one amendment they'd have to include. Right after they deported all the blacks, fags and foreigners!

Today, they were nearly fifty strong, counting the three who were being hustled away from the rear of the procession by the brown-shirted Gestapo. By the end of the week, as others arrived for the Congress of Leaders, they would number over one hundred, representing nearly every state. The AAFF had reserved an entire campground up on Sugarloaf Key, welcoming their brothers for a week of strategic planning, weapons training and carousing in Key West's myriad bars. The Keys had been chosen for their warm weather, the scarcity of black faces, and for Florida's liberal gun laws. And here was some stupid, fag pig telling him he had no rights!

The Key West bike cop pushed his helmet from his brow with a thick thumb. He sighed at Rolf. "Look, pal. You guys are breaking at least three city ordinances. Either you disperse now or you'll spend the rest of your vacation in the Monroe County jail."

A red haze descended over Rolf's eyes, blazing white anger filling his head. He stared into the cop's tanned face defiantly, but knew that, as First General, he had to be smarter than the enemy, play by their rules if necessary, at least for now. He noted the cop's badge number and grew calm. He'd remember this pig when they began the round-up of the traitors. His day would come.

Without another word, Rolf turned to his men on the sidewalk and raised his arm in the air. He spun it in a circle, their battlefield signal to disperse and rendezvous later at designated point Beta. Grumbling, but raggedly obeying orders, the shaven-headed men and boys drifted away in small groups, laughing, flipping off the cops and cursing the system. Rolf was left with two of his senior lieutenants, Bobby from Georgia and Ray from California. The bike cop looked satisfied and nodded at them. Rolf gave him the finger and led his two remaining men away.

The police split up too, trailing the scattered knots of skinheads to the various bars around Old Town, keeping a lid on things. Rolf and his associates were followed by their bike cop shadow who slowly pedaled along behind them. The First General of the Aryan-American Freedom Forces led Bobby and Ray up Duval Street, where they settled into the first dark bar they came to. They ordered long-neck Buds. The cop sat astride his bike outside the bar and kept a vigil on them through the open doorway. He wondered again why he had left that cushy deputy job back in upstate Minnesota where nothing ever happened. Except, he remembered, for that homicide with the wood-chipper a few years back. He shuddered.

\* \* \* \* \* \* \*

Daiquiri Taylor parted the front window curtain with her long red nails and gazed out on the Duval Street scene. Today's deck party at the Rainforest Resort had gone splendidly. The manager had made her the permanent hostess afterward, and she celebrated now in her apartment with a glass of white wine, enjoying the satiny feel of the revealing dress that clung to her smooth black body. And, there was the excitement of signing on aboard the *Key Monster*, a name Taylor had suggested, a couple of afternoons a week. Things were working out wonderfully.

Below on the street, weekend tourists strolled toward the busy end of Duval, returning to their cruise ships, hunting for an inexpensive meal, or on their way to Mallory Square for the sunset celebration. But a black cloud was about to obscure the festivities.

The swarm of Bermuda-shorted and tee-shirt-garbed visitors abruptly dispersed, fleeing into open shops and doorways, hurrying to yield the sidewalk to a thick throng of men marching from the opposite direction. Daiquiri stared down in revulsion.

There were about fifty of them, acting as though Old Town was their own. In mismatched uniforms of steel-toed work boots, stained tee-shirts and torn blue-jeans, they swelled up the street under the late-afternoon sun, shaved heads unprotected from the burning rays. Daiquiri held her breath and shuddered. Skinheads!

She'd seen them before, in New York and Miami. Maybe not this particular group, but others of their ilk, bashing gays and harassing people of color and other so-called non-Americans. Trailing a short distance behind, three Monroe County Sheriff's vehicles kept an eye out, waiting to head off trouble. Tourist families crossed the street, out of the skinheads' path, as they approached. Two Key West bike cops paralleled the punks, keeping them confined to the sidewalk as they threatened to spill into the street. A sick feeling knotted Daiquiri's stomach as she witnessed the intrusion of the intolerant into this tolerant community.

She stared in horror as two beautiful men, holding hands, blundered unsuspecting from the doorway of a gift shop into the tail end of the mob. Daiquiri could see the expression of surprise and fear on their faces as they found themselves surrounded by a jeering host of neo-nazis. Brown-uniformed deputies spilled from the cruisers and broke up the disturbance before any real damage was done, and the pair of men fled down the street to safety. The deputies hauled several of the skinheads to the idling patrol cars. One of the bike cops pedaled to the front of the crowd and conducted a heated discussion with a squat, beefy man, who sported a swastika tattoo on his bare shoulder. Daiquiri saw gesturing, but their words were inaudible through the closed windows of her apartment. Nevertheless, it became clear the officer had made his point.

The tattooed man waved at his men. He shouted mutely at them. Grudgingly, the group splintered into gangs of three or four and melted away up the sidestreets. The cops split up too, keeping the clots of skinheads in sight. Daiquiri gulped the last of her wine and felt her brow break out in a cold sweat despite the chill of the air conditioning. She stumbled to the kitchen and poured an uncharacteristic second glass of chablis.

How could this possibly happen in Key West? Except for Angel and Samantha, she'd felt safe and unmolested up until now. Daiquiri returned to the big picture window and gazed back down upon the restored peace of her little adopted town. There was no longer any trace of the hate, as though it had only been a very bad dream. She gently probed the slight swelling around her eye, hidden by layers of make-up, and silently prayed that the skinheads might happen to encounter her two tormentors. Let hate deal with hate, she thought as she pulled the curtains shut against the nightmare.

## KEY MONSTER

\* \* \* \* \* \* \*

Miami was closer than he'd thought, Marco mused as the steel and glass skyline came into view. The little Suzuki whined as he banked through an intersection at the directional marker for Downtown. He slowed as he entered heavy traffic, searching for the intersection of US 1. At this rate, he'd be in the Keys before midnight, and Winch would be coughing up dollar bills by sunrise. He chuckled as he swerved to avoid a pothole and then slammed on both brakes, skidding onto the shoulder.

Breathing heavily, he shook his head beneath his helmet, refusing to believe the sign he'd just passed. He used his legs to push the bike backwards until he had brought himself even with the green and white metal signpost planted next to the road. He read it twice and hung his head. It said, "Welcome to Jacksonville."

After a moment to gather himself and to await the next break in traffic, Marco wheeled around in a U-turn and aimed the Suzuki back the way he had just come. He grimmaced and spit out a flying bug that had lodged between his teeth. A little while later, he passed, again, the Marineland Motel and another notice which read, "Miami, 290 miles." You're a dead man, Winch, he thought. A dead man.

# CHAPTER 12

They are dancing that tentative, teasing waltz that will lead them to that most intimate of dances. Cautiously circling, diving and rising, tenderly brushing their bodies against one another. They test, they tickle and tumble beneath the embrace of the soft blue water.

She is ready now, as ready as he has been all along. Coiling and caressing, kissing the sandy sea-bottom, the intricate courtship ritual is coming to a close. She is sleek, black and waiting for him, ready to submit at last. The days and nights of pursuit are at an end. With a touch of a fluke she flips to her side, raising a curtain of fine silt and he gently lowers himself upon her. Bright fish scatter from the waters that are disturbed by their mating motions.

In the time it takes to swallow a tarpon, it is over. He lolls dumbly exhausted on the bottom, watching her swim lazily away toward deeper waters, her long tail swishing back at him in farewell. She carries his seed.

A new stirring grows inside of him. Hunger. He stretches himself, drifting upwards upon the current and through a school of unsuspecting snapper. He fills his belly and has already forgotten the old urges which have brought him to these tropical seas. He munches on a small sea turtle and waits for nature to tell him what to do next.

\* \* \* \* \* \*

Her feet were killing her. She'd been up one side of Duval and down the other, leaving stacks of fliers in stores, restaurants and galleries. She'd covered the waterfront, Mallory Square and the motels and guest houses near Southernmost Point. Laura was down to a handful of fliers now as she trudged along Whitehead Street, the dappled shade of papertrees and oaks soothing her and offering protection from the late-afternoon sun. She passed Blue Heaven and left a few fliers at the bar where she and Steve had had their first drink together.

Try as she might, there was no denying the spark of attraction Laura felt toward the reporter. Her husband, left behind with his bucks, his booze and his bimbos in Maryland, had already receded to a dull toothache of a memory. She tried to conjure his face, but the details of his chin, his eyes, his hands were all slipping away.

It had been a long time, she realized, since she had studied his features carefully, her interest in Big Jim waning over the last year or two. Desperately, she had even signed them up for Marriage Encounter, sitting alone in their ornate living room, bags packed for a weekend of marital rediscovery, only to receive the inevitable last-minute phone call, offering his weak apologies and a lame excuse about some clients who needed to be entertained on the boat.

Laura shivered at the remembrance despite the sub-tropical heat which embraced her. Big Jim was the past. Perhaps, she thought, Steve was the future. Oh, maybe not a long-term future, because she refused to look that far ahead. But today, and maybe next week, there were possibilities open to her that never existed before. Soon she would phone her attorney in Baltimore and they would take care of the simple details of the break-up. She wanted nothing from the marriage except for the nearly seven years she had lost, wasted away on Big Jim Quinn.

At the corner of Caroline and Whitehead, Laura climbed the steps of Kelly's Caribbean Bar & Grill in the old Pan-Am building. She stepped into the shade of the veranda and searched the premises for her dining partner. Paddle fans overhead stirred the air, ruffling her blonde tresses. Beyond the veranda, a yard full of people dined al-fresco under the buttonwood and mango trees. To her right, inside, a cool wood-paneled bar beckoned her. She hauled open the heavy oak door and entered the taproom, letting her green eyes adjust after the intense glare of the Key West sun.

Leaning on one corner of the bar, Steve Stevens nursed an icy gin and tonic, waiting patiently for her. He wore his regulation khakis and a perfectly pressed gray sports-shirt. His salt and pepper hair was freshly barbered, combed into a studiously nonchalant wave over his lightly tanned face. Laura ran a moist hand down her skirt, smoothing a wrinkle, and, smiling, approached him. He beamed at her as she came to him, utterly irresistible in her bouncy yellow pleated skirt and casual sky-blue blouse, and when he leaned forward to greet her with a kiss on her cheek, this time she didn't duck. Maybe not a long-term future, she caught herself thinking, but she'd worry about the future tomorrow.

\* \* \* \* \* \* \*

Big Jim shoveled in his stone crab salad and worked on his third vodka martini. Liza picked at her cracked conch salad and barely tasted her glass of wine. The sun found its way through the leaves and scattered weaving spots of white light upon the linen tablecloth. The gay Cuban busboy scooped up an empty martini glass from the table and sashayed away, humming something bright and Latin. Big Jim set down his fork and stared at the servant with naked hostility.

"Christ, they're everywhere in this town," he muttered. "Fuckin' freaks." He looked at his plate suspiciously, the stone crab and lettuce wilting in the heat. "How do I know it's safe to even eat this?"

Liza glanced up at him questioningly.

"I could get AIDS or something," he explained in a too-loud voice. At nearby tables, heads turned in his direction and then away. Liza continued to stare at him.

"And did you see what they're charging for this stuff?" he added indignantly. "It's worse than Baltimore! This whole town is one giant rip-off. God, I can't wait to get my hands on the boat so we can get the hell out of here."

Liza slapped her fork on the table and sat back in her chair, crossing her arms defensively. "So, that's the only reason we're here? Your goddam boat?"

Big Jim looked up at her, startled. Hey, he'd only been making conversation. What the hell was *her* problem? He decided to ask.

"What the hell's your problem? You wanted to go out for a nice dinner, we're out for a nice dinner. What, that's not enough now?"

Liza gave him a long measured look. "No," she said petulantly, then leaned forward, resting her elbows on the table. Big Jim leaned forward a little too, and she caught him trying to look down the front of her dress. She pinched the fabric around her shoulders, tugging the clingy garment higher over her bosom and sat back with a grunt. She took a long drink of her wine.

Big Jim sat back too. "So, what? Ya wanta do somethin' after dinner?"

"For starters, yeah." She raised her arms in the air and waved them around at the scenery. "Look at this place. It's gorgeous! Hibiscus, palm trees, always eighty degrees, and all you can do is bitch about your boat, the homos, and all the money you're spending. And what about me, huh? What the fuck about me?"

Big Jim's head tried to retreat into the collar of his shirt, turtle-like. Shit! He'd never seen Liza pissed off before. It reminded him uncomfortably of Laura.

Laura. Now there was a whole other problem. He wondered where she was and whom she was doing it with. Once this problem with the boat was settled, well, then he'd deal with his runaway wife. Dump him, huh? No fucking way! He was dumping *her*! He gulped some more martini and signaled his undoubtedly fag waiter for another. He dared another glance at the seething Liza.

"What?"

"I want to do something fun, together, the two of us. I'm sick of sitting around waiting for you."

"You went shopping today, didn't you? Isn't that something?"

"Yeah, alone. And thanks for the dress, by the way," she answered snidely.

"Oh, izzat new? S'nice." For the first time he looked beyond her cleavage and noticed the crisp white cotton of Liza's new sundress. Her newly browned skin contrasted nicely with the material and Big Jim mentally drooled over the flesh that was hidden within its folds. Liza recognized that look in his eyes and knew she had the upper hand. She wasn't above using sex as a weapon.

Liza dug into her purse and produced a gold Visa card. She flipped it across the table at him. "I've got the receipt, too, if you want it." He declined.

"How about we go back to the room after dinner?" he winked at her. She smiled back at him smoothly.

"I bought some new underwear today too," she said, perfectly aware of what she was doing to him. "But if you want to get a peek you're gonna have to try a little harder."

Big Jim gulped. Something in his pants stiffened. "Um, what did you have in mind?"

Liza sat up straight, triumphant. It always worked, it always would, at least as long as she had these breasts, these legs. Men. She pitied them.

"Three things," she whispered. "Tonight, we go out dancing. That's non-negotiable. Tomorrow, you'll pick something for us to do. Parasailing, the treasure museum, biking, whatever, as long as we do it together." Big Jim nodded, thinking of some deep-sea fishing. Yeah, that would be okay.

"What's the third thing?"

Liza bit her crimsoned lip and stood up. "Then I get to pick another thing to do, for later in the week. Do we have a deal?"

"Deal," he agreed eagerly. She picked up her purse.

"Where're you goin'?"

"Ladies room," Liza answered. "Maybe I'll see if there are any brochures in the lobby, find something fun for us to do." She walked away from the shaded table, mounting the steps to the veranda. Big Jim watched her tight little behind wiggle up the stairs, wondering what color underwear she'd bought. He hoped it was black.

\* \* \* \* \* \* \*

It was too hot outside to eat a big meal, and the air-conditioned bar was crammed. Steve and Laura opted to share an appetizer of chilled shrimp over a bottle of cold Riesling on the veranda. Steve sipped his wine and stared across the cozy table for two at Laura's emerald eyes, watching her delicate fingers pull the pink shell from a morsel of white flesh. He knew he was a helpless sucker for cute blondes. He tried to pay attention to Laura's words, but his mind kept drifting away, picturing them alone together in his trailer.

At her elbow, the last half-dozen advertising handbills threatened to scatter in the breeze. Laura tried to snatch the fliers before they took flight, but a few got away, fluttering across the veranda. She held on to the rest of them and handed one to Steve.

"I've got these out all over town," she said proudly. Steve read the handbill, photocopied on light blue paper: *The Save the Reef Foundation, offering tours of the local reefs aboard the Key Monster. Leaving daily from Stock Island at 2pm, $25 per-person, cash bar, free hors d'oeuvres and* *complimentary use of snorkeling gear.* He handed the flier back and she waved it off with sticky fingers.

"Keep it," she said. "I wanted to ask you about advertising the tours on your radio station. Would it be very expensive?"

Steve shook his head. "I'm afraid I don't know our current rates. That would be the sales department, but I could find out for you. Maybe get you a discount."

She smiled at him and munched more shrimp. God, this was exciting! Pulling this whole enterprise together, setting it all up, seeing that it was successful. And to be doing it with Steve's help, that was an extra bonus. Laura knew she damn well wasn't ready to embark on anything serious with the newsman, but she found herself pulled into his orbit, circling him at a safe distance, not quite ready to fall into the gravity of a real relationship, but not really doing anything to prevent it either. She would let nature take its course, and either the planets would align or they wouldn't. Brushing her fingers, Steve helped himself to a shrimp and asked a question.

"Are you still doing your media tour Wednesday?"

Laura nodded between bites. "Yes, but so far you're the only positive reply. Channel 8 said they'd send a cameraman if they could, but no one from Miami's called back. Even the editor I spoke with at the *Citizen* said he couldn't promise anything."

Steve dabbed his lips with his linen napkin. "Maybe I could make a few calls for you," he offered. Laura grinned at him.

"I was hoping you'd say that."

Steve returned a weak smile, knowing how empty his offer was. In the world of Miami television, two years was an eternity and most of his friends and contacts had moved on to bigger, or smaller, markets. Doug Johnson might still be producing at Channel 4, or might not. He'd call and find out. Though, truthfully, he'd prefer to keep Laura all to himself.

A striking brunette in a skin-tight white sundress strode across the veranda and passed close by their table. Steve couldn't help but notice her, and Laura couldn't help but notice Steve noticing. She bristled a little as the attractive woman disappeared into the ladies room.

"Pretty girl," Laura remarked stiffly. Steve's attention snapped back to his tablemate.

"Not bad," he lied, his brain fumbling for the words to save himself. "But nothing at all compared to my companion this evening."

The sentence hung in the silence between them. Finally Laura shook her head and smiled to herself. Men. But it was a nice diving catch Steve had made, and to be honest, the woman *had* been quite a looker. She secretly forgave this unsuspecting male and chastised herself for her annoyance, reminding herself that she had no claim on Steve. Yet.

\* \* \* \* \* \* \*

Liza coated her lips with a fresh layer of gloss and brushed her black hair in the mirror. She stared at her reflection. Here she was, 28 and single, with a body that could make men beg. So why the hell was she wasting her time with Big Jim Quinn?

Oh, sure, he had money to burn and he wasn't too overweight for a man of his advanced age. He was even kind of distinguished looking, in a Jack Nicholson sort of way. His long-promised divorce was in the works, thanks to Laura, who'd finally run out on him. According to Big Jim, it had only been a matter of time before his wife ran off with one of her many indiscretions. Now he'd be free to marry her. But did Liza really want him?

*No!* a voice within her resounded. Jim was a graying lump, except when he was in bed, when he somehow became an Olympic athlete. During their first time, she'd understood why he was called Big Jim. She smiled at the memory, then frowned. But sex, though it was great, wasn't enough. In time, he'd tire of and abandon Liza for some even younger hot-to-trot flame, just as he'd done to Laura.

Liza wondered about Big Jim's wife. They'd never met, thank God. Liza didn't think she could stand the guilt. But how had that poor woman stood almost seven years of this man? It had only been a few months for Liza and she was growing disenchanted already. The cute sales clerk who'd sold her this sexy dress today had made no secret of his desire for her. He couldn't have been more than 22 and was built like Adonis. Very flattering, and for a moment tempting. But Liza had a firm rule never to cheat on a boyfriend, even when the boyfriend was cheating on a spouse.

Liza exited the stuffy restroom and browsed the adjacent gift shop, wondering if every bar and restaurant in Key West had a gift shop. She chose a few tourist brochures, searching for something fun to do. Back outside, on the veranda, a gust of wind lifted the hem of her sundress a few inches higher. A pile of papers stacked on a nearby table fluttered to the floor at her feet.

Despite the turns her life had taken lately, Liza had been well-raised by her adoptive parents. Politeness and helpfulness had been household hallmarks, and her training had been thorough. Sometimes, like a few minutes ago with Jim, her temper got the best of her, but her pique was always quick to pass. Already she was feeling sorry that she had argued with Big Jim.

Liza reflexively bent and scooped the papers up before they could go any farther, and approached the table from where they had escaped.

A pretty blonde, maybe five years older than Liza, sat at the table across from a man with graying hair, in his early forties perhaps. Another younger woman-older man scenario, she thought tiredly. Maybe that 22-year-old sales clerk was still around somewhere? Liza held the papers out to the couple at the table.

"Excuse me," she interrupted their love-struck gazes. "I believe these are yours?"

The woman looked up at her.

"Oh, my fliers. Yes, thank you."

Liza handed them over and noticed that the man was trying not to examine her too closely. He glanced down at his shrimp. As Liza placed the blue papers on the table, she read for the first time what was printed on them. The woman saw Liza reading and spoke up.

"It's a great tour! Lots of sun and fun!" she enthused. "Best reef tour in the Keys." Liza looked over at the blonde and smiled back.

"Sounds like fun. Do I need a reservation?"

"Oh, no, we've always got room for one more on the *Key Monster*! How long will you be in town?"

"Probably til the end of the week," Liza answered, still perusing the flier. It did sound interesting. This could be the third fun-thing she and Big Jim could do together. She glanced up. "Mind if I keep this?"

"Please!" the reef-tour woman replied.

"Thanks," Liza said as she turned and walked back toward the steps to the outdoor tables. Her earlier doubts faded. Yes, she thought. This was it-- a romantic day on the water with Big Jim. She reminded herself to buy him a tube of sunblock. He burned so easily.

\* \* \* \* \* \* \*

"Our first passenger!" Laura exalted. Steve returned a half-smile and wagged a finger at her.

"Can't count it until the money's in the till," he admonished her, but Laura refused to be discouraged. In fact, she felt almost cocky. She caressed Steve with her eyes.

"C'mon," she teased. "Drive me home and I'll buy you a nightcap at the pool bar. I feel rich tonight."

Steve met her challenging gaze and stood up, taking her hand.

"An offer far too good to pass up," he grinned.

He steered Laura out of Kelly's and into the cooling Key West evening.

\* \* \* \* \* \* \*

Liza took her seat across from Big Jim and handed him the pastel-colored flier. He hardly glanced at it.

"What took you so long? I thought maybe you'd run out on me." It was supposed to have been a joke, but the remark had a mean edge to it. The sting of Laura's abandonment was still fresh and he felt somehow vulnerable. The woman on the veranda had reminded him vaguely of his wife. Same shape, same hair color, but too far away to make out her face.

Liza let his barbed comment pass.

"I found something for us to do later this week," she told him, indicating the flier in his hand. He didn't look at it, setting it on the table.

"Who was that you were talking to?" he probed. Big Jim glanced up at the veranda in the distance. He was slightly nearsighted and had left his glasses in the hotel room. The table he'd seen Liza hovering over was vacant now, just a glimpse of the tall man and the skinny blonde receding into the nightfall as they left the restaurant, hand in hand.

"A lady gave me this flier," Liza replied frostily, "and we talked about it a bit, that's all. Jeesh, you're insecure!"

Big Jim looked at her and shook his head. "No, it's not that. It's just that, well, I couldn't see her too clear, but she looked a lot like Laura." Whoops! The words were out and the evening had been wrecked. Big Jim recognized his tactical error and cringed.

"Laura, Laura, Laura!" Liza spat and threw down her napkin. Politeness be damned, her temper always won out. "You're down here with me, remember? You called *me*, said you didn't want to be alone? 'How about a trip to paradise, baby?' Remember?"

There was more on Liza's mind and on her sharp tongue, but Big Jim managed to tune most of it out. He gazed into the empty spaces of the veranda and pondered.

No, it couldn't have been. The woman he'd seen was too happy, too carefree, dressed way too sexy. Laura was uptight, wore her dresses no more than an inch above the knee. Maybe she had left him, but Big Jim would have bet his left nut that Laura was too scared of life to run any farther than her mother's house in Michigan, where he expected to eventually find her cowering. The incessant drone of Liza's voice brought him back to reality.

"And another thing," she was saying. "You can forget any whoopie tonight, but we're still going out dancing after dinner, got it?"

Big Jim nodded absently and raised his finger to signal the homo waiter for a vodka refill. He glanced once more at the veranda and wondered.

# CHAPTER 13

The approaching storm made its presence known with rapid bursts of heat lightning, low on the horizon. Small craft out on the Gulf scurried before the setting sun, seeking shelter from the rising wind in the lee of the Keys. From far off, trembling across the gray water, echoes of thunder washed over the island town. Mothers hurried to take their laundry in from backyard clotheslines, towels, shirts and underwear snapping in the freshening breeze. Wise bartenders rolled down rain curtains. Clerks hurried their racks of tee-shirts off Front Street into the shelter of their cramped shops. Tourists sought refuge in whatever tavern, boutique or ice-cream store was handy. The first fat drops of rain pattered on the pavement.

The remnants of the sunset cast faint light upon the violet anvil-shaped clouds storming in from the west. A burst of hot white light and a concussion of rapidly expanding gasses trumpeted the arrival of the storm. Torrents of fresh, cool water swept the gutters, washing away the weekend's array of trash, scrubbing the town clean. Key West battened down for the Sunday night thunderstorm.

*******

In the pouring rain, yet oblivious to it, Winch sat on the bow of the *Key Monster*, watching the storm. His long blonde hair was matted, water cascading down his naked back as he sat cross-legged on the slippery deck. Soft music from the all-weather speakers competed with hard rolls of thunder across Cow Key Channel. Steely Dan sang of love lost and love squandered. In the steady rain, Winch was unable to discern which drops fell from the sky and which fell from his eyes.

Below, in his vee-berth, the tourist girl from Dothan, Alabama slumbered. She was not yet twenty, and Winch had swept her from the hardscrabble roadside bar along Route 1 and brought her back to his boat just ahead of the wind and rain, laughing drunkenly and tugging at each others clothes before they were even aboard. He'd pointed out the freshly repainted transom, the words *Key Monster, Key West, FL* neatly lettered in his own hand, and she'd giggled and fallen into his embrace.

A half-bottle of wine, a couple of bong hits, and she was naked and playful. She'd teased him with her small, pointed breasts, and he'd led her back to the rumpled berth in his cabin, kicking discarded shorts and socks out of the way.

She'd made love. He'd had sex. And when it was mercifully over, she'd rolled onto her flat belly and murmured that he'd been pretty good, for an old guy.

In the pre-dawn, with the big boat gently riding the swells of the storm, Winch listened to the music mocking him, Donald Fagen singing "Hey, Nineteen" and reminding him that they couldn't dance together or talk at all.

\* \* \* \* \* \* \*

Sheets of rainwater coated the motel window, washing the salt from the glass. Laura lay on her bed in the dark, the only illumination coming from the arcs of lightning stitching the black sky. Thunder rattled the panes and pierced her.

After another romantic glass of wine at the pool bar, Laura had allowed Steve to walk her back to her room. Pausing in the threshold, deftly blocking his passage, she'd brushed his stubbly cheek with her lips and sent him on his way with muttered, confused apologies. Too much. Too soon. Without bothering to undress, she'd fallen onto the bedspread, clutching the pillow to her breast, and gazed out into the storm, wishing that sleep would come. It would not.

Instead, her mind was a riot of unbidden, unwelcome images. She saw Steve, handsome and attentive. She saw her husband, bloated and preoccupied. She saw herself, torn between the two, between freedom and failure, the failure of her marriage, her life and her dreams.

A flash lit up the window, and she saw a reflection of herself, for only an instant. She didn't like what she saw.

\* \* \* \* \* \* \*

Almost imperceptibly, the aluminum-skinned trailer rocked in the wind. Rain tap-danced on the ceiling, echoing the length of the hollow tube Steve called home, just two blocks north of Laura's motel room. Over a glass of mineral water and two aspirins, Steve tugged his bathrobe tighter and repositioned the bucket next to the sofa to catch the rainwater that dripped relentlessly from the faulty roof. It splashed in perfect time to the beat of Willie Nelson, the soft guitar strains crossing the eight feet of black, rainy night that separated him from the trailer next door. Steve sat back on the couch and smiled, though he knew he needed to sleep soon. Another morning shift at WRKW in just a few hours, and the insufferable Maxx Rock to suffer.

Nodding in time to his neighbor's plaintive music, he thought of Laura, of how she was slowly drifting toward him. Not tonight, certainly, but soon. He could wait. He could be patient. And when the time came, he would be gentle.

He reflected upon his exile in Key West, how it hadn't really been so bad after all, an un-terrible place to pass one's life away in the slow lane. And he thought of Armand Pringle, the possible key to his escape from this paradise and his return to the rat-race of a big-city newsroom. Tantalizing visions of Mrs. Pringle danced before his eyes. His thoughts became a confused jumble.

Steve thumbed the TV remote and switched to the Weather Channel, wondering how soon this unexpected storm would pass.

\* \* \* \* \* \* \*

The bedroom door was locked. Thick walls and double-paned glass kept the thunder from disturbing her. Liza had danced and danced with every good looking guy in the club, fending each one off as he got too close to her and exchanging him for the next, until she was exhausted and it was closing time. Big Jim had remained chained to the bar, drinking bourbon and watching TV. She hadn't cared a whit. It had turned out to be a most interesting night for her.

Wordlessly, they had returned to their room, the silence between them as loud as the storm. There had been no question that tonight she would sleep alone, unmolested. She awakened but once, briefly, and returned to bed quickly and softly, having caught Big Jim in the act.

Liza pulled the covers higher over her shoulders, stirring just slightly at the soothing rumble of thunder, a remembered pleasure of childhood, and returned to her deep, untroubled slumber.

\* \* \* \* \* \* \*

A bolt of lightning etched the glass of the balcony door, throwing the dark hotel suite into a crazy pattern of light and shadow. Big Jim Quinn drank twelve-year-old scotch, straight-up, from a twelve-ounce glass. His bulk rested comfortably in the padded recliner, which faced the view of the rain-pounded harbor. Thunder beat against the windows and bled through, matching the pulse in his temples. For a while, after Liza had gone to bed and locked the door against him, he'd tried to concentrate on the business news on CNBC, but the cable had gone out shortly after reporting that the Dow Jones would start the new week down 113 points.

Each flash of lightning brought a new image to his bloodshot eyes. He saw his wife, languid and lean, lying sprawled across some asshole's bed, her legs spread wide and waiting. He saw the *LauraLee*, desecrated by the presence of a scruffy, long-haired freak. He saw Liza, grinding her hips against some over-jeweleried jerk from Ohio in some Old Town bar. He saw his mother, smiling as she removed a hot apple pie from the oven in his boyhood kitchen.

He blinked. What?

Big Jim gazed at the glass of scotch in his hand and slowly poured it onto the carpet. Let the maid clean it up; he'd had enough tonight.

He glanced at the bolted bedroom door, filled with hate. "You can forget any whoopie tonight," she'd told him after dinner. He'd see about that.

With a grunt, Big Jim struggled out of the chair and switched on a lamp. He found the local phone directory in a drawer, a thin volume, and leafed through the yellow pages. With a fat finger, he punched a series of numbers and spoke softly, slurringly, into the receiver.

Twenty minutes later, with a fresh glass of booze and a more optimistic outlook, he ushered the young woman from the escort service to the couch and indulged his appetites. Twenty minutes after that, she was gone, credit card imprint in hand.

Big Jim dozed on the sofa, his immediate needs slaked, while the storm swept across the island.

*******

The phone rang again. Reluctantly, he answered, knowing already to expect the now familiar voices. Thunder shook the walls of the apartment, nearly drowning out the hissing words that bled into his ear.

"Get out now, nigger!"

He slammed the receiver down on it's cradle. It was past 3 A.M. The sixth-or was it the seventh?-call tonight. Not always the same voice. Two different voices, actually. One tough and hard, the other lilting, teasing, the trace of a lisp. Angel and Samantha. Taylor stared at the phone, breathing hard.

What had he done to them? Come to Key West to seek a new life? Been a better dancer? Been born black and beautiful? They hated him, despite his efforts to cultivate their friendship and forgiving them for the rude pranks they had visited upon him.

The telephone rang, insistent. Four, five, six times. Taylor snatched it from the hook.

"Leave me alone!" he cried into the mouthpiece, and once more slapped the phone down. He contemplated tearing the wires from the wall, hurling the apparatus down the dark stairwell into the alley, but he was a practical man. His tormentors would revel in the knowledge that they had goaded him into damaging his own property just to spite them. He'd never succumb to their bait. He waited in the darkness, hating himself for his inability to stand up to them, and sweated.

Another series of summons. He flipped the phone over and lowered the volume to its minimum, allowing it to buzz unanswered. So much hate of late, invading his island sanctuary. The girls from the club. Skinheads! The

KEY MONSTER

soft chirping of the telephone continued on and off for another two hours. When would they tire of this game?

Taylor was not a plotter, but plot he did. Somewhere there was a solution, and he used his scientifically trained mind to experiment, test and analyze. And in the moments before dawn, as the thunderstorm slackened, he proofed out a formula which would offer him relief from the nightmare of hatred that ensnared him.

\* \* \* \* \* \* \*

There was no rain yet, thanks to God; only the distant flash of lightning and the subsequent peel of thunder over the black horizon. But he was alone, unprotected from the elements should nature turn her wrath upon him, and he clung helplessly to the rough mast as the *balza* pitched up and down over the ten-foot swells.

With each burst of crackling white light, Felix scanned the seas for signs of land, an indication of a passing boat, or, most worrisome of all, the bubbling, roiling water that would prove that he was not alone upon the ocean. The horrid memories of his encounter with the black sea serpent tormented him, forcing him to question his own sanity after days adrift at sea, solitary and dried to a husk with thirst.

Felix felt the sting of undrinkable seawater wash over him as he hugged the mast with his powerful pitching arm. He clasped his hands together in supplication, and prayed as the pelting rain swept in.

\* \* \* \* \* \* \*

The rain gently tickled the thick glass over his cell window. Just an evening shower, but tonight he was warm and dry and not forced to endure the weather by the side of the road or in some cheap motel room. The blanket over his body was soft and the pillow contained actual feathers. Dinner, hot and tasty, had been served promptly, a repast of steaming beef stew, fresh bread, milk, and apple cobbler for dessert.

Marco rolled over on his bunk, thankful that the Palm Beach police had seen fit to arrest him for failing to signal a left turn and for being a Latino, lingering after dark in this enclave of exclusivity. It was the first time in his entire life that he had been officially discriminated against, enduring the handcuffs, mug shots, fingerprinting and racial slurs he'd been denied back in Maryland. And he had Winch to thank for it.

Marco's one phone call had been to Maria, who'd fussed over him and promised to wire the modest bail, telling him that she and the children missed him. And he missed them. This crusade against the man who owed him nine hundred paltry dollars had become less important than the feeling he had for his family, separated from them by a thousand miles and his own proud, foolish vendetta against Winch. He yearned for the pleasure of tucking his littlest into her bed and whispering sweet *buenos noches* to her. The remembrance of the warmth of his wife's embrace before he drifted into sleep sustained him upon the comfortable mattress as he recalled her ample body.

As he drifted off, his last thoughts were of Winch. The captain had always been a good customer, maybe needing a little reminding now and again, and Marco's heart softened. His client, his friend, wouldn't have skipped out on him without a good reason. Perhaps the cause of his flight had been the ugly fat *gringo* who had made such dire threats against the blond seafarer.

Marco slipped off into peaceful sleep, the soft south Florida rain tapping on his wire-reinforced window. He resolved to finish his conflict with Winch peacefully. And, he knew, at the end of his quest lay his emerald isle, his ancestral homeland, that palm-fringed place called Puerto Rico.

# CHAPTER 14

"Hey, Steve! Are you allowed to say *frigate* on the air? Frigate, frigate, frigate!"

Steve paused in the middle of his morning news report on the port call being made by the Navy's newest warship, the *USS Robert Dole*. He'd known that Maxx wouldn't be able to let the word *frigate* slip by unremarked upon. The greasy, coffee-stained slob in the next booth leered through the double-paned glass at Steve. The newsman felt the familiar flutter of a developing headache.

"While we're on the subject of boats," Steve pressed on, "we have part two of our special series, 'Saving Houseboat Row.'" He clipped his mike and hit the reel-to-reel playback for the pre-recorded three-minute package, but he wasn't fast enough. Maxx still managed to jump in with one more *Frigate!* before the tape rolled.

Steve Stevens settled back in his chair and slipped off his headphones. A three minute break from Maxx Rock's moronic blatherings. He sighed and rubbed his temples.

His Sunday dinner date with Laura was still fresh in his mind. He remembered every detail, what she wore, how her hair was fixed, the intoxicating aroma of her perfume. The recollection of the way she tilted back her head and laughed and the feel of her fingers entwined in his as he walked her to her motel. And that sweet, sudden brush of her lips against his cheek just before she'd sent him home. It had been maddening! It had been a long time since Steve had been in love with someone, but he still recognized the symptoms. And it looked like 'ol Cupid had shot him once again. He resolved to be patient and understanding. Laura was going through a divorce and would need time to heal before she was ready to fall into his arms. Steve just wished she would heal a little faster. Lost in his reverie, Steve stared vacantly at the turning reels on the tape deck.

"Steve! Earth to Steve!" Maxx broke into the sudden silence. The report had ended and the newsman dove for his mike key. "Just fascinating," Maxx's voice came, dripping with sarcasm. "Ya got a weather report for us?"

"Another perfect day for the Lower Keys, sunny and breezy, 82 degrees our high. Chance of a late-day thunderstorm, 30 percent. Tonight, partly cloudy and mild, lows in the upper 60s, and more sunshine tomorrow with highs in the mid-80s. Currently, it's mostly sunny and 78 degrees at 8:55. I'm Steve Stevens, Key Rock News!"

The stacatto guitar of Blondie's "One Way or Another" crept under his outro as Maxx Rock jumped back in. "Ah, here's a little lady I'd like to show around my frigate! This is Debbie Harry and Blondie on the Maxx Rock Morning Mess at Key Rock 102, WRKW!" The music came up at a post and the red on-air light winked out in the hallway.

Steve rewound his taped report and tossed his cans next to the mike. He picked up his news copy and exited the booth where Grant Davies lay in wait for him, arms crossed and scowling. Steve had to tilt his head down to look the station manager in the eye.

"Hey, bucko," Grant sneered up at him. "I thought I told you to deep-six those reports on Houseboat Row? Now you're doing a *series*? And whatever happened to that feature on the Save the Reef people I told you to put together?" The little dictator wore a suit jacket, vest and tie despite the unhospitable climate. Why the hell was he all dressed up, Steve pondered? "I'm working on the SuRF piece," Steve defended wearily. "I've got one interview on tape and there's a special briefing set up on their boat Wednesday. Now, if you'll excuse me, Grant." He pushed past his boss in the narrow hall. Grant called after him.

"No more dead-air, Steve! And I want to hear more banter between you and Maxx! Got it?"

Steve entered his office and slammed the door. He stared at the phone knowing that he needed to make some calls but couldn't bring himself to lift the receiver. His mind fogged over with thoughts of a double homicide, Maxx Rock and Grant Davies lying stiff and bloody in the studio. His lip curled in an unconscious smile.

A soft tap on his office door snapped him back to the real world. He glanced up as the door slowly swung inward.

"Busy, Steve?"

The news director rose and grinned, extending his hand to the middle-aged man in the sports shirt and slacks who entered his office.

"I'll be damned! Bob Davies! How the hell are you?"

The owner of WRKW-FM, Steve's old roommate, grinned back and pumped Steve's hand. "Never better. I just sold three stations and bought five more in Atlanta, Orlando and Macon. Closed the deals yesterday and thought I'd take some time to see how Grant was doing with WRKW."

The newsman grimaced at the mention of Bob's son. Why had Bob given Steve a job, only to saddle him with his evil spawn? He was about to avoid the subject when the face of an angel appeared over Bob's left shoulder. The station owner glanced back and motioned her into the office.

"Steve, I'd like you to meet a friend of mine, Janet Sullivan." Armand Pringle's wife, the naked woman in the hot-tub, offered Steve a limp handshake, her cool gray eyes flicking absently about the office, noticing everything but Steve himself. All thoughts of Grant, Maxx and houseboats fled in the face of this vision before him. He took in the enticing red sweep of hair pulled back into a frizzy ponytail and the skintight blue bodysuit that molded itself over her outstanding breasts.

"We've met before," he reminded her, smiling his best.

"Really?" she replied dryly, with only a subtle glance at his face before she turned away. "I don't recall."

They had seen each other twice in the last week and she didn't remember him? She'd *stripped* for him! Steve's mouth hung open, unable to form a coherent sentence. Janet Sullivan turned to the station owner.

"Bob, do you mind if I visit that announcer, Maxx? Whenever I'm in the Keys it seems I just can't start my day without his program."

Bob Davies touched her silky shoulder. "Of course, Janet. You know where the studio is?"

"Uh-hmmm," she purred and left the newsroom upon her four-inch stiletto heels, the sound clicking down the tiled hallway. Steve let out a breath. She didn't remember him, a crushing blow to the ego. That performance in the hot-tub could have been for anybody.

"Quite a woman," Bob said admiringly. "Her husband, Armand Pringle, is the man I just bought those five stations from. He had some other business today and asked me to show Janet around." He sighed, glancing wistfully up the hall. "If only . . ."

Steve grinned and punched his old buddy on the arm. "You dog." They both laughed.

"So, Steve, how are things going? Still trying to get back to television, or are you happy here in Key West?" The owner gazed openly at his friend.

Steve thought about the question for a second. Working at Key Rock was a far cry from Miami, but the town really seemed to suit him, eccentric as it was. There were no earth-shaking stories to cover, but it was becoming comfortable. A future with Laura was a possibility, and the laid-back atmosphere of the Keys had put an end to the minor ulcer which had plagued him on the mainland. Except for the dual annoyances of Bob's son and Maxx, things were going pretty well, he had to admit.

"It's not too bad here," he confessed. "I've met some interesting people, the food's good and I don't have to deal with the traffic on the interstate."

"That's good to hear, Steve. But, I wanted to tell you that one of the TV stations I bought is a UHF up in Macon, Fox affiliate, I think. I need a news director up there, wondered if you might be interested?"

"Macon, Georgia?" Steve shook his head immediately. "Sorry, but I'd rather stay here; that is, if you still want me."

"Hell, yes! Your newscasts are the heart of WRKW as far as I'm concerned." He rubbed his shaven chin thoughtfully. "Personally, I can't stand the format Grant instituted. Classic rock. Bah!" Steve smiled again. Back at the University of Florida, Bob's taste in music had begun and ended with jazz. He'd hated the Stones, Zep and the Who equally, even when the old songs had been new. "So why don't you make him change it?" Steve ventured.

"I'm thinking about it," Bob admitted. "The station is about breaking even and I've got to put Grant somewhere in the organization." He raised his eyebrows a little sadly. "Who else would hire him?" A tough thing for a father to admit about his only son, but an admission Bob seemed used to making.

"You know, Steve," he went on. "There are two other rock stations in Key West. So I ask Grant, why are we going head to head? He gives me some BS about the differences between modern rock and alternative rock and classic rock. Well, it's all garbage to me. If I were GM, and not just the owner, I'd give this town some jazz, or maybe all-news. But as long as he isn't losing money, I guess I'll stand it."

"What do you think of our morning man?" Steve asked, seeing an opening. His friend scowled.

"Maxx Rock?" He spit the name out as if it were a piece of bad meat. "A total jerk. A disgrace. But, he has the ratings, the only daypart we're beating the competition."

Steve's heart sank. It looked as if he'd never be free of Maxx, unless he wanted to move to Macon. Not an option.

"But I didn't come by to just talk business," Bob Davies said. "I wanted to say hello and see if you were free to join Janet and me for lunch today. About one?"

Steve snickered. "I thought you'd want to keep her all to yourself."

"I wish," Bob grinned. "Grant's mother would kill me!"

Steve checked his schedule and agreed to meet them at one o'clock at Camille's on Duval.

"I have to go talk to Grant, but I'll see you at lunch," Bob said, checking his expensive wristwatch. A Rolex Oyster, Steve noticed with a twinge of jealousy. He thanked Bob for stopping by and sat back down at his desk as his old buddy left.

That Janet Sullivan is a piece of work, Steve thought to himself. Stripping naked right before his eyes, literally behind her husband's back. And that trick with the banana! He shook his head in wonder and turned up the volume on his monitor. Ranting bled from the speakers.

"So, were there a lot of guys in the room when you were flashing your boobs for *Knockers*? Camera people, lighting, all that?"

"Oh, Maxx," Janet Sullivan giggled on the air. "I'm just sorry *you* weren't there when I did my video! You know I'm your number one fan."

Steve nearly gagged.

"Same here, baby! Hey! Are those things real? Can I touch them?"

Steve threw his coffee cup at the monitor.

\* \* \* \* \* \* \*

Marco stood next to his Suzuki 250, parked beside the highway at the western tip of Marathon. Before him, disappearing over the horizon, stretched the Seven Mile Bridge. There was no other land in sight.

Marco didn't mind bridges, he just didn't like not being able to see land. He glanced again at the sign by the road that announced the landmark.

## KEY MONSTER

Could it really be seven miles across open ocean? He shuddered, picking at the memory of an Arnold Schwarzenegger movie he'd seen. The Seven Mile Bridge had been blown up, collapsed into the sea. Had they repaired it? Would it collapse again? Reluctantly, he saddled up and kicked the sputtering engine to life.

Somehow, he thought, he'd get across this impossible span, make it to Key West and find Winch. At this point, Marco would be glad just to see a familiar face. He could almost forget the debt the captain owed. He'd had it with fast food, beachfront jails and roaring truckers. All he wanted to do now was cross this bridge and get a cold beer, his reward for surviving seven miles of land-free hell. If he made it across.

At a break in traffic, Marco pulled out slowly onto Route 1. He coaxed the bike up the gentle incline as Marathon receded in his cracked mirror. He kept the gearbox in second up the long slope, knuckles white on the handgrips, his eyes sweeping ahead for any sudden breaks in the pavement, any missing section of bridge. Brakes screeched and horns blared as other vehicles came from behind at speed and were suddenly forced to squeeze around the barely moving motorcycle. Marco stared sternly ahead, refusing to look at the panorama of the sweet blue ocean to his left and right. He maintained a cautious 25 miles-per-hour and swore to sell the Suzuki and take the bus home.

\* \* \* \* \* \* \*

He'd told Winch that it would be a snap to sell. But it hadn't just been easy, it had been huge! Skip Miller leaned his vast bulk back in his office chair and scanned the sales contract again. Bending forward, he ran his pudgy fingers over the calculator keys, figuring his commission, and beamed. This was big, the biggest in three or four years!

Skip flipped through his Rolodex and found the number he'd been given. He lifted the receiver and punched eleven digits. The phone began ringing, distantly. After seven unanswered rings, he hung up. His eyes drifted to the print on the wall of his office, the waterfront view of Key West. He shook his head and smiled. "Gene, you lucky bastard," he mused and then set about cutting Winch's check.

\* \* \* \* \* \* \*

Liza had been pretty drunk Sunday night, but not so drunk that she hadn't heard the unmistakable sounds of copulation outside her bedroom door. Masked by the thunder of the tropical storm, she'd peeked into the livingroom and glimpsed Big Jim wrestling with some bimbo on the sofa. Who she was, Liza didn't care one bit. Because now she had him by the short hairs.

She asked Big Jim to please pass her another mini-muffin from the silver tray. He did so silently, keeping his red-rimmed eyes on his plate. His temples throbbed. He'd had a long night and was paying the price this morning. Liza had always been a good drinker. A full night's sleep and two aspirins always refreshed her no matter how many drinks she'd consumed. Last night, though, had been a whopper!

Sometime after midnight, at some bar whose name she couldn't recall, Liza had danced, danced, danced, while Big Jim sat sullenly at the bar. Dancing made him sweat, he'd said, so she had danced with anybody who'd asked. College boys, sailors from the base, even an elderly local. She'd shocked them all, dirty dancing, grinding herself up and down their sweat-slickened bodies. Big Jim had barely paid attention once he'd tipped the bartender ten bucks to put the TV over the bar on CNBC for the business preview.

Liza applied a glob of key lime jelly to her muffin and popped it in her mouth. The tender, rain-freshened morning air wafted across the pool, and the dazzling sun shone off the water, making Big Jim's eyes smart. Good.

A little before closing, she'd been slow dancing with some guy who'd been buying her drinks all evening. He'd had short dirty-blonde hair and three earrings in each lobe. As they swayed to the music, hidden from Big Jim by the crowd
and the smoke, her ear had been nibbled expertly, and she had returned the gesture with a long, wet, passionately sloppy kiss. The voice in her ear told her to meet in the hallway near the bathrooms, next to the pay phones.

Moments later, in the relative privacy of the back hallway, she'd allowed her new friend to slip a hand up her skirt, caressing the crotch of her new bikini underwear. She'd moaned in pleasure, driving her tongue past narrow lips. She hadn't made out in a bar like this since her senior year of high school, and it was delicious.

Liza had fumbled for the pants zipper and eased it down. She'd slid her hand through the gap and felt around. Nothing. She continued to kiss as her eyes slowly opened and then went wide. Her partner broke away and whispered, "How about we go back to my place, Lipstick?"

Liza ran an exploratory hand across the front of the guy's shirt. Definitely boobs in there.

"You're a woman," Liza had said, stupefied.

"And so are you," breathed the tenor voice in her ear. "Lets get out of here." The tongue washed Liza's ear. The room spun.

"Can't," Liza had managed, still caught in the embrace. "Gotta go." She took half a step away and smoothed her skirt back down. The handsome lesbian pulled a pen and paper from her denim pocket and scribbled. She lifted Liza's skirt and tucked the note into the front of her underwear. Liza was too drunk to resist.

"My number," she sighed, disappointed. She kissed Liza again, quickly. "Call me."

Liza had stumbled back into the barroom. The crowd was thinning. Big Jim still sat at the bar, his eyes riveted to the television. She'd wiped her lipstick with a cocktail napkin and tapped him on the shoulder.

"We can go now," was all she'd said. Big Jim left a twenty on the bar and drove her back to the Pier House. As she'd undressed, locked alone in the bedroom, Liza found the scrap of paper in her panties. She'd balled it up and aimed for the wastebasket, then paused. She wasn't about to give up men. Yet. She smoothed the paper and dropped it into her purse. Bobbie might be a woman, but she kissed better than Big Jim. Liza fell asleep to the rhythm of the storm, awakened only briefly by the panting and moaning outside her door.

She was beginning to see that there were all sorts of alternatives to Big Jim Quinn, even things she'd never before considered. But for now, as long as he was footing the bills for this vacation in paradise, she'd stay with him, squeezing him for all he was worth. There'd be time enough to dump him when they got back home.

"Headache?" she asked much too brightly. Big Jim didn't reply, the hammering in his head drowning out any answer he could give. "Poor baby," she soothed, with a hint of mockery in her voice. She sat back, full of breakfast, and gazed across the shimmering hotel pool.

"I thought we'd start today with a little shopping," she said evenly. She pulled a handful of tourist brochures from her purse. Big Jim groaned. She ignored the sound.

"Then we can do lunch. I heard about this fantastic Italian place on Duval. After that, I want to take the Conch Train Tour, see the Shipwreck Museum, oh, and the aquarium! The sunset cruise on the *Rumrunner* looks like fun..." The words became a droning buzz to Big Jim's ears. Feebly, he signaled their waitress for another bloody mary.

"Oh, and Jim?" Liza interjected. "Don't try anything else with any hookers again, okay?" She paused a beat. "Now, where were we? Oh, sunset cruise, and dinner at Louie's Backyard..."

How did she know? Big Jim wondered.

How could I not? Liza telegraphed with her eyes.

She smiled across the table and tortured him with more tourist brochures.

# CHAPTER 15

Laura cast the bow line toward the pier. It fell short by a good three feet and splashed into the green water. At the helm, Winch shook his head. Laura had been right. They definitely needed the practice.

The low grumble of the twin diesels fell a notch as the captain engaged reverse and edged the *Key Monster* away from the dock. Taylor scrambled forward with a gaff to snag the fallen line.

"Forget it," called Winch. "We'll get it later." He shoved the throttles ahead and angled the big cruiser out into the channel.

Winch's headache, and the heartache of the night before, dissipated in the cool seabreeze off the Atlantic. He was back in his own element, piloting his boat across the expanse of green and gray ocean, the swell and roll of the water precisely matching the rhythm of his body. He'd been born alongside the water, he'd lived on the water and he hoped that, when his time came, and like his old man, he would die on the water. Had his passengers known this, they might have been more nervous with him as captain than they already were.

Winch peeled off his black tee-shirt and donned a pair of cheap sunglasses against the killer glare reflecting off the whitecaps. Strings of unraveling denim fringed his thighs, the remains of his favorite pair of cut-offs. His feet were bare upon the non-skid deck.

The girl from Alabama had disembarked before ten, and Winch had been relieved when she'd gone. He was a thirty-eight year-old stoner, twice her age, but the distance between them had been caused by more than just years. It had almost been a cultural thing, as though they were from two entirely different countries, speaking mutually unintelligible languages. She had left bleary-eyed and hung-over, with only the slightest peck on his stubbled cheek and leaving behind no promises to see him again. He'd not been sorry to see her go. Winch shook the painful image from his cloudy brain and unrolled the chart next to the helm.

In the bright midday sun of the Keys, Taylor sat cross-legged on the bow, finding it hard to reconcile the nightmare of skinheads and the telephoned threats from Angel and Samantha with the clean, crisp air of the open sea on this gorgeous day. The *Key Monster* planed off nicely, gliding over the light chop and Taylor's night terrors fled into the slipstream.

Taylor wore modest blue bathing trunks and a fresh linen shirt. He kicked off his deck shoes and leaned back on his elbows, allowing the cool air to rush over his body. Laura picked up the unused gaff and cautiously edged her way back to the stern. She hopped down onto the deck, landing beside Winch, and was thrown off-balance, unfamiliar with the predictable movements of a pitching boat. Winch shot out a skinny arm and seized her around her waist before she could tumble to the deck.

For a moment, their eyes locked, blue versus green, the colors of the ocean. Here, thought Winch, are eyes I could lose myself in, eyes nearly as old as my own. But that was the limit of what they shared in common. They too, like the girl from Dothan, had grown up in different worlds, seen different things through those mismatched eyes. Gently, Winch released her and returned his attention to the chart.

"Gotta work on those sea-legs," he muttered to her, hiding his feelings and musing that her legs were actually just fine.

Laura rested a hand on the back of his chair to steady herself. The look in Winch's eyes, before he'd turned away, was a look she'd recognized, and it saddened her. The captain was a nice guy, a little off-kilter perhaps, handsome in an off-beat way, but there was no spark between them. Damn it! She didn't want any sparks! Not between her and Winch, nor between her and Steve. This is what had kept her up half the night during last night's storm. I have to rule this out now, she thought, tell him where things stand between us, that this is merely business and that I have no desire to run my hands across his smooth, bare chest and tangle my fingers in that long golden hair . . .

A thump on the deck beside her startled her. Taylor had jumped down from the gunwale, an excited smile playing around the corners of his mouth. He patted Laura on the shoulder and slid next to Winch.

"So," he said to the captain, "you've picked out a good reef?"

Winch turned the wheel, aiming the boat in a southeasterly heading, and pointed to a spot on the chart he'd circled. Taylor crowded in for a better look.

"Pelican Shoal Reef?"

"About 4½ miles offshore," Winch nodded.

"How deep?"

"Chart says ten feet."

"Good for an easy dive," Taylor mused. "Provided there's anything to see."

"Four and a half miles," breathed Laura, peering between the two men. "Wouldn't that be, what do they call it, in international waters?"

Winch smiled and checked the compass. Behind them, the Keys were fading in the haze. "Actually, the territorial waters extend three nautical miles beyond Pelican Shoal."

"I've never been outside the country," she said.

"Not a problem," Winch grinned. "After we check out the reef, we'll take a little spin out to sea and you'll be officially out of the U.S.of A. You won't even need a passport."

"Cool," Taylor added. "I could get to like this seafaring life."

"Here," Winch said to Laura, taking her hand and placing it upon the wheel. He pointed to the compass. "Keep it steady on 120 degrees." He stepped away and Laura looked flustered.

"Where are you going?" she called worriedly to his back. "What if I hit something?" But Winch had disappeared through the cabin door. Laura licked her lips and stared hard at the numbers on the compass, her fingers white on the wheel. Taylor grinned helplessly.

"So, what do you think of our captain?" he asked her.

"He seems to know what he's doing, once we're on the water. On land," she shrugged, "that's another story."

There came a slight clatter from below and a moment later Winch popped back on deck with an armful of beer bottles. Laura chanced a glance away from the compass to give him a disapproving look.

"Since this is supposed to be our practice run," he explained as he opened a beer, "I stocked the bar. You know, for realism." Taylor declined the offered beer. Winch cracked open a second and set it on the console next to Laura.

"Please," she said, "no drinking when we've got customers on board, okay?"

Winch nodded reluctantly, but he understood. Back in Maryland he'd usually observed the same rule, at least until the dock was in sight. But he noticed that Laura, thrilled with the power of piloting the big boat, lifted the open beer and took a short sip. He glanced at the chart and looked off to port where the water was flatter, a softer shade of blue. He tapped her on the shoulder.

"I'll take it now," he said, and Laura turned the helm over to the captain, just slightly relieved.

Winch throttled the *Key Monster* down, gazing over the side as the water grew shallower. He steered in a wide arc, searching the sea until he was satisfied and dropped the engines into neutral. They bobbed peacefully upon the slow swells.

"We're here," he announced.

Taylor gazed raptly over the side into the clear water. "Oh, she's a beauty!" Beneath the boat, in less than ten feet of water, grew a multi-colored coral reef, thriving in the warm waters washing over the shoal.

Taylor grabbed a duffel bag from near the transom and untied the drawstring. He spilled a pile of masks, flippers and snorkels upon the deck. Stripping off his shirt, he selected his equipment and slipped it on.

"Come on, Laura," he offered her a mask. She looked doubtful.

"I think I'll wait here where it's dry."

Winch was annoyed. "Hey, you said we were here to practice. I got us here, now Taylor's got to do his little speech and take the tourists down to the reef. And you, boss, are the tourist today."

Laura sighed. Winch was right, she had to admit. There was no other good reason for her to be on board today, except to get in the way. She shuffled to the transom and took a seat.

"Okay," she said to Taylor in resignation. "Educate me."

Taylor started his monologue, explaining how reefs were formed, the various types of coral that were native to the Keys, and the varieties of fish they could expect to see. He was instructing the "tourist" on the proper use of her snorkel when his rap was interrupted by a startled yelp from Winch.

The engines raced beneath their feet and the boat lurched backwards, white foam kicking up behind the stern and splashing onto the deck. Taylor grabbed for a handhold and Laura rocked violently on the transom. In a moment, the engines resumed their previous steady hum and Winch looked up from the helm, wearing a sheepish grin.

"Sorry. Tide's going out and the current is a little tricky here. Nearly put us on a rock."

"Can't you drop the anchor?" Laura demanded.

"No, he can't," Taylor said patiently. "It could damage the reef." He looked over at the captain. "We're all right now?"

"Yeah, I think I got the sucker figured out."

"Okay," Taylor turned to Laura. "Then lets get our feet wet."

Still looking pretty uncertain, Laura accepted the set of snorkeling gear, setting it on the transom. She crossed her arms over her chest, gripping the hem of her long tee-shirt, and tugged it up over her head. She kicked off her yellow shorts. Winch gaped.

Flimsy didn't begin to describe the bikini she wore. Bright red with black trim, three tiny triangles of material. Winch batted discreetly at the rising bulge in his shorts and looked away. Taylor eyed the suit appraisingly. He touched a forefinger to his lips.

"You know," he said to her, "I have a camisole in those same colors."

Laura reddened, almost matching her bikini. "Come on. Let's get in the water."

Taylor fastened the collapsible ladder to the gunwale and showed Laura how to drop into the sea. She followed, a little awkwardly, and the two of them paddled slowly across the surface, sprays of water spurting from their breathing tubes. Winch watched them for a moment before he dipped his hand into the pocket of his cutoffs and extracted an orange tab of LSD. He popped it into his mouth and opened Taylor's bottle of beer to wash it down. The tide had slackened and he had little to do but wait for their return.

\* \* \* \* \* \*

The reef was breathtaking, the clarity of the water shimmering with refracted sunlight. Parrotfish nibbled at the edges of the coral and a small nurse shark rested brownly on the bottom in the shadows of the reef. Taylor pushed Laura's hand away just before she reached to caress a fire sponge, shaking his head at her and pointing toward the surface.

They broke the barrier between sea and sky and flipped back their masks, treading water. Laura laughed delightedly.

"That was great!" she enthused. Taylor agreed but warned her never to touch the coral. He added that he had saved her from a nasty sting had she come in contact with the orange fire sponge.

"Just like the song says: 'Keep your hands to yourself.'"

Laura grinned. "You'll have to add that to your spiel."

They swam the few feet to where the *Key Monster* drifted, and clambered up the ladder. Winch reached down to assist them on board. Laura stood dripping on the deck.

"Darn! I forgot to bring a towel," she complained. Winch indicated the cabin door.

"Below, in the first stateroom, there's a couple on the bunk." Laura vanished through the hatchway and Winch called after her, "And grab me another beer!"

Laura made her way forward, passing through the opulent cabin with the couch, stereo system and wet bar. In the first stateroom, she located the towels where Winch had said they'd be. She dried herself off, working the soft terry through her long wet hair. She was about to pick up a second towel for Taylor when she spied a large pad of paper which had been tossed upon the bunk. Curious, she picked it up and opened to the first page.

It was a sketchbook, done in a talented hand. She sat damply on the bedspread and examined the drawings. At the bottom of each was a scrawled signature which might have read, "Brant."

The first page was graced by a charcoal rendering of a harbor, boats with tall masts lying at anchor. She flipped to the next sheet and found a portrait of a grizzled old man, a beer bottle in his hand, sitting on a barstool. His eyes, despite his apparent great age, were alive and bright.

The next picture was of a group of men seated at a bar, all wearing fishing caps and looks of satisfied exhaustion after a day of hard labor on the water. She turned the page again and found a rough sketch of the same creature which had been painted upon the side of the *Key Monster*. It seemed to have been hastily drawn and lacked the fine detail and vibrant colors of the finished product, but it was nevertheless brilliant. She admired the work of this artist named Brant, whoever he was.

Intrigued, Laura turned to the following page and gasped. Her hand trembled.

Cruel eyes leapt off the paper and wounded her. The hard lines of a down-turned mouth, the slightly oversized ears, the ski-slope nose, all these details were frighteningly familiar. In her shaking hand she held the unmistakable portrait of her husband, James P. Quinn.

Barely able to rise to her feet, Laura fought the rocking of the boat as she retreated to the afterdeck. The engines thrummed louder and the big boat--Jim's boat, she realized--made headway across the ocean. Laura emerged on deck, fighting for a breath of fresh air.

"Where's my beer?" Winch demanded from the helm. When Laura didn't answer right away, he added, "We should be in international waters in about fifteen minutes. I suppose we should have some kind of ceremony or something."

He looked over at her, noticing how pale she was.

"Hey, you okay?" Taylor called from the stern. He too could see that she wasn't right.

"Feeling a little seasick?" Winch asked.

Laura held the sketchpad up for Winch to see.

"Oh, you found Brant's drawings," he said brightly. He squinted at the portrait. "That's the guy from back in Maryland who was shooting at us."

"You were being shot at?" Taylor asked, eyes wide. Winch shrugged.

"No big deal. I think he's the father of the girl I was, uh, dating. Hey, I didn't know she was a minor and . . ."

"It's a picture of my husband." Laura's words hung in the salty air.

Winch's acid-addled brain tried to sort this new information into some kind of logical order. It failed.

"Then she was your daughter?" he reasoned. "What were you, twelve when you had her?"

Laura slapped the pad onto the seat in anger and frustration. "No, you moron! There is no daughter!" Winch looked shaken and she took a step closer. Taylor watched from a distance.

"Listen," she hissed over the beating of the engines. "You bought this boat at a tax auction, right? Jim's boat, one *just like this one*, was seized for back taxes. Are you getting this yet?"

Winch stared hard at the horizon. Rusted cogs slipped across corroded gears in his head. He put one and one together and came up with eight. He thought harder, fighting the effects of his Miller-reinforced LSD buzz. Finally, a very dim light came on.

"So, you're saying, this was *his* boat?" he mumbled, unsure of his conclusion.

"Eureka!" Laura cried, flinging her arms in the air. She spun on Taylor. "I think he's finally gotten it!" Taylor waved her off in a leave-me-out-of-this gesture.

"But I paid for her, I've got the pink slip," the captain protested. "She's mine now."

Laura sighed loudly and rubbed her face with her hands.

"Yeah, legally. But you don't know Big Jim."

"I know he shot at me."

"Exactly. He was devastated when the IRS took his boat. And he's been obsessed with getting it back ever since."

"So," Winch said cautiously, "it's got nothing to do with the girl I slept with?"

"I doubt it, very much." This was exasperating. "It has everything to do with Big Jim tracking you down and getting his boat back."

"*My* boat," Winch said firmly. He made a slight course correction with the wheel.

"Your boat, his boat, same thing." She gazed over at Taylor. "You know, I bet my husband's more upset about losing his boat than he is about me."

Taylor returned a pitying look.

Laura thought about it a moment and she came to realize something dangerous. She touched Winch on the arm.

"Tell me," she asked. "When did you see him? When did he shoot at you?"

Winch stared into eternity, trying to remember. "It was a week ago Sunday, the day I left for Key West. Yeah. Brant, he's the kid who drew the pictures, came to warn me and we just got out of Solomons Harbor in time. He's a real lousy shot." Winch smirked. "His car rolled into the water, too."

Laura stared hard at the captain. Jim's Mercedes 500SL had been his second-most prized possession. She, herself, had been a distant third. She could almost picture the anger and determination on her husband's face.

"Winch," she said as softly as she could over the engines, "this is important. Tell me. Is there anybody back home who knew where you were going?" Please, no, she prayed.

"Um, well, Brant, but he'd never tell. Let's see... Skip, my real estate agent, he's got the address for SuRF. I can't remember if I told Donna Jean or Gil."

He trailed off. Laura hung her head, her long blonde hair brushing the top triangles of her bathing suit. Great. Big Jim was an asshole but not an idiot. If he could track the boat to Solomons Island, he'd find Winch's house, then the real estate agent, and finally her office on Stock Island. He'd figure it out, put it all together like assembling a portfolio. She half feared he'd be waiting for her when they arrived back at the dock. Suddenly she was in no hurry to return to land.

The engines wound down and the *Key Monster* slowed and settled into the water. The swells were larger out here, easily six-feet, the effects of last night's storm still roiling the ocean. Winch looked about, not a whisper of dry land in sight. He clapped his hands once, the threat of Laura's errant and crazed husband already forgotten. Good drugs will do that for you.

"We're here," he announced. Laura and Taylor looked around at the empty sea.

"We're where?" queried Taylor.

"Out of the country, international waters! So, what d'ya want to do? Gamble? Find an unclaimed rock and set up our own country?" He grinned. No one answered him. He shut down the engines, allowing the boat to drift. The *Key Monster* bobbed, the only sound coming from the waves slapping against the hull and the occasional screech of an errant gull. Laura couldn't take it anymore.

"I need a beer," she muttered and headed for the galley.

"I'll take one, too!" Winch called after her.

"A Coke, please," added Taylor from the transom.

Laura paused in the hatchway and shot them both poisonous looks. She went below, shaking her head.

Winch unrolled the chart and examined it. Taylor settled back in his seat and stared off at the horizon under the white-hot sun. Far across the water, just above the tops of the waves, two black specks appeared. Taylor watched them as they grew noiselessly larger, sprouting narrow appendages on each side, coming closer, becoming winged objects.

Taylor stood up, shading his eyes against the afternoon sun. They were coming on fast, the slightest whisper of rapidly displaced air reaching his ears. Winch looked up from the console, listening, trying to understand the odd sound that had nothing to do with the boat or the open sea. At last he identified the noise and glanced to the west.

The two specks had become black dots, rushing at them at better than two hundred miles per hour. Winch was familiar with the Navy jets flying over the Chesapeake out of NAS Pax River and had seen the daily flights from the base at Boca Chica next to Stock Island. He nodded at Taylor and reassured him.

"Navy jets," he said. "Probably out of Key West NAS." He peered at the looming objects which were heading straight for the *Key Monster*. "Most likely Tomcats," he added, though in truth he had no idea. He knew boats, not planes.

The two jets closed the final short distance to the *Key Monster*, their frantic roar ripping the fabric of the air as they passed barely overhead, nearly scraping the flying bridge and radio masts with their silver underbellies. Taylor covered his ears for protection as he stared up at the flashing wingtips barely fifty feet overhead. He got a good look at the wing decals and the almost antique outline of the aircraft. The *Key Monster* rocked savagely in the buffeting slipstream and a loud crash resounded from below deck.

"What the hell was that?!" hollered Laura from the galley. She dashed back on deck, grabbing for a handhold against the pitching of the boat. An opened bottle of beer in her shaking hand foamed madly from it's longneck, sudsing on her bare feet.

"Uncle Sam's Navy, playing games," Winch sneered as the two planes shot off to the east and then banked into a neat, coordinated turn.

"I don't think so," said Taylor flatly, watching them as they set up for another run. Laura and Winch looked in his direction.

"What do you mean?" Laura asked. Taylor glanced at her.

"I don't think they're American," he replied, "unless the US Navy has started flying MiGs."

The three of them searched the sky, watching as the pair of jets screamed toward them once again.

# CHAPTER 16

The MiGs completed their graceful arc and powered down to nearly sea-level, coming dead-on. They'd spoted him, and now they were coming back.

Felix glanced around the raft in a panic, seeking a weapon, the stone-age versus mid-twentieth century technology. The weathered *balza* slid down the crest of a swell into a deep trough, and he lost the jets from view for a moment. Then the next roller came through and Felix and the raft were propelled to its peak, a rise of at least three meters. The planes were impossibly close now.

They hadn't fired on him yet. Perhaps they wouldn't. Maybe they would only radio his position and the *Marina* de *Guerra* would be sent to pick him up to return him to his homeland and one of Fidel's prisons. Or it could be that the navy was busy and these two pilots would open fire and finish him off. In either case, Felix resolved to go down swinging.

Despite the predictable and rapid change in altitude as the raft rode the waves, the motion of the *balza* was fairly smooth. It was like riding in one of the old elevators at the Hotel Habana, only this *ascensor* was malfunctioning, racing from the lobby to the second floor and back again, over and over. Felix was used to it by now after days adrift at sea and he had no trouble balancing upon the deck.

The MiGs were drawing ever closer, barely ten meters above the waves. Felix imagined he could see the eyes of the lead *piloto*, the man's finger tightening on the trigger, ready to put an end to Felix's life and career. The *refugiado* reached down to the canvas bag lashed to the broken mast and pulled from it the only weapons he had on board.

Felix used his batter's eye to gauge the distance to the second jet. In his left hand, he firmly grasped his lucky bat. With his right hand, calculating the elapsing distance and the rise of the swells, he gently lofted a baseball into the air. The first plane screamed by without firing. The ball hung suspended in the air as the raft sank into the next trough. Felix brought the bat around with all his strength and connected for a line drive to center field. The white ball hurtled toward the second plane and vanished.

The MiGs swooped over him, the jetwash blowing his few remaining supplies into the sea. The second jet made a funny popping noise as it pulled away.

Down into the trough again, the MiGs lost from sight. And then up, up again, in time to see a puff of white smoke from the exhaust of the second MiG. A half second of silence, followed by the sound of tearing metal. Felix stood stunned, anger seeping into jubilation. The trailing MiG skittered across the sky, powerless, the piloto too low to eject. The avion nosed down at two-hundred miles an hour, and dove into the sea.

Miracle of miracles, the baseball had found the jet's intake, shredding the turbofan to pieces. The lead pilot, unable to comprehend what had happened to his wingman, pulled around in a tight circle and reduced his speed, coming in over the wreckage. A package fell from beneath a wing and bright yellow smoke billowed upon the surface of the water. The jet climbed a thousand feet or so and began to circle the crash site lazily, awaiting assistance.

And help would come, Felix knew. Maybe the *Marina de Guerra* was too busy to bother with a lone *refugiado*, but they would undoubtedly respond to a downed *avion* of the *Fuerza Aerea de Cuba*. Now, he realized, it wouldn't just be prison if he was taken. In the post-Soviet era, MiGs and pilots were too rare and valuable to the State. No, if they took him now, it would be to his death.

His life was over. There would be no major league career in America after all. His eyes filled with tears, blurring his vision. And as he rose upon the next wavecrest, he was confronted by yet another recent nightmare, no more than a dozen meters away.

The black, beady eyes of the sea serpent bore into his, the long slender body uncoiling from the frothing waves. The *balza* dipped into a trough again and Felix lost *el montruo marino* from view. Oh, nightmare of nightmares! First the jets and now the creature! He stared in horrid fascination as the raft rose upon the swell.

He glimpsed it again, but something about it was wrong. The *nariz*, that was it. The nose was too long. And it didn't move, except for the rising and falling of the sea. And the horizon beyond it was blocked by a vast white object, while black numbers and letters floated above the monster's head.

The serpent was fastened securely to the hull of a large white boat. With nowhere else to go, with no other choice available, Felix dove into the *oceano* and swam towards the bobbing vision of the monster.

\* \* \* \* \* \* \*

The two men on the boat were too busy gaping at the spot where the Cuban jet had splashed down to notice the tiny raft wallowing nearby. It was Laura who spied the fracturing craft off the port beam. A waif-like figure dove from it into the water and swam toward the *Key Monster*, and her shriek of surprise drew the attention of Winch and Taylor.

"Man overboard!" she yelled appropriately and because she could think of nothing else to say. Her two friends scrambled to her side and stared over the gunwale.

A swarthy, sunburned young man struggled hopelessly against the waves and the tide, repeatedly sinking below the surface as his stamina waned. Winch grabbed the boathook and stood ready to snag the swimmer, but the current was only pushing the man farther from the boat.

"He must be a Cuban," he shouted.

"He's not going to make it," Laura cried back in horror.

Taylor saw the man's distress and didn't think twice. He leaped over the side and hit the water. Winch dropped the gaff on the deck and began hurling orange life vests towards the drowning man. Laura looked about for some way to help.

Taylor was a powerful swimmer and it was only moments before he was alongside the man from the raft. He dove under and grasped the refugee around the chest and brought him back to the surface. The rafter sputtered and coughed up seawater as Taylor gripped him in a rescue hold and stroked steadily towards the boat. A line, thrown by Laura, splashed the water just ahead of them and Taylor seized it with his free hand, dragging the unresisting body in his wake. Winch and Laura hauled them to safety.

The dark-skinned man allowed himself to be reeled in, relaxing in the reassuring grip of the negro who'd saved him. Taylor thanked God that the man wasn't a thrasher.

*KEY MONSTER*

"You're okay," Taylor encouraged him as the whitecaps slapped at them. "We're almost there!"

The half-drowned man tried to speak, but took a mouthful of seawater for his trouble. He spit it out and coughed out a short question in accented English.

"You are Bahamas man?" he croaked.

Taylor bumped against the side of the *Key Monster* and grinned. "No," he replied, spitting out his own mouthful of salt-water. "I'm from Jersey."

\* \* \* \* \* \* \*

Four white arms stretched over the gunwale and grasped him by the wrists. Wearily, dejected, Felix felt himself lifted out of the water that for so many days had been both his constant companion and mortal enemy. He flopped over the rail and landed upon the dry deck on his sunburned back. He squinted up and saw a beautiful apparition.

A comely blonde woman in a shockingly small bathing suit hovered over him. She was absolutely unlike the women he had known at home and without question was a *Norte Americano*. And the black man had said he was from Jersey.

Oh, the agony! He was in the hands of Americans! No, this couldn't be!

She helped him sit up against the bulkhead and covered his shaking body with a soft towel. Another *hombre* with a scraggy beard handed him a bottle of cold, fresh *agua*. Felix drank greedily, the liquid spilling down his chin and coursing over his blistered, salt-encrusted body.

"Gracias," he gasped between gulps.

The black man who'd saved him from the sea pointed over the side and yelled something in complicated English. The bearded man who'd given him water dashed to the helm and Felix felt the powerful rumble of the engines beneath the deck. The big boat lurched into motion, coming about and rapidly picking up speed. Felix stared over the stern and saw the remaining Cuban fighter-jet rushing at them. He closed his eyes and wondered if the plane would strafe them.

The jet screamed by to starboard, just above the waves.

"Almost there!" the bearded man at the helm shouted over the jetwash. The big boat skimmed across the sea at high-speed, but there was no way it could outrun the plane.

Where were they taking him? Not to America, he prayed. Perhaps they were Americans on vacation in the Bahamas and they would land in Bimini or Andros. *Por favor*, not Miami!

More shouting in English among them, excited sounds. Felix watched the negro scramble up the ladder to the flying bridge with a bundle of cloth in his hand. He attached the cloth to a line and pulled a rope. Up the banner rose, unfurling into a streaming pattern of stars and stripes. Felix's heart sank. They would take him to America, he knew, if they survived the pursuing warplane.

He closed his eyes again and rested. The *monstruo marino* he thought. Had he seen it again? No, he reminded himself, it had only been a picture painted upon the hull of this big boat. But how had the creature come to be depicted upon the *bote* of his rescuers? Did they too know of the monster? After all his prayers that he never see the creature again, here he was, upon a boat which honored the beast! It was all too much. He shook his head and tried to rise.

The *rubia señorita Americano* helped him to his feet, whispering soft words of encouragement. The exact meaning of her words escaped him as his rudimentary English skills fled before his state of shock. Felix trembled uncontrollably and she supported him tenderly.

"There!" cried the captain, pointing. Ahead of them, just breaking the wash of the ocean, rose a series of rocks. Once more the jet swooped in at them and then, surprisingly, banked away, leaving them behind. The Americans whooped and cheered, the MiG abandoning the chase as the boat slipped into U.S territorial waters. Moments later, a pair of jets, wearing Navy blue, screamed over them heading south, pursuing the Cuban intruder.

The captain eased back on the throttles and strode to where Felix weaved on the deck. He spoke a few words to the *chica bonita*, who replaced him at the wheel. The captain looked Felix up and down and extended his hand. Felix took it and shook.

"Do you speak English?" the captain shouted.

"Little bit," Felix answered carefully, his loose command of the foreign tongue returning. The captain grinned broadly at him.

"Welcome aboard the *Key Monster!*"
What little color was left in Felix's face drained away.

* * * * * * *

The low skyline of Key West appeared on the horizon. Felix sat in the shade of the canopy near the helm eating crackers with cheese that sprayed from a can, the only food they had on board. He was conflicted, happy to be alive, but devastated to know that his dreams of major league free-agency were not to be realized. He had to convince his rescuers to deliver him to the Bahamas, without touching American soil. He'd almost rather face the Cuban Air Force, or even the sea serpent, rather than suffer the indignity of being the draft choice of some losing team and earning only a fraction of his worth as a ballplayer.

As they closed on the American shoreline, Felix tried to calm himself enough to remember his grammer school English. The pretty lady with the golden hair was trying to explain to him that there was a Cuban refugee center at a place called Stock Island where *Marielitos* would care for him and help him apply for asylum in the United States.

"No, no," he kept telling her, struggling for the words to express himself. "Not America. Bahamas."

"What's he saying?" Taylor asked her. She shrugged.

"He seems to have something against going to the U.S. If I were him, I'd say any port in a storm."

Felix touched his hand to the plastic bag hanging from his belt, his most precious and last remaining possession. It had hung there all during his perilous crossing of the Florida Straits. He unsealed the bag and extracted his baseball mitt, holding it aloft for the crew to see.

"Baseball?" Winch asked, and Felix nodded eagerly. "You play?"

"*Si*, yes! I, I pitch. *Por* Diablos Rojos de Pinar del Rio."

"Cool," said Winch. "I used to play catcher, in high school." Taylor and Laura looked at him funny.

"You played baseball?" Taylor smirked. Laura stifled a laugh. It was hard to picture Winch doing anything athletic.

"What's so funny about that? I was a kid once, ya'know." He returned his attention to the Cuban. "Are you any good?"

"*Si*! I want to play in American leagues, make *mucho dinero*."

"Well, the people at the refugee center will help you, I'm sure," Laura assured him. Felix shook his head.

How could he explain? The words in English were beyond his ability. "No. Bahamas I must get. Free agent, no draft! You take me?"

Taylor looked puzzled, but a dim light went on over Winch's shaggy head.

"*Comprendo, amigo!*" he exclaimed in the only Spanish he knew. Winch tried to explain the concept to the baseball-ignorant.

"I've read about this. It's how the major leagues work. If a Cuban lands in America to play baseball, he can be drafted by any team. They can pay him the minimum." Felix's eyes shone. Yes, this one understood! "But if he gets to the Bahamas or some other island first, then he's a free agent and can sign with whoever he wants, take the best offer! Right, amigo?"

Felix nodded happily. "Much dollars!"

"That's stupid," scowled Laura.

"That's baseball," shrugged Winch.

The captain smiled and patted the ballplayer on the back. "What's your name?" he asked loudly.

"Felix Munoz. Play for Yankees, play for Cubs! Do not care. But first Bahamas, not America!"

"Well, I'm Winch. This is Taylor, and this is Laura." Everybody shook Felix's hand again. "We're almost home, and maybe the refugee people can help you get to the Bahamas."

Felix was distraught. Taylor saw the pained look on his face.

"Maybe," he suggested, "we could run him over to Bimini. It wouldn't take that long, would it?"

Winch tapped the fuel gauges above the wheel. "Not enough in the tanks for that."

"And I don't think the Bahamian police would look very kindly on our smuggling in a Cuban," suggested Laura.

"She's probably right," Taylor confirmed. "They'd probably deport him and lock us up."

"The other way around would work better," Laura observed.

"So what do you suggest?" Winch asked them as he angled the *Key Monster* between the first pair of channel markers on the approach to Cow Key. The crew fell silent. Felix stared over the bow, watching America looming ever closer.

"You know," Taylor supposed. "If he doesn't actually get off the boat, stand on U.S. soil, is he still in America? Technically, I mean?"

Winch gave him a long hard look. "You mean, keep him aboard the *Key Monster*?"

"Just until we figure out how to help him."

"We've already helped him," Winch countered. "We pulled him out of the ocean and outran the Cuban Air Force!" He swung his eyes toward Felix. "Now we've got to hide him out on my boat? Sheesh!"

"We can refuel, take him over to Bimini at night and drop him off near a beach or something," Laura prodded.

"*Capitan* Weench," Felix implored. "I like what *bonita señorita* she says. I help on *bote* until then. I clean fish, I clean *bote*, I work for you! No, what is word? No freeload?"

"Shit," Winch muttered. He piloted the *Key Monster* alongside the SuRF pier. Laura sidled up to Winch and put her hand on his bare shoulder. As usual, her touch sent a current through him.

"He could help out with the reef tours, you know," she said quietly.

"Taylor, grab the bow lines," Winch called, but Felix was already leaping to gather the ropes.

"See?" urged Laura. "He could do all your grunt work. Polish stuff, clean the galley, serve drinks, organize the gear. All you'd have to do is steer. Less work for you."

The gentle squeezes she gave his shoulder and the warmth of her breath on his cheek were more persuasive than her words. Winch sighed deeply.

"Do we have to pay him, too?" he whispered.

"I'm sure room and board would be good enough. I mean, if he's not going to get off the boat, where would he spend a paycheck?" Laura grinned at her logic.

The *Key Monster* settled gently against the Uniroyal fenders along the dock. At the stern, Taylor made the boat fast. Ahead, on the bow, Winch watched his prospective first mate expertly lasso the cleat on the pier and tie it off, leaving just enough slack to counter the rising and falling of the tide.

It was done exactly as Winch would have done it himself. Probably a little neater, too. Felix diligently coiled the extra line on the deck.

Winch thought of sharing his floating home with a Cuban they'd plucked out of the sea who barely spoke English. He resented the loss of his privacy for a moment, and then thought of the balky marine toilet which was forever in need of cleaning. And the greasy, filthy job of changing the oil and filters. And the dozens of other dirty, tedious chores that came with running a boat as large as the *Key Monster*.

Felix made his way back to the helm, standing on the edge of the gunwale and staring down at the captain hopefully. Winch glanced at Laura and Taylor, who were wondering if the captain would put the Cuban ashore. Winch shut down the engines and flicked his eyes to the refugee, who waited nervously in the sudden stillness.

"One question," he asked Felix. "Can you cook?"

Felix answered slowly. "*Si*."

Winch sucked in a deep breath. Laura was right. He had to agree. He pointed below, to the galley. "Get me a beer, mate."

Felix was back in seconds, a broad smile covering his sunburned face. Winch guzzled an icy Rolling Rock and watched as the Cuban grabbed a mop and began to swab the afterdeck. The captain set his beer on the console and stood up. He reached over and took the mop from the man's hands, shaking his head.

"Later," Winch told him. "Get yourself a beer."

Laura smiled. She gave Winch a peck on the cheek.

"Not exactly Captain Bligh," she giggled. Winch swatted her playfully on the rump.

"Get off my boat."

\* \* \* \* \* \* \*

"Winch."
"Weench."
"No, Winch."
"Weeench."

Winch sighed and took another hit of the joint. He passed it to Felix who was sitting beside him on the bow. Felix waved him off and sipped a cold Budweiser.

"Well, your English ain't half-bad for a Cuban."

"*Si*. I mean, yes," Felix answered drunkenly. It was only his first beer, but dehydration will do that to you.

Winch let out a lungful of smoke. "You learn it in school?"

"A little bit. Mostly, I teach myself. I listening to Radio Marti, *beisbol* games from Miami and Chicago, WGN. And I study English books, too."

Winch looked at Felix in the sunset. "You listened to Cubs games on WGN?"

"Holy cow!" Felix replied and laughed. Winch smiled.

They had passed the late afternoon sitting on the *Key Monster* drinking beer. Laura had left with Taylor in the Caddy just a few minutes ago. She'd been relieved to find that her husband hadn't staked out the dock, and congratulated the crew on a successful practice trip and rescue. She deemed the SuRF Reef Tour ready to go.

Felix had eaten the last of the food on board and Winch had used the phone in the office (he'd borrowed a spare set of keys when Laura hadn't been looking) to order two pizzas. Ravenous, Felix had devoured the pizza despite the fact he'd never seen one before. He'd discarded only the anchovies, claiming he'd eaten enough fish for a lifetime.

"How long were you out there, drifting?" Winch asked. Felix shrugged, mentally counting.

"Six days, 'cept when I land back in Cuba accidental. Mos' *refugiados*, two day, but I am *lanzador*, not sailor."

"Six days," muttered Winch. "Must have been tough. I guess those two jets were your worst moment, huh?"

Felix stayed still, remembering. "No," he finally said. He looked over at the captain. "When I first saw your *bote*, was worst time."

"Why?"

Felix cocked his head toward the side of the bow. "Your picture on the side."

"The sea monster painting? It scared you?"

"I only saw *pintura* of thing first, not *bote*. I think it is real."

Winch nodded and mumbled, "You ought to see the real thing, you think the *painting* is scary." He immediately regretted his words.

Felix spilled his beer on the deck. "You saw too? *Monstruo marino?*" There was an edge of panic to his voice.

Winch shook his head stubbornly. "No, no, I just imagined it." He held up the joint, abashed. "Too many drugs."

Felix was shaking his head too. "I do not use the drugs," he whispered urgently. "But I see it out on *oceano, uno, dos* day ago!"

"Bullshit!" Winch got up angrily. "It's a hallucination, just something in my head."

"No! It is just like picture on your *bote*. I see it, I am not drunk or, how you say, stoned."

Winch stared over the rail, into the west. The sun was starting its nightly show for the tourists at Mallory Square. Across Cow Key Channel, the last Cape Air flight of the day took off, heading to Ft. Myers.

"You were lost at sea, starving, thirsty," Winch insisted. "You were seeing things."

"Yes," Felix nodded wisely, "things I see belong at bottom of *oceano*." He finished mopping up the spilled beer with his shirt and joined Winch at the rail. "Is no trick of the eye," he added.

"You think so?"

Felix took a deep breath. "Back home, in Los Palacios, is legend of *monstruo marino*. I never believe, is story to scare *niños*. But now," he turned and looked Winch squarely in the eye, "I believe."

"Crap."

"What is *crap?*"

"Crap is shit."

"Oh. Is no crapshit."

Winch stifled a laugh. He put a comradely arm over the Cuban's shoulder.

"So, no crapshit?" he said.

Felix nodded out to sea with his chin. "I know what I see. And if you see too, then no crapshit." Felix waited a heartbeat and added, "Tell me."

Winch slowly pulled a fresh jay from his shirt pocket and fired it up, inhaling deeply. After a moment, he confessed, coughing on the smoke.

He told about first seeing the monster on the Chesapeake Bay ("That's in Maryland, one of our states.") and how the creature had seemingly pursued him south to the Keys. Felix listened intently to Winch's description of the hurricane and the subsequent reappearance of the sea monster in the Gulf Stream.

Then it was Felix's turn, relating how the monster had bellowed and nearly wrecked his raft. "That, *mi amigo nuevo*, was no dream, no crapshit."

Winch let out a long stream of smoke and dropped the roach over the side.

"Then either we're both *loco*," he told the Cuban sadly, "or there really is something out there." Winch wasn't sure which alternative he preferred.

The two men, one blond and lean, the other dark and powerful, stared over the bow rail, watching in silence until the sun had extinguished itself beyond the profile of Key West.

"Baseball," Winch said in the enveloping dusk. He glanced at Felix. "How good are you?"

Felix continued to stare at the horizon. "*Muy bueno*." He was exhausted now, and his English was failing him. "I want to pitch for American team."

Winch nodded and looked back out to sea.

"Tomorrow," he said. "We'll scrounge up a ball and a catchers mitt and we'll see how good you are." He patted Felix on the back and inclined his head toward the stern.

"C'mon, mate. I'll show you where to bunk."

Gratefully, Felix followed his rescuer below to one of the vacant staterooms. He barely managed to fall onto the softest mattress of his life before he was fast asleep.

Winch extinguished the light in the cabin and paused in the doorway, looking back at the ballplayer slumbering on the bed.

"*Buenos noches*," he whispered, and closed the door.

# CHAPTER 17

They'd done the Conch Train, the Aquarium, some shopping, the Secret Garden, even the goddam cemetery! Big Jim's gut rumbled. He was hungry, sunburned and thirsty. Now, late on this relentlessly sunny Monday afternoon, he crept the Mercedes through gridlocked traffic in search of a parking place within walking distance of Liza's artsy-fartsy restaurant along the south shore. He'd lost the entire day squiring Liza around the island, but it had been the only way to placate her after she'd nailed him fooling around with that hooker last night. Tomorrow, he thought, it was back to business, back to the search for Winchell and the *LauraLee*.

Stalled in traffic, Big Jim drummed his fingers on the steering wheel, keeping an eye out for a free curbside space. Liza lounged in the passenger seat, sunglasses on, face tilted up to the sun through the open window. His own window was closed, the air conditioner running full-blast, but he had been unable to persuade her to roll up her's. She was getting on his nerves again, dragging him around all day, wasting his time and money. All he wanted to do was park somewhere, find the restaurant and grab a fat, medium-rare steak and a cold beer.

The pink taxicab in front of him inched forward at the intersection. He started to follow, but the sudden gap between the cars left just enough room for another car to squeeze in ahead of him as it turned from the side street. The driver waved a casual thanks. Big Jim saw it was a classic '66 Cadillac convertible, in mint condition. It was being driven, top down, by a big black man and a blonde woman. He hated seeing that kind of shit. He admired the automobile for a split second before the anger at being cut off by a nigger exploded.

"Look at that shit," he muttered, and Liza glanced over at him. "Big nigger stud with a white chick. Disgusting." Liza, without a truly racist bone in her body, looked away, bored with her lover. Everytime he opened his mouth lately, she found herself a little more repulsed by him.

Pissed off by the Caddy cutting in front and the spectacle of a white woman riding with a black man, Big Jim leaned on the horn. The driver's white eyes glanced in the rearview mirror. The woman turned in her seat to stare back at the Mercedes.

Big Jim Quinn's heart stopped for a beat. The woman turned away from him again. No. *Laura* turned away! Holy shit! It was his wife! It *had* been her he'd seen at dinner last night! There was absolutely no doubt, and as she swiveled her head to speak to the colored man, her familiar features were in perfect profile. That sculpted face he'd fallen for years ago, her shiny blonde hair, and the way she tilted her head back to laugh at something her dark companion said. Goddam it!

Whatever snarl had been blocking the street ahead unwound and traffic began to move. Big Jim willed himself to remain calm as he stayed on the Caddy's bumper. He flicked his eyes at Liza. He didn't want a confrontation with his wife in front of his girlfriend.

So, he'd been right after all. Laura *had* run away with another guy. But a nigger? Big Jim had never figured on that. It was revolting. But the serendipity of it all gave him pause.

If he'd seen Winchell and the *LauraLee* here, and now his runaway wife, well, that was too much to be a coincidence. Somehow, he surmised, it was all tied together. One would lead him to the other. Total victory was at hand!

Big Jim was glad he'd sprung for the extra cost of a tinted windshield on the Mercedes, knowing he could stay right behind them without being recognized, at least if Laura didn't notice the Maryland tag on the front bumper. A silver Mercedes 500SL was not an uncommon car in South Florida. He dropped back a ways and allowed the Cadillac some room, matching its movements through traffic.

"There's a space," Liza pointed at the curb, but Big Jim ignored her, concentrating on tailing the convertible. They were nearing Southernmost Point and running out of road. Finally, the car ahead of him signaled a left onto a dead-end street. The Mercedes went straight and Big Jim glanced down the road, which led to a row of motel rooms and a bar at the end of the block by the water. He braked in the middle of the intersection, oblivious to the honking horns behind him. Something was going on down there. Police cars with flashing strobe lights choked the narrow street and a crowd milled about. Big Jim lingered just long enough to see the Cadillac pull to a stop in front of one of the motel rooms before the blare of horns behind him became too much. He'd seen enough for now and he shot the Mercedes forward, glancing at the sign displaying the name of the motel. He memorized it.

At the next corner he made a left and found on-street parking half-a-block from Liza's restaurant of choice. Suddenly light on his feet, Big Jim exited the car and stared up the beach to the motel, just a block away. He smiled, sat down with his mistress, and ate a very pleasant dinner.

\* \* \* \* \* \* \*

"What a jerk," Taylor was saying as he wheeled onto Simonton Street, glad to have the annoying silver car off his tail. "One of those drivers from the northeast, no doubt."

"What's going on?" asked Laura, straightening in her seat as she saw the commotion of police cars at the foot of the street.

Taylor slipped the Caddy into a parking space near Laura's door. They got out and stood by the side of the car, staring.

It was a mob scene in front of the adjacent bar. The Key West cops were trying to restore order, holding back the curious and trying to keep the lane clear. An ambulance, with lights and siren, rushed up the street. A patrol car sped in the opposite direction with a pair of bald young men occupying the screened-in rear seat. Laura and Taylor stood by the Cadillac and watched. Laura spotted a familiar face in the crowd. She waved to get Steve's attention.

Steve Stevens had suffered through a distressing late-lunch with Bob Davies, Janet Sullivan, and, as a surprise guest, Maxx Rock. Janet had invited the shock-jock along after his show, a development that Steve learned of only after they'd been seated. Steve discovered that the only thing more disgusting than the words that came out of Maxx's mouth was what he put in it. The man was a total slob, apparently being completely unacquainted with utensils, napkins or any form of etiquette. Janet had found him charming, much to Steve's dismay. At Maxx's dare, and after a full bottle of wine, Mrs. Pringle had even flashed her tits at the table. Bob had reddened in embarrassment. Steve had choked on his Cuban coffee. Maxx had whistled in admiration.

Steve couldn't get back to the radio station fast enough, and it was over the newsroom police scanner that he'd heard the call for back-up at the Deep, where a riot was in progress. He'd grabbed his cassette recorder and made it to the scene in under five minutes. At least fifteen city and county cops were dragging an equal number of skinheads from the bar, tossing them upon the trunks of their cruisers, patting them down and cuffing them. An ambulance surged through the crowd and paramedics tended the wounded, including four scantily-clad male dancers sporting sundry cuts and bruises. The reporter fought his way through the policeline, flashing his credentials, and found the sergeant in charge, Bill McReady. They spoke for a few moments about the riot.

With the basic facts on tape and in his notebook, Steve stepped back out of the way to observe. He spotted one of the skinheads, hands cuffed behind his back, sitting sullenly in the back seat of an unattended brown and white. The rear window was halfway down, as far as it would go, and the police were still too busy to notice the reporter as he whipped out his mike and approached the patrol car. He rapped on the partly open window to get the prisoner's attention.

Cold blue eyes under a stubble of light hair glanced up at him. A small, bloody cut oozed beneath a bandage along his chin. Steve shoved the mike in the man's battered face.

"Hey, pal! I'm from Key Rock News. What happened?"

"Fuckin' faggots," the man glowered. Whoops, couldn't use that on the air, but at least the guy was a talker. Steve let him.

"My buds and me are out for a little R&R, right? We hear about this bitchin' strip bar. Only, they gets on stage and starts to take it off and, *fuck*, they're guys! One of 'em wagging his dick right in my face!" He shrugged. "Nuthin' we hate more'n fags, so we took 'em out. Next thing ya know, the goddam bouncers are all over us, but it's like three against twenty, so no problem. Then the cops come, five of 'em on me, but I got in my shots, too!" He spit on the front seat, managing to aim through the wire-mesh screen. "Fuckin' pigs!"

"What's your name?" asked Steve, holding the mike steady and looking over his shoulder for deputies. Cops didn't like reporters interviewing suspects before they were booked, but Steve grabbed the opportunity anyway. He was a pro.

"Gus Schmidt, from Bad Axe, Michigan."

"You guys all from Michigan?"

"Nah," the prisoner said, shaking his head. "From all over. I'm a Captain in the Aryan-American Freedom Forces an' we're havin' our leadership convention."

"Aryan-American Freedom Forces," Steve repeated carefully. "What's that?"

Prisoner Schmidt puffed out his chest as best he could with handcuffs on. "We gonna save the fuckin' country when the revolution comes. Kick out the kikes an' niggers an' spics an' homos!" He glanced back at the bar savagely. He hissed, "'Specially the homos."

"Who's your leader? Can I talk with him?" Steve was excited now. This was a huge story. Nazis in Key West!

"General Schenk," Schmidt replied. "He ain't here, though. He's up the campground on Sugarloaf. Most the guys stayed up there for weapons training today. Guess I shoulda stayed there too 'steada comin' down to Fag City." He leaned back in the rear seat of the cruiser and sighed. "Fuck Florida."

Out of the corner of his eye, Steve saw a deputy striding meanly in his direction. He extracted the microphone and rereated to the sidelines, losing himself in the crowd.

He'd gotten some good stuff on tape, but the real story was up on Sugarloaf Key. Steve flipped open his notebook and scribbled a few lines. When he looked up, he noticed his friends, Laura and Taylor, waving at him from the other side of the street. He tucked away his notes and, after a last glance at arrestee Schmidt, who was busy cussing out a black paramedic, ambled over to them.

"What's up?" asked Taylor, shaking Steve's hand. Steve smiled at Laura and hooked a thumb over his shoulder.

"Just your run-of-the-mill, all-American Nazi scum. Had a little to-do with some gays, got out of control."

"Skinheads? *Here*?" gasped Laura worriedly. She eyed the Key West police as they shoved a couple more into the patrol cars. The lead car pulled out. As it passed them, one of the skinheads in the back seat hurled abuse at Taylor. He flinched. Steve shot the car a deadly look.

"Nice bunch of fellas," Steve said sarcastically. He told them about General Schenk and his group's philosophy. "There's a lot more of them camping up at Sugarloaf, call themselves the," he checked his notes, "Aryan-American Freedom Forces, the AAFF."

"Just a bunch of AAFF-holes," grumbled Laura, and Steve grinned.

But Taylor looked worried. He glanced at the bar, at the motel and then at Laura. He shook his head.

"You shouldn't stay here," he told her. "Not with these jerks around."

Laura patted him on the arm. "I'm a big girl," she countered, but then thought about it. There were always bikers and other lowlifes hanging around outside the bar half-a-block down. And at nearly a thousand dollars a week, winter-rates, the resort was far too expensive. She'd been thinking of moving somewhere cheaper but hadn't had the time to look for anything.

"Taylor's right," Steve urged. He saw an opening and went for it. "My place is just up the street. You could stay with me." He looked at her hopefully and she met his eyes.

"And I have an extra bedroom," Taylor interjected. "You're more than welcome to be my guest." Steve scowled to himself. Laura shook her head.

"Thanks, but I should really find something on Stock Island. It's closer to work and the rents are cheaper." Both men looked disappointed. "I promise, just one or two more nights here and I'll find an apartment. Really, I'll be fine."

The last of the patrol cars with prisoners pulled away. Only the sergeant in charge and a couple of deputies remained to take statements. Laura looked up at the two men who worried about her and smiled. She kissed each on the cheek and assured them again that she would be okay. She unlocked the door to her room and closed it behind her.

The two men looked at each other. Steve was uneasy. Taylor was amused.

"Your place?" Taylor smiled at Steve.

"Oh, shut up. It was worth a try." And he smiled, too.

"Now what?" Taylor asked.

"Back to work," Steve answered. "I've got a few more questions for the police, then over to the jail to get names and charges and then back to the station to put together the story. No rest for the ambitious. How about you?"

Taylor looked thoughtful. He gazed at the strobe lights of the remaining cruisers parked in the street and watched as the last injured dancer was loaded into the ambulance. He looked pretty banged up.

"I've got some things to do," he said distractedly.

The two men shook hands again and parted company. Steve walked back through the thinning crowd and Taylor climbed into his '66 Caddy and backed out. He cruised up the street and headed for Duval.

\* \* \* \* \* \* \*

Taylor parked the convertible on Petronia and strode into the familiar surroundings of the Riding Crop Bar. He found the manager in his office next to the dressing room, and had no trouble securing an agreement to rent the bar for a private party the next night. The Crop was normally closed on Tuesdays and the manager was happy to do a favor for his favorite dancer. He gave Taylor a break on the usual fee but reminded him that the renter was responsible for booze, breakage and bartenders. Taylor agreed, but had one more request. The manager looked puzzled for a moment, but promised Taylor that he would indeed phone Samantha and Angel, offering them double wages to dance at Taylor's bash. They'd be added to Taylor's bill.

But remember, Taylor warned the manager, not to mention his name to them. If they asked, the manager was to say it was for a convention. Taylor signed the rental form and waiver and strolled back to his car, a smile on his lips. He'd had the shadings of this plan from the first afternoon he'd seen the skinheads from his apartment window. And now that plan was in motion. He had one more thing to do: the Invitation.

The sun had set and the heat of the day dissipated as the moon rose over Stock Island. Taylor steered the Caddy into the SuRF parking lot and then walked down the splintering pier to where the Key Monster lay. He found Winch sitting alone, drinking a beer on the afterdeck.

"Ahoy," he called, and was welcomed aboard. Taylor, to Winch's surprise, accepted a beer and the two men talked quietly under the moonlit sky. Taylor inquired after their new Cuban crewmate, and Winch assured him that Felix was below, sleeping like your typical tired, poor, huddled mass. Winch listened seriously as Taylor outlined his plan. He never hesitated, just told his visitor that he'd do it. They drank a toast for luck.

As Taylor got back in his car for the drive home, he heard the *Key Monster*'s engines rumble to life. A moment later, the big boat slipped away from the dock and swung out onto Cow Key Channel, her running lights winking red and green against the black water. Taylor's little surprise party was going to be a smash.

\* \* \* \* \* \* \*

There'd been bad news from town this evening. More than a dozen AAFF troops were in custody. A collection had been taken up among the rest of the men to bail out their patriotic comrades. Rolf Schenk rubbed his bald head in consternation beneath the dull glow of the overhead light in his camper. A half-dozen weapons leaned against the wall next to his chair. On the table before him, a disassembled Ruger gleamed with oil, freshly cleaned after a day on the target range. He'd sent Lieutenant Bobby down to Key West in his Econoline van to post the bail and fetch his men. But as annoying and as costly as their misadventure in town had been, Rolf was proud of them. Bashing gays and fighting cops was good practice for the coming revolution.

It was nearly midnight when a rap came at the door of his command post.

"Come," he barked, and he glanced up from his work with the pistol.

A disheveled, skinny man with long hair climbed the steps and entered the camper. Following a goosestep behind, with an M-16 trained on the stranger's back, came Lieutenant Ray.

"Sorry to disturb you, sir," Ray said, "but a patrol found this intruder near the perimeter. He said he wanted to see the general. Asked for you by name."

Rolf looked the prisoner up and down. His hair was long, but blond, and he possessed the distinctive features of Germanic descent. He was unarmed, middle-aged, with red-rimmed eyes, and the smell of salt and diesel fuel clung to him. Rolf didn't sense this guy was a cop or a fed. Nobody would go *this* deep undercover. The general leaned back in his chair.

"Who are you?" he demanded.

"An admirer," the prisoner answered in a nervous voice. Rolf waited in silence. He indicated for the man to go on.

Winch glanced over his shoulder at the rifle still trained on his back. He licked his lips. "I'm Eugene, up from Key West? I heard about you guys in town." He paused.

"And?"

"And I wanted to stop in and say howdy and welcome." He leaned forward over the table, dropping his voice. "You guys really tore hell out of those faggots today. I just wanted to tell you that I thought it was about time someone did something about all those queers down here." Winch had rehearsed that line all the way to Sugarloaf. He'd only had four beers and a joint, so he was pretty straight tonight.

Rolf allowed himself a small smile and relaxed a bit. "That's nice of you to say. Lieutenant, at ease. And bring a chair for Eugene here."

Lt. Ray cautiously lowered his rifle and shoved a chair toward Winch with his booted foot. But his eyes remained wary. He was responsible for the safety of his general. Winch folded himself into the chair.

"First-General Rolf Schenk, at your service." Winch thought the man, sounding like a German officer, had watched too many World War II movies. At least he didn't click his heels. Then Winch noticed the swastika banner hanging on the back wall of the camper. He tried not to show his nervousness.

"Nice to meet you, General." He found himself staring at the cashe of guns by the desk. Rolf's eyes followed his.

"You shoot, Eugene?"

"Only coloreds," Winch improvised after an awkward pause. The two skinheads bawled with sudden laughter.

Rolf stood up from the table and extended his hand. "Ah, a patriot!" he exclaimed. "Are you here to sign up?"

Winch shook the general's hand tightly, trying to impress. He found talking to these men more distasteful than he had imagined, but he'd promised to help Taylor.

"Well, I'm a bit old for hunting coons," he demurred, "but I wanted to at least do something to let you know how much some of us 'preciate what you stand for."

Rolf nodded sagely and sat back down. "Thank you, we're always in need of support from the people. Tell me, Eugene, where is your family from? Originally, I mean."

"Wales and Holland," he answered, the first truthful thing he'd said since he'd tied up the *Key Monster* at the campground wharf. The general nodded approvingly.

"Yes, I thought there was some Welsh in you, but I would have guessed German instead of Dutch." He waved a hand at Lt. Ray. "Small difference." There was a beat of silence in the cramped room.

"Anyway," Winch said, anxious to get this over with and get out of there, "a couple of us have arranged a party for you."

"A party?" Rolf's eyebrows shot up.

"Yeah. Nothing fancy, but we've rented a bar in Key West for tomorrow night. Some food, music, open bar, strippers . . ."

"Strippers?" Lt. Ray breathed excitedly behind Winch's back.

"Uh-huh," Winch confirmed. "Nice ones, do whatever you want with them. I mean, just to show our appreciation."

The general smiled warmly. "That would be very kind of you. You know, my men haven't exactly been greeted with open arms down here. Not too many niggers around, but Key West is swarming with fags. Do my men good to relax without any deviates around. What about the police?"

"Not a problem," Winch assured him. "Like I said, it's a closed party, just for you and your men and other real Americans." If his mother was in heaven eavesdropping, Winch prayed she'd forgive him for this. He promised her he'd wash his mouth out as soon as he got back to the boat.

Rolf shifted his eyes to Lt. Ray. "What do you think?" he asked his aide.

Lt. Ray was beside himself at the prospect of getting off this mosquito-infested key and partying with some good ole American strippers. "Sounds like a great idea to me, General," he drooled.

"Me too," Schenk agreed. "We've been working pretty hard and the men need a break. Lieutenant, cancel night maneuvers for tomorrow and spread the word."

Lt. Ray snapped to attention and saluted. "Yes, sir!" He took his weapon and sprinted out the door, happy as a kid on the last day of school.

Winch fed the general the address on Duval and told him that the doors would open at 10 P.M., "2200 Hours," he remembered to say. Rolf pushed the pieces of the Ruger aside and reached for a bottle on the shelf behind him.

"Schnapps," he said proudly, pouring them each a glass. He lifted his in a toast. "To the revolution!"

"L'chaim," chimed Winch. He couldn't help himself. The general glanced over the rim of his glass in suspicious puzzlement. "Old Welsh toast," grinned Winch just before he knocked back the golden liquor. The general smiled back.

"Then, l'chaim!"

\* \* \* \* \* \* \*

The ringing of the bedside telephone brought Laura running from the bathroom where she'd been brushing her teeth. She snatched it up. "Hello?"

"Ms. Chadwick?" came a woman's thin voice. "This is the front desk. Sorry to disturb you so late, but we have a plumbing emergency in the room next to yours. We need to send our maintenance man over right away to check the pipes in your room."

"But there's no problem here," Laura protested. It was midnight. There was a longish pause at the other end of the line, and a muffled conversation with another voice, before the woman spoke again.

"Well, the plumber needs to get at the pipes from your side of the wall. I'm very sorry, but he says it will only take a few minutes. Otherwise, he says, your room might flood, too."

Laura sighed deeply. "Yes, okay," she relented. "But please make it fast. I was about to go to bed."

Without another word, the connection was broken. Laura shook her head ruefully and buttoned up her pajama top. It was fairly long, hanging to mid-thigh. Modest enough for a midnight call from the plumber. She hoped this wouldn't take too long. She was bushed.

In less than two minutes, there was a knock on the door. Laura threw back the deadbolt and pulled it open. She stared up at the repairman, well-lit by the porch light. Her mouth fell wide open in shock. The man took a forceful step into the room, preventing her from either closing the door or escaping. He gazed down at her malevolently.

"Hello, Laura," leered her husband, Big Jim Quinn.

# CHAPTER 18

Laura tried to speak, but her throat constricted and no sound could escape. Big Jim had always had this effect upon her, treating her as a naughty child, a little girl standing guiltily before a scolding parent, and she'd despised the way he made her feel. This was precisely why she had slunk away during his absence, leaving only a letter behind. Had she attempted to leave her marriage by confronting him, enumerating her reasons face-to-face, she would have crumbled under the weight of his penetrating, haughty gaze. It had been Dr. Judy, her therapist, who had suggested that she abandon her husband without giving him an opportunity to shame her into staying. And it had nearly worked. How the hell had he found her?

She backed deeper into the motel room until her calves bumped against the side of the bed. Big Jim stepped through the threshold and held her eyes.

The son-of-a-bitch had done it somehow, tracked her to Key West. Laura hadn't told anyone-not even her best friend-- not even Dr. Judy--where she was going. Yes, she'd mailed Mom a note last week, but she'd been vague as to her exact location, sending a generic Florida postcard announcing her pending divorce, along with a promise to phone soon. Her mother wouldn't have told Jim where Laura was even had she known. She hated her son-in-law. It must have been Winch and the damn boat that had drawn him to Key West!

Damn it! Why hadn't that burnt-out freak of a captain gone to some other island, like Jamaica or Nantucket or Greenland? And why had she remained entangled in Winch's life once she'd known that he was in possession of Big Jim's boat? It was exactly as she'd feared, finding the boat and then finding her. Laura wished she'd had a day or two more to plan what she would have done or said before she had to face her husband. Now time had run out. She was scared, confused and exhausted, not the best of circumstances to have the argument of a lifetime.

Big Jim looked mildly around the motel room and then directly at his wife. "Nice place you got here," he said sarcastically. He didn't wait for an invitation. He pulled out a chair and sat down in front of the door, leaving it ajar but cutting off the only way out of the room.

He indicated she should sit also, and Laura lowered herself upon the turned-down bedspread. They stared at each other in silence for a long moment. This was very bad, Laura knew. When he was quiet, it always presaged the worst. He lowered his eyelids and for a moment she thought he had nodded off. He looked tired and rumpled. With his eyes half-closed, he spoke, softly, controlled.

"Long time, no see," he said banally. Laura stared at him. He dipped into the pocket of his sportscoat and extracted a cigar. He peeled the plastic wrapper and lit it up, pulling the virgin ashtray on the tiny table under the front window within reach. He exhaled smoke and considered the finely shaped corona. "Man in the store said this is a real Cuban, smuggled in. Very good, I tend to believe him." He blew out more smoke. "Let's see if I believe you." He waited.

Laura found her voice, barely. "I'm not coming back, Jim. It's over."

He nodded through the cigar smoke. "Maybe it is, maybe it isn't. I haven't decided yet." He leaned forward and tapped the glowing end in the ashtray.

"How did you find me?" she asked.

"Funny story," he answered without smiling. "I've been following your friend, Eugene, who, as you surely know, has my boat."

Laura was genuinely confused. Eugene? Big Jim saw the puzzlement on her face and scowled.

"C'mon, Laura. The *LauraLee* is here, I've seen her. Winchell is here, I've seen him, too. And now, *you're* here. That's all too much to be a coincidence." He leaned back in his chair again. "I've got two questions: How did you meet him, and did the two of you think you could get away with it?"

Laura clamped down on her tongue. Her anger had overcome her fear. Doctor Judy's training came back to her. She did a quick breathing exercise, felt herself steady, and looked into her husband's eyes. She told the truth.

"I met him three days ago, and yes, the whole thing *is* a coincidence."

Big Jim snorted, another indication of his controlled anger. Laura wondered how long her husband had been watching her and how much he knew. Had he really found Winch and the boat? The hell with her therapy. She decided to play dumb.

"Look," she offered, "I met him down here, he's helping out where I work."

"You're working?" Big Jim seemed amused. "Where?"

"I'm the Director of Public Information at the Save the Reef Foundation," she answered a little proudly.

"Save the Reef Foundation," Jim mused as he pulled on his cigar. "Why does that sound familiar?" And then it came to him and he pointed the hot ember at her. "Reef tours! That's it! You were handing out fliers at that restaurant the other day. You gave one to . . ." and he stopped himself. "I thought that was you, but I wasn't sure." He glowered at her, remembering. "Who was the guy you were with? Tall guy, kinda gray-haired. Another boyfriend?"

Laura was too angry to speak, so Big Jim kept on.

"And today, I see you cruising around in a Caddy with a big black guy. You doin' him, too?"

Laura tried to figure out what he was talking about. Then she remembered how Taylor had driven her home after their practice tour. She barked an involuntary laugh.

"Taylor?" Laura shook her head, smiling sardonically. "You have no idea how far off-base you are on that one."

"Maybe doing all three of 'em, huh?" Big Jim rose suddenly from his chair by the door, pacing the entryway, puffing on his cigar and working himself up. Laura flinched as he crossed to the bed.

"Yeah," she dared him, hating him. "We all do it together, on the deck of your goddam boat, every night!"

Big Jim lost it, she could see it in his eyes as he drew back his hand above her.

She'd pushed him too far. But a beating would be worth it if it would get him out of her life once and for all. She steeled herself for the blow.

"Excuse me," threaded a woman's meek voice through the doorway. Big Jim's fist hung in mid-air. Laura tore her eyes from his red face and looked to see who had saved her.

A young, shapely, dark-haired woman in a see-through blouse stood beneath the porch light just outside the room. Her made-up face was a mixture of desperation and relief. She looked vaguely familiar to Laura. Big Jim slowly lowered his hand and made a show of smoothing the front of his jacket. He glanced over his shoulder at the woman.

"What?" he hissed.

"I really gotta use the ladies room," the newcomer whined.

"Wait in the car," Big Jim ordered.

"Come in, please," Laura countermanded. She used the opportunity to clamber off the bed and put it between herself and her husband. But there was no clear path past him to the door, to freedom.

Without a second glance at Big Jim, the brunette hurried into the motel room, passing in front of the table-lamp which backlit her and revealed a peek-a-boo bra cradling proud breasts beneath the gauze-thin material of her white blouse. She smiled sadly at Laura, muttered a grateful thanks and disappeared into the bathroom, closing the door.

Laura folded her arms and stared hard at Big Jim, who seemed to have shrunk an inch or two. It came to her, the woman she and Steve had met at Kelly's, the one who had stopped to inquire about the reef tour. Big Jim's bimbo. Gotcha!

"Look," Laura said, finding some strength. "You might as well take your girlfriend and leave. I'm not going back with you." She let her final statement hang in the air.

Big Jim moved to the door and pressed it shut. He stubbed out his cigar in the ashtray and reached under his coat. In a smooth motion, he leveled his .38 at her belly. Laura tried not to react. The bathroom door snicked open and the brunette stepped back into the room.

"God, that's so much better," she breathed. "I thought I was gonna pop!" She turned to Big Jim and her pretty face went slack.

"Enough of this bullshit," he growled, and waggled the pistol at the door. "Let's go, Laura. Get in the car."

"Where are we going?"

"I want to see where you work. I want to see if my boat is there and find that Winchell guy you say you're not sleeping with."

Liza made a whimpering noise and started for the door.

"Not you," Big Jim commanded. "There's no room in the Mercedes." He fished out his wallet and tossed a twenty on the bedspread. "Call a cab and wait for me at the hotel. I'll be back later."

Liza took the folded bill and looked at the floor. She whispered guiltily, "I'm sorry, Mrs. Quinn."

Big Jim made a face. "Wait till we're gone, then call a taxi from here. And don't use one of those faggy pink ones! You," he told Laura, still pointing the gun at her. "Let's go."

"Can I change first?" Laura asked, trying to buy time. She had to stall and warn Winch somehow. But how? They'd never gotten around to installing the phone line to the dock, and her wild-eyed husband would never have let her make a call anyway. She considered the problem in desperation. Maybe she could lead Jim somewhere else, an empty dock, but she didn't know where to go to find one. She sure wished he'd let her get dressed first.

"You're fine as you are," he interrupted her thoughts. "We're just going for a ride. In fact," he added, "you drive."

The brunette never lifted her eyes from the carpeting as Big Jim herded his wife out the door to the parking lot. Liza heard the car doors slam and the balky, seawater-infested engine cough to life. She sat down on the bed and pulled the slim phone book out of the drawer of the nightstand. She never hated a man so much in her life as she did at that moment. Worse, she was starting to fear him. Big Jim was acting crazy now. He was slipping over the edge. She needed to split this scene, get outta Dodge, but her luggage and remaining money was back at the hotel.

Liza spied the mini-fridge in the corner and helped herself to a bottle of mineral water, then looked up the number of a cab company. She called the pink one anyway, out of spite.

*******

The engine sputtered, gave a final lurch, and then quit completely. Marco pulled in the clutch and coasted the bone-dry Suzuki to the side of Route 1. In his excitement at finally nearing Key West, he'd completely forgotten that he'd switched to the reserve tank back on Marathon. He should have stopped for gas at Big Pine, and he hadn't passed a single open station since.

Marco lowered the kickstand and dismounted. In the early hours of a Tuesday morning, sometime past midnight, traffic was sparse on the Overseas Highway. A salty mist shrouded the road, dampening his clothes. Alien swamp-sounds echoed from the mangrove. Without the light from the headlamp, the darkness was nearly total.

"Fuck," he whispered, and removed his helmet, setting it on the saddle. Marco looked up and down the fog-shrouded highway. Not a light in sight.

He sighed and crunched down the gravel shoulder in his boots, kicking dispiritedly at stray pebbles, walking west.

About a half-mile or so on, a dim light showed itself from the opposite side of the road. He angled toward it and paused at the entrance of a shell-paved trail leading into the mangroves. The small spotlight illuminated a weathered wooden sign which announced his arrival at the Bide-a-Wee Campground. Faintly, through the tangle of tropical undergrowth and trees, a series of lights shone, and he could hear the muted sounds of laughter and country music.

Someone here must have some gas to spare, he thought. Marco trudged down the narrow track, the night sounds growing louder all around him, and he worried about gators and snakes and panthers. Oh, my.

As he emerged from the mangrove into a large salt-meadow, he found dozens of travel-trailers, tents and rough-wood cabins spread out before him. Marco was about to take another step when he got the creepy feeling that there was someone behind him. Before her could turn, he felt the distinctive poke of a gun barrel in his back, hard steel against soft muscle.

"Don't move," a low voice ordered, and Marco obliged. A pair of rough hands ran over his body and relieved him of the switchblade in his hip pocket. The rifle barrel in his back prodded him forward.

\* \* \* \* \* \* \*

"You know," Laura said glumly, "this is the first time you ever let me drive the Mercedes." The engine missed. "What's wrong with it?"

"Your boyfriend Winchell is what's wrong with it. Engine's still full of seawater." Big Jim held the gun in his lap, staring out the windshield.

"I told you, he's not my boyfriend. And he doesn't have your boat!" She glanced at him as she drove along A1A near Smathers Beach. "Face it Jim. The *LauraLee* is gone. Give it up already!"

"Uh-uh," he huffed. "I *saw* it, and he had it. Liza traced the registration and I traced him."

They rode in silence through the nearly deserted early-morning streets until they were passing the airport. Then Laura spoke.

"Liza. That's your little friend, then? Nice looking girl. A bit flashy, though."

Big Jim didn't answer. He was trying to work up enough hate to blow away Winchell as soon as he saw him. Then he'd fish the keys off the corpse and he'd have his beautiful yacht again. As for Laura, well, he hadn't figured out that part yet. He didn't particularly want to kill her too, but he couldn't allow any witnesses either. Perhaps he could kill Winchell out of her sight, get Liza and disappear.

Liza. Screw her! Barging in on them when he'd told her to stay in the car. At least she'd been useful, calling the motel, asking for Laura Chadwick's room so his wife would unlock the door. The first time they'd called the Rainforest Resort, he'd foolishly and automatically asked for Laura Quinn's room. Hearing that there was no one registered by that name, Big Jim had correctly surmised she was using her maiden name, shrugging off their seven years of marriage like an old winter coat. How could she betray him like that, after all he'd done for her? Women, he decided, just couldn't be trusted. Even Liza had become a real bitch over the last week. Who needed her? The Mercedes was ruined, so maybe he'd abandon it and his mistress, and sail the boat out alone. Maybe he could even take Laura along, show her what a mistake she'd made leaving him. They'd had some good times, though none came immediately to mind, and she was still fairly young and good-looking. He stole a look at her bare legs as they worked the pedals.

Yeah, first he'd waste Winchell and get the keys to the boat, then he could take Laura down to one of the staterooms and have a little reunion. He licked his lips, tasting victory.

Laura drove over the short bridge to Stock Island and Big Jim shifted in his seat to relive the bulge in his pants. He was getting himself all worked up. "How much further?" he asked.

"Not far," his wife answered. Laura hadn't yet come up with a diversion. All she could hope for was that she would have enough time to yell to Winch to warn him. Grabbing the gun from Big Jim's lap was out of the question. Unless . . .

She moved her hand from the gearshift to Big Jim's thigh. Let him think things were going his way. She slid her fingertips towards his crotch, towards the weapon. With his right hand, he drew the pistol back out of her reach. With his left, he grabbed her groping hand and pulled it against his hard dick. He leered at her.

"I knew you missed it," he said, leaning toward her ear. Then he pushed her hand away and smiled. "Later. After I get the boat."

Laura shuddered. She made the last turns that took them into the SuRF parking lot and pulled to a stop at the foot of the pier. Along the dock, empty black water rippled under moonlight. She stared. The *Key Monster* was gone!

Big Jim looked around and then at her.

"So, where the fuck is my boat?"

Laura's mind raced. Good question. Finally, she said, "I told you, we don't have your boat. The Foundation boat sank last week and we don't have a replacement yet. See? There's nothing here!"

Big Jim thought for a moment, his arousal subsiding.

"Where's Winchell live?"

Laura shook her head. "I don't know. I hardly know the man. He just works for us." She tried to keep her voice steady, forcing a tone of annoyance into her words. "Now can I please go home and get some sleep?"

He pounded the dashboard in frustration, making Laura jump. "Shit!" He swung his poisonous gaze at her. "He's coming to work tomorrow?"

"Yes, I mean, I don't know. Until we get a new boat, there's nothing for him to do, and who knows where the guy hangs out?"

Big Jim chuckled dryly. "Still sticking to that bullshit story." He mimicked her: "'We don't have your boat, Big Jim. I don't know *where* Winchell is.' Cut the crap. C'mon. Drive."

"Where?" she asked weakly.

"Back downtown. I'm not lettin' you outta my sight until I get this straightened out."

Big Jim gave her directions to the Pier House. Winchell would show up tomorrow, he was sure of it, could feel it in his bones. Or in his boner.

He watched Laura from the corner of his eye as she guided the Mercedes back into Key West. The wet-bar in the suite was well-stocked, Liza was well-built, he was well-hung. And Laura? Well, Laura would do whatever he wanted her to do, as long as he had the gun. Yeah, he hoped, the evening might not be a total loss yet.

Big Jim relaxed in the leather bucket seat and, staring at his wife, painted lascivious thoughts in his head.

\* \* \* \* \* \* \*

Rolf Schenk and Eugene "Winch" Winchell had just drunk yet another toast to the coming revolution. The schnapps bottle was emptying rapidly. It was bottom-shelf booze, and Winch thought of it as the Thunderbird of schnapps. It was giving him a headache. Rolf had set up another round for his guest when a knock resounded upon the door of his trailer. It echoed in the small room.

"Come!" he said loudly. Winch rubbed his ears and wondered again how to get out of here gracefully. It was past 1 A.M. and he wanted to get back to the *Key Monster*, tied up at the campground pier, before Felix awoke.

The door swung open and Lt. Ray stepped in. He saluted crisply and stood at attention.

"General," he announced. "We have found another intruder and taken him prisoner, sir."

"What?" choked a clearly startled Rolf as he pulled himself unsteadily to his bare feet.

"A Spic, sir," the lieutenant boasted. "He was snooping around out front."

Winch closed his eyes tightly and prayed that Felix hadn't chosen this moment to step onto American soil for the first time.

Rolf rubbed the bridge of his nose. Damnation! They couldn't go around taking prisoners! That was kidnapping, and the cops would certainly get involved! He sighed. "Where is he?"

"Outside, sir. He had this on him." He dropped the switchblade on the table. "Should I bring him in?"

Rolf nodded, deciding to be strong in the presence of a guest, show Eugene just how tough the AAFF really was.

"Bring him in!" Lt. Ray called outside to the guard detail.

With a shove, the Puerto Rican tumbled through the doorway. Winch gagged on his drink. Marco looked up from the floor at the general, and then swept his eyes 'round the room, taking in the stack of weaponry and the Nazi banner draped on the wall. His heart was in his throat. And then he saw Winch.

"Winch!" he gasped. Winch, unencumbered by serious drugs for a change, and fueled by the cheap schnapps, leapt to his feet. He smacked the drug dealer across the scar on his cheek.

"That's *Captain*," he bellowed. Marco was vastly confused. All he had wanted was a little gasoline. Now here was Winch, a secret Nazi, the last person he expected to see here, smacking him around at gunpoint. Winch turned to Rolf, who looked a bit confused himself.

"I have to apologize," he said stiffly to the general. "This is one of my crewmen, from my boat." Partly to keep up the charade, and partly because it had been so satisfying the first time, Winch slapped Marco again. Marco felt the rifle barrel in his kidney, and was too stunned to speak anyway.

"What are you doing off the boat?" the captain screamed in Marco's face. "I told you and Felix to stay on board! How dare you disobey my order!" He drew his hand back again and Marco flinched. The general grabbed Winch's wrist, arresting the blow. Winch looked at the head skinhead.

"This is one of your men?" Rolf asked.

Winch nodded. "It's so hard to get good white help nowadays," he replied. "I pay them practically nothing and remind them if they misbehave I'll have them deported. Isn't that right, Marco?"

"*Si*," the shanghaied man managed.

Winch swatted at Marco's head again, but he ducked the blow. "Who told you to speak?" Winch bawled. Lt. Ray and the man holding the gun on Marco grinned.

"General," Winch said more calmly. "I believe I've imposed on you long enough. With your permission, I'll take this sub-human back to the boat and see that he's punished for disobeying my orders."

Rolf nodded, relieved to see any potential charge of abduction evaporate. It would not be his responsibility. "It's been a pleasure," he told his guest.

Winch took Marco by the arm and headed for the door. He paused and looked back at the general.

"Tomorrow night?"

"We'll be there," Rolf promised. "Oh, and before you go, I almost forgot." He rummaged through the bottom of his tiny closet and handed Winch a catcher's mitt and a bat. "You asked for these?"

Winch grinned and accepted the items, handing them to a puzzled, bruised Marco to carry.

"Yeah, thanks! Can't play in the church softball game without 'em!"

And he pushed Marco out the door ahead of him and down the path to where the *Key Monster* rocked on the water.

# CHAPTER 19

"Hey, man. This stuff is beginning to melt."

Marco looked at the folded towel he'd been holding against his cheek. It was stained a sticky green from the leaking can of frozen margarita mix, nature's icepack. The bruise just beneath his right eye was a puffy purple.

Winch fished a fresh can of concentrate from the galley freezer and handed it to Marco.

"Why'd ya hafta hit me so hard? And twice?"

"Sorry," Winch smiled and headed for the companionway to the afterdeck. "C'mon up and I'll tell you about it."

Reluctantly, still holding the makeshift compress to his wounded cheek, Marco followed the hippie topside.

Winch helmed the *Key Monster* up Lower Sugarloaf Sound and underneath the Harris Channel Bridge, retracing his route. Marco joined him alongside the wheel and stared off into the black tropical night, the horizon an uncertain blur between sea and sky. Winch piloted slowly, picking out the channel markers with care. The *Key Monster* drew a lot of water. This wasn't at all like sailing the Chesapeake, deep water almost anywhere you cared to go. Instead, the captain was forced to creep along, winding among scattered keys of mangrove and sudden sandbars, circling all the way around Sugarloaf until they'd navigated Bow Channel and popped out into the Atlantic. A trip that would have taken no more than thirty minutes by car cost almost two hours on a boat this big. Winch produced a six-pack and they had a mini-reunion. Marco told him about his trip, skipping a few highlights.

"I really am sorry I had to hit you," the captain nodded as they rolled into the Atlantic. He goosed the throttles.

"Well, I guess you owed me one," Marco conceded, remembering the sucker-punch he'd greeted Winch with outside the Oarhouse last week.

"Those guys back there would've ripped you to shreds if I hadn't kept you quiet." He glanced at Marco seriously. "White supremacists. Hate blacks, Jews, gays, and spics, no offense."

"And you're hangin' out with 'em?"

Winch smiled again. "A friend of mine in Key West is planning a little surprise party for them. I'm not exactly sure what he has in mind, but I'm going to be there. He said I could bartend if I promised to duck for cover at the appropriate time."

Marco stared at Winch, standing behind the wheel, lit only by the green glow of tachometer and pressure gauge lamps. He looked a little scary, with wild, unkempt blond hair flying loose in the wind. Marco took a conciliatory tone.

"So, what you doin' down here? You ran out on me, you know."

Winch bit his lip. "The nine hundred?"

Marco nodded, unseen in the darkness. "Your pal, Brant, told me you'd come down here."

"Didn't he tell you that I promised to send you the money?"

"No," Marco admitted. "I guess we didn't give him the chance."

"We?"

"Yeah, some big dickhead was roughing him up when I got to the Oarhouse, looking for you."

Winch blanched. "Is Brant okay?"

"Yeah, he's fine. He's a good kid."

"Who was this guy?" Winch asked, relieved to hear Brant hadn't been hurt.

"Dunno. We didn't swap names. Said you stole his boat and he was comin' down here to get you. Big guy. Looked like an insurance salesman. He had a gun, .38, I think."

Winch remembered the dude from the Harbor Lights Marina, shooting at the *Stuffed Ham* as he and Brant made their getaway. Not an angry father. Laura's deranged husband.

"Does he know where I am?"

Marco shrugged. "Knew as much as I did, just that you were goin' to Key West. He an' I kinda made a bet about who would find you first."

"Guess you won," Winch admitted. "I haven't seen him down here." He pounded the wheel. "Man, I *knew* this boat was too good to be true!"

He peered at Marco through the tropical darkness, a neon-green pallor washing his stubbled face. With a deep breath, Winch said, "Now I suppose *you* want your money."

Marco stilled himself for a moment, thinking.

"Ya know, man? I don't even really care anymore."

Winch looked at the drug dealer suspiciously.

"I mean," Marco went on, "you saved my ass back there. I know what a skinhead is, I figured they was gonna string me up or somethin'. I was shittin' my pants! You coulda let 'em kill me, but you didn't." He placed a hand on Winch's shoulder. "Guess I owe you another one."

"Look," Winch said. "How long've we known each other?"

Marco thought for a minute. "Fifteen years?"

"Sixteen," Winch corrected and grinned. "You even came to my mom's funeral. How many scummy drug dealers would've done that? I really appreciated it. Listen. I've got some money coming in real soon, and I'll pay you like I said I would."

"Thanks, man," Marco told him. And then he wondered, "Hey, could we get to Puerto Rico on this boat?"

Winch gazed levelly at Marco and the two of them hammered out a deal to forgo Winch's debt in exchange for a passage to San Juan. Marco confessed that he'd had enough dealing drugs, it wasn't a reliable way to raise a family. Pushing forty himself, it was time to get out of the game. He'd decided, somewhere back in the Everglades, to get to Puerto Rico and follow in his parent's footsteps, open a flower shop and send for his wife and daughters. Winch had to agree, it sounded like a good plan.

"What about your bike, back on Sugarloaf?" Winch reminded him.

"That beat-up piece of Japanese shit? Screw it. When I get to Puerto Rico, I'll get myself a Harley. Damn Suzuki nearly killed me gettin' down here. Bikers made fun of me!" Winch laughed.

While the sunrise heralded the arrival of another perfect Tuesday morning, they talked the rest of the way back to Stock Island, Winch filling Marco in on some of the craziness he'd encountered in Key West. He even found himself talking about the sea monster he kept seeing. Marco scoffed and advised Winch to stay off the acid for awhile.

The captain told him about Laura, and their plan for taking the tourists out for reef tours on the *Key Monster*. Winch chuckled and added, "And wait till you meet my friend Daiquiri! You like your women big and dark?"

"Weench?" interrupted a hollow voice from below. Marco started.

"Oh," Winch calmed him. "That's just Felix. We pulled him out of the ocean yesterday. He's a Cuban. Here, hold the wheel," he added as he stepped to the hatchway.

"I'm up here, Felix," he called below.

"The *baño* is crapshit," Felix called back.

Winch sighed.

\* \* \* \* \* \* \*

With one hand, he turned over the keys to the Mercedes to the valet. With the other, Big Jim steered Laura by her upper arm across the lobby to the elevator. "Don't make a scene," he hissed, but people were staring anyway. How could they not at the beautiful blonde woman striding barefoot across the tiles in only a thin pajama top and panties? "Sleepwalker," muttered Big Jim to the rabbit-faced desk clerk as they hurried past.

Upstairs, he slipped his keycard in the slot and turned the handle. He pressed Laura through the doorway. The living area was dimly lit. Most of the available light spilled from the open door to the bedroom, where Big Jim found Liza tossing her clothes into a suitcase.

"What the hell you doing?"

"Packing," she said flatly, never looking up. On top of a silk blouse she threw her curling wand.

"Seems like all your women are leaving you," remarked Laura from the doorway. Her husband seethingly ignored her.

"I'm not going to be part of any kidnapping," Liza declared as she folded a skirt. "You're on your own from here on. I'm going back to Maryland."

"Babe," he said soothingly.

"Shit," snorted Laura, and turned away.

"You wait right here," Big Jim commanded Liza and hurried after his wife.

"Fuck you," Liza muttered after him.

Laura had found the wet bar and was pouring herself a bourbon, neat. Big Jim strode to the door and double-locked it before he faced her.

"Yeah. Good idea, a drink. Pour me a scotch while you're at it." Laura took her drink and sat down on the couch. Big Jim poured his own drink and took a seat in the chair opposite her. He pulled the .38 from his jacket pocket and set it on the table beside him, within easy reach. He couldn't imagine using it on his wife, but she didn't know that, and its mere presence, he hoped, would be intimidation enough to control her.

He studied his errant wife. She'd changed in the week or so since he'd last seen her. Not just the new tan, something else. She didn't cringe when he threatened her. She sassed him back. She'd never done *that* before! And her green eyes had a jagged, dangerous cast to them. He swallowed some scotch and waited.

"So," Laura said, cradling her own drink in her lap. "That's your latest bimbo?"

"I'm not a bimbo!" Liza chided from the bedroom.

"Sor-ry," Laura called back sarcastically. She gazed at Big Jim.

"Why'd you leave?" he asked her quietly, staying in control.

"My question is, why did I stay so long?"

"Ah, crap," he mumbled and took another drink.

"So, how come you're here in Key West?" Laura leaned forward, glaring at him. "You couldn't have known where I'd gone. Did you come down here to find *me*, or your goddam boat?"

Big Jim glanced away to the sliding glass doors overlooking the light-spangled Gulf. Laura shook her head. Just as she'd suspected, her husband couldn't answer her, not without a blatant lie. She sat back again, but continued to stare at him. In their deadly silence, from the adjoining room came the distinct sound of luggage locks snapping shut.

"So," Laura said finally, "now what do we do? Sit here until the next hurricane hits and knocks down the hotel? That's just the way my luck is running."

"We wait till morning, then we're going back to the dock to get the boat."

"Ahh," Laura nodded wisely. "Then it *was* the boat you came here for."

"Yeah, smart mouth," he growled. "It was. But I got lucky and found you first. I was gonna do it the other way around, but this works out just fine. Saves me a trip to Michigan, to your mother's."

He was interrupted when Liza appeared, holding her suitcase and wearing a lime sweater over a lemon pantsuit in the bedroom doorway,. "Hey, where you think you're going?" Big Jim barked.

"I told you," Liza spat back. "Home."

"You can't get a flight out till morning. It's fucking two-thirty in the middle of the night!" His earlier fantasies of a menage-a-troi vanished.

"Then I'll wait in the lobby," Liza informed him and walked to the door. Big Jim stared hard at her back as she fumbled with the deadbolt. Laura kept one eye on Big Jim's gun; with the other, she watched Liza go. Good riddance, she thought sourly.

Liza paused in the open door and glanced back over her shoulder. "Goodbye, Jim. And don't ever call me again." And then to Laura she said, more gently, "I'm really sorry about all this. I must have been out of my mind."

And she left.

Laura was genuinely surprised. That had been a pretty classy exit. She glanced back at her husband and saw the wounded look spreading across his face. Good, she thought. Serves him right.

Big Jim sighed deeply and drained his scotch, tinkling the melting ice cubes. He got up to pour himself another. Damn it, he brooded, if just one more fucking thing goes wrong . . .

The telephone rang. Maybe it was Liza, calling from the lobby to apologize. He picked up the phone, keeping an eye on Laura, and found out he was only half-right. The call coming from the lobby part. He listened for a moment, squeezing the glass in his hand to within a degree of shattering.

"HE WHAT?" he screamed into the receiver. Laura could hear a frantic and clearly terrified voice from the phone as Big Jim listened. "I'm coming right down!" he barked and slammed the phone down. He scooped up the gun and replaced it in his pocket.

"Come on," Big Jim ordered his wife. "We're going downstairs. Fucking valet wrecked my car!"

\* \* \* \* \* \* \*

When Liza emerged from the elevator, the relative peace of the middle-of-the-night lobby had vanished. A hotel employee in a red jacket was sprawled on a chair holding a bloody mess of gauze to the bridge of his mangled nose. The night manager was bending over him, alternating between making sure the man was alright and promising to fire him. The rabbit-faced desk clerk stood at his station, white as a hotel sheet, the phone in his clenched fist held slightly away from his ear. A sparse crowd of rubbernecking staff and guests murmured around the periphery. Outside, past the front doors, red strobe lights painted the foot of Duval Street. The clerk grimaced and cradled the phone. "He's coming right down," he called, sounding a little fearful, to the manager. Liza set her suitcase next to an unoccupied chair and approached the desk.

"What's going on?" she inquired.

"Just a minor accident," he replied, regaining some composure. From here on his boss, the night manager, would deal with the car's owner. He'd only been told to deliver the bad news. "Everything is under control. Can I help you with something?" he added, hoping her request would remove him from the lobby and the coming storm. The staff had been enduring the pompous Mr. Quinn for a week now. Then suddenly, the clerk recognized Liza.

"Oh, *Mrs.* Quinn!" he gasped mistakenly. "We're so sorry about your husband's car! Of course, the hotel is insured and . . ."

"His car?" Liza asked, puzzled.

The desk clerk lowered his voice. "We had a slight accident. The parking valet hit a delivery truck head-on. We're so sorry, Mrs. Quinn."

The elevator doors swept open. Liza glanced in that direction and then back at the clerk. She, too, lowered her voice, but smiled a little as she said, "Can you keep a secret? I'm *not* Mrs. Quinn." She pointed to the woman wearing nothing but a pajama top and panties, and whispered, "*That* poor woman is Mrs. Quinn."

The desk clerk hooded his eyes and nodded. "I understand." Of course he did. He worked in a hotel in Key West. He'd seen it all.

Liza turned toward Laura and gave a discreet little wave and a sly smile. Mrs. Quinn was going to just love this.

\* \* \* \* \* \* \*

Laura and Liza stood together in the shadows of the veranda outside the front door. Staying within arms reach of them, Big Jim talked agitatedly with a Key West cop and the hotel's night manager. The silver Mercedes squatted in the middle of Duval, the front of the car battered and dented against the grill of a Volvo truck. The truck was hardly marked. The Mercedes was banged up pretty good, but still looked like it could be driven.

"He had it coming," breathed Liza.

"I always hated that car," Laura whispered back. They observed a small truce in the wake of Big Jim's automotive disaster, united against a common foe.

The clearly annoyed policeman was taking notes as the paramedics arrived to tend to the injured valet. Laura mused that it would be so simple to walk up to the officer and tell him that her husband had kidnapped her and that he had a gun in his coat. But Big Jim was raving, threatening to sue the hotel, punch out the manager and finish off the stupid valet who had damaged his car. His hand was already in the pocket with the gun, and Laura was beginning to suspect that her husband had become a little unbalanced since she'd left him. She'd seen him angry before, plenty of times, but never like this. She actually feared that he might do something crazy if she tried to get the cop's attention. Maybe better to wait a bit and see if Big Jim talked his way into jail on his own.

Liza stood grinning, enjoying the unfolding scene. The wrecker, with yellow lights flashing, struggled to separate the two vehicles. Laura shivered in the chilly night air. It couldn't have been more than 55 degrees, the coldest part of the night. Liza noticed Laura's discomfort.

"Here," she said, slipping off her sweater. She offered it to the ill-clad Laura.

Laura looked at it for a moment at the end of her enemy's outstretched arm. The wind blew right through her and up the hem of her pajama top.

"Thanks," she reluctantly accepted and slipped it on. It smelled of lavender.

Liza looked away, back at the accident scene. "It's okay. I've got another in my bag."

They stood in silence a moment, listening to Big Jim blather. The cop was losing patience. Under the cover of the argument Laura mumbled, "I'm sorry I called you a bimbo."

"S'okay," Liza said quietly. "I guess I am."

"Why?" whispered Laura. "I mean, why Jim?"

Liza just shrugged. She looked over at Jim's wife. "I really am sorry. I didn't know when we met that he was married. Said he was a widower."

"Humph," grumped Laura.

"By the time I found out about you," she went on, "well, I guess I was in pretty deep with him. You know how he can be, turn on the charm when he wants something. And I've never seen someone throw money around like he does! I grew up poor, I'm just a data entry operator now, and having money like that, well, it's like doing opium, you get hooked."

Laura didn't want to understand, but she did. Liza was telling Laura's own story. She, too, had not found out for a long time that Jim had only been separated, not divorced as he'd claimed to be, the whole time they'd dated. When she'd confronted him, threatening to break it off, he'd flown to the Caribbean and gotten a quickie-divorce that same week. At the time, Laura had been touched by his apparent sincerity. She'd taken him back, stupidly, and they were married the next weekend at the beach in Delaware. Laura had never met Jim's first wife, never had the courage to face her. Why she had gone ahead and married him anyway, against her mother's better judgement, was the very story Liza was telling her now.

"He'd told me you'd left him," Liza said.

"I had."

"When he found out you were in Key West, he went bananas! He made me call your motel room with that stupid story about the plumber." She stole a glance at Laura. "Of course, I didn't know at the time it was you I was calling. He hadn't told me he'd found you, just that he had a friend he wanted to play a joke on. I didn't know that you were Miss Chadwick."

Laura shivered again, but not from the breeze. *That conniving bastard*, she fumed. She took a long look at Liza. About Laura's height, but a fuller bosom, slimmer hips, and younger, of course. Short dark hair, looking a little like Marisa Tomei. Probably about half-a-dozen years between them, mid- to late-twenties. Too dumb to know any better, falling for Jim's smooth lines, just like she had almost seven years ago.

"I was gonna leave him anyway," Liza continued in a whisper. "I mean, even before tonight. I was pretty much fed up with him. Only," she paused, "I don't have enough money to get home. My Visa is maxxed out and all I've got is thirty-five dollars cash."

"Well, don't look at me," smiled Laura grimly, indicating her outfit. She looked back at Liza sadly. "Did you love him?"

"Yes," came the barely audible answer, and Laura hated that it made her heart ache anyway.

The circus was winding down. The policeman had put away his notebook and Big Jim was calmer now, casting wary glances at the two women in his life while he tried to listen to what the manager was saying about insurance. Laura sidled a little closer to Liza.

"If you have no money, where were you going tonight?"

"Don't know. I just knew I couldn't stay here, make more trouble for you. Just . . . away."

"I can't blame you for any of this. If it hadn't been you, then it would have been someone else, sooner or later." Laura was talking faster now. "Listen. You have enough money for a cab. I've got a friend, where I work, over on Stock Island. Will you help me?"

Liza answered with a secret squeeze to Laura's hand. Laura explained how to find Winch and the *Key Monster*. "Warn him that Jim's going to come looking for the boat tomorrow, he's got to get out of there. And tell him to call Steve and Taylor. They'll think of something." She didn't want to leave the planning of her rescue to Winch.

The cop left and the night manager personally steered the Mercedes to a parking space. It still seemed to be driveable, though the front end had a noticeable shimmy. Big Jim took a step over to the two women and said, "C'mon, ladies, party's over. Back upstairs." He waggled the gun through the material of his jacket pocket.

Liza looked at Laura for a moment and then at Big Jim. She picked up her suitcase and told him, as smoothly as she could, "Three's a crowd. I'm outta here."

Big Jim glowered at Liza as she hiked over to the cab-stand. Then he turned to Laura and took her by the arm again.

"All right, let's go."

He steered her back through the lobby, where the desk clerk cowered, and muttered darkly about the fuckin' valet, hoped he could die from a fuckin' broken nose. Laura glanced back through the lobby doors and glimpsed Liza as she slipped into a cab.

Another pink one.

# CHAPTER 20

Deep in the water, in the wide strait between the chain of islets and the great island he has already circled twice, he swims. Plenty of fish here. Big, tasty fish that he must stroke hard after in order to catch. No sign of the she who carries his pup, but there is no surprise, no disappointment in this. He feels only hunger, then fullness, and the occasional longing to drift on the powerful northward current to a place that a tiny spot in his brain recalls faintly as his ancient home.

It is a place he has never visited in the many seasons he has wandered the oceans. He knows, somehow, that it is very far away, where the water is cold and deep. Though he doesn't understand this, all of his kind, the last hundreds who remain, know of this place, buried in their collective memories. He has dreamt of a long, narrow stretch of sheltered water, difficult to reach, and surrounded by barren, windswept hills. It is a place he will attempt to reach when his time of freedom in the seas is close to an end, and he will go there to pass his final days, much as elephants return to a certain spot to die, though he knows nothing of elephants.

He knows only of food, and his pursuit of a new meal takes him ever deeper in these warm waters. The tarpon he chases is tiring, and with a last flick of his tail, he closes the gap and the unfortunate fish is his. He gulps, stops swimming and drifts along, digesting. A shiny object on the seabed attracts his eye. He approaches it, cautiously.

It is a mancraft of some sort, but it is not on the surface where it belongs. Nor is it in one piece. There are bits of dull metal strewn about the bottom. And it is most odd because, when he examines it, he sees that it has two great flippers sprouting from each side. A jagged hole on the dorsal side near the mancraft's head is evident, as is the man itself, strapped into the seat, his foreflippers waving limply in the wash of the tide.

But this is not food, and he loses interest and swims on. He hears churning in the water and peers up toward the surface where dual propellers thrash beneath another large mancraft, this one on top of the dawn-lit water where it belongs. Familiar shape, this one, distinctive. For some reason he thinks of food again, and pushes himself forward to follow.

## KEY MONSTER

\* \* \* \* \* \* \*

Winch felt the hair rise on the back of his neck. He swept his eyes over the chop nervously in the first light of dawn. There was nothing to see other than the blue-gray ocean and the distant line of keys to the north. Yet, he couldn't shake the feeling that he was being watched. He rubbed his eyes, tired and grainy from lack of sleep, and hollered down the companionway to Felix to bring him his morning beer. Instead, Marco poked his head out of the hatch and handed Winch a cold one.

"Man, it's really beginning to stink down there," he told the captain.

"Felix wants to know when you're gonna come down and fix the toilet."

Winch scowled. He was sleepy and short-tempered. He snapped the bungee cord into place on the wheel and stomped below, brushing past Marco.

In the salon, sprawled comfortably on the leather sofa, Felix juggled a baseball from hand to hand. He grinned up at Winch.

"Weench, it smell so bad. You fix?"

Winch clamped his nostrils shut and pulled open the door to the head. He found the plunger and stalked back to the couch, tossing the device at Felix.

"Here," he grumped. Felix looked at the plunger.

"You no *reparar*?"

"I no *reparar*. You fix," Winch told him. "You're supposed to be the mate, and unclogging the head is the mate's job."

Winch left without another word and returned to the helm where he found Marco finishing the beer he had brought for the captain.

"You were kinda rough on him," Marco observed. Winch looked at him narrowly, still unable to escape the feeling that a pair of dark, reptilian eyes was tracking him.

"Just get me another beer, please," was all he said. Marco shrugged and shuffled to the galley.

With the sun above the horizon finally, and after his two customary morning beers and a few eye-opening tokes, Winch was feeling much better. He was sorry that he had been ugly with Felix, but the truth was he'd never had a crew before and didn't really know how to handle one. In addition,

Winch was a loner by nature. Suddenly, in less than twenty-four hours, he'd acquired two roommates. But what could he do? Kick them into the ocean? He decided to try to be a better friend and shipmaster. Winch glanced at the baseball equipment atop the console and grinned. There'd be no work today, aside from the usual maintenance, and after a nap they'd see if Felix was really as good a ballplayer as he claimed.

He spun the wheel to port and aimed the *Key Monster* toward Cow Key Channel and home. He called below to Marco and Felix, "Come topside and prepare to man the lines!"

The two Latinos scrambled onto the deck. Marco took up a station in the stern and Felix climbed over the gunwale to make his way to the bow. Winch stopped him.

"Felix? Sorry I got mad," he said over the thrum of the engines. "I'll help you fix the head later, okay?"

Felix paused, then smiled and nodded. He hurried up to his position on the bow.

Idled down, the *Key Monster* glided over the protected water of the channel, angling in toward the splintered wood of the SuRF dock. Winch checked to be sure Marco and Felix were ready to snag the lines from the pilings. They were. An unexpected feeling of pride grew in him. A crew! He had an honest-to-God crew! He took a look at the pier to gauge his approach and was startled by what he saw.

She was lovely, about five-feet-six, short, dark hair swirling in the morning breeze, back-lit by the rising sun. A body he'd very much like to explore molded into a yellow pantssuit. He threw the engines into reverse to stop the drift and the boat kissed the bumpers along the dock. He shut down the diesels and shaded his eyes, peering across to the woman. "Ahoy!" he called.

"Ahoy yourself," she called back with an unfriendly edge to her voice. "You Winch?"

Uh-oh, he thought. Is this someone I should know? Is this someone I *have* known, in the Biblical sense? He decided to be cautious. On the bow, Felix was doing a credible job of tying up, leaving enough slack in the line to counter the rise and fall of the tide. Winch grabbed the spring line amidships and tightened it around a cleat. In the stern, Marco had created an incredible snarl of rope and the transom was starting to drift away from the dock. Winch hurried to assist the drug dealer, quickly untangling the line and tossing the loose end toward the pier.

"Grab the line!" he urged the woman standing there. She did as she was told. Marco, embarrassed, stared at her. She looked a good deal like his wife, but trimmer and younger. Suddenly he missed Maria deeply.

Without waiting for an invitation, the woman jumped from the dock onto the deck. "Welcome aboard," Winch said doubtfully. She looked up at him, hard.

"Where the hell have you been?" she rasped. "I've been freezing my ass on that dock half the night!"

"Uh . . ."

"You're Winch, right? And this is the *Key Monster*?" She gazed about the vast 57-footer, biting her lower lip. "Now I see why he wants it back."

"Excuse me?"

"Big Jim's been looking for this boat all week, said you stole it from him."

"Who?" Winch struggled. The name was familiar, something Laura had said. He held out his hands before she could yell at him again. "No, wait. First, who the hell are you?"

"I'm Liza Benedetto." No bells went off in Winch's head. Felix and Marco gathered around to study this gorgeous apparition that had appeared on the afterdeck. She looked from one to the other and asked of them, "Are you Steve and Taylor?"

"Who?" stuttered Marco.

"*Quien?*" stammered Felix.

"No, they're not," replied Winch. He tilted his shaggy head toward them. "Felix and Marco, my crew. Yeah, I'm Winch. Now, you want to tell me what you want before I throw you off my boat?" Winch just hated when someone boarded without permission. It was an old seagoing tradition, one his father had taught him and one Winch still respected.

Liza sagged a little, the anger in her eyes dissipating, replaced by fatigue and relief. "Sorry," she said. "I've been up all night."

"Me, too." Winch said. "Beer?"

Felix heard the magic word and dashed below. After being reprimanded by the captain earlier, he was anxious to please. Marco took a seat on the transom, gazing at Liza and daydreaming about his wife.

"I've got an urgent message for you," Liza said. "From Laura."

Oh, she was a friend of Laura's, Winch thought. She probably worked for SuRF. He ambled over to the helm and began to wipe the console down with a rag. "What's up?" he asked while he worked.

Liza realized she wasn't getting through. She'd imagined that Winch would look more like one of the men from the covers of the romance novels she devoured, and that her devastating message of distress would launch the captain into forceful action before he swept her down to his cabin to ravish her. No. Ugly thought. She shook her head and tried again, straightforward.

"Laura's been kidnapped."

Winch stopped polishing. Felix reappeared and handed Liza a beer. He held another out to Winch, but the captain didn't even see it dancing before his eyes. "What?"

Liza took a long swallow, cold and delicious.

"You know about her husband? Big Jim Quinn?"

*That's* where he'd heard the name! Winch nodded.

"Well, we came down here looking for his boat, only he found Laura instead. Now he's got her over at the Pier House and won't let her go and he's going to come here this morning to kill you and steal the boat, too!"

Winch furrowed his brow, trying to follow her story, but his beer-soaked brain thwarted him. Had he heard the word *kill*?

"Is this guy about six-feet, 250 pounds, drives a silver Mercedes 500SL?" interjected Marco from the transom. Liza looked at him.

"Yeah," she said in wonderment.

"Got a nasty-looking .38 in a shoulder holster?"

Liza nodded. Marco let out a long breath.

"Winch? This guy might be a problem."

\* \* \* \* \* \* \*

Felix proved to be an excellent cook. Despite the scarcity of actual food on board, he'd whipped up a satisfying breakfast of tunafish and rice covered with a spicy sauce made from the canned tomatoes he'd found in the locker. With the hatch to the forward part of the boat closed, the stench from the overflowing head was hardly noticeable.

While Felix scrubbed in the galley, Winch, Marco and Liza sat around the dining table drinking beer and reviewing their options. Liza was adamant that they cast off and get out of there as soon as possible, before Big Jim arrived to seize the *Key Monster* and shoot Winch.

"He could be here any minute," she exclaimed, checking her watch. It was nearly eight.

"She's right," added Marco. "I talked to him at the Oarhouse for more than an hour. I don't think he's wrapped too tight."

Winch sat back, disturbed. If Laura was in danger, he couldn't just sail off and forget about her. She might be a little bossy at times, but he'd grown very fond of her. A mask of resolve crept over his face.

"We'll have to go over there and get her back," the captain declared.

"What, are you nuts," sneered Liza. "You'd be dead two seconds after he sets eyes on you."

"Then someone he doesn't know will have to go."

"Don't look at me," Marco deflected.

"Could we call those other guys she asked about, Steve and Taylor?" Liza wanted to know.

"No phone," Winch replied. "I don't have their numbers anyway." He didn't want to admit that, although the *Key Monster* was equipped with the latest marine radio-telephone gear, he'd never been able to figure out how it worked. He was forever an analog man in a digital world.

"Call the cops?" suggested Marco.

Winch shuddered. "Not yet." He looked sidelong at the dealer and knew Marco didn't really want to have to mess with the police any more than he did. After numerous brushes with the law over the years, they both possessed a natural aversion to cops. "C'mon, let's think about this!" They lapsed into silence.

"Ahoy the boat!" came a muffled voice through the hull. Three heads snapped around.

"He's here!" gasped Liza.

Marco blinked. "Now what?" he whispered to Winch. Winch stood up and paused at the bottom of the companionway.

"I guess I go see what he wants. Stay here."

He disappeared up the steps. Liza mewled in fear. Marco hurried to the galley, muttered a few words to Felix, and began to search for something to use as a weapon. Through the skin of the boat, they could hear Winch and another voice, conversing in muffled tones.

The companionway steps creaked. Marco, having selected a filleting knife, hid behind a bulkhead, sweating. Felix held his baseball bat in a hitter's stance in the galley. Liza ducked under the table for cover.

Winch rounded the corner and recoiled at the weaponry aimed at him.

"Whoa!" he exclaimed, raising his arms defensively. In his hand was a white envelope. Felix and Marco relaxed.

"Mailman," said Winch innocently. Liza crept from her hiding place. Winch shoved the envelope into his back pocket. "Thanks for the back-up, crew," he smiled, "but I think we're still okay."

"For the moment," mumbled Liza.

Winch told them all to sit down. "I've got an idea. I'll be right back." He left the galley, heading forward.

Liza grimaced. Laura had warned her about letting Winch do the thinking.

The captain returned moments later carrying a small brown bottle with a rubber-tipped cap. He had Felix fetch another round of beers to top off their breakfast and explained his plan. Liza finally agreed, reluctantly, and Marco had some severe misgivings, but Winch brought him around.

"You sure this will work?" Marco asked the captain.

Winch grinned. "Do you remember the first time you did it?"

Marco nodded glumly. "I couldn't function for two days."

"Exactly," said Winch. He turned to Liza. "So all you have to do is slip him the stuff, wait until the right time, and you and Laura just walk out the door. No one gets hurt, no one gets busted."

"Why me?" argued Liza. "Why do *I* have to go back there? Why can't he," pointing at Felix, "go?"

"'Cause it's gotta be someone who can get close to him. All you hafta do is pretend you've gone back to him."

Liza wrinkled her nose in distaste. "But he'll still come looking for the boat eventually."

"We'll deal with that in a day or two. For now, at least, we'll get Laura away from him. Okay?"

Winch took their silence for agreement. He handed the bottle to Liza and winked at her. "Meet back here. We'll lie offshore and watch for you, then come in and pick you both up. We'll go to sea for a few days until he gets tired of waiting and goes home."

He lifted his beer bottle and offered a toast.

"Here's to Timothy Leary," he chuckled.

Marco and Liza exchanged dubious looks and drank.

\* \* \* \* \* \* \*

Until closing time the night before, Taylor had covered all the gay hotspots Key West offered. He'd gone home, caught a few hours of sleep, and resumed his mission after a leisurely breakfast at his favorite Cuban cafe.

Dressed in fresh khaki shorts and a green linen shirt, Taylor dropped by the pool at the Rainforest Resort and left a freshly printed stack of fliers with Dave the bartender. While he was in the neighborhood, he stopped at Laura's door and rapped brightly. No answer. Probably already at work over on Stock Island, he considered. Taylor moved on, down Simonton, visiting the various gay-oriented guesthouses along the way. Whenever he had the opportunity, he chatted with the men and women he met, inviting them to join him in his campaign. Nearly all of them were highly receptive to his idea, united as they were in their common crusade against intolerance. They'd all been victims themselves at one time or another. But hardly ever here in Key West. Now it was time to strike back.

Taylor was in a buoyant mood this morning. Everything was going perfectly. He'd had a nice chat with Dave at the Rainforest. Cute guy, who said he'd be glad to help Taylor out tonight. He dropped off some more fliers at the ManGrove and grinned. It promised to be one hell of an evening.

\* \* \* \* \* \* \*

Crunching to a sudden stop in the gravel parking lot along Garrison Bight, Steve grabbed his notebook and recorder from the back seat and dashed to the pier. He was late. After his last newscast of the morning, he'd been forced to deflect the barbed criticisms of his work which had been leveled by his diminutive boss, Grant. Now, he saw with relief, the great blue and white yacht of Armand Pringle was still idling placidly alongside the wharf. Steve hurried up the gangway and remembered to ask for permission to board. It was granted.

He found Armand in his usual seat, checking his watch with impatience. Pringle looked up at the newsman and tapped the crystal with his index finger before picking up a telephone handset and saying, "Take her out, Mr. Morgan." As he hung up the phone to the bridge, crewmen were already casting off the last of the lines and, seconds later, the yacht edged away from land.

Steve accepted the proffered coffee from the steward in his crisp whites as the yacht made her way around the tip of Fleming Key and out into the Gulf of Mexico. They steered a zig-zag course up the Northwest Channel, passing a series of sandbars and low, mangrove-dotted keys along the way. Pringle noted that this was the route by which they would depart Key West tomorrow, sailing for San Juan and the Leeward Islands. With the sun at his back, the cool breeze of the Gulf ruffling his thinning hair, Steve finally relaxed a bit, the persistent annoyances of Maxx and Grant slipping from his thoughts.

And slipping into the hot-tub and his line of vision was Mrs. Pringle, up to her old tricks again. Without a moments hesitation, she expelled from the tub her bikini top, releasing her amazing globes to soak up the sun. Steve believed himself to be immune to her, now that he had found she was a fan of Maxx Rock. All he had to do was picture her in the shock-jock's company and a shiver of revulsion ran through him.

"Are you chilly, Steve?" Armand inquired pleasantly. "The last time you were aboard, I recall, you'd had too much of this wonderful sun."

Steve Stevens smiled and tried to ignore Janet Sullivan frolicking in the hot-tub. "Are you ready to begin, Mr. Pringle?"

They cruised slowly out past Fort Jefferson in the Dry Tortugas, Steve making careful notes as Armand Pringle delivered a boastful monologue of his life. A lot of this Steve already knew, but there were enough good tidbits revealed to provide a framework for a fascinating story, one he hoped he could sell to a network. They cruised and talked for two hours.

Mrs. Pringle, clad in a white terry robe and a pout, joined them for a light lunch in the salon. Steve noticed that the couple did not address each other during the entire meal. He found that interesting and made a surreptitious note to that effect. What was the story with these two, he wondered? Stunning woman married to a billionaire, and they don't speak? Steve had promised during the pre-interview that he wouldn't poke into their private affairs, but that didn't mean that he couldn't keep his eyes and ears open. It would make for an interesting angle.

After lunch, Armand politely excused himself. He needed to visit his office and conduct some pressing, confidential business over the satellite phone. He told Steve to feel free to explore the yacht and promised to rejoin him soon. Pringle said not a word to his wife before taking his leave. Somewhat mysteriously, the crew seemed to have vanished also. Steve found himself sitting alone across the table from the amazing Mrs. Pringle.

Mrs. Janet Sullivan Pringle, one-time star of the *Sorority Girls Go To . . .* series (. . . *Go to Rio, Go to Amsterdam, Go to Mars*, et al), leaned forward in her seat and allowed the front of her robe to gape open. Despite himself, Steve gasped.

Mrs. Pringle licked her lips and purred. Steve half-expected her to start grooming herself with her tongue. She gave him a sly smile and settled back again, stretching her feet under the table and inching her painted toenails up Steve's leg. He caught her foot with one hand just before it buried itself in his crotch and he gazed at her meaningfully.

"Miss Sullivan," he scolded. "What would your husband think?"

Janet tilted her head back and laughed softly, a deep, throaty sound. He let go of her bare foot, which, he found to his dismay, he had been stroking with his fingertips. He tried to force himself to think of Maxx. He was just forming that disgusting image in his mind when Janet stood up and dropped her robe to the deck. Steve swooned.

She turned her sculpted back on him and padded over to the bar on the far side of the salon. Steve glanced about nervously. There was not a soul in sight. *Help me*, he thought desperately. There is a Siren luring me onto the rocks ahead and I can hear the crashing waves announcing my doom!

Mrs. Pringle tonged some ice into a glass and splashed some gin over the top. The rocks, the waves. She plucked a wedge of lime from the cutting board and teasingly rubbed the piece of green fruit across her erect nipples. Steve shifted in his seat, mightily uncomfortable, and watched her drop the lime into the drink. She stirred it with her pinkie and offered it to him.

Steve's eyes flicked from the glass to Mrs. Pringle's alpine breasts, and back to the glass. With a shaking hand, he accepted the drink and swallowed. But his eyes returned involuntarily to those creamy mounds, wet and sticky with fresh lime juice. She squatted next to his chair.

"Do you have enough lime in your drink?" she whispered in his ear. Her tongue flicked at his lobe.

"Oh, my God!" he managed before he lunged forward and buried his face deep in her cleavage. *I tried to be a good boy,* he kept thinking. *I tried to ignore her!*

"Oh, my God!" he repeated, coming up for air.

In the doorway, behind them, the steward nudged the first mate and murmured, "There she goes again."

The mate scowled and turned to go. "I'll go see that the boss stays busy for awhile."

The steward caught him by the sleeve and whispered, "Better make sure it's a long while." He nodded toward Steve, who was scrambling out of his boxers. "This one looks like he got stamina."

\* \* \* \* \* \* \*

An hour later, Armand Pringle stepped out onto the deck and glanced around. He found Steve relaxing in the hot tub. And Steve was totally relaxed. The steward had provided him with a pair of bathing trunks and a knowing wink. Janet was back in her bikini, sunbathing on the foredeck. Everything looked normal, except for the red in Pringle's face.

"Damn it to hell!" shouted Armand, and Steve recoiled. Pringle pulled up a chair next to the hot tub and sat down, accepting a glass of chablis from the steward.

"Something wrong?" Steve managed. Pringle looked steamed.

"Oh, that damned baseball team I own." He waved his hand in the air in exasperation and drilled the reporter with his cold eyes. "I'll never understand *that* game. Now, football, or, as you Americans say, soccer, that I understand. But, baseball? Bah! Full of overfed egos, boys playing a game, who always demand too much money!"

*KEY MONSTER*

Steve eased himself back down into the bubbling water. He'd been contemplating making a break for it, diving overboard and swimming to safety if he had to. He was relieved that Armand's rage was directed at some other target. Not that he wouldn't have deserved it.

"What's the problem," Steve asked, amazed that his voice didn't shake.

"Three of my best throwers . . ."

"Pitchers?" Steve corrected.

"Pitchers, yes, are free agents now that the season is over. We achieve the play-offs, which we lose thanks to them, and they have the nerve to demand even more money! Not ask. Demand! I told their agents to go to hell."

"Good for you."

"Yes, only now, what do I do?" He scowled again. "Baseball!" He made the word sound like a curse.

As if summoned by Pringle's words, something small and white splashed into the hot tub, smacking Steve lightly on the thigh. Steve stared at the bubbling water in mute surprise. A smooth, white ball with curvy red stitching popped to the surface and floated amongst the foam. Armand, sipping his wine and gazing aft, hadn't seemed to notice the splash or Steve's mild yelp of bewilderment. Steve Stevens lifted the baseball out of the water and examined it.

From across the water, over the low hum of the yacht's engines, came the distictive sound of a stick of ash striking a sphere of cowhide. A solid hit. All that was missing was the roar of a crowd. A small splash rose in the water about fifteen yards off the starboard beam.

Steve stood up in the tub and looked over the rail. He saw half-a-dozen or so baseballs drifting on the tide. Another one fell from the sky not far away. He glanced at Armand Pringle, who was now pre-occupied by an incoming call on his cell-phone. He really should witness this amazing sight, mused the reporter. Another ball landed in the Gulf. Steve raised his eyes to the horizon.

He couldn't help but wonder. Did Jesus and the Disciples play baseball? Because there seemed to be three silhouettes engaged in a pick-up game upon the surface of the Gulf of Mexico. And that was impossible, wasn't it? He regarded the very solid, very real baseball in his hand.

Steve stared hard at the three figures dancing upon the surface of the sea over a hundred yards distant. Two dark-skinned men pitched and batted.

Another, tall, long-haired and possibly bearded, crouched upon the water wearing a catchers mitt.

Does Jesus catch for the Angels?

\* \* \* \* \* \* \*

"Swing, batter, batter, batter!" laughed Winch from his crouch.

"What is this crapshit you saying?" asked an exasperated Felix, who had just been struck out by a thirty-seven year old dope dealer from Maryland. Winch laughed again and waved Marco in.

Marco strolled down the sloping sandbar and sloshed through ankle-deep water. "Your turn," he called to Felix, passing him his glove. "My turn to hit." Winch juggled the baseball in the air while he waited for them to trade places. Man, this Cuban was really something! Winch had dared Felix to try to hit that passing yacht, and--damn it--he'd done it! Winch figured it at 400 feet, easy. And, Felix had done it barefoot while standing on a submerged sandbar! The Cuban sloshed back out to the mound, a sandbar just a little bit higher than the one on which the batter and catcher waited, paced out sixty feet away, more or less. Coming out here had been the only way Felix would agree to play, resisting the idea of stepping onto actual American soil and blowing his chance at free-agency. Winch knew they were still well within U.S. waters, but he figured Felix didn't need to know that.

"C'mon, Munoz!" Winch shouted, easing into a crouch. "Tide's coming in, and we're gonna have to call the game!"

Winch felt great! He hadn't enjoyed the satisfying smack of a real baseball meeting a leather glove in more than twenty years. He was just slightly buzzed, taking the occasional hit from the fat joint he kept tucked behind one ear. Tethered nearby, the yellow emergency life-raft from the *Key Monster* bobbed, filled with extra baseballs, ice and a half-case of Miller.

Liza was off on her secret mission, carrying the magic potion to poison the evil Quinn. She'd told him that it would likely take a few hours at least before she had a chance to snatch Laura and escape back to SuRF. In the meanwhile, to pass the time, the captain had decided that a little baseball was in order. He'd taken the *Key Monster* to the shallows west of town and coaxed Felix and Marco into the water, where a spirited practice was now underway. But a tiny corner of his brain worried over Laura. He wished he could be more directly involved in her rescue. He tried to push the fears from his mind, trusting Liza to do her job. Either his plan would work or it wouldn't. If it failed, well, he'd come up with Plan B later.

Winch waved his glove at the passing yacht in farewell as it steamed away, and a man in bathing trunks standing by the rail returned the gesture.

"C'mon, baby, burn one in here!"

Felix went into his windup, glanced at the imaginary runner on first, and delivered a breaking ball. Marco lurched back in terror and fell into the water on his ass.

"Hey!" he objected.

"What's the matter," Winch declared, grinning. "It was right over the plate!" He pointed at the empty shell of the horseshoe crab they'd embedded in the sand.

Marco rose drippingly to his feet and took a few practice swings. Felix caught Winch's toss to the mound and wound-up again, sending a perfect fastball right through the strike-zone. The ball burned into Winch's mitt. Marco never even swung.

"I can hit this guy," Marco muttered angrily through gritted teeth.

Felix Munoz, late of los Diablos Rojos de Pinar del Rio, took pity on his fellow Hispanic and lobbed one in. Marco swung with a grunt and connected, a high pop-fly to center-ocean. He smiled.

Winch laughed. He was having the best time of his life.

# CHAPTER 21

Spewing oil, the mistreated Mercedes chuffed into the SuRF parking lot around half-past nine. The pier was vacant. Big Jim spat on the ground and settled against the smoking hood of his car to wait for Winchell to show up with the *LauraLee*. Laura marched to the front door and unlocked it.

"Where the fuck you think you're going?" he growled, seizing her by the arm. He was royally pissed that his boat wasn't here. He'd worked himself up to blow the boat-stealing bastard away.

"To work," she answered defiantly. He released her arm and grunted. At least they'd be inside and out of this killer sun.

The *Key Monster* was nowhere in sight, Laura had noted with relief. She hoped Liza had found Winch here and warned him to stay away from SuRF. There was the chance, of course, that Liza had changed her mind about helping and had just left town. Perhaps Winch was off gamboling on the *Key Monster* even now, smoking who-knows-what, about to come blundering into Big Jim at any moment, completely unaware of the peril he was in. Stay away, Winch, she prayed. Stay away.

This morning, back at his suite at the Pier House, Big Jim had ordered them breakfast from room service, a meal heavy on starch and grease. They'd chewed sullenly, too worn out by a sleepless night of marital contention to argue anymore. The plan for the day, Laura had guessed, was to return to Stock Island and lay in wait for Winch to come back in. Laura had been able to persuade Jim to stop by her motel room on the way to SuRF so she could change into something more appropriate for the day than the peejay top and panties she'd been wearing.

When they'd gotten to her room at the Rainforest Resort, Laura had insisted upon a shower and a careful application of make-up. She'd dallied over her wardrobe, killing time, selecting and rejecting several outfits. What did one wear to a kidnaping? Big Jim had paced nervously, checking his watch and ammunition. Laura dressed slowly and fussed with her hair, trying to buy time. Finally, in a bright yellow sundress and blue tennis shoes, and with her blonde hair swept back behind one ear, she'd realized she could stall no longer. Either Liza had found Winch or she hadn't. The boat would be there or it wouldn't. It was out of her hands. Never in a million years would she have dreamed that, at that moment, Liza was heading back to the Pier

House to rescue her single-handed, or that Winch was playing baseball on a sandbar in the Gulf of Mexico.

On the rest of their drive to Stock Island, Big Jim had insisted that they have the same old argument all over again. Laura's heart hadn't been in it. "You're coming back home with me." "No, I'm not." "You're just a dumb blonde housewife." "You're a fat pig." And so on.

Inside the cool cinder-block building, Laura busied herself with the remaining filing while Big Jim glared out the single dirty, salt-caked window, which afforded a view of the dock. They passed the day in silence. Once, the telephone rang. Jim forbade her to lift the receiver. She did anyway. He dismantled the phone against the wall.

Finally, at six, Laura stood up. "Time to go," she announced as if this had been just another day at the office. Big Jim, loading and unloading his .38 over and over, glanced at her.

"Not until the bastard gets back with my boat."

Laura shook with frustration. "There *is* no boat! I keep telling you that!"

"Bullshit," he said with a yawn.

So they waited some more. Until after eight, when Big Jim's stomach began to growl audibly. Laura was hungry, too. Though not as sleepy now. She had been able to catch a few winks sprawled across her desk while her husband stood guard. He woke her and ordered her to close up and get back in the car.

"That little shit'll come back here sometime. We'll do this again tomorrow, and the rest of the week if we have to," he grumped. Right now though, he wanted to get back to the Pier House, get something to eat, tie up his wife and catch some shut-eye.

Big Jim coaxed the wounded Mercedes to the hotel, forced Laura upstairs, and unlocked the door.

\* \* \* \* \* \* \*

Liza heard the electronic bolt snap open. She sat up straighter on the couch and smoothed her skirt, making sure that the little brown bottle was still secure in her blazer pocket. Her make-up was perfect, lips a glossy cinnamon, eyelashes extra long. She'd had all day to sit and wait and plan out exactly what she was going to do. She hoped Laura would get the idea and play along.

Laura stumbled into the room first, Big Jim right on her heels. His perpetually angry face went slack when he saw Liza. Laura wore a look of bafflement. Liza leapt from the couch and ran to her one-time lover.

"Oh, Jim," she crooned, burying her face in his shoulder. "I couldn't leave." She kissed him on the cheek.

The expression on Big Jim's face turned from surprise to vindication. Laura stared at the rich beige carpeting, feeling betrayed.

"I knew you'd be back," he lied, and cast his wife a triumphant leer.

"Did you find your boat?" Liza asked, nuzzling him. He pushed her away and headed for the wet bar.

"Not yet," he bitched, pouring himself a scotch-rocks. Behind his back, Laura shot Liza a frozen look. Liza returned her glare with a subtle wink, startling Laura. Liza joined Big Jim at the wet bar.

"Pour one for me, Sugar?"

Big Jim grinned through his fatigue. Liza was back! Soon, after dinner, he'd tie Laura up. Maybe order a bottle of good wine, have his way with both of them, the willing Liza and the unwilling Laura. But his wife would come around, he fantasized; and if she didn't, well maybe she'd just have to watch, remember what she was missing. He poured a third drink and set it on the coffee table in front of his wife, who pushed it away. Yeah, time for a little party to celebrate Liza's return, Big Jim thought, and licked his lips.

\* \* \* \* \* \* \*

Steve slumped back in his chair, studying the words he had just written as they floated on the desktop monitor. He had the beginnings of a great feature story on the elusive Armand Pringle. He'd decided to abandon the marital angle, feeling that he was possibly too biased now to explore any difficulties between Armand and Janet.

He dwelt on the amazing Mrs. Pringle and recalled the friendly pat on the back he'd received from the steward as he'd disembarked late this afternoon back at Garrison Bight. He guessed correctly that the crew knew all about Mrs. Pringle's games and that he had been just one of many players. He shook his head ruefully and reminded himself again to get tested as soon as possible.

The ringing phone on his desk interrupted his daydreams.

"Newsroom, Steve Stevens," he answered.

"Hello, Steve," came a rumbly, dark voice. "It's Taylor."

"Hey! What's up?"

"I wanted to tip you off to a story tonight. Thought you might be interested."

Steve was. "The skinheads?" He leaned forward and grabbed a pen, jotting down details.

"That's sorta manufactured news," the reporter warned. "And what you're suggesting kinda puts my ethics on the line."

"Are you in or out," said the dark voice slowly.

"In."

"Another thing," Taylor added over the line. "I've been trying to reach Laura all afternoon. There's no answer at the Foundation or her room. Have you seen her?"

"Sorry, I've been out all day."

"Well, actually, I need to get in touch with Winch, but there's no phone at the dock and I couldn't find Laura to get a message to him. Do you think you could swing by the boat and give him a lift on your way into town? He's bartending for me tonight. I'm running a bit late and I've got a million things to do."

Steve grimmaced. It wasn't "on his way" and the besotted captain was not his favorite person in the world. But he reluctantly agreed to do this favor for Taylor in exchange for this golden tip.

He suddenly realized that, although he knew he was speaking to Lamont Taylor Jackson, he kept picturing Daiquiri Taylor on the other end of the line. Key West was playing with his mind again.

After promising Taylor to come by the club tonight with Winch, Steve hung up. He saved his draft on a disk, checked his Colt, and made the drive out to Stock Island.

\* \* \* \* \* \* \*

It was long past dark when Winch saw, through his battered binoculars, the silver Mercedes scratch out of the SuRF parking lot. After batting practice, he, Marco and Felix had laid offshore for a couple of hours watching for Laura and/or Liza to appear. It had been a bad omen to see the bruised Mercedes parked by the dock, and they held off their approach until the madman's car had gone. There had been no sign of the girls, and that concerned the captain. Even after Quinn's car had left, they still hadn't shown up. What was going on?

Winch cranked over the engines and motored in, gliding the *Key Monster* to the pier. This time, Marco managed to tie up the stern without any major snags.

While Felix scrubbed down the deck, Winch sent Marco up to the grocery on the main road to pick up some food for dinner. He grimaced as he handed Marco a twenty dollar bill. The last of the advance on the house was disappearing fast. He was going to need money soon, especially with all these mouths to feed. He stomped below, worried about finances. It wasn't supposed to be this way here in Paradise.

Winch took a shower and found some clothes that weren't too dirty, while Felix worked his magic in the galley. The three shipmates dined on a spicy pork roast, with new potatoes and a fresh garden salad. The meat must have cost a fortune!

"What's the plan for tonight?" Marco asked the nearly destitute captain around a mouthful of roast.

"You guys can hang out here," Winch chewed. "But I've got a gig in town tonight, bartending for a friend." He was wondering if he had enough cash left over after the grocery run to get a cab into Key West. He'd spent most of his remaining money refueling this pig of a boat on the way back in from their baseball game. She needed to be topped-off and ready to go for Laura's media tour tomorrow. The thought made him stop chewing. He forgot about money.

Where the hell were they? Liza should have accomplished her mission by now. Maybe they'd gotten away, as planned, and were hiding out somewhere? Maybe they were still in big Jim Quinn's clutches! Winch was becoming seriously worried about them.

"Mind if I come along tonight?" Marco said, breaking into Winch's thoughts.

"I don't think you'd like it," Winch replied, wiping his mouth with a paper towel. "It's a party for our skinhead friends."

"Pass," said Marco as he stabbed another slab of pork. He nodded at Felix. "Hey, man. You sure can cook! And you're no slouch with a baseball, either."

Felix smiled and gathered up the dirty plates.

"Hell of a pitcher," agreed Winch. "My hand is still sore from catching fastballs. Too bad we didn't have a radar gun. Some of those pitches must've been ninety miles-per-hour, easy."

"Good hitting, too," added Marco. "You see him peg that yacht? Wonder what they thought about baseballs landing on them in the middle of the ocean?"

All three of them laughed.

"Anyone aboard?" filtered a deep voice through the hull. They stopped laughing immediately. Marco looked alarmed.

"Bet that's not the mailman," he said.

Winch went forward to the salon and peered through a curtain. "It's only that dude from the radio station," he assured them after seeing the reporter out on the dock. "I'll go see what he wants."

Winch went above, trailed by his curious crew, and hailed the reporter.

"Taylor called me, asked if I'd give you a lift into town," Steve explained. He noticed the other two men in the shadows by the helm. "Got company?"

Winch gave Steve permission to board and introduced his crew. "Marco is an old friend from back north. We pulled Felix off a raft the other day. He's a big Cuban baseball star, right Felix?"

"Funny you should mention baseball," Steve said, rubbing his jaw. "Weirdest thing happened to me today." He outlined his day on Armand Pringle's yacht, leaving out the part about his tryst with Janet Sullivan, and told them how he had witnessed a shower of baseballs while sitting in a hot-tub. Marco, Felix and Winch convulsed in laughter.

"That was you?" gasped Winch, holding the stitch in his side.

"Felix here can really bat 'em out of the park," Marco pointed with pride.

"And you should see him pitch!" Winch added.

Steve gazed at Felix, thinking. "No," he said. "There's someone else who should see him pitch. Would you be interested in trying out for a major league team?"

Felix's eyes sparkled.

"I'm his agent," Winch invented. He guided Steve by the arm, up and over the gunwale onto the pier. "Let's talk. You drive."

It occurred to Winch that he should mention Laura's troubles to Steve. But then, Steve would want in on the plan or, worse yet, do something rash on his own. He might even be successful! Winch wasn't prepared to share the credit for Laura's rescue with his rival. He elected to keep his mouth shut for now.

Winch waved to his crew, told them to defend the ship at all costs, and he'd see them later. He got into Steve's car and rode away toward town.

Marco glanced at Felix as the tail lights disappeared into the night. "Hey man. You think you can help me with my Spanish? I'm moving to Puerto Rico."

"And you help me with English?" Felix smiled. "I'm moving to America."

\* \* \* \* \* \* \*

Sinatra melted from the bookshelf speakers and Big Jim lumbered clumsily across the tiles, clutching Laura tightly against his bare chest. He could feel her moderate breasts rubbing him through her sundress. She could feel his bulge pressing against her through his pants. Over his shoulder Laura saw Liza fooling with Jim's drink.

Big Jim hadn't slept now in over thirty-six hours, but somehow he found the stamina to be horny. He seemed to have it in his head, Laura realized with disgust, that he was going to go to bed with two women tonight. In your dreams, she thought as he tried to dip her. He lost his grip and Laura fell painfully to the carpet. "Asshole," she muttered.

"Whoopsie-daisy!" Big Jim wheezed and laughed stupidly. He was on his third glass of wine, on top of the booze he'd been swilling. He'd barely picked at their room service dinner. The two women had wolfed down their meals and only pretended to drink from their goblets. But they hadn't yet had a chance to talk. Laura was still clearly under the impression that Liza had betrayed her. She cast nasty looks at Jim's harlot.

Then, from her awkward seat on the floor, Laura spied Liza unscrewing an eyedropper from the top of a small brown bottle and squeezing several drops into Big Jim's wineglass. Knockout drops, she wondered? Vitamins? Big Jim suddenly danced around to face Liza on the couch. Liza was just able to palm the tiny bottle in time.

"Liza, honey," he slurred. "Why don'cha go slip into somethin' more comf'erble?"

Liza forced back a gag and smiled sweetly instead. She stood up from the couch and touched his cheek with her finger, tenderly. "I'll be right back," she breathed. "Why don't you have another glass of wine?"

She picked up the glass, the one she had doctored, and handed it to him. As she flounced across the floor to the bedroom, Big Jim picked up a second wineglass from the coffee table.

"Let's have a lil' toast," he urged, handing Laura a random goblet.

Which glass? Laura dreaded. She'd seen Liza do something to one of them. Both looked exactly alike, and she'd lost track of which was which when Big Jim had shuffled them! Her drunken, sleep-deprived husband nuzzled her earlobe.

"To ol' times an' new 'speriences." He drank the wine. Laura hesitated. He weaved on his feet, looking at her. "C'mon, honey, loosen up! Drink!"

Laura sipped gingerly. Big Jim reached out a fat index finger and raised the base of the stem, tilting the glass back so that she had no choice but to take a swallow. He took her glass away and set them both down on the table by the couch.

The bedroom door whisked open and Liza swept back into the livingroom clad only in a semi-sheer babydoll nightie. Laura gaped at her and was secretly ashamed that her own body didn't measure up. Then she worried about what Liza had in mind. *My God!* she thought. Liza couldn't be thinking what Big Jim was thinking!

Liza slyly grinned at Laura, a smile Laura couldn't interpret. "Any wine left?" Liza asked brightly.

Big Jim waved at the half-empty bottle. "Gotta pee first," he mumbled and looked over at his wife. How was he going to do this, he wondered? He couldn't leave Laura unattended, even with Liza here to stand guard.

Couldn't trust women. Tying her up would take too long, he had to pee *now*! He glimpsed the balcony through heavy-lidded eyes.

"C'mon, you two. Outside."

He ushered them onto the balcony, into the cool night air. Liza's nipples went to attention immediately in the breeze. Big Jim placed his meaty hand on Laura's backside while he leaned over and stuck his sour tongue in Liza's mouth. She fought the urge to bite. He pulled away.

"I'll be right . . . back," he hiccupped, sliding the door shut and locking it from within. Liza spat over the railing and wiped her mouth.

"That does it," she griped. "I'm switching to women." It was meant as a joke and she looked over at Laura to see her reaction. "Laura?"

There was no reaction. Laura was gripping the railing with both hands, white knuckled. Sweat beaded on her forehead and her bare knees trembled below the hem of her sundress.

"I'm going to fall!" Jim's wife wailed in terror.

Liza blinked, then whispered, "Shit!" Suddenly, she knew that the three glasses of wine, two pure and one dosed with Winch's LSD, had gotten mixed up. Laura was on the upward curve of what was most likely her first acid trip. The poor woman had no idea what was happening to her.

Liza put her arm around the frightened woman and pulled her close. "It's okay, Laura, I'm here. You're gonna be all right." Liza steered her away from the railing and made her face the outside wall of the building, where Laura began to minutely examine the texture of the stucco.

"Shit," Liza breathed again.

Big Jim sloshed back from the bathroom and fumbled with the lock. He'd neglected, purposely or not, to zip his fly and tuck himself back into his slacks. Liza shuddered and guided Laura back inside to the couch. Laura went willingly, mumbling about how tiny the room was all of a sudden. Liza sat down next to her, protectively.

"Wha's she sayin'?" gurgled Big Jim as he plopped down on the sofa alongside the women.

Liza could tell Big Jim was only drunk and not stoned. "She was saying how good the wine was and that we should all have some more."

"Good idear," Jim agreed and grabbed the bottle from the table, topping off all three glasses.

Damn! They'd been moved around, and Liza had no idea which glass held the magic potion! Before Liza could select one, Big Jim picked up a glass and handed it to his wife, who was content to giddily stare into the blood-colored fluid. He handed a second glass to his mistress, and kept the third for himself.

Liza was no stranger to LSD. She'd done a little experimentation in school, and found it didn't appeal to her. So it didn't really worry her that her chances were one in three picking the laced glass. She could handle it. But she was pretty certain that Big Jim had never had anything stronger than a vodka martini. And Laura looked pretty dosed-out already. Liza couldn't take the chance of completely stoning her out. They would need to be functional later. By "accident" she elbowed Laura hard enough to make her drop the glass of wine. It shattered on the floor. Laura gazed at the broken glass refracting the low light on the blood-red carpet. She said nothing, just stared. And then started to giggle.

Big Jim attempted to rise from his seat, but Liza pulled him back down. "Let's drink first," she soothed. "Then I'll clean up the mess."

Big Jim grinned sloppily and they clinked glasses. One chance in three, shrugged Liza. What the hell? They both drank. Liza waited, fending off Big Jim's gropings.

After a few minutes (had it been only minutes?), Liza saw Laura float up from the couch and drift across the room to the stereo above the console TV. Sinatra dissolved into a squeal of static as Laura spun the tuner, landing on a severe groove by Earth, Wind and Fire. "Boogie Wonderland." Perfect. Liza joined her in the middle of the room and they danced together. *I'm sooooo stoned!* Liza thought. I must have gotten the wrong glass. Oh, well. Laura gyrated and laughed maniacally.

At the first blast of disco from the twin speakers, Big Jim curled his lip in a snarl. But the snarl evolved into a look of decadent excitement as the two women danced with each other. He snaked his hand down into his lap and massaged his limpness into firmness.

Liza was no LSD neophyte, she knew how to maintain a tenuous grasp on reality in spite of the acid. So she tried to keep her improvised plan in motion. She knew she could take care of herself. The problem would be protecting Laura from Big Jim.

From the corner of her eye, Liza saw Big Jim pause mid-stroke and reach for one of the wine glasses. Good boy. He finished it in one gulp. Was that the right one, her leftovers?

As he drunkenly set the glass down on the coffee table, he leaned too far forward, heavy with drink, and crashed into the remaining goblet, sending it flying onto the floor. Laura didn't notice a thing, lip-synching along with the lyrics and absorbed by the LED display on the compact stereo.

Liza decided to up the ante. She reached both hands over her head and pulled her nightie up and off, allowing her breasts to swing in time to the funk. Laura laughed and whistled at Liza dancing in only her panties. Big Jim rubbed himself harder and yelled, "Take it off!"

His mistress danced her way around the couch and into the doorway of the bedroom. Liza snatched the tiny brown bottle from her blazer, hanging on the doorknob, and shoved it down the front of her peach-colored panties, dancing back into the livingroom. When she faced Laura again, she whispered, "Stay with me, girl." Laura looked puzzled for a moment and then laughed again. Liza crouched down and lifted the hem of Laura's sundress. With two deft moves, she slid Laura's panties off and tossed them to the drooling Big Jim Quinn, now abusing himself with gusto.

Laura, a rush of air streaming up her skirt, forgetting who she was and where she was, spun to the music. Her dress flared out around her, drawing Big Jim's eyes like a magnet. Liza boogied over to the wet bar and poured an unhealthy amount of scotch in a tumbler. She was buzzing now and didn't even try to hide the fact that she was extracting a small brown bottle from her panties and dumping its entire contents into the Johnny Walker Black. Besides, Big Jim's attention was elsewhere, as she'd hoped. Liza vamped back to the sofa and offered the drink to their enemy.

"Gotta keep up your strength, big boy," she scolded him. As an extra inducement, she ran her hands across her breasts.

Big Jim complied, gulping acid-laced scotch. Before he had even set the glass back down, the room was swimming, but he still felt wonderful, renewed, full of energy. He, too, found himself up on the livingroom floor, dancing to a jungle beat with two half-naked women, his dick flopping back and forth through the gap in his pants. He leaned forward to nibble on Liza's nipple. She allowed it. After all, this was for a good cause. He ran his fingers through Laura's soft hair as she danced by, oblivious to her surroundings.

Liza murmured in his ear. "You know Jim? You got two of us, but I don't think that'll be enough for you."

"Yeah, two," he stammered.

Liza stole a peek at the digital clock on the stereo. It shimmered 10:15 P.M.

"It's still early, and I know another girl downtown who'd probably like to have some fun, too," she suggested. She was thinking of Bobbie, and the thought was actually making her wet. Stay on top of things, she ordered herself.

"Yeah," he moaned. "Yeah! Three!" Things rushed in and out of focus, but the idea of *three* women was almost too much. Liza tickled his ear with her tongue as Laura danced past again.

"Let's get dressed and go down to the car," she whispered. "We'll pick up Bobbie and the four of us can go do it on the beach."

"Yeah! Four! D'beach!"

Quickly, before anything happened to distract him from the potential realization of his lifelong dream, Liza threw on a mini-skirt and the blazer and made a fast search for Laura's panties. The girl would not cooperate, though, so Liza shrugged, giggled and warned Laura to keep her legs crossed.

"Like this?" Laura asked, and promptly fell down. Big Jim roared with laughter and then stopped, staring at the sparkly car keys in his hand. Where had they come from? They were fascinating!

Liza stood by the door, smiling, escorting them into the elevator, where Big Jim and Laura stood side by side, entranced by the blinking numbers over the door.

"Amateurs," she huffed in a pleasantly buzzed manner.

\* \* \* \* \* \* \*

A little more mascara, just a hint of blush. Ice-blue sequinned gown. Matching heels. And that lovely diamond pendant her grandparents had given her on her twenty-first birthday. Daiquiri Taylor gazed in the mirror, liking what she saw. Hell, she liked herself for who she was, skinheads and bigoted drag queens notwithstanding. She checked the clock, saw it was time to go. This was not only *her* night. This would be a night for all those Conchs who wanted only to live in peace, free of hatred and intolerance. If she had to resort to some of the tactics of the enemy, so be it. After all *they* were the ones who had made the rules.

Daiquiri turned out the lights in her apartment over the art gallery and descended the stairs into the madness of Duval Street.

It was show time!

# CHAPTER 22

Strobe lights flickered spastically, a thousand lightning bugs trapped in the smoky, deafening confines of the Riding Crop. The band, bass, guitar and drum, struggled through the unfamiliar territory of Stevie Ray Vaughn, Bad Company and Steppenwolf, having abandoned for tonight their usual glam-rock repertoire. Hidden behind the massive speaker column, the fire door was propped open with a broomstick, venting some of the smoke and affording the band a quick escape route should one become necessary. The guitarist kept glancing that way nervously, misfingering chords. The crowd, fueled by free beer and liquor, never noticed or cared.

Power riffs drowned out the *click-click* of billiard balls chasing across green felt and barely masked the smash of the occasional beer bottle splintering on the oak floor. Brown and green shards of glass crunched under heavy, steel-toed boots. Stubble-headed men in combat fatigues, dungarees and tee-shirts played drinking games, swapped bawdy stories and insults, and ordered refills from the grungy, long-haired bartender. It could have been any blue-collar roadhouse on a Saturday night in the Upper Midwest, but it wasn't. This was Key West, Fag Town, home of the enemy, and tonight it was theirs.

First General Rolf Schenk smiled boozily and surveyed the scene from his barstool perch at the rear of the Crop. Lieutenants Bob from Georgia and Ray from California hovered nearby, guarding their commander from the unruly, jostling troops. These are my officers and men, Rolf thought with satisfaction. Over by the jukebox he spied Colonel Brown, commandant of the Free Missouri Militia. He was chatting with Major Duncan of the Nevada Posse and Bud McGhee, adjutant to the Grand Dragon of the East Texas Klan. McGhee stood out in the crowd in his sparkling white robe, though he'd removed his hood for the occasion. All these men here tonight were from the upper echelons of the white-power movement, all veterans of busting heads, cross-lightings and other assorted mayhem.

The only thing that had made the General uneasy was the four NFL-sized bouncers by the front door who had patted down each man and relieved them of all weapons, dropping each pistol and knife in a large box and handing out chits for their return, a bizarre variation of a coat-check. But as

*KEY MONSTER*

Rolf looked over his men at play, he decided that it had probably been a good idea to disarm them as the unceasing flow of alcohol spurred fraternal rivalries. Already, the bouncers had broken up a scuffle between a pair of anarchists and a trio of fascists. No telling what might have happened had these men been armed.

One hundred and fifteen members of the Aryan-American Freedom Forces, the umbrella group of these disparate organizations, partied hard in the bar on Duval Street. Another seventeen men had been unable to attend, as they were currently guests of the Monroe County Sheriff's Department. General Rolf leaned over the bar and snagged the bartender by the sleeve to get his attention.

"Another beer, General?" Winch grinned.

"Eugene, I thought you said there'd be girls?" Rolf shouted over the heavy-metal music. The bartender nodded.

"They'll be here." He handed up three more bottles of Bud for the general and his aides.

"Who'd you say that guy is?" asked Rolf, pointing to the middle-aged man in a tie, blazer and pressed khakis standing near Winch behind the bar. He was taking pictures and scribbling notes on a spiral notepad. Winch glanced at Steve.

"Friend of mine. Reporter for the Florida Free White Press."

Rolf was mildly impressed as the bartender dropped the name of the biggest rightwing newspaper in the Southeast. "Well, tell him to stop taking pictures, would you? It makes me nervous."

Winch nodded and eased over to speak to his friend.

"General said to stop taking pictures," Winch shouted in Steve's ear.

Steve put the camera away. He'd already photographed nearly everyone in the bar anyway. Reflexively, he patted the bulge under his blazer, feeling the reassuring lump of his weapon. Taylor had made sure the bouncers would overlook the holster the reporter wore.

The final, crashing chord of an opus by Rush rang through the bar and a chorus of clapping and stomping filled the void. "We want the girls! We want the girls!" The chant started by the edge of the stage, banked to the pool tables and caromed across the bar. "We want the girls! We want the girls!"

Winch checked the time on the bar clock. He winked at Steve and told him to hold the fort. The reporter put down his notebook and pen and began filling orders as Winch slipped from behind the bar and headed to the back room. On his way, he signaled the band.

The bartender stuck his head past the curtain which separated the manager's office from the dressing room. "You girls ready?"

Angel and Samantha huddled together, looking worried. "We're not going out there, not with that crowd," Angel stammered.

Taylor had anticipated this and had prepared Winch. The bartender reached into the pocket of his jeans and pulled out a wad of bills. He peeled off six one-hundred dollar bills and handed them over. The two girls looked at the money, then at each other. They paused, indecisive.

"C'mon," Winch insisted. "They're really a good crowd, and we've got bouncers to protect you anyway. Three hundred each, plus tips, for a twenty-minute set."

"Who'd you say these guys were?" Samantha wanted to know. Out in the barroom, they could hear the band launching into their opening music, Gary Glitter's "Rock and Roll, Part 2." Rhythmic clapping and the crash of breaking bottles punctuated the heavy beat.

Winch repeated Taylor's lie. "They're from the Ontario Gay Lumberjack Association." Winch didn't have anything in particular against these two guys, but Taylor had said they must be punished, and Taylor was the one with the master's degree.

"Well, they *do* look like lumberjacks," sniffed Angel. "So crude!"

"C'mon," urged Winch, shoving the money into their reluctant hands. "They came all this way just to see you two dance!"

The money and the flattery worked, as Taylor had predicted. The two dancers doubtfully followed the bartender down the hallway.

Winch resumed his place behind the bar next to Steve. He leaned into the reporter's ear and stage-whispered, "Get ready to duck!"

He glanced at the front door. As Angel and Samantha pushed their way to the stage, slapping away groping hands, Winch noted that the four beefy bouncers had, on cue, slipped outside, taking the box of weapons with them. No one else seemed to notice their departure, all eyes riveted on the only two women in the bar.

Twin spotlights hit the stage, framing the pair of lovely ladies. Deafening applause and war-whoops greeted their appearance. Angel was wrapped in a tight mini-skirt of blue and gold spangles, her tiny breasts covered by a matching halter-top. Samantha wore a black-leather, zippered catsuit which showed off her boyish curves. They spun and twirled senuously to the music before the wildly appreciative crowd of Canadian lumberjacks. Eager men surged forward with dollar bills in outstretched fists, desperate to slip their hands into garters and g-strings. First General Schenk clapped and wolf-whistled. He clambered onto his barstool, Bob and Ray supporting him. From the back of the bar, through the haze of cigarette smoke and several beers, the two dancers were the most beautiful women the General had ever seen.

With the assistance of his two lieutenants, who cleared a path through the mob, Rolf made his way to the apron of the stage. He pulled a ten-spot from his wallet and beckoned to Angel. Angel pursed her lips and smiled at her partner. They were going to make out like bandits tonight, entertaining this group of gay backwoodsmen from the Great White North.

Angel sashayed her way across the stage, teasingly, and squatted down before the man with the ten. Her hips bumped in time to the music. She licked her bright red lips and planted a long wet kiss on the General's mouth.

"Get down," Winch warned Steve, and the two men sank out of sight, and out of the line of fire, behind the protection of the bar.

Rolf, swooning from the effect of the dancer's tongue flicking across his chapped lips, raised a shaking hand and slipped the ten dollar bill down the front of Angel's g-string. The men around him roared in delight. His fingertips brushed something wholly unexpected.

The General turned white. Then he vomited on the floor.

\* \* \* \* \* \* \*

"The hate is behind those doors! Hidden now, but awaiting a chance to persecute you! Disgusting, slimy scum who would kick your heads in just because you're gay, or black, or Cuban. They have infested *our* town! Are we going to just cower? Are we going to let them frighten us?"

"NO!" shouted the answer.

"Are we going to back down in the face of their intolerance?"

"NO!"

"Are you ready to defend your rights as proud gay men and women and people of color?"

"YES!"
"Are we a rainbow?"
"YES!"
"Are *we* the real Americans here?"
"YES!"
"Will you join me in expelling these gutter-dwellers from the Conch Republic?"
"YES!"
"Are you afraid of them?"
"NO!"
"Then say it with me! Down with hate! Down with hate!"
"DOWN WITH HATE! DOWN WITH HATE! DOWN WITH HATE!"

Daiquiri Taylor stepped down from the makeshift dais across the street from the Riding Crop and was replaced by Dave, the bartender from the Rainforest Resort. Dave wore his favorite black bicycle shorts with a white muscle shirt. His sandy blond hair was capped by an old US Army combat helmet he'd found at a flea market. He led the crowd in the chant.

"DOWN WITH HATE! DOWN WITH HATE!"

Daiquiri stood tight-lipped on the sidewalk, watching her creation. She'd spent a small fortune bringing this demonstration together. A forest of signs she'd had printed waved above the crowd. They all said "Down With Hate!" and were carried by gay men, lesbians, local writers, artists and businesspeople. Even a Key West councilman had shown up. They had been joined by a contingent of black men and women from Bahama Village and another group representing the island's Cuban community. Stretching for more than three blocks along the west side of Duval Street, Daiquiri made sure that the demonstrators remained on the sidewalk. Key West Police cruisers and bike cops patrolled the roadway, keeping a wary eye on the loud but well-behaved crowd. A sergeant demanded to see the required permit, which Daiquiri produced for him. Resplendent in a purple, off-the-shoulder evening gown, Daiquiri checked her watch and gazed at the front door of the bar across the street. It was just about time. She could hear the music of Gary Glitter leaking from the building.

Suddenly, the music stopped mid-verse. There was a squeal of feedback. From the alley fire door, three panic-stricken musicians stormed their way to safety. A burble of angry voices, mixed with smashing furniture and breaking glass, spilled from the bar. The chanting of the demonstrators died out and the police snapped their attention to this new disturbance across the street. At the repeated crack of gunfire, the cops reacted as one and sprinted across Duval.

\* \* \* \* \* \* \*

It was Lieutenant Ray who raised the incredulous alarm.

"Christ! They're *guys*!"

The band dropped their guitars and drumsticks and fled through the fire door. Samantha shrieked. The mob of skinheads shook themselves out of their momentary shock and rushed the stage. Angel's high-heeled foot connected with the chin of a lumberjack who was trying to crawl onto the platform. Bottles flew through the dark, smoky air. One of them bruised Samantha on the shoulder, just missing her head. Bud McGhee swung a pool cue at Angel, drawing a long welt across her stockinged thigh. Lieutenant Bob helped Rolf back to his feet, and then slipped and fell in the general's pool of puke. The fall saved his life as a barstool flew by exactly where his shaven skull had been only a second before. From behind the relative safety of the bar, Winch and Steve peered at the chaos.

"Now?" asked Steve, drawing his pistol from his shoulder holster.

Winch watched as the two dancers, cut, bruised and bloodied, scrambled for an exit. One of the skinheads grabbed Angel by his halter-top, tearing it off. He fell to the floor and crawled through a forest of boots toward the exit. Samantha was wielding his spiked heel as a weapon, drawing blood as he fought his way through the mob. But there were too many of them. The dancers were losing.

"Now!" shouted Winch over the din.

Steve raised his .45 over his head and fired four well-paced shots into the ceiling. The effect was immediate.

All movement in the bar was arrested. Arms cocked to throw punches froze. The side-battle between the anarchists and the fascists screeched to a halt. Stunned skinheads groped for guns and shivs that weren't there. And into the empty silence crept the growing noise of an army of people outside the door, chanting.

Steve hauled a weaving Winch to his feet behind the bar, where the captain had been greedily sucking dry a fifth of twelve-year-old scotch, afraid that it might be his last drink. Using the Colt, Steve covered their retreat to the front door, allowing Angel and Samantha an opportunity to flee ahead of them. Over a hundred puffing, panting, extremely angry skinheads watched the bartenders slip toward the exit. With the gun making quick, sweeping movements around the room, no one dared move against them. Even outnumbering Steve and Winch fifty-to-one, no one wanted to be the first to fall in the name of his race.

At the door, Winch paused. He snapped a short salute and smiled widely. "Goodnight, everyone!" he crowed. "Thanks for coming!" He caught General Rolf's bloodshot eye. "And, thanks for the baseball equipment, General!"

And he and Steve hurridly backed out the front door and onto Duval Street.

\* \* \* \* \* \* \*

"Look!" someone in the crowd yelled, and hundreds of pairs of eyes focused on the Riding Crop. Two bloody, battered drag queens stumbled from the building and collapsed on the sidewalk. The demonstrators roared in anger. Here was the evidence of the evil within! Policemen rushed to assist the two injured dancers. Two other men, one well-dressed, the other long-haired and scraggly, fled from the bar behind the victims.

"Someone's got a gun!" Winch yelled. He and Steve jogged across the street to join the safety of the crowd. A couple of cops intercepted them but recognized the reporter, who explained that he was covering a story and Winch was merely the innocent bartender. The Conchstables let them go.

Skinheads streamed out the front and fire doors. Some of them spotted the picketers and police and attempted to beat a retreat back inside but were thwarted by the continuing exodus of their brethren from the disastrous party. The sight of the two beaten transvestites lying on the pavement enraged the demonstrators past reason. The forces surged toward each other, meeting in the center of Duval Street. The police, outnumbered and caught in a no-man's land between the two sides, tried to defend themselves.

Punches were landed. Noses were bloodied, teeth were chipped, hair was pulled. The brawl escalated. Daiquiri was aghast. She hadn't wanted it to go this far! Her hope had been that the skinheads, faced with the reality of hundreds of reasonable, peaceable, protesting citizens, would slink back to whatever sewer they had crawled from. But she hadn't considered the effect on the crowd of seeing Angel and Samantha bleeding on the sidewalk. Now they were beyond her control. Signs denouncing hate were swung as weapons. Fists flew on both sides. Blood flowed. The cops waded in, futilely trying to segregate the combatants. Sirens wailed in the distance. Angry men in dresses wrestled men with swastika tatoos. Someone shoved Daiquiri to the gutter.

"No!" she cried and wept. A hand yanked her wig askew. She kicked out a leg and caught a skinhead square in the chest. Two men seized her by each arm and dragged her away, and she struggled futilely against them.

"Taylor! Take it easy! It's us!"

Daiquiri swiveled her head from side to side. Winch and Steve eased her back to her feet in the shadow of a doorway. She glanced back at the battle in horror and fell against Steve's shoulder, weeping.

\* \* \* \* \* \* \*

Laura sat in Liza's lap in the two-seat Mercedes while Big Jim drove. The grill of the 500SL was missing and the radiator fan screeched against some torn piece of metal with every revolution. Only one headlight still worked, the bumper was askew, and the car had developed a distinct pull to the right. The misfiring engine sputtered worse than ever.

Liza toyed absently with Laura's long blonde hair as their would-be lover cruised the side-streets, looking for a parking place. He was in no condition to drive, having consumed the better part of a fifth of scotch, two bottles of wine, and an unknown quantity of LSD. Hence, though it seemed to him that he was navigating the narrow streets of Old Town at raceway speeds, he had in fact been traveling no faster than seven miles per hour since leaving the hotel fifteen minutes ago.

"Turn here," instructed Liza aimlessly. She was awaiting an opportunity to bail out of this mess and had no particular destination in mind.

"Here?" Big Jim asked merrily as he drove straight through a stop sign which actually seemed to ripple a little in the passing breeze.

"Yeah, there," laughed Laura. She squirmed in Liza's soft lap.

Big Jim tittered too, maniacally, and stole a slobbering glance at the two women. What was it they were doing? Where were they all going? Oh, yeah. They were looking for another woman 'cause he was too much man for just the two of them. That was it. He turned left at the next intersection, narrowly missing a tourist-ridden moped. Police cars screamed by in the opposite direction. Laura watched their bubble lights in fascination.

Liza, more in control of herself than she was letting on, was waiting for a chance to pop the door so she and Laura could make their escape. It should have been so easy. But Big Jim kept the car moving just fast enough to make bailing out dangerous, especially with the stoned-out Laura in her lap. She'd have to wait until he stopped completely, but Big Jim continued to blow through stop signs, never varying his seven mile-an-hour pace.

"Here?" the driver asked in response to an imaginary instruction, and he turned left onto Duval Street. Big Jim's red-rimmed eyes widened, trying to understand what he was seeing. He slammed on the brakes.

"Wha' the fuck?"

He had somehow driven into some kind of intricate street ballet, all moving in slow-mo. An amazing array of people in all manner of costume swirled around the Mercedes. A man in high-heels swung a sign at a short guy with tatoos. A huge black man was busy punching out a skinny guy with a bald head. Another skirmish filled the space behind the car, cutting off any escape. Big Jim fought with the fog in his brain and made a face at the freakish scene. He reached for the power-door-lock and flipped the switch. *CLICK.* The doors to the Mercedes locked shut against the mayhem. Liza groped for the switch on her side. *CLICK*, the locks popped open. *CLICK*, Big Jim jabbed the button again. *CLICK*, as Liza unlocked them. *CLICK*, when he re-locked the doors.

"Click," said Laura dreamily.

*CLICK* went the latches as Big Jim unlocked the doors. Liza dove for the handle and sprung the door before her captor could react again. A puzzled look crossed his face as Liza unceremoniously dumped Laura into the street and then scrambled out after her. Big Jim leaned across the center console and snatched hungrily at Liza's clothes.

"Bye-bye, honey," she said to him just before she kicked the door shut, denting it.

Big Jim raged. It came over him like a gunshot. He fumbled his way out of the car and glared over the roof in time to see Laura and Liza disappearing into the mob. The battle swirled around him like a kaleidoscope, and his menage-a-quatre dreams vanished into the night.

Someone pushed him from behind and he banged his chin against the open car door painfully. He spun around to see who had hit him. An ugly woman in a tube-top was grappling with a bald guy sporting a swastika earring. The woman landed a roundhouse, knocking the guy onto the trunk of the Mercedes where his skull made a considerable dent in the metal. The woman adjusted her tube-top, sliding it back up over her hairy chest to cover breasts that weren't there. Big Jim reeled. A dyke broke my car! Big Jim thought in shock.

"Fuckin' dyke!" he yelled and tackled her from behind. At this moment, Big Jim hated every woman who'd ever lived. He hated fags, niggers and anyone else who wasn't Big Jim Quinn. He punched blindly, assaulting anyone within reach. Other nearby patrons of the riot piled on.

Liza dragged Laura through the crowd, only stopping to catch her breath once they were safely on the fringe of the riot. Monroe County deputies poured in from the side-streets. Big Jim was lost to her view, but Liza could see the silver Mercedes rocking ominously from side to side in the middle of the street. With a cheer arising from the exultant crowd, one side of the sportscar rose almost gracefully off the ground. Strong arms tilted it from beneath, and it tottered on two wheels, one tire spinning uselessly in the tropical night. The car wavered for a moment before a final, fatal shove toppled the vehicle completely over. It came to a rest upon its crushed-in roof. The anti-theft alarm finally went off, adding to the pandemonium. From somewhere in the vicinity of the wreckage pierced the anguished shrieks of a devastated, and very freaked-out, man.

"Quite a party, huh?" said a voice next to them. Laura turned to see who had spoken from the blue, and she launched herself into Winch's surprised arms.

"Winchie!" she laughed.

Winch, with Laura entwined about him, looked at Liza questioningly.

"Her first trip," Liza shrugged.

The police were regaining some control now. The riot ran out of energy with the intervention of the cops. Everyone fled as deputies moved in to make arrests.

"Let's get out of the way," Winch said urgently. He led the two women over to the sheltered doorway where Steve and Daiquiri huddled. The five of them gazed at each other in wonder.

Steve hugged Laura. "Hey, what's a nice girl like you doing at a civil disturbance like this?"

Laura laughed, a high-pitched squeal. Steve glanced at her oddly. Something here wasn't right. Laura had a weird look in her eyes. She took hold of his tie and began to examine the pattern.

Steve glanced over her shoulder at the remnants of the riot and then at his friends. Laura began humming an old disco hit. Steve disengaged Laura's hand from his tie and put his arm around her protectively. "Come on," he invited the others. "I'll give you all a ride home."

Half-reluctantly, Winch, Laura, Steve, Liza and Daiquiri left the carnage behind. Steve dropped a weepy Daiquiri at her apartment a few blocks away. She passed the rest of the night staring out her front window at the rubble of Duval Street. She called the hospital repeatedly, trying to find out the conditions of Angel and Samantha. Finally, by claiming she was a reporter like Steve, Daiquiri discovered that both dancers had been treated and released, their bumps and scratches not as bad as they'd looked. She breathed a sigh of relief and finally fell asleep on the couch sometime before dawn.

On the drive to Stock Island, Steve and Winch got the story of Liza and Laura's escape from Big Jim's clutches. Steve was aghast to learn that he had been kept in the dark, never knowing that Laura had been kidnapped by her deranged husband. He berated Winch for not telling him about Laura's plight, and tried to make Laura understand that he would have helped rescue her if he'd known.

Laura was still too stoned to care. She scrunched herself sideways in the front seat next to Steve and forgot she wasn't wearing any panties. Her short skirt rode up. Steve glanced over at her and nearly swerved into a parked car.

In the backseat, Liza rested her head and closed her eyes. They'd screwed Big Jim good tonight and she was satisfied. True, she was broke and stuck in Key West, but she'd worry about that later. For now, she was content to revel in her success. The image of the overturned Mercedes was a balm to her soul.

Winch stared hostilely at Steve from the back seat. Why was *Laura* riding shotgun? He was the one who'd put together the plan that had saved her. It had been *his* acid he'd sacrificed for the cause. Laura should be falling all over the captain in gratitude for banishing her monster. Winch sat silently and fumed all the way back to Stock Island.

Steve deposited Winch, Laura and Liza back at the *Key Monster* before he left for the radio station to file his story about the riot for the morning news. And for the wires and the nets. His call to the Key West Police revealed that twenty-nine skinheads had been arrested, eighteen were at the hospital under guard, and the rest had slunk away into the night. Six Conchs had been arrested, nine others were being treated for minor injuries. And four police officers had been slightly wounded in the melee. Steve spent a long, full night pulling together the biggest story to hit Key West in ten years, praying this would turn out to be his ticket out of paradise.

Winch tucked Laura into bed in one of the staterooms on board the *Key Monster*. He kissed her on the cheek tenderly as she slipped into sleep. He found Liza in the galley with Marco and Felix, drinking coffee and trying to stop shaking, a delayed effect of her adventure and the acid. Winch, using soothing tones, finally talked her down from her trip.

The captain and his three guests passed the night talking quietly on the afterdeck. They watched the lights of Houseboat Row reflecting on the calm water, passing around a couple of fat joints Winch had rolled. Long before dawn, everyone had curled up somewhere and was fast asleep, except for the captain.

Winch sat alone, cross-legged on the forward deck, sipping from a bottle of rum. The houseboat lights across the channel twinkled until, one by one, they were extinguished by their sleepy owners. Winch leaned back and stared up at the stars. Two of those stars, he imagined, might be his parents. *Did I do good tonight?* he wondered at them. *Would you have been proud of me? We drove away the bad people. I hope . . . I hope . . .*

Winch fell asleep propped against the forward hatch, the last of the rum spilling along the deck and dripping down the side, across Brant's mural of the sea monster, and into the water, mixing with the tide.

# CHAPTER 23

The morning breeze ruffled the curtains over the bulkhead windows. They were navy-blue cotton, printed with white anchors and white seahorses. The sunlight of a new day spilled through the open windows and illuminated the port stateroom. Under the toasty blanket, Laura wiped her eyes with balled fists and stretched like a newly-woken kitten. Her eyes popped open and she took in the unfamiliar, sunstreaked room. Where was she? This wasn't the Rainforest or the Pier House.

Contented snoring, almost a whisper, rose from under the blanket beside her. Laura propped herself up on an elbow and peeled back the covers, fearing who she might find. Tuesday night was a blank.

Liza stirred in the cool breeze and sudden morning light. She was nude except for a pair of blue bikini panties. She groaned in protest against the bright coolness of the day and fumbled the pillow over her head. Laura flipped the warm blanket back over the sleeping woman and slipped out of the berth.

She perched on the edge of the bed and tried to reassemble last night. Laura looked down at herself, puzzled by her outfit. A cheerful yellow sundress and no underwear. She wondered where she'd lost them. In fact, she seemed to have lost the entire preceding evening. Laura stood up from the bed and peered into the companionway. She was on board the *Key Monster*, that was obvious, but couldn't remember how she had gotten there. The aroma of coffee filled the companionway and her stomach rumbled.

A dozen questions nagged her. If she followed the scent of that coffee, who would she find perking it? Very possibly Big Jim and, at this moment, Winch would be floating facedown in the Gulf. Or, Laura counseled herself, Winch just might be safe in the galley, pouring rum into that coffee. She needed to calm down and be smart.

Laura shut the door softly and glanced about the cabin. At the foot of the bed she'd apparently shared with Liza (*There's a switch*, she thought, *now I'm sleeping with my husband's mistress!*), she spied Liza's travel bag. Laura stooped and rummaged through the overstuffed outer-pocket and came up with a fresh pair of panties for herself. She slipped them on under the creased and stained sundress.

Getting off the boat was priority number one. Establishing who currently commanded her was secondary. Laura vaguely recalled seeing Winch sometime last night, but the exact outcome of the evening eluded her. There were dim images of mobs of people; Daiquiri; the Mercedes; Liza; but she couldn't put it together. She drew open the stateroom door and peeked into the empty hallway. The coffee smell was stronger than ever. Cautiously, Laura made her way aft.

The salon was clear, but now she could hear kitchen sounds. Laura crabbed her way around the salon, edging toward the aft doorway. The steps to the afterdeck and freedom lay just past that door, but within sight of the galley. She'd have to be quick and quiet. She took a deep breath, prayed it was only Winch in there, and propelled herself forward.

"*Buenos Dias*," smiled Felix, just as Laura stepped through the hatch. "*Cafe, señorita?*"

Laura froze for an instant, a sudden feeling of dislocation overwhelming her. She'd completely forgotten about the refugee they'd plucked from the sea. Yet, if Felix was here, that was a good sign. Big Jim wouldn't have tolerated his presence for a second. Did this mean she'd been rescued? Was her ordeal over?

Hesitantly, Laura accepted the proffered steaming mug. It, too, was navy-blue with little white anchors and seahorses. She sipped, peeking at the dark-skinned man over the rim of the cup.

"You like the eggs?" he questioned in a thick Cuban accent. "Marco, he steal them fresh las' night."

Marco? Who was Marco? Laura nodded tentatively. "One please. Scrambled." The man, in a white tee-shirt, white boxer shorts and white apron, turned his attention to the grill. He hummed something fast and Latin while he worked. Laura leaned against the bulkhead.

"Where's Winch?" she finally asked, half-afraid of the answer.

"Weench, he *dormido* on top of *bote*," the Cuban replied, pointing upward. "I cover him up."

Laura refilled her mug and backed out of the galley, climbing the steps topside. Poking her head out on deck, she carefully glanced around. No sign of her husband. In fact, no sign of anyone. The *Key Monster* was bobbing peacefully alongside the SuRF pier. Moving forward, balancing herself and her coffee as she navigated the narrow catwalk above the gunwale, Laura managed to locate Winch, snoring beneath a damp blanket, propped against the forward hatch. She was happy as hell to see him. She peeled the blanket away from his face and held the coffee beneath his nose. An empty liter of rum rolled across the deck.

Winch's eyelids flapped. "Aaacckk," he uttered against the morning light. Laura smiled.

"Come on, big boy," she purred. "Time to get up. I've got some things to ask you."

Winch came awake all at once. He smacked his mouth noisily and squinted against the offending sunlight. Without a word, he groped for Laura's coffee mug and took it from her hand, swallowing the hot beverage in two gulps. When he handed back the empty cup, he reopened his red eyes and looked about in bafflement.

"Damn," he breathed. "Fell asleep on deck again." He peered at Laura with concern. "You okay?"

"Slept like a baby," she assured him. "Though I do have an interesting roommate. You want to tell me about last night?"

Winch gathered the dewy blanket around himself and stiffly led Laura back below to the galley. Felix was adding chunks of green pepper and splashes of Tabasco to Laura's congealing egg.

"*Buenos dias*, Weench," the Cuban cook called, much too cheerily. Winch collapsed onto the bench next to the galley table. Felix handed him a fresh mug of coffee and cracked some more eggs for the captain's breakfast. Laura sat down opposite him and waited until he'd drained half the mug.

"Since *I'm* here, and you, Felix and Liza are here too," Laura began, "my basic questions are, where is Big Jim, and how did I get here last night?"

Winch wiped sleep from his eyes and poured coffee down his gullet. "Steve drove us back. After the riot."

Riot. Laura thought about that for a minute in silence. Felix placed her perfectly cooked egg on the table.

"What was I drinking last night?" she ventured.

Winch shrugged. "You'll have to ask Liza. I was tied up somewhere else." He looked at her curiously. "How do you feel?"

"Pretty good. But I don't remember most of last night."

Winch got up to pour another cup of Felix's coffee. "That would be from the acid."

Laura dropped her fork, spraying scrambled egg across the table. "Acid?!"

Winch sat back down and nodded. "Liquid Sunshine. I gave it to Liza to spike your husband's drink. She said that you'd accidentally been dosed too. Sorry about that. Probably why you don't remember much."

Laura opened and closed her mouth like a gasping carp. Winch shrugged and reassured the jittery Laura that she would be okay, she wouldn't be having acid-flashbacks and that her chromosomes were probably still fine. Laura shook her head and tasted her eggs.

"I'm on my own for two weeks, and I end up doing acid, staying out all night, and finding myself sleeping pantyless with a nearly naked woman."

"Welcome to Key West," offered Winch, hoisting his coffee mug. Felix bustled over with another plate of eggs.

"So, do we know what happened to Jim?" Laura asked between bites. The eggs were delicious.

"Nah. Last we saw of him, he was under a pile of skinheads while his car was being flipped. My guess is, he's either in the hospital or jail."

Laura chuckled. "Good."

"The point is, you're free of him, and so am I." Winch jogged Laura's fuzzy memory, filling her in on the Duval Street riot and its aftermath. Hazy details returned. She vaguely recalled dancing with Liza at the Pier House, and riding in the Mercedes. Drinking some wine. Seeing Taylor in a sparkly dress. A big fight. Sirens. It must have been some Tuesday night.

Tuesday night? Then, if today was Wednesday . . .

"What time is it?" Laura demanded suddenly.

Winch glanced at the tiny clock over the stove. "Eight-fifteen."

"A.M.?"

"Well, yeah." Winch looked puzzled.

Laura jumped to her feet. "Shit! We've got a million things to do!"

"Huh?"

She glared down at him. "It's Wednesday! The media tour is in less than six hours! Hurry up! We've got to get the boat ready!" She looked down at herself, at the soiled, rumbled sundress. "I've got to shower and find something to wear. And all my bags are still at the resort."

She was still mumbling to herself as she swept out of the galley, heading for her stateroom. Winch rubbed his temples.

Silently, Marco floated into the galley and took a seat beside Winch. He wore only a pair of graying boxers and his black hair stood up in sleepy spikes.

"*Buenos dias!*" Felix crowed, delighted to be among his new friends on this sun-shiny morning.

"Coffee," Marco coughed. He swallowed from the mug Felix set before him and tried to wake up. He was not a morning person. Just ask his wife. "Who was the blonde?" he finally managed.

Winch sighed against his hangover. "Another damn mouth to feed," he replied.

\* \* \* \* \* \* \*

My, this boat is getting crowded, Laura mused as she passed the strange man wearing only boxers coming through the salon. He'd barely glanced at her through heavy-lidded eyes and grunted as he'd gone by. Possibly Marco the egg-thief? He seemed harmless.

She slipped quietly into her cabin and tiptoed to the pile of luggage on the floor, careful not to awaken Liza. From the bag, Laura pulled a pair of white shorts and a red tee-shirt. Judging by what she'd seen Liza wearing up to now, these were most likely the best garments she could hope for.

Across the narrow hallway, she squeezed herself into the tiny shower and let the warm water wash away the trauma of her kidnapping. So, Big Jim was probably either in the hospital or in jail? Perfect. She hoped he'd experienced both last night and she'd never lay eyes on him again.

After toweling off, Laura dressed in her borrowed outfit. The shorts fit all right, though they were shorter than she cared for, and the tight red top glowed like a stoplight. And as much as she tugged and pulled, her involuntary cleavage refused to submit to propriety.

She found the keys to her office still in the pocket of her ruined sundress and poked her head into the galley to tell Winch she was going up to SuRF. He offered her a brief introduction to the still unresponsive Marco and then she hurried up the companionway, excited about the new, Big Jim-free day ahead of her. A day that would make or break the Save the Reef Foundation, she thought as she unlocked the office door. Briefly, as she entered the office, she had a fleeting thought of monsters. It seemed she had vanquished hers.

Using an extension her husband had failed to disable, Laura dialed a number. Taylor answered groggily on the fourth ring, and she reminded him that the media tour was at two and she expected him to be at the boat no later than one. Taylor reluctantly promised he'd be there, in an oddly remorse-tinged voice. The Key West Police had been by at first light, clutching a copy of his demonstration permit and a summons. Laura consoled him, though she didn't have the slightest idea what he was talking about. The fuzzy image of Daiquiri sobbing amidst a raucous mob chewed at the corner of her after-shocked brain. She had work to do. Laura thanked Taylor and hung up. She was about to place a call to Steve when line two rang.

\* \* \* \* \* \* \*

The ringing in Steve's ears would not abate. The noise in his head had been torturing him since he'd fired those four shots into the ceiling last night at the Riding Crop. He'd been up since then, writing, editing and filing stories with AP, NBC and Mutual. The riot in Key West was big stuff, and he led his morning newscasts with the gory details.

"So, tell us bub, what was all that hubbub?" asked Maxx the half-wit, over Steve's headphones.

"It's 8:52, and I'm Steve Stevens, Key Rock News," he intoned, ignoring Maxx's question. Steve hit a button on the cart machine and the riotous sounds of screaming, fighting and gunshots leapt off the tape. The sound quality was excellent. He'd recorded it himself inside the Riding Crop. He faded the actuality under and re-opened his mike.

"That was the scene on Duval Street last night as members of the Aryan-American Freedom Forces clashed with protesters outside an Old Town bar. A coalition of citizens had assembled to protest the presence of about one hundred skinheads who were holding a party inside the Riding Crop Bar. After allegedly assaulting two male dancers at the party, the skinheads surged onto Duval Street to confront the protesters, where a riot ensued. Sergeant Bill McReady, of the Key West Police:"--Steve hit another cart. Bill McReady's voice barked from the monitors--"At about 11:45, we responded to a call of a disturbance on Duval Street. Responding officers and deputies from Monroe County encountered numerous fights in progress and heard shots fired. We made a total of thirty-five arrests and transported thirty-one victims to Lower Florida Keys Hospital, mostly with minor injuries." Steve flipped his studio mike back on.

"Six cars were damaged during the riot, including a late model Mercedes-Benz which was flipped and destroyed by the mob. The unfortunate owner of that car has not been located.

"I spoke with Rolf Schenk, self-styled leader of the Aryan-American Freedom Forces, who had this to say:"--Steve punched the play button again, starting a sound-bite from an interview he'd recorded at the county jail--"We were just minding our own business when about a thousand people jumped us! We put up a good fight, white Americans against some of the worst scum we've ever seen, fags, colored and spics. And you know what? You can keep Key West! What a *BLEEP*ed-up place to live!"

"Aw, c'mon, Steve," Maxx Rock cut in. "You bleeped out the best part!"

"Sorry, Maxx," Steve ad-libbed, "but we've got some tender young ears out there." He returned to his copy.

"This morning, Duval Street is peaceful again as city crews work to clean up the debris. The Monroe County Sheriff's Department reports that they have swept the Bide-a-Wee Campground on Sugarloaf Key, arresting twelve alleged neo-nazis on a variety of weapons violations and evicting dozens of others from the campground. I'll have further details on this breaking story in one hour."

Steve did the weather without any more interruptions from Maxx. He signed off over the opening beats of the Stone's "Street Fighting Man." Maxx had finally come up with an appropriate segue out of the news.

Steve slipped off his headphones and returned to his office. He had other things on his mind beside the riot. The first thing was Laura was safe. Another thing he thought of was that Cuban ballplayer he'd been introduced to yesterday afternoon. Munoz, Steve mused. He'd heard that name somewhere before.

Steve flipped through his Rolodex and found the number of an old buddy of his, a sportscaster in Miami. He called his friend at home, chatted about old times a bit, and then asked about Felix Munoz. Steve listened to the sportscaster's information, thanked him, and hung up.

Well, well. It seemed that Winch's refugee was a cousin of Arturo Munoz-Torres, starting shortstop for the Marlins. So, Felix had a baseball pedigree, and if he was even half as good as his cousin, he belonged in the big leagues. Steve thought about this while he checked his meticulouly-kept calendar for the day. The main appointment scheduled for Wednesday was Laura's media tour at two. He slapped his forehead with the heel of his hand and cursed himself. The tour had completely slipped his mind. He'd also neglected to call the TV stations and newspapers as he'd promised. Hurridly, Steve made some calls but, this late, he received only flacid, unenthusiastic replies. Well, *he* would be there, tired as he was. He dialed Laura's number at the Foundation.

"Hi," she said brightly after he'd gotten her on the first ring. "I was just about to call you. Are you still coming to the media tour?"

"Two o'clock, I'll be there," he stifled a yawn. "Did you catch my newscast this morning?"

Laura confessed that she hadn't, and Steve felt a stab of disappointment. But she vowed to listen to his last report at 9:50. He bounced back.

"By the way," he asked, "is Winch around?"

"He's on the boat, having breakfast."

"Could I talk to him?"

Laura put Steve on hold and left to fetch the captain. Steve grabbed his cell phone and dialed Armand Pringle's sat-phone number. He got the billionaire on the line and made a brief proposal. Pringle seemed agreeable and rang off. On the other phone, Steve heard a click and then Winch's voice.

"Hello?"

"Winch? It's Steve Stevens. Remember what we were talking about last night on the drive to the bar? About your friend Felix?"

Steve outlined his idea and Winch laughed. Yeah, he'd see Steve at the sandbar at 11:00. Big white yacht. They hung up.

The newsman placed another call to the Key West police, in an unofficial capacity, and asked to speak with his pal Bill McReady. The sergeant was reluctant at first but at last agreed to loan Steve a certain piece of law-enforcement equipment for the day. Steve grinned and told him he'd be by to pick it up in about an hour, on his way over to Armand Pringle's yacht.

*\* \* \* \* \* \* \**

The enormous white boat churned out of Garrison Bight at eleven o'clock sharp. Through red, bleary eyes, he tracked its movement until it disappeared behind the new development on Sunset Island, across the narrow channel. Jealousy surged. He wanted *his* boat, *his* wife, *his* mistress, and *his* car! What the fuck was going wrong? His pale hands shook and his stomach boiled. Two days of beard erupted from his sunken cheeks and his mouth tightened in what was becoming a perpetual scowl. His oily, unwashed hair stiffly resisted the tropical breeze washing across the balcony and Big Jim Quinn wiped his runny nose with a tattered, grimy sleeve.

That's it, he realized, gazing at a great white yacht slipping past the breakwater. To find a boat, you need a boat. Big Jim turned away on sleep-deprived, hungover legs. He checked for his wallet and the .38, still snug in its holster against his chest. Last night, when he'd finally remembered to draw his weapon, while he was being stomped by about a dozen people, he'd found that the gun wouldn't fire. It had only been later, after he'd extricated himself from the mob and had watched them destroy his car, that he'd discovered the safety had been on the whole time. What had he been thinking? And that was no ordinary scotch he'd been drinking. Someone had slipped him a mickey, and he guessed he knew who.

The thought of his wrecked Mercedes drove a spike through his brain. Somehow, in some way, he was positive that Winchell was to blame for all of this. And today he would nail that son-of-a-bitch and retrieve the *LauraLee*. Big Jim buttoned his torn jacket over the holster and trudged to the elevator.

On the way down to the rental docks behind the Pier House, he attempted to recapture the events of Tuesday night. What the hell had they done to him? He'd been blasted enough for Liza and Laura to give him the slip right in the middle of Duval Street! And then he'd been in the midst of some huge street-brawl, punching out a guy in a flower-print dress. Big Jim shook his head, trying to drive out the dust. He had to get out of Key West before he lost it completely. The hell with the women and the car. He'd just find the fucking boat, kill Winchell, and go home.

With his gold card, Big Jim rented a fifteen-foot Boston Whaler sporting a 110-horse Merc. Ignoring the advisory to wear a life-vest, he shoved the throttle forward and the little boat leapt into the Gulf. He hardly gave a second glance at the lumbering white yacht off his starboard beam as he rounded Fort Zachary Taylor at 30 knots. Quinn sped along the south shore, off Smathers Beach, and aimed for Stock Island. It was payday.

# CHAPTER 24

Two men stood side by side at the rail, peering through binoculars. "Incoming!" yelped Steve, and they ducked. The snow-white baseball thudded against the hull and bounced harmlessly into the sea. His sportscaster friend in Miami had been one-hundred percent right. Munoz was dynamite!

"What a hit! Didn't I tell you? This kid has some real talent!"

Armand looked impatient. "Yes, very well, I agree he can hit a baseball. But I need a pitcher."

"You got it," Steve assured him. He picked up the walkie-talkie from the table next to them and keyed the mike.

"Steve to Winch," he transmitted.

"I hear ya, Steve," crackled Winch's voice through the tinny speaker.

"Mr. Pringle wants to see him pitch."

"Roger," said Winch, and he hooked the radio to his belt. He waved at Marco to trade places with Felix. "Show 'em your stuff, Felix!"

Marco splashed through the shallow water toward the captain. He passed his mitt to Felix as the Cuban plodded by, heading for the mound of sand. Marco took up a position behind Winch, who was catching, and aimed the radar gun at Felix.

It was only a little past eleven. Winch had told Laura that he was taking the *Key Monster* out to get fuel and run an errand. Preoccupied with last-minute details, she'd warned him to be back before two, and he'd promised he would.

He'd piloted the boat back into Northwest Channel, determined that the tide was right, and launched the inflatable, puttering out to the sandbar. The giant white yacht steamed into view moments later, just as Steve had said. Left back on board the *Key Monster*, Liza enjoyed some of Felix's leftover eggs and coffee and changed into a swimsuit. It was peaceful to have the big boat all to herself, rocking at its anchorage, and she found a pleasant spot on the foredeck for a little sunbathing. Occasionally she glanced over the side to watch the boys at play.

"Tell me again why we are out here instead of on a baseball field?" inquired Armand aboard his yacht, anchored in deep left field.

Steve, watching Felix through binoculars, replied, "Because Munoz is a Cuban national. He can't enter the United States unless he surrenders his free-agency. So he refuses to step on U.S. soil. Unless he goes through a third country first, that is. It's one of the rules of the major leagues."

Pringle gave Steve a sidelong glance. He sighed. "I'll never understand America, and I'll never understand baseball players."

"Okay," crackled Winch's voice. "He's ready."

"Fastball," Steve ordered.

"Okey-dokey," came the reply. Armand arched an eyebrow.

Felix took his windup and powered the ball into Winch's outstretched glove. The report echoed across the placid blue water.

Marco checked the LED read-out on the borrowed police radar gun and said, "Eighty-nine."

"Eighty-nine miles-an-hour!" yelled Winch into the transciever. Felix threw another strike. "Ninety-two!" relayed Winch.

"That's good?" Pringle asked Steve.

"That's great, considering he's pitching in ankle-deep seawater in his bare feet!" He hit the radio again. "Let's see some curves!"

Felix got the signal and delivered a breaking ball that appeared to be outside until it suddenly jigged to the right, smack into Winch's catcher's mitt. The captain grinned at the trick.

After another dozen pitches, Armand turned to Steve and said, "I've seen enough. You may bring them aboard. I'd like to speak to this ballplayer."

Steve broadcast the message. From across the water, he could hear Winch's whoop of delight. In moments, the *Key Monster*'s inflatable was whipping across the flats.

Marco lay in the bow ducking the spray as they sped toward Pringle's yacht. Winch handled the little outboard, with Felix sitting next to him. Over the whine of the motor, Felix spoke clearly so the captain could hear him.

"Weench? I want to thank you for everything. Most of all for pulling me out of the *oceano*."

"No problemo, *amigo*."

"You know," the Cuban went on, "the picture of the *monstruo marino* on your *bote* look *muy* real. I think for a moment it is real."

Winch's hand wavered on the throttle and the engine sputtered. "There are no sea monsters," he said evenly, trying to convince himself.

Felix shifted uneasily. "You may think I am *loco*, but I see it too. Out there."

Winch didn't want to hear this. He glanced at Felix from the corner of his eye.

"Only he's nose, it was not like that," Felix finished.

Winch gunned the outboard a little harder. And he couldn't stop himself from scanning the calm surface of the Gulf, hoping that he would not see what he did not want to see.

The inflatable swamped to a stop alongside Pringle's yacht and the three soggy men climbed aboard.

Pringle welcomed them and faced Felix, switching effortlessly to Spanish. Winch was baffled, while Marco tried to follow along. Presently, Armand signaled the steward to supply his guests with whatever they cared to drink while he and Felix had a private discussion in his office. Pringle patted the Cuban on the back and steered him through a doorway.

"What was all that about?" Winch asked Marco.

"Something about his cousin in Miami and money," Marco answered and shrugged. "They were talking pretty fast and my Spanish isn't what it should be."

Winch gave him a sly look. "I thought you were the Puerto Rican here?" Marco reddened.

"I'll get better," he mumbled, "once you get me to San Juan."

They ordered refreshments and the steward returned a moment later with a Coke for Steve, a Corona for Marco, and a Rolling Rock for Winch. They clinked glasses.

"Here's to America's great national pastime," offered Steve.

As they drank, Steve noticed, from the corner of his eye, the Amazing Mrs. Pringle approaching the hot-tub. She was wearing a new bikini, red and white and consisting of less material than one would find in a handkerchief. He elbowed Winch.

"Have you met Miss Sullivan?" he asked wickedly. "Why don't I introduce you?"

Winch was already gaping as pieces of bikini were flung from the hot tub. Marco thought guiltily of his beloved wife back home in Maryland and faced away, out to sea.

"No need," grinned Winch, brushing off Steve's guiding hand. "I can say hi by myself." He smoothed back his long blond hair and strolled casually over to the hot tub. Steve, too, turned his back, and in seconds he heard the distinctive giggle of Janet's voice.

The steward passed by and Steve stopped him.

"You will tell us when Mr. Pringle is done in his office?"

The steward glimpsed Winch and Mrs. Pringle naked together in the hot tub and said stonily, "Most assuredly, sir. Would you care for refills?" He left to alert the first mate that Mrs. Pringle was at it again.

"I don't think we've been introduced," Steve said to Marco. "Steve Stevens, news director at WRKW."

Marco shook his hand. "Marco, drug dealer, retired."

After that, Steve couldn't think of a single thing to say. They stood at the rail watching the horizon and tried to ignore the laughing, splashing and, finally, frenzied moaning that emanated from the hot tub. There was a pause and then a final small splash of water. Winch squished up to the rail, re-buttoning his cut-offs.

"Nice girl."

The steward returned with more drinks, looked Winch up and down, sniffed in distain at Mrs. Pringle's obviously slipping standards, and departed to sound the all clear.

"What's with him?" asked Winch.

Steve made a dismissive gesture. "Ah, he's just jealous." Winch nodded sagely.

"Gentlemen," came Armand's accented voice from behind them. It made them all jump. "After consulting with my baseball people, Mr. Munoz and I have come to an agreement. It seems that Felix Munoz has a reputation in baseball circles that is not merely confined to Cuba. I'm told by people who know these sort of things that he is the best pitching prospect to come out of the Caribbean in ten years, and I was urged to sign him immediately. I have done so."

Felix stood next to Pringle, grinning wildly.

"Since we are sailing for Puerto Rico, and will be passing Santo Domingo anyway, I have agreed to transport Mr. Munoz. I will put him ashore there with the explanation that I rescued him from his raft at sea. Once in the Dominican Republic, he will apply for entry into the United States. I promise him a try-out with my baseball club next spring." He patted Felix on the shoulder.

"Until then, he will play winter baseball with a team that I'm told I own in Puerto Plata."

Winch stepped forward and high-fived Felix. "Way to go, *amigo!*"

Steve smiled and made mental notes. This would make a great human interest story, if he could get it past his boss. If Grant hated stories about houseboats, he'd really flip-out over a non-blood-and-guts story like this one. But, somehow, he'd get it on the air.

Only Marco seemed downcast. Nervously, he raised his eyes to the billionaire. "Mr. Pringle, sir?"

Pringle looked down his nose at Marco, who cleared his throat and forced himself to speak. What could he lose?

"Ah, since you're going to Puerto Rico anyway, could you, um, maybe, give me a lift?"

Pringle's brow darkened. Felix leaned in and whispered in Spanish in his new boss's ear. The storm clouds fled from Armand's face. "Well," he said pleasantly, "since Mr. Munoz says that you are his personal trainer, I suppose it would be a disservice to separate you. But will you not join him in Santo Domingo?"

"Mr. Marco has pressing business to attend to in San Juan," jumped in Winch. "I'm sure he'll join up with Felix as soon as he can, won't you, Mr. Marco."

Now it was Marco's turn to grin. He leaned against Winch and whispered, "Don't forget. You still owe me $900."

The steward reappeared by Armand's elbow, bearing a tray of champagne. Glasses were passed around.

"To my new pitcher, and a championship next year," toasted Armand.

"*Brindemos por Estados Unidos,*" said Felix.

"To San Juan," crowed Marco.

"To pretty girls everywhere," offered Winch, taking a sip, with a side-glance at the hot-tub.

"To Mrs. Janet Sullivan Pringle," cheered Steve.

Winch choked on his wine.

# CHAPTER 25

A̲rmand Pringle's big white yacht disappeared up Northwest Channel, heading out to sea. Sadly, Winch gazed at the vanishing shape as it bore his old friend Marco and his new friend Felix toward promising lives on other islands. He'd miss his crew, but wished them the best.

He finished stowing the inflatable and kicked over the twin diesels, rocking the *Key Monster* gently to free the anchor. Upon the bow, Steve guided the chain up and secured the anchor. Liza popped through the main hatch from below and handed Winch a cold beer.

"Thanks for staying aboard and keeping an eye on her," the captain smiled.

"Hey, a day on the water, getting an all-over suntan in private? It was my pleasure!" Liza took a sip of Winch's beer and grinned.

When Winch and Steve had pulled alongside the *Key Monster* after bidding Marco and Felix farewell, Liza had been caught scrambling back into her bikini bottom. Now, she stood beside the captain, still topless, unashamed of her proud, brown breasts. Winch took back his beer and admired her well-honed figure. Janet Sullivan might have the shape of a goddess, he considered, but there had been something cold and distant about her. Liza was real, more like the girl-next-door with her soft, tanned figure and short, black hair billowing in the breeze. She caught Winch checking her out and laughed, suspecting what he was thinking. She ruffled his dirty-blond hair and walked away, her barely-clad bottom clicking left and right before his gaping eyes.

Men were so easy, Liza chuckled to herself.

Steve finished stowing the anchor and made his way aft. He gazed at Liza's retreating form and whistled softly. She flicked an amused smile over her shoulder and went below to find her bikini top.

"I just love Key West," Steve said over the purr of the engines.

Winch had to agree.

The captain hoisted himself up onto the narrow bench behind the helm. As he slid onto the seat, a long, white envelope escaped from his back pocket

*KEY MONSTER*

and fluttered to the deck. Steve stooped and scooped it up. "Dropped this," he said to Winch, handing it back to the captain.

Winch squinted at the crumpled, damp envelope, blurry ink on the front addressed to him.

"Forgot all about this," he muttered, recalling yesterday's visit from the mailman. He tore it open and scanned the contents. A small smile spread across his features.

"Good news?" Steve asked at Winch's elbow. Winch handed the papers to the reporter. Steve read.

It was a letter from a real estate agent in Solomons Island, Maryland. The agent, Skip Miller, was advising Winch that his house and half-acre of waterfront property had just been sold to a Qatari holding company that planned to develop a restaurant and mini-marina on the site. Enclosed, find a check for . . .

"Eight-hundred and seventy-three thousand dollars!" Steve gasped.

Winch smiled broadly. "Guess I can afford to take the day off, huh?"

Steve refolded the letter and the check and stuffed them back into the envelope. "Congratulations," he said, patting Winch on the back. "But I don't think you should skip out on Laura's media tour today. Not if you want to live to spend this." He checked his faux Rolex. If they hurried, they'd just make it. He pointed the time out to Winch and the captain responded by adding more power to the diesels.

The *Key Monster* plowed through the light chop as they rounded Southernmost Point. Winch piloted his boat east toward Stock Island and daydreamed of naked women in Tahiti.

\* \* \* \* \* \* \*

A nearly frantic Laura awaited the arrival of the *Key Monster* at the pier. As Winch, Steve and Liza tied up, she berated the captain for his tardiness. He shrugged her off, pointing out that it was still twenty minutes before the scheduled start of the tour at two. What had Laura tied in knots was the dismaying fact that not a single member of the press had accepted her invitation. The media tour was turning out to be a giant failure.

Taylor, having arrived in his Cadillac more than an hour earlier, was more than happy to trade places with Steve on the *Key Monster* while the reporter walked Laura back to the office. They made a half-dozen last-minute calls to various newsrooms, only to find that Laura's media tour had been overshadowed by last night's riot on Duval. Reporters from all over the Keys and from as far away as Atlanta were streaming into Key West. But they hadn't come to attend some rinky-dink briefing about a boring reef. No blood was ever spilled for the cameras on a press junket. Laura was devastated.

Steve insisted gently that they proceed with the media tour anyway, promising that he would devote a multi-part report to the Foundation. Reluctantly, tearfully, Laura relented and ordered Winch to take the *Key Monster* out to sea. Instead of the hoped-for swarm of reporters aboard, Laura and the captain were accompanied only by one radio newsman, their transvestite tour guide and her ex-husband's ex-mistress. The Save the Reef Foundation's director went below and raided the captain's liquor cabinet, drowning her disappointment with a couple of shots of tequila.

Riding slow swells, just yards from Pelican Shoal Reef, Winch worked the throttles to hold the boat in position. In the forward stateroom, Laura dejectedly changed into a bathing suit borrowed from Liza's travel bag. She had three or four to choose from and selected a relatively modest, teal-blue two-piece. Across the passageway, in the opposite cabin, Steve changed also, pulling on the red and black trunks he'd brought along. Lastly, he placed his holster and the Colt atop his carefully folded clothes in his overnight bag and carried it up to the afterdeck. He placed the bag beneath the gunwale, out of the way.

Liza, finding that there was no crush of media on board after all, had once again jettisoned her top in order to soak up the sun and, incidentally, to confound Winch. She toyed with the captain and the strap on a diving mask, slipping it over her head, trying to get a snug fit. Winch smoked a cigar at the helm and pretended not to look.

Taylor unfolded and hooked the ladder to the side of the boat in preparation for their dive to the reef. He checked his meticulous notes and paced the deck, waiting for Laura to appear from below. Steve peeled off his shirt and soaked up some sun while he chatted with the topless Liza.

At last, Laura moped her way up the companionway to join them. "Come on, Taylor," she huffed irritably.

"Let's get started." One reporter, she fumed. And from a radio station, at that. It couldn't have been TV or print. The Foundation would be history by Monday. She had failed.

Taylor gathered Steve, Liza and Laura together by the transom. Steve started his cassette recorder and made notes while Taylor explained the ecology of the reef they would be exploring today. Laura tugged repeatedly at the straps of the too-large bikini top, reliving in her mind the August she was thirteen, newly-budded, and had lost the top of her swimsuit while diving into Lake Huron. She'd surfaced, to her embarrassment, amid a cheering throng of teenage boys. Mortified, she'd fled to the safety of her beach blanket. It had taken five years before she'd worked up the courage to wear a two-piece again.

Finally reaching the end of his lecture, Taylor distributed snorkling gear and led his three charges to the swim ladder. He slipped over the side into the warm water and waited as each of the other swimmers dropped into the sea. Laura hit with a splash, and Winch glanced overboard in time to see two teal-blue triangles connected by a narrow strap pop to the surface. Laura's head rose above the water. Annoyed, she grasped the bathing suit top and flung it over the gunwale, where it landed on the deck with a squishy plop.

"Screw it," she muttered, and shoved the snorkel in her mouth. She paddled away after Taylor, Steve and Liza.

Winch picked up the dripping bra and hung it over the back of his bench to dry. He took a last look at the four snorkels cutting through the waves and edged the *Key Monster* into reverse, correcting for the drift, making sure the hull was clear of the reef.

Satisfied, and knowing that they would be happily exploring underwater for the next twenty minutes or so, Winch left the engines idling and slipped below for a cold beer and a toke or two.

\* \* \* \* \* \* \*

Big Jim Quinn lowered the binoculars and gently pressed the throttle forward, moving stealthily. Thirty minutes ago, he'd spotted the familiar outlines of the *LauraLee* cruising southward out of Stock Island. Tailing her at a distance of a thousand yards, he'd watched as she slowed and stopped dead in the water, miles from the coast.

The sun beat down relentlessly on his arms and scalp, but the slight breeze created by his forward motion dried the sweat from his sunburned forehead as it formed. He trembled with excited anticipation, his goal within his grasp at last. Through the glasses, he'd seen four people clamber over the rail and into the water. A black man, a man with graying hair, and two women, almost certainly Laura and Liza. And then he'd seen that long-haired, hippie freak leave the cockpit and go below. On deck now, nothing stirred. There wasn't a thing to stop Big Jim's impending act of piracy on the high seas. He idled the little Boston Whaler closer to his prize. Big Jim groaned in real pain when he spotted the mural of the sea monster which disfigured the hull of his beautiful yacht. Winchell would pay for that too. He'd kill the bastard, slowly.

The Baltimore investment banker shut down the outboard and glided the last few feet in silence. Noiselessly, the Whaler bumped against the bigger boat. He felt for the stock of his .38 and, reassured, gripped the stern-rail of his recaptured boat and heaved himself aboard, allowing the Whaler to drift free. He wouldn't be needing it anymore.

Big Jim stood on the deck of the *LauraLee*. He drew the gun and glanced around. She was in better condition than he'd expected to find her. He noticed a soggy bathing suit top dripping on the pilot's seat. He'd seen that particular item before, on Liza. He smiled and moved quietly to one side of the companionway hatch. From below, over the soft rumble of the twin diesels at idle, he heard bottles clinking and the tread of bare feet mounting the steps to the afterdeck.

With his jaw set tightly, Big Jim thumbed off the safety and waited for his quarry.

\* \* \* \* \* \* \*

Alongside the *Key Monster*, four masked heads broke the surface of the Atlantic near the swim ladder.

## KEY MONSTER

"That was so cool!" Liza laughed, spitting out a mouthful of seawater. She grasped the rungs and hauled herself aboard. Laura followed behind, while Steve and Taylor treaded water and awaited their turns.

Laura pulled her dripping self over the gunwale, long wet blonde hair hanging limply in her eyes. She flicked her head back to clear her vision. Liza stood frozen next to her on the deck, mute and trembling. Laura, able to see finally, looked at Liza and followed the direction of her gaze.

Huddled beneath the starboard gunwale, shivering, Winch sat with his back propped against the inner hull. His normal bronze tan was fading, his face a pasty white. He kept his right hand clamped against his upper left arm, and dark red blood spilled through his fingers, dripping upon the teak deck where it mixed with the puddle of Coors and broken glass. He gritted his teeth against the pain and stared blankly across to the captain's seat by the helm, at the man with the gun.

Big Jim lifted the damp bikini top with one finger and faced the two dripping women. He smiled cruelly.

"I believe this belongs to one of you?" He flung the top at them casually. It landed damply at their feet.

Rage, fear, and shock coursed through Laura simultaneously. Liza stood rooted to the deck, unable to move. She glanced repeatedly between Big Jim and the wounded Winch, who grimaced in pain.

"Goddam you!" Laura howled in outrage.

Big Jim ignored her outburst. "Where's your friends?" he said as he hopped off the seat and strode to the stern. A hand reached blindly over the side of the boat. Big Jim hefted the revolver and brought it down on Steve's unsuspecting fingers. With a yelp, the reporter let go and splashed back into the water, landing on top of Taylor. Big Jim gazed over the side at the two men floating in the ocean. He aimed his revolver at them.

Taylor instinctively dove for safety. Steve, two of his fingers broken and a wave of pain spreading up his arm, was slower to react. He prepared himself to die.

Instead, Laura's husband wiggled the .38 in the direction of the drifting outboard. Steve got the message and kicked away from the *Key Monster*, holding his battered and bleeding hand above the water. Taylor surfaced nearby and swam over to Steve, who was having a difficult time pulling himself one-handed aboard the smaller boat. Big Jim turned to face Winch and the two topless women.

Laura and Liza knelt next to the captain, trying to stop the bleeding from the ragged hole in his bicep. Laura looked for something to wrap around the wound to staunch the flow of sticky blood. She spied Steve's valise and groped for something to use, her fingers brushing against a cold, hard object. She extracted a tee-shirt and wrapped it tightly around the captain's arm.

"Don't waste your time," Big Jim sneered at their efforts. "I ain't done with him yet."

"Can you stand," Liza whispered in Winch's ear, ignoring the implied threat. Winch nodded weakly and his two friends helped him to his feet. With their support, he shuffled over to the bench seat and collapsed in it.

"He's in shock," Laura stated flatly.

"Won't matter soon anyway," Quinn replied, leaning against the transom. "After we're underway, he'll be fish food."

Laura left Winch's side and marched fiercely across the wide deck, coming face to face with her insane husband.

"Damn you, you bastard!" she roared at him. "Okay, you've got your damn boat back. Yes! It's true! This was *your* friggin' boat! So take it, and let us go!" She pointed to the Boston Whaler bobbing fifty yards away with Steve and Taylor, watching wide-eyed.

Big Jim scowled and gave her a shove backwards. Laura retreated a step, but no more. Half-naked and defenseless, she proceeded to verbally tear him a new asshole.

At the helm, Liza cradled Winch's feverish head against her bare breasts. *Mmmm, nice*, dreamed Winch, growing ever more lightheaded as his blood leaked out. Laura's pathetic pleadings grew hazy in his ears. He raised his head from Liza's chest and gazed out upon the endless blue sea, the light drone of idling diesels lulling him to the edge of the abyss.

A ripple in the seascape appeared off the starboard beam, a V-shape splitting the surface of the water. Winch smiled placidly as the sea foamed and parted, and a familiar black head glided upward from the waves. A long black, coil-like body trailed behind, and Winch suddenly realized how beautiful Chessie was. Traces of deep aquamarine flashed in the bright sunlight, the monster undulating with astounding grace. Mysterious, sentient dark eyes swung in his direction, meeting his own. Winch offered a friendly little wave. And with the softest whisper, the beast dipped its head below the surface once again and vanished into the depths.

Winch wobbled his head back and grinned foggily at Liza. Liza's mouth described a perfect "O" as she too stared raptly at the vacant surface of the ocean, now smooth once again. Winch tasted satisfaction. It was nice to die knowing that he wasn't crazy after all.

From the stern, the fight raged on. It had devolved into your standard domestic argument, both of the combatants throwing the past into each other's faces. Liza made sure that Winch was securely seated by the wheel and tromped over to the transom to give Laura some support, to talk Big Jim out of the gun.

"We've got to get him to a hospital," Liza argued. "I think you hit an artery. He's going to bleed to death!"

Big Jim glanced at the pool of blood forming below the captain's chair. Laura saw too, and gasped. Pints of it. How could Winch still be alive?

"He needs another bandage," she said and turned to help him. Big Jim grabbed for her arm. Laura shook him off. "What are you going to do," she spat, "shoot me too?"

Laura glared at the gun for a heartbeat and resolutely padded over to Steve's bag. As she bent down, the entire boat shuddered and rocked violently. A tearing, scraping sound reverberated from beneath the hull. The *Key Monster* lurched drunkenly.

Laura fell flat on the deck, gashing her knee. Liza spun around on one foot, off balance, and crashed into Big Jim. He, in turn, fell hard against the transom, cracking a rib.

"Fuckin' reef," muttered Winch in a bloodless daze. The captain knew instictively that they had run aground on the coral, and he reacted accordingly. He raised a leaden arm and reached for the throttle levers.

Big Jim fought to regain a firm footing on the sloping deck. He brought the pistol to bear on the back of Winch's head. "Don't touch that!"

Liza rolled across the deck and looked up at Laura, who was scrabbling through Steve's overturned bag. Clothes, socks and shoes spilled out. And something else.

Big Jim applied pressure to the trigger. Winch, in a world of his own, threw the engines into reverse, trying to wrench the *Key Monster* free of the reef. The twin diesels screamed and the boat vibrated under the strain. Laura closed her hands around the grip of Steve's Colt .45 and rolled onto her side, aiming squarely at her husband.

"Jim?" she sang out.

He swung his piggy eyes at her, taking in the bikini botttom, the long, tanned legs, her perky breasts, and the matte-black weapon in her hands. Perspiration dripped in his eyes.

"Fuck you," she said softly, and squeezed off a single round.

The recoil shocked her. The gun kicked back and up, flying from her grip, the bullet completely missing Big Jim's wildly beating heart. The shot punched high and wide of its intended target, creasing the side of her husband's head, just above his right ear.

Spun by the impact of bullet against bone, Big Jim Quinn fell hard against the transom as blood and sweat streamed over his eyes, obscuring his vision. His head rang, he was deafened and blinded, and he toppled limply over the stern-rail.

The *Key Monster*'s engines revved in reverse, yet the reef held the boat fast. Dual vortices formed in the water around Big Jim's legs as he gripped the rail with all his strength. Laura and Liza pulled themselves to their feet and raced to the stern, staring down into the foaming water roiling about Big Jim's flailing legs. He looked up at the two women pleadingly, and reached a hand up to them. Laura flexed her fingers outward, in spite of herself. And, at that second, Big Jim's last, the mighty diesels of the *Key Monster* succeeded in their task. With a terrible rending sound, the boat lurched backwards, free of the reef. Laura and Liza were pitched backwards, onto the blood-slicked deck.

Big Jim Quinn disappeared beneath the stern, yielding to six shining blades of spinning brass.

Laura rolled to her knees. She cradled her face in her hands and wept silently.

*  *  *  *  *  *  *

He has been following the mancraft all day as it crosses the surface of the sea. It is the familiar one, the mancraft that occasionally offers up a fine pre-digested meal for him. Shedding his natural shyness, he has even risen to the surface for a moment to be sure that the man--yes, the same man, with the unkempt yellow features--has seen him and knows that he is hungry. And it has worked.

Above him, the mancraft backs away quickly from the reef, and he sees that it is mortally wounded. A finely ground meal of fresh food drifts bloodily through the water. He knows not what kind of food he eats, nor does he care. It is delicious.

He dines in satisfaction and swims back down to the seabed, searching for a nice crunchy turtle for dessert.

\* \* \* \* \* \* \*

The *Key Monster* listed hard to starboard, her stern rising higher in the tropical sky. Shredded bits of clothing hung wetly on the stilled propellers as the bow of the big boat settled heavily into the sea. Through a fatal gash, torn by coral claws, salt-water rushed into the forward cabins. Steve and Taylor had worked frantically to grab as many of Winch's belongings as they could before they were forced to abandon ship and retreat to the Boston Whaler bobbing alongside the doomed vessel.

Steve dropped a soggy cardboard box in the bilge next to Winch. His hand was throbbing. The captain, bandaged properly from the first-aid supplies on the rental-boat, had refused to leave his ship until his box of memories had been salvaged. Taylor cranked the wheel hard to port and pushed the throttles to their stops, aiming for the hospital on Stock Island. The small boat pounded across the choppy ocean.

"Help me . . . sit up," Winch groaned.

Laura assisted the captain to an upright position beside her. He stared astern, forlornly.

With agonizing slowness at first, and then more rapidly, the *Key Monster*'s stern rose high into the sky, and then gracefully, completely, and with sudden finality, slipped beneath the waves. She was gone.

The spot where the *Key Monster* had gone down became indistinguishable from the rest of the vast, unrelenting ocean. Winch bit his lip and wiped away a tear. In the back pocket of his cut-offs, a white envelope flapped merrily in the wind. Steve reached out with his good hand and gently pressed it deeper into the captain's pocket. Winch raised his eyes and and managed a faint smile.

Liza continued to apply pressure to the captain's wound, though the bleeding had subsided. Carefully, so the others couldn't hear, she spoke softly under the masking whine of the outboard motor.

"Did we really see what I thought we saw?"

Winch turned his head slowly and looked into Liza's wondrous eyes. He blinked once and nodded nearly imperceptibly.

"Aye," was all he said before he looked away.

Laura stroked a wind-whipped lock of long blond hair from Winch's tired face. She brushed her lips across his stubbly cheek. She, too, looked astern at the final, watery resting place of her husband.

"It's over," she soothed, to both Winch and herself.

Gazing at the southern horizon, Winch thought of his parents, his lost boat, and sea monsters. He tilted his head down as the tears came freely now.

Laura took his hand in hers. "It's all over," she repeated softly through the salt of her own tears. He looked up to her in gratitude.

With guarded relief, Winch had to agree.

# EPILOGUE

Between the gently sloping hills of the Great Glen, a place that, coincidentally, both man and his own kind know by the same name, he slumbers. It is a sleep of weariness and finality. Upon the powerful current he has swum across the cold Great Sea and then, in darkness, in secret, a last rush up the channel to his resting place.

He cannot recall the last morsel he has swallowed, nor does the thought of food entice him. He feels that it is almost over now, and he lies patiently in the deep, frigid water. The faint sounds of slowly moving mancraft, and their distinctive *pings*, reach his ears. They are criss-crossing the surface, beneath a damp, gray sky, searching for him, seeking proof, but even if they are very lucky, they will find only his bones.

It has been uncounted seasons, during which he has ranged powerfully up and down the Shore of the Setting Sun. Here, beyond the Shore of the Rising Sun, is the ancestral lake he has always known of, somehow. With his own failing eyes, he has seen the bones of his forebearers littering the bottom. He is home. He is at peace.

His gills ripple asthmatically in the salt-free water. His four flippers steady his weakened body upon the silt. A milky haze clouds his vision. It is done.

He rests his head upon the soft floor of the loch and sleeps. Forever.

\* \* \* \* \* \* \*

More than four miles south of Stock Island, the *Key Monster* surrendered to slow disintegration. The yacht lay on her side in the muck of the seafloor, timeless. Over the passing years, tentacles of coral sprang from the damaged hull, attracting parrotfish, rays and crabs. The coral spread over the dead piece of fiberglass, bringing new life. Parties of snorkel-breathing tourists visited the wreck frequently, swimming amongst the golf ball and rose corals, and stinging probing fingers on the fire coral.

This nondescript spot in the ocean, just south of Pelican Shoal, came to be known to the local guides as Key Monster Reef.

\* \* \* \* \* \* \*

Rolf rang up the total on a carton of Marlboros and a twelve pack of Bud Light. He counted out the customer's change and closed the register. The Gas'n'Go was empty again but for himself, the assistant night manager. Former First General Rolf Schenk wiped his hands on his orange and blue apron and pulled his pilfered copy of *Modern Warrior* from beneath the counter. He studied the cutaway diagram of an AK-47 and then glanced up as the bell chimed over the doorway.

From out of the humid night air choking suburban Ocala, a hulking black man entered the convenience store and helped himself to two quarts of Bull and a couple of Ding Dongs. Rolf smiled up at the gentleman.

"Anything else tonight, sir?"

\* \* \* \* \* \* \*

The pounding *thump-thump* of a re-mixed Diana Ross hit washed over the bar. Angel, in a natty, white-linen suit, leaned against the rail and watched his partner working the crowd. Samantha, wearing a fabulous red mini-skirt, slow- danced with a mark. She slipped a slim hand into the tourist's back pocket and deftly extracted his wallet.

Angel strolled through the mob of dancers and took the handoff from Samantha. He faced the wall, quickly rifled the wallet, removing cash and credit cards, and discretely returned the empty billfold to the dancing Samantha, who guided it back into her victim's pocket. Later, while strolling along a secluded part of South Beach, they would split tonight's take, then cross the causeway to their one-bedroom apartment in Miami Springs.

They were larcenous and in love, but in the months to come, one of them would die of jealous stab wounds and the other would become a permanent guest of the State of Florida.

\* \* \* \* \* \* \*

In the pleasant tropical town of Juana Diaz, not too far outside of Ponce, the shopkeeper supervised the first of this week's deliveries. Flats of tulips, roses and baby's breath were carted into his store. When the unloading was done, Marco found Juanita in the greenhouse and asked her to mind the shop for the day.

"I have to drive to the airport," he told her in his rough, but improving, Spanish. Juanita beamed up at him.

"Then they are arriving today?" she prattled excitedly.

"*Si*," the florist agreed. "At one o'clock, on the American flight from BWI."

Marco left his flower shop and strode past his classic Harley Davidson Sportster 1000, a gift from an old friend. He slipped behind the wheel of the fifth-hand used car he'd recently purchased and cranked the stubborn engine. Flowers and gift-wrapped boxes crammed the back seat as he puttered out of town and made a series of wrong turns.

Marco steered the rattletrap Toyota across the mountainous spine of Puerto Rico, toward San Juan. He was excited, because today he would welcome Maria and his little girls to their new home on his tropical island.

\* \* \* \* \* \* \*

It was a frightfully long, and ultimately frustrating, trip to the top. From winter ball in the Dominican Republic, to spring training in Sarasota, through a difficult summer in Boise, he worked to prove himself. And then, finally, on a crisp autumn night in Kansas City, Felix Munoz threw major league baseballs.

In the third inning of his first big-league start, fresh from the minors, Felix felt an ominous tug in his right shoulder. In the fifth inning, after a third-strike fastball, he felt something pop near the joint and experienced exquisite pain. In the clubhouse, the team doctor examined him and made his diagnosis. Felix's career was ended, as certainly as if a fat man from the Sports Ministry had read him a document from Fidel.

American citizenship came the following year. He had been sworn in by a federal judge in Billings, Montana, where Felix still worked for Armand Pringle, teaching younger and more promising pitchers the mechanics of throwing the perfect slider. Pringle had been good to his word, and Felix's contract provided a nice disability settlement. Years later, after Castro's death, Felix returned to Santa Clarita a relatively wealthy man and spent his fortune bringing clean water, manicured baseball fields and a new schoolhouse to his people. He grew old among his many friends and regaled the *niños* of his adopted hometown with stories of his cup of coffee in the major leagues, and of *monstruo marinos* lurking in the blue sea. The children laughed at Felix Munoz, but they loved the old man.

\* \* \* \* \* \* \*

Once he had paid for the extensive damage to the Riding Crop Bar after being fired, Lamont Taylor Jackson was all but wiped-out financially. He gratefully accepted a partnership with the owner of the Duval Street art gallery below his apartment, dressing now as Daiquiri Taylor full-time. Few of his customers suspected the truth, charmed by the tall, honey-voiced black woman who helped them select pieces of local art from the gallery's walls.

Peace had returned to both her heart and the streets of Key West. And Daiquiri's pulse quickened each afternoon at five o'clock when the front door would tinkle open and her beau, Dave the bartender from the Rainforest Resort, would escort her to their favorite cafe for a light, romantic dinner.

\*\*\*\*\*\*\*

Locking the front door securely at five, Liza Benedetto left her assistant director job at the Save the Reef Foundation and strode across the gravel parking lot to the waiting GMC longbed. She popped open the passenger door and slipped into the cool interior, gracing Bobbie with a quick kiss on the cheek. Bobbie smiled back and placed a rough hand on Liza's thigh, giving it a gentle squeeze.

They drove home to their cottage on Big Coppitt Key, Liza flicking coy glances at her girlfriend as Bobbie droned on about her day putting a new roof on the ManGrove House hotel. Liza was crazy in love and wondered if it would last. This was a radical change for her, but there was something very special about this relationship. Men were too easy, she thought to herself. And there was an unexpected complexity involved in loving another woman.

Liza snuggled against Bobbie's meaty shoulder and smiled happily.

\* \* \* \* \* \* \*

There were fitful stays of execution, court battles, petitions and protests, but in the end Houseboat Row was doomed. With the fate of the colorful vessels docked along Cow Key Channel sealed, it signaled a sea-change in the unique character of the city at the end of the road. Downtown, the tee-shirt shops continued to bloom like runaway algae. Behemoth cruise ships packed the tiny harbor and disgorged thousands of sunburned tourists into the already clogged streets. Historic conch houses were torn down and replaced by pink concrete timeshares. Overcrowding set people on edge, Conch versus tourist and man versus his environment. The cordial, tolerant atmosphere that made Key West what it was withered.

Someone had forgotten what Key West meant, and other someones set about turning this placid piece of coral and limestone into Fort Lauderdale South.

\* \* \* \* \* \* \*

Having done his part for the developers and speculators, Grant Davies accepted his father's new job offer and left Key West. The diminutive, former general manager of Key Rock 104 packed his belongings and moved north to the Deep South, installing himself as the new Sales Manager at his dad's Fox affiliate in Macon, Georgia.

He met and married a cocktail waitress from the Holiday Inn out by the interstate. They had three girls and took frequent vacations to Atlantic City, Nassau, and Vegas, where Grant was hit by a pick-up truck and died at the age of 36.

\* \* \* \* \* \* \*

In the wake of his coverage of the Duval Street Riot, Steve was offered not one single job by the networks. He did, however, earn over $3,900 in talent fees. And a life in Key West, he came to realize, wouldn't be so bad after all.

After liberating WRKW's News Director from the tyranny of his Georgia-bound son, Bob Davies promoted Steve Stevens to Grant's old job. Steve's first action as General Manager entailed a complete change of format. He sold the old rock music library and purchased a new one, consisting entirely of jazz. Next, he beefed up the newsroom, hiring three full-time reporters. And finally, he summoned Maxx Rock to his office on a gloriously perfect afternoon.

Steve's old, aching ambition to return to the big time had evaporated in the Key West sunshine. He lost a little weight, learned to appreciate the taste of conch and grouper, and moved himself into a spacious new ranch house on Eagle Avenue, leaving his old leaky trailer behind for the next unfortunate tenant.

Steve decorated his new home with Daiquiri's tasteful guidance. They remained close friends, and he gave the bride away when she married Dave on the pool-deck of the Rainforest Resort.

\* \* \* \* \* \* \*

He left Key West angry and unemployed, a stack of tapes and resumes in the trunk of his decrepit Honda Civic. For four months, Maxx Rock, aka Gregory Bitzer, mailed applications to any radio station that had advertised for a jock and to a few that hadn't. He collected unemployment benefits until they ran out. And then, not surprisingly for a man of his self-imagined talent, he landed on his feet. He always did, he thought smugly. He'd show that asshole Steve. He'd been the number one morning man in the Florida Keys and he'd be number one here!

Maxx watched the second hand sweep past midnight and keyed open the mike.

"Hey, hey, hey! It's the Mad Maxx Midnight Mess here at WSUX-AM, the Voice of Sussex County, Delaware! Let's get things rollin' with a big oldie from one of my favorites, Debby Boone on WSUX-AM!"

The first piano notes of "You Light Up My Life" rolled under his intro and he flipped off the mike. Outside, a snowstorm shrouded the flat Delmarva landscape. Maxx stared blankly at the piece of vinyl spinning on the turntable and sipped his lukewarm coffee, hating his life.

\* \* \* \* \* \* \*

Mrs. Winters died in Boca Raton a few days after Christmas. Her formidable will left a sizable bequest to her pet project, the Save the Reef Foundation in Key West.

With this unexpected windfall, Laura Chadwick purchased a used thirty-five foot excursion boat for her twice-daily reef tours. Now that Winch was unavailable, she was learning how to captain the boat herself. She'd discovered that she loved the freedom and challenge of piloting your own ship on the open sea, and Laura blessed Winch for that lesson.

Lured by the sudden success of the Foundation, volunteers returned and Laura was able to hire a small office staff, including her new friend Liza Benedetto.

Thanks to her late husband's life insurance policy, and the proceeds from the sale of their house in Maryland, Laura acquired a newly-refurbished conch house on White Street on the edge of Old Town. The blue, two-story, gingerbread-trimmed, tin-roofed house became the place to be, if you were anyone in Key West. Laura hosted all the Foundation's charity balls in her home with the assistance of Liza, Daiquiri and Steve, all good friends still.

And it was Steve who, after a respectable period of mourning had passed, asked Laura to dinner one evening. Eventually, the dinners turned into weekends, the weekends became long vacations, and the vacations culminated in a happy lifetime together in the Keys.

Laura and Steve were wed at the Chapel by the Sea on a bright June morning. Daiquiri served as Laura's maid of honor and cried happily through the entire ceremony.

\* \* \* \* \* \* \*

With his left arm in a sling, Winch waited in the tiny terminal at Key West International Airport. Gulf Stream flight 1014 touched down right on time from Orlando and fifteen passengers sweated through the midday humidity into the comfort of the low, air-conditioned building. A young man with spiky, blonde hair stepped through the gate and set his bag on the floor. He looked about, lost.

"Brant!" Winch called and pushed his way upstream against the tide of deplaning tourists. The captain and the student embraced warmly.

Winch drove Taylor's borrowed Cadillac convertible through the traffic of Old Town, pointing out the sights to his friend. At last, they pulled to a stop beside a slip at Garrison Bight. Winch led Brant along the pier and swept his hand with pride, showing off his brand new boat.

She was a beauty. Thirty-eight feet of sleek lines, a comfy cabin below and a solid aluminum mast rising high above the deck. "No more stink-pots for me," Winch told him. "She's all outfitted, loaded and ready to set sail."

Brant looked the sailboat over with an appreciative eye. He glanced up at the captain. "What did you name her?"

Winch guided the young man to the stern. Painted neatly upon the transom were the words, *Stuffed Ham II*. Brant smiled with approval.

"She just needs one more thing," Winch added.

"What's that?"

"There, on the bow," he indicated. The captain looked levelly at Brant. "I want you to paint another monster. But get the nose right this time." His lip curled in a grin.

They boarded the sailboat and Winch offered Brant a cold soda. "No beer?" asked Brant, amazed.

Winch shook his head. "Nore more dope, either. Cold turkey. Time to grow up," he said. "Getting shot changes your perspective on life."

Between the check from Skip Miller for the sale of his parent's house and the insurance money he'd collected after the loss of the Key Monster, Winch had bought his new boat for cash at a yard up on Marathon. For a few hundred dollars more, he had paid for Brant's flight to Key West during spring break. Winch explained all this over a couple of ginger ales in the cockpit, and touched upon some of his recent adventures here in the Conch Republic.

"One thing I don't get," said Brant. "You only sent me a one-way ticket."

Winch grinned mischievously. "'Cause me and you are setting sail in the morning. For Rio."

Brant stood up sharply, almost cracking his head on the boom.

"I can't do that! I've got classes next week, and finals coming up! What'll my parents say? They'll kill me!"

Winch put a protective arm around Brant's shoulder. "Don't sweat it. You know, there's more than just going to school and getting a job and wasting your life in Maryland. You and I are gonna go out and see the world!"

Brant looked doubtful.

"Besides," Winch went on, holding up his wounded wing. "How can I sail her alone with just one good arm?" He shook his head insistently. "I need you, man."

"What about money?"

"Not a problem. I paid off Donna Jean and Gil last month, with interest. I also sent ten thou to Marco for his flower shop in Puerto Rico. And I got enough left over to keep us afloat for a couple of years."

"Years?"

Winch shrugged innocently. "It's a long trip to Rio," he said simply.

"And after that, there's Hawaii, and Fiji, and, hey! Didn't you ever wanna go to Australia?"

The two sailors sat on the deck under the lowering sun, sipping sodas and talking long into the evening. And when dawn broke over the Florida

Keys, they ran up the sails of the *Stuffed Ham II* and drifted away on an outgoing tide, moving placidly toward the sunrise.

* * * * * * *

Disoriented, he slips free from the hot, slippery birth canal. He spills into the cool water and wriggles his new body. Mother has already abandoned him, as is perfectly natural for the species. His gills start to flutter for the very first time, filtering oxygen from the warm blue water.

"What am I?" he thinks before he tentatively wiggles a pair of foreflippers against the tide, and then forgets the question. He swallows the first food that swims by, a small barracuda, though he has no name for this first meal.

Light shimmers down from the surface and he rises slowly, examining his new environment. A tiny voice in his equally tiny brain whispers to him, telling him to find another of his kind. But what is he? What should he look for?

A shadow passes above, blocking momentarily the bright light of the surface. A shape drifts by, long and sleek, like himself. "Mama?" he wonders.

He turns his lithe body in a tight circle, paddling clumsily with his newly-formed flippers, and follows the sailboat out into the great, blue sea.